Also by Alex Hay

The Housekeepers

Praise for Alex Hay's *The Housekeepers*

"*The Housekeepers* is a treasure trove of contradictions: fast-paced but thoughtful, vengeful but compassionate, satisfying but completely unpredictable.... You'll never have so much fun cheering on grand larceny."

—**Nina de Gramont, *New York Times* bestselling author of *The Christie Affair***

"Rollicking fun and entirely original... Anyone who relishes a good party gone wrong will devour this."

—**Sarah Penner, *New York Times* bestselling author of *The Lost Apothecary***

"[A] quick-fire, almost whimsical story of class and privilege.... Mischievous, suspenseful, and just plain fun from start to finish."

—*BookPage* (starred review)

"Hay brings a lively tempo and an elegant wit to this zippy thriller that is also a social commentary on the plight of the powerless."

—*Washington Post*

"[A] glittering debut... The ensemble cast is a delight of this delicious, *Downton Abbey*–like tale of the reversal of fortunes."

—*Shelf Awareness*

"Wonderfully inventive...full of shocking secrets, suspense, hidden identities, flamboyant characters, and subtle humor... Fans of historical fiction, strong female characters, and twisty, pacy thrillers will love it."

—*Booklist*

"Readers will delight in the shenanigans. This lighthearted romp is a treat."

—*Publishers Weekly*

"If *Ocean's 8* took place at a *Bridgerton* ball instead of the Met Gala, you'd have *The Housekeepers*."

—*PopSugar*

THE
QUEEN
OF
FIVES

A NOVEL

ALEX HAY

GRAYDON
HOUSE

GRAYDON HOUSE®

ISBN-13: 978-1-525-80985-9

ISBN-13: 978-1-525-83046-4 (International edition)

The Queen of Fives

Graydon House
22 Adelaide St. West, 41st Floor
Toronto, Ontario M5H 4E3, Canada
www.GraydonHouseBooks.com

Printed in U.S.A.

For Tom

A confidence scheme, when properly executed, will follow five movements in close and inviolable order:

I. THE MARK.
Wherein a fresh quarry is perceived and made the object of the closest possible study.

II. THE INTRUSION.
Wherein the quarry's outer layers must be pierced, his world peeled open...

III. THE BALLYHOO.
Where a golden opportunity shall greatly tempt and dazzle the quarry...

IV. THE KNOT.
Wherein the quarry is encircled by his new friends, and naysayers are sent gently on their way...

V. ALL IN.
Where all commitments are secured, and the business is happily—and irrevocably—concluded.

A CODA: there may be many counterstrikes along the way, for such is the nature of the game; it contains so many sides, so many endless possibilities...

RULEBOOK—1799.

Prologue

Quinn

August 6th, 1898
Berkeley Square, London

There was no suggestion that Quinn might be allowed to dress herself. The boudoir was packed with people: maids and waiting women, ladies hovering behind painted screens. They'd peeled off her nightdress with fingers like spiders; they'd bathed her, ornamented her hair, added stain to her lips. And now they were arranged around the room in a circle, waiting for her next move.

Quinn could sense their nerves. This was a day of supreme importance, after all. The newspapermen were gathered on the pavement outside; the sketch writers had arrived en masse to take notes on the breakfast. The lawyers were on the landing, and the whole house was thick with the scent of orchids and pink roses and kippers. This day had been oiled, stoked, heated—readied for her.

"Come along, then," she said to the room, extending her arms, beckoning for the wedding gown. "Bring me the dress."

This boudoir was like all the rooms in the house: low-ceilinged, dark-lacquered. It was octagonal in shape, like a jewel box or crokinole board, full of cunning holes and gaps and hidden doors. The mirrors were age-spotted, marked with holes and scratches. Quinn perceived motion in the reflection: housemaids in dark uniforms, bringing out the dress.

It was a brutal-looking gown—constructed at great expense, according to Quinn's design. She touched the tangled, coruscated beading around the waist, letting the fabric glide from her fingers and ripple into creaseless folds. This dress was very ugly. Which was a good thing. Now was not the moment to be seduced by this wedding, nor this house. Quinn would not be lulled into false security by hot baths and swan-feather pillows and an army of servants. She had come too far, had been working too hard, to grow soft today.

"Lovely," she said, and stepped into the gown.

This was it: the final move in the game. She felt the pleasure of it, low in the gut. Ribs: hers. Spine: hers. Voice, changing. Expression, smoothing out. It wasn't acting, or not simply that: it was bigger and more important altogether.

Eyes down, lips pressed, waist tight, face becoming more famous by the hour. A face that in the past week had been photographed, sketched, scrutinized for flaws, praised for its beauty, decried for irregularities. A face for every occasion, a face that revealed nothing.

Her dress struggled, buckles snapping—as if it recognized her for what she was. A fraud. The best confidence woman in London. Queen of her very own underworld. But Quinn smiled. Arranged her skirts.

"Thank you," she said to the maids who laced her in. They flushed, pleased.

But they weren't on her side.

The clocks began chiming, right on schedule. This house

was filled with clocks, a hundred shimmering faces, a thousand points and alarms.

Time to get married.

"Where is the duke?" she murmured, breathing through her veil.

"His Grace is waiting for you downstairs," they said, as if to imply, *You need to hurry.*

It didn't matter how long you watched someone, spied on them, tried to learn their habits—you never really knew what was in their mind. But there was no time to doubt herself. Quinn was not someone who hesitated. She hated waiting; she despised it above all things. She had marched into that room to get her life back, to do what she had been trained to do. She adjusted her bouquet gingerly, wincing at a small pain in her wrist.

She—Quinn Le Blanc—dissolved. The person Berkeley Square needed, expected, *believed* her to be shimmered into view.

Day One
The Mark

1

Quinn

Five days earlier

Here was how it began. Four miles east of Berkeley Square, a few turns from Fashion Street and several doors down from the synagogue, stood a humble old house in Spitalfields. Four floors high, four bays across. Rose-colored shutters, a green trim to the door. A basement kitchen hidden from the street, and a colony of house sparrows nesting in the eaves, feasting on bread crusts and milk pudding scrapings.

On the first floor, behind peeling sash windows, stood Quinn Le Blanc.

She changed her gloves. She had a fine selection at her disposal, per her exalted rank in this neighborhood—chevrette kid, mousquetaire, pleated gloves for daytime, ridged ones for riding, silk-lined, fur-edged. All shades, too—dark, tan, brandy, black, mauve. No suede, of course. And no lace: nothing that could snag. The purpose of the glove was the preservation of the skin. Not from the sun, not from the cold.

From people.

She pulled on the French kid—cream-colored with green buttons—flexed her fingers, tested the grip. For she was the reigning Queen of Fives, the present mistress of this house; the details were everything.

"Mr. Silk?" she called from the gaming room. "Have you bolted the rear doors?"

His voice came back, querulous, from the stairs. "Naturally I have." Then the echo of his boots as he clumped away.

The gaming room breathed around her. It was hot, for they kept a good strong fire burning year-round, braving incineration. But now she threw cold water on the grate, making the embers hiss and smoke. She closed the drapes, which smelled as they always did: a tinge of tobacco and the sour tint of mildew. Something else, too: a touch of cognac, or absinthe—one of the prior queens had enjoyed her spirits.

Quinn examined the room, wondering if she should lock away any valuables for the week. Of course, she had no fears of not returning on schedule, in triumph, per her plan—but still, she was venturing into new and dangerous waters. Some prudence could serve her well. The shelves were crammed with objects: hatboxes, shoeboxes, vinegars, perfume bottles, merino cloths, linen wrappings. But then she decided against it; she despised wasting time. The most incriminating, valuable things were all stored downstairs, in the bureau.

The bureau contained every idea the household ever had, the schemes designed and played by generations of queens. It stood behind doors reinforced with iron bolts, windows that were bricked up and impassable. It was safe enough, for now.

"Quinn?" Silk's voice floated up the stairs. "We *must* be punctual."

"We will be," she called back with confidence.

Confidence was all they had going for them at the Château these days.

The Château. It was a pompous name for a humble old house. But that was the point, wasn't it? It gave the place a sense of importance in a neighborhood that great folk merely despised. There were tailors and boot finishers living on one side, cigar makers and scholars on the other, and a very notorious doss-house at the end of the road. Quinn had lived in it nearly all her life, alongside Mr. Silk.

Quinn descended the creaking staircase, flicking dust from the framed portraits lined along the wall. They depicted the Château's prior queens, first in oils, later in daguerreotype, with Quinn's own picture placed at the foot of the stairs. Hers was a carte de visite mounted in a gilt frame, adorned with red velvet curtains. In it, Quinn wore a thick veil, just like her predecessors. She carried a single game card in one hand, and she was dressed in her inaugural disguise—playing the very splendid "Mrs. Valentine," decked in emerald green velvet, ready to defraud the corrupt owners of the nearby Fairfield Works. She was just eighteen, and had already secured the confidence of the Château's other players—and she was ready to rule.

That was eight years ago.

Quinn rubbed the smeared glass with her cuff. The house needed a good spring clean. She'd given up the housekeeper months ago; even a scullery maid was too great an expense now. Glancing through the rear window, she caught her usual view of the neighborhood—rags flapping on distant lines, air hazed with smoke. The houses opposite winked back at her, all nets and blinds, their disjointed gardens tangled and wild. She fastened the shutters, checking the bolts.

Silk was waiting by the front door. "Ready?" He was wearing a bulky waistcoat, his cravat ruffled right up to his chin. His bald head shone in the weak light.

Quinn studied him, amused. "What have you stuffed yourself with?"

"Strips of steel, if you must know."

"In your jacket?"

"Yes."

"For what reason?"

"My own protection. What else?"

Quinn raised a brow. "You're developing a complex."

"We're living in a violent age, Le Blanc. A *terribly* violent age."

Silk was forever clipping newspaper articles about foreign agitators, bombs being left in fruit baskets on station platforms.

"Stay close to me, then," Quinn said, hauling open the front door, squinting in the light.

Net curtains twitched across the road. This was a quiet anonymous street, and the location of the Château was a closely guarded secret, even among their kind. But the neighbors kept their eyes on the Château. Nobody questioned its true ownership: the deeds had been adulterated too many times, sliced out of all official registers. In the 1790s, it was inhabited by an elusive Mrs. B—(real name unknown). Some said she'd been a disgraced bluestocking, or an actress, or perhaps a Frenchwoman on the run—a noble comtesse in disguise! She caught the neighborhood's imagination; they refashioned her in their minds. B—became "Blank," which in time became "Le Blanc." Her house was nicknamed *le Château*. Smoke rose from the chimneys; queer characters came and went; the lights burned at all hours. Some said Madame Le Blanc had started a school. Others claimed it was a brothel.

In fact, it was neither.

It was something much cleverer.

The Queen of Fives. They breathed the title with reverence on the docks, down the coastline. A lady with a hundred faces, a thousand voices, a million lives. She might spin into yours if you didn't watch out... She played a glittering game: lifting a man's fortune with five moves, in five days, before disappearing without a trace.

The sun was inching higher, turning the sky a hard mazarine blue. "Nice day for it," Quinn said, squeezing Silk's arm.

Silk peered upward. "I think not." He'd checked his barometer before breakfast. "There's a storm coming."

Quinn could feel it, the rippling pleasure down her spine. "Better and better," she replied. "Now, come along."

———

They made an unassuming pair when they were out in public. An older gentleman in a dark and bulky overcoat, with a very sleek top hat. A youngish woman in dyed green furs, with a high collar and a sharp-tilted toque. He with his eyes down, minding his step. She with her face veiled, gloves gripped round an elegant cane. Always listening, watching, rolling dice in their minds.

Silk and Quinn had a single clear objective for the day. Audacious, impossible, outrageous—but clear. He showed her his appointment book: *Three p.m.—Arrive in ballroom, Buckingham Palace, en déguisé.*

"In disguise? Doesn't that go without saying?"

"You tell me. Has your costume been delivered?"

"Not yet. But we have a more serious impediment."

"Oh?" he asked her.

"I've still not received my invitation card to the palace."

They turned into Fournier Street. Silk tutted. "I've dealt with that. Our old friend at the Athenaeum Club will oblige you."

"You're quite sure? We've never cut it so fine before."

"Well, you might need to prod him a little."

"Just a little?"

"The very *littlest* bit, Quinn."

Unnecessary violence was not part of their method. But persuasion—well, that was essential. Let's call a spade a spade: the Château was a fraud house, a cunning firm, a swindler's palace ruled by a queen. It made its business by cheating great men out of their fortunes. In the bureau stood the Rulebook, its marbled endpapers inscribed with each queen's initials, setting the conditions of their games.

And this week the Queen of Fives would execute the most dangerous game of her reign.

Quinn paused outside the Ten Bells. "Very well. We can't afford any slips. I'll go to the Athenaeum now. Anything else?"

Silk shook his head. *"Rien ne va plus."* No more bets.

They gripped hands. He gave her his usual look: a fond gaze, then a frown. "Play on, Le Blanc."

She grinned at him in return. "Same to you, old friend."

They parted ways.

And the game began.

———————

Quinn hailed a hansom cab at the junction of Aldgate East and Commercial Street.

"Which way, love?" said the driver. His eyes fixed on her fluttering ribbons, bright lincoln green, whipping in the breeze.

"Piccadilly," she said. "The Athenaeum Club. Fast as you can."

She worked in the back of the cab, chewing her pencil, marking up fashion sketches sent by her seamstresses on Hanbury Street. Quinn paid better wages than the sweating system, and her people worked quickly. Plus, the Château had a good string of haberdashers on their books to supply lace and trimmings at knockdown prices. Even so, this job required a significant wardrobe—fresh garments by the hour, on a need-to-wear basis, for all occasions. She willed herself not to think about the costs. Dwelling on her debts would only distract her at a time when she most needed to hold her nerve. The first day of a job was a delicate one. It needed to be handled with care.

The cab slowed, heading downhill, avoiding the broughams rolling out from St. James's Square. Quinn glanced through the window, watching the buildings expand, become grander. As she arrived at her destination, she fished out her purse, handed the driver his fare. "Keep the change." She leaped from the cab, avoiding the muck in the road, adjusting her veil.

The Athenaeum Club stood at the foot of Pall Mall, its stained plasterwork braced against a cloudless sky. A carriage drew up on the opposite side of Waterloo Square. A clergyman, evidenced by his dog collar, descended rather blearily to the pavement, also arriving on schedule for his luncheon. Quinn aimed straight for him, letting out a friendly cry. "Archdeacon!"

Quinn always liked to keep a churchman onside. One never knew when one might need someone to vouch for one's character, particularly on a job like this one, where she would have to penetrate the upper circle of society. The Château had clocked the archdeacon long ago, noting his more lascivious tastes, guarding his secrets. But they never *blackmailed* him. As long as people remembered what they owed to the Château, there was no need to tighten any screws. So Mr. Silk said, at any rate, listing obligations in the ledger.

The archdeacon swung around as Quinn approached. "Surely *not*," he said, looking round fast, trying to see whether they'd been observed. "This is my *club*. My own personal domain! Whatever are you doing here?" Then his face paled. "I suppose you've come about that dreadful woman. Well, I won't have it. She simply hurled herself upon me, absolutely without provocation, against my wishes. I would have every right to press charges against *her*..."

Quinn laid a gloved hand on his sleeve. "I'm not calling about your indiscretions, Archdeacon. I need your assistance."

"Absolutely not. I've signed more than enough credentials for one year. You're pressing me too hard."

Quinn dug her fingers into the crook of his elbow. "I'm not pressing at all, Archdeacon. I'm simply asking for your help."

He shook her off. "Regarding?"

"We are trying to procure an invitation to this afternoon's Drawing Room. We intend to present a young lady to the queen."

"Impossible."

"Quite possible."

"But what are you coming to *me* for? I can't give you access to Buckingham Palace—and certainly not at this hour. You'd need to speak to the Lord Chamberlain."

"We have tried—without success. Hence my request."

The archdeacon's lip curled. "I fear he may be rather out of your reach, Madam. Even *your* charms have their limits."

Quinn studied him coolly through her veil. "But yours don't. Go to the Lord Chamberlain at once."

"Look here, enough is enough. I can't possibly…" The archdeacon shook his top hat at her. "Extortion is one thing. But to poke a chap's social currency, ask him to call in favors from his friends? It simply won't *do*. I shall have to go to the police."

They'd been through this a hundred times before. Quinn unfolded a banknote from her sleeve. "First payment, Archdeacon, as a goodwill gesture. And the next to follow later this week. I need an admittance card."

Sometimes Quinn wondered if it would count against her at the gates of paradise, offering so many bribes to men of the cloth. Apparently, it didn't worry the archdeacon.

"You really are quite an extraordinary young woman," he said, folding the banknote into his pocket. "Silk's trained you so remarkably well. You *appear* perfectly well bred."

Quinn ignored this. "How quickly can you get me the card?"

"I can't make you any promises. You shall have to supply me with all the references: moral character of the girl in question, the name of a lady to make the presentation…"

"Naturally. But I shall expect the card to be in my hand the moment I arrive at the palace. You have five hours."

"You are asking me to move heaven and earth, Madam. I can guarantee you nothing."

"Do you wish to repay your advance, Archdeacon?"

He studied her for a long moment. Then sagged, beaten. "Very well. I shall try my very best. Who's your victim this time?"

"Victim?"

"Your quarry, your kill? Who do you intend to ruin *this* week?"

Quinn saw no harm in telling him. They had him by the throat; he was employed by the Château under indentured servitude.

"The Kendal family," she said. "Do you know them?"

The archdeacon began to laugh in disbelief. "Know them?" he repeated, slapping his thighs, as if the joke were too good to be true. "Do I *know* them?"

Quinn would have quite happily shoved him into a passing omnibus. But his face suddenly became serious.

"You don't stand a chance."

2

Tor

Kendal House was once considered a handsome building: one of the oldest residences in Berkeley Square, Palladian in its lines, constructed from honeyed limestone. Now it was transformed. A house so lavishly remodeled it might have been stricken with scarlet fever, fronted with crimson sandstone and blood-colored brick. It was wide and flat-faced, seven bays across, adorned with dark pediments and moldings that looked like devils' wings. But Tor thought it was a perfect house, the best in London. It stood vast and aloof on the north side of Berkeley Square, running to its own rhythms, containing myriad wonders: the orchid house heated with steam pipes; the oak staircase crenellated in the medieval style; the magnificent smoking parlor, festooned with rich silks and giltwork. Its perfection transferred itself on to the servants and the horses; it ran through every polished, lacquered line and flickered in the electric lights.

It was the best house anywhere.

Every time Tor Kendal ascended the broad front steps, spread out her arms, ran her fingers along the tips of those vicious up-thrusting railings, she felt the deep, pleasurable sensation of knowing she was *home*. Her blood existed in the bones of this house. She would never leave.

Tor liked to say these things out loud, even though such frankness made other people uneasy. Of course, she understood this. She knew she was one of society's most detestable creations: a well-born woman of thirty-five, not married, too rich to bear. But Tor spoke her mind, regardless of censure. After all, being a Kendal was not like being any other sort of person. This family was not like other families.

Tor's neighbors went to church every Sunday and tried to pray their sins away—or else pretend they had no sins at all. Tor didn't care about sinning. Her sins belonged to her; she was not afraid of them. Sometimes the neighbors—fellow members of the nobility, members of Parliament, illustrious bankers—stared at her askance, or tutted as she rode by—not toward St. George's, or St. James's, or the Church of the Immaculate Conception, but in the other direction altogether. To the park, to the wide-open sky, to freedom. She didn't know why they needed to *demonstrate* their judgment. To frighten her? To remind her that she was alone in the world? To discourage her independence? Well, Tor was not discouraged and she was unrepentant.

She would not change for anybody.

———◆———

The day had opened with a message from Tor's stepmother. It was inscribed on a small card, delivered to her rooms on a silver platter. They did a lot of message sending in this household. Kendals traveled in a pack—stepmother, brother, sister, shifting from Kendal House to Loch Lomond, the Peaks, the Isle of Wight, Biarritz, Paris, Cowes—but they maintained separate quarters,

interests, hours. Communication was managed through intermediaries; they didn't need to *talk* to one another.

The note card from Lady Kendal had been stamped with the
family crest: bloodred, dripping. The words had been copied out
in a secretary's rigid hand, presumably by dictation: /

> *Darling Victoria. Today we will attend the Queen's Drawing*
> *Room. No need at ALL to accompany. With love. M.*

Tor had woken as she always did, at six o'clock, to the sound
of the girls scuttling up the servants' stairs lodged between the
walls, cleaning the grates in her private parlor. She had eaten no
breakfast to speak of, only a few slices of fruit placed on a dish
with a Kendal-monogrammed napkin. Then she'd dressed herself
in her riding habit. Every morning, irrespective of the weather,
she circled Hyde Park and Rotten Row. Afterward, she would
return for a scalding hot bath, change—without the assistance of
a maid—and then attack the day. She was the first up, the first
out, and she would do all this without seeing or hearing from
her stepmother and brother at all. So the arrival of this message
gave her a prickle of surprise.

"Any reply, my lady?" the footman asked.

The card was embossed, gilded, thick. Tor turned it over.
"Lady Kendal sent this?"

"Yes, my lady."

Tor frowned. "They're going out?"

He nodded.

"Together?"

"Separately. Lady Kendal has appointments in town. The duke
will leave at noon; he has ordered the landau."

We are attending the Queen's Drawing Room.

For what reason? The Kendals were *known* for never attending
society functions; Tor declined invitations for balls and suppers
and breakfast parties all the time; they never went to the races

or diplomatic receptions. Tor couldn't think of the last time her brother had visited a presentation ceremony at the palace— probably not since her own coming-out, more than fifteen years before.

"*Why* are they going?" she asked the footman.

Of course, he was unable to answer this. The family didn't explain itself to anybody. *Our blood, our laws.* He looked at her helplessly.

"No reply, then," Tor said, and closed the door.

She locked it, as she always did, to avoid any prying eyes.

———

The best thing to do, when unsettled, was to seek further information. So Tor sent a message of her own to someone who would be compelled to tell her the truth. Not one of the servants: they were not easily compromised. But one of the lawyers, secretaries, and moneymen. "Send for Mr. Willoughby," Tor told the housekeeper. "Tell him to come riding with me."

The air in the stable yard was humid. These stables—plastered, plumbed, illuminated by electric lights—were the best in London. Tor had ordered portraits of the family's ponies to be put up on the interior walls: a whole gallery of dun mares, wild-eyed and lovely, bearing the names she'd chosen for them—"Beauty" and "Amulet" and "Cousin Emmeline." Tor kept hunters and jennets in London, as well as some very superior Flemish mares, and a rare little Scotch Galloway, *and* a collection of Barbs and Turkoman descendants, purchased at quite unimaginable expense. Well, not wholly unimaginable. Mr. Willoughby kept an eye on the bills. He'd already given her several warnings about the dangers of profligate spending. Tedious—and quite unnecessary. Kendals could indulge every whim, every fantasy they could conjure, and they'd still have a fortune left over.

"My lady?"

Tor turned. Willoughby was trotting out from the stables

to greet her, tipping his top hat. The grooms had saddled Patience for him, one of her favorite mares. She approached, and he halted. She ran her fingers down Patience's crest, knuckled the mare's forehead gently. "Poor girl," she said in a low voice, leaning against the horse's shoulder. "You slept badly, did you not? We will take care of you."

She glanced up. Willoughby was sleekly dressed in a bright blue coat, a little garish for a man of his age—past forty, Tor was certain, though his smooth face and polished skin belied it. He grinned down at her, his teeth white and glinting.

"How nice of you to send for me."

She studied him seriously. "You do *know* how to ride, don't you?" she asked. He was a town creature, she realized—slender in his build, delicate around the wrists and ankles. He might have no seat on him.

His smile faltered fractionally. "Of course! One adores to ride."

Tor checked Patience's straps. "Not right," she said to the horse, adjusting the buckles. "Not right at all. Our grooms must want you to break your neck."

They brought out her own horse: she lifted herself smoothly into her own saddle. "Now, tell me," she said over her shoulder, getting straight to the point. "What are my brother and Lady Kendal up to?"

She saw it: the brief contraction in his expression—as if calculating. And then she knew, she *knew*: something was happening.

◆

The quickest way to Hyde Park was along Hill Street, and they rode together without the grooms, Tor leading the way. The sky was blue, almost cloudless. Tor wore her tricorn hat, pressed down hard upon her brow; she could feel sweat prickling against her scalp as the constable halted the traffic coming round Hyde Park Corner. People stopped and stared at her from the pavement. She understood this: she was a great lady, riding out in state. She expected she made a very fine sight.

"I don't know that Their Graces are *up to* anything," Mr. Willoughby said. They turned leftward toward the riding track.

"No?" Tor nudged the mare, moving it neatly into a canter, lining up to the smooth curve of the carriage drive. "Then *why* is my brother going to the palace? He never does."

"Don't you think it's rather nice that His Grace wishes to go abroad in society a little? The season is almost over, after all. The world will start to forget about the Kendals if they never go out, my lady."

Tor snorted at this. "When did we ever depend on society's interest in our actions? *You* can sing for your supper if you like. I don't wish to."

Willoughby appeared to take this placidly. "There comes a time, Lady Victoria, when even a duke must go hunting for favors."

"Favors?" The crowd by the railings thinned out; they cantered to the long stretch of the track beyond, the mud dry and burned by the sun. "What favors does my brother need?"

The breeze tossed Willoughby's voice toward her. "Friends. Allies. Votes."

"Votes? Max can't bear going to the lords. That has nothing to do with it." Dust rose in huge clouds around her. "And what will he do with himself at a presentation ceremony? Talk to a collection of chinless debs?"

"He might enjoy meeting some of the new young ladies at court."

"No," Tor said firmly. "He won't. He'll stand in the corner and talk to nobody. I know my brother." She gave Willoughby a sharp look. "Are you trying to provoke me?"

"Why should it anger your ladyship, to see the duke happy?"

"He is happy."

"A little courting could make him happier still."

"Courting?" Tor reined her horse in. "Is that what he's doing?"

Willoughby shifted in his saddle. "Would it be a very bad thing?"

Tor felt a headache coming on. This, again? Over and over, the subject came up from the household—the lawyers and the secretaries and the money people. Marriage, always marriage. Not hers: that topic had been closed long ago. But Max's.

"My brother will not marry," she said shortly, adjusting her tricorn hat. "Whatever you say about it."

"You sound so certain."

"He is too old."

"He is thirty! Or about to turn so."

"Precisely."

"Well, what better time to settle the matter? Lady Kendal's ball could provide the perfect occasion to make a happy announcement."

"Oh," Tor said with a shudder, "the ball." The servants were in a frenzy over it. Her stepmother had decided they ought to celebrate Max's birthday in some style—although Tor could not think of the last time they'd opened their doors to a crowd, not even for a card party. She dreaded it: the house would be overrun by interlopers. "I am sick to death of hearing about it." She turned. "What *is* Lady Kendal's part in all this?"

He remained neutral. "Naturally the household has spoken to Her Grace about the merits of His Grace getting married. It is a rather pressing topic. The duke's succession will protect you all."

"Not all," Tor said fiercely. "Not *all* of us." She gripped her reins tighter. "Discuss it between you as much as you like. I'm certain my brother won't bend on it."

"I think he will, your ladyship."

"Then you shall be proven wrong."

Willoughby's expression darkened. "I wish your ladyship would leave the matter alone."

"I am sure you would. But perhaps I shall raise it with my brother instead."

Willoughby revealed a flash of discomfiture. "*Strictly* speaking, the duke has not yet made up his mind to go to the palace this afternoon. The lawyers and I intend to raise it with him this morning."

Tor reined in her horse. She stared at Willoughby in astonishment. "Lady Kendal's note said the appointment was settled."

"And so it shall be! Once we discuss it with His Grace."

"So my stepmother is leading the matter."

"I think Lady Kendal's motives are to be commended. Her Grace desires peace and prosperity for both of you, and for the whole estate."

Tor flicked her horse's reins. "I've heard enough. Don't speak of this again. There will be no marriage. We don't need any strangers in Kendal House."

———————

Yet, on the return journey, she began to grow anxious. Lady Kendal loved Max quite as much as she loved Tor: her word, her guidance, her suggestions—these things would carry weight with the duke. If she *did* take Max to Buckingham Palace, they would have every opportunity to inspect the young women being brought out into society. But it perplexed Tor utterly. Why would Lady Kendal push for Max to marry—now, after all this time? She had never interfered in their personal affairs before. "Darling Tor," she always said, expression misty. "All I *ever* want is to see you perfectly happy."

Tor *was* perfectly happy. She would be absolutely and fully content if things remained exactly as they were. Was that so very much to ask? Of course, she had her grievances; who wouldn't, in her position? She was the eldest child of the House of Kendal, but her brother had been the heir to the estate from the day he was born, the repository of the family's hopes and expectations, filled with Latin and Greek and all the right opinions. He would inherit the earth and she would inherit nothing. So far so typical. Naturally, Tor had been advised to marry, for her own welfare—but she didn't wish to acquire security through marriage. What she *wanted* was to keep her home. She wanted the land, the rocks; she wanted to stay dug into *her* soil.

Here was the source of her fear. If her brother married, sired a child, and an heir, then Tor's position would be supplanted. A new Duchess of Kendal would never put up with Tor's omnipresence in the house. Her rooms would be stripped and remodeled and transformed back into nursery quarters.

But she and Max had made their agreement: they would *never* marry. Years had passed; they had both held fast.

It was bad enough that she was expected to join the birthday ball. To break the customs of this house—to throw open the doors, just to celebrate the hour of his birth. Nobody held a dance for Tor when she turned thirty. The very notion would have made her sick.

Things were moving in a disagreeable direction. They required direct intervention. Back at Kendal House, Tor took out a note card, scratched out a message in navy ink—and made an appointment to see her stepmother.

3

Mr. Silk

Mr. Silk knew that some people thought him dour, even stuck in the mud. But he understood his own capacities. Some showmen wore big capes and handled lions. They loved the stage; they needed applause. But Silk prided himself on being a faithful lieutenant. Pulling levers, mending gears, fixing lights—from the wings.

And today he was in his element, ready to run an auction.

It would not take place in an auction house. Rather, it would be conducted from the back parlor of Mr. Russo's Luncheon Rooms on Lisle Street, where Silk kept regular appointments at his favorite table. He liked to do business on this side of town—while it was no less smoggy than Spitalfields, and in some corners very badly paved, holding meetings here preserved a proper distance from the Château. And doing things properly was Silk's watchword.

He grew sentimental as he crossed Shaftesbury Avenue. He'd

spent his boyhood in Soho, and it was hard not to mourn the things that had vanished from this neighborhood: Cantelo's Chicken Establishment, and the coffee shop on Berwick Street that smelled of marjoram, and the ability to order a good piece of roast beef for sixpence. Sixpence! But those things had been replaced with everything modern and convenient: market stalls selling Milanese stockings, and eating houses that served lamb cutlets *à la Constance*, and waiters who spoke very intelligent German. Quite right, of course, and Mr. Silk was the last person in the world to impede progress. But he would have enjoyed a little of that shrimp sauce they used to serve on Beak Street.

"You're growing soft," Quinn had told him amusedly, when he expressed this opinion.

"Good," he replied. Too many men were brutes. A certain pathos was necessary in their line of work. "We need to see into people, right down to their bones. We need to feel *everything*, to slide under someone's skin."

"How ghoulish."

"I'd rather be a ghoul than be hanged."

"Oh, you won't be hanged." Quinn had laughed. "We've made it this far in life. Nobody can possibly catch us now."

This was so utterly not true that it had almost made Silk lose his temper—until he realized that Quinn was bluffing, testing him. Some people presumed Silk was the paterfamilias of the Château: a kindly uncle, a gruff tutor, a tetchy majordomo. This missed the mark entirely. Silk was Quinn's chief counsel, her liege man. The oldest, most loyal servant to her crown. It was he who guarded the Rulebook, who took care of the bureau.

The bureau had always resided in the fortressed gloom of the back parlor at the Château. It was a Flemish cabinet, made of dark oak. It contained a dozen drawers, the knobs hung with tassels, and bits of shipyard rope, and desiccated conkers, and gemstones wrapped in black thread—symbols and reminders left by other queens over the years. Inside the drawers were the note cards and the indexed games. Each one carried precise particulars. A proposed game: "False Prince," "Vanishing Act," "Firework Surprise," "Death of a Countess," and so on. Notes: engineering, acts of coercion required, estimated payouts, necessary costs. It was the Château's brain. It was the source of all their trade.

Mr. Russo's waiter greeted him at the anonymous door on Lisle Street, conducting him to a back parlor illuminated by lanterns flooding the crimson-patterned wallpaper. The windows were so heavily swagged with velvet as to eliminate both the sunlight and the view of the dingy yard beyond.

"Allow twenty minutes for each visitor, please," Mr. Silk told the waiter. "If they're blathering, burn something in the kitchen."

"Very good, sir." The waiter put a large glass of champagne on the table, adding, "Particular compliments of Mr. Russo."

Silk inclined his head. "You may tell Mr. Russo we appreciate his courtesy very much." He made a reminder in the margin of his appointment book: *reduce Mr. Russo's levy by six shillings per annum.* When it came to managing their suppliers and informants, Silk always played fair. Mr. Russo had been paying gifts to the Château for years, and this was a most excellent glass of champagne. Silk could loosen the shackles.

He allowed the waiter to unfold his napkin with a flourish, and a bell tinkled in the hall. "Your first companion, Mr. Silk."

Silk smiled, admiring the glinting surface of his knife. "Do send him in."

The first meetings went swiftly. Each visitor arrived punctually, was seated by the smooth-mannered waiter, enveloped by their napkins. They were of a similar type: land agents and private secretaries and attorneys retained by powerful gentlemen. They picked at the dishes waved under their noses: eggs *à la Villeroi*, potatoes *aux truffes*, a little roast fowl, some of Mr.

Russo's delicious risotto. When eighteen minutes had passed, the waiter would murmur, "Perhaps you wish to wash your hands, monsieur?" and the fellow would rise from the table, make his clipped farewells, and depart.

The fourth man to arrive was a chap called Mr. Lancer, who had a long thin face and fussed endlessly with his cutlery. "What are you hawking?" he asked Silk, trying to catch an asparagus spear on his fork. "Stocks? Bonds?"

In normal circumstances, Silk would have nodded and passed over a written prospectus. This time, he dabbed his mouth with his napkin and said, "I'm representing a lady. In a personal matter."

Lancer grimaced. "A *lady*?"

Quinn had planned her latest part with care. She and Silk had rehearsed all the details. "A lady of very good stock, residing near St. James Garlickhythe."

"Cheapside?"

"The daughter of a merchant banking family, long-established in the city."

"Name?"

Silk smiled. "White," he said. "Miss White."

"And what does she want with me?"

"Nothing at all, Mr. Lancer. But you represent Lord Rochester's affairs, do you not?"

"What of it?"

"I hear those affairs have been a little—*turbulent*, of late."

Lancer's expression became flat. "The earl's finances are in perfect order."

"Really? I caught word of quite monumental debts. Of course, I understand. The price of coal beggars belief." Silk sipped his champagne. "I presume his lordship would like to turn his fortunes around?"

"We're always looking to invest, sir," said Lancer, swigging his own claret. "But I presume your *Miss White* is not selling stock options."

"Miss White is looking to be married."

Mr. Lancer fell silent. He ran his fingernail around the circumference of his claret glass. "Married?" Lancer said. "Goodness." But there was a light in his eyes now. "I'm not sure I can oblige you. Lord Rochester is a sentimental man. He'd only ever marry for love."

"Of course," Silk replied, chewing his cold beef contentedly. "Quite right."

"And he's a widower, of course."

"Indeed."

"*And* fastidious. He doesn't go dipping in any old tuppeny-ha'penny ponds."

Silk said, more curtly, "No."

"Are we brokering a marriage?"

"At this moment we're just enjoying our lunch."

"And are you talking to anyone else?"

Silk tilted his head. "I do have a number of appointments."

Mr. Lancer put down his fork. "Lord Rochester is one of the principal peers of the realm. He does not need to enter competition for *any* bride."

Silk cleared his throat. "I should tell you, Mr. Lancer, that Miss White's parents are sadly deceased."

Lancer glanced up. "She's an heiress?"

"She is."

"How much?"

"In dowry?" Mr. Silk reached down, picked up a leatherbound folder. He had produced ledgers and balance sheets, a labyrinthine account of bonds and settlements, assets traded and sold. Falsified, naturally—but extremely convincing.

Lancer was alert now. "Dowry—and the rest."

"In general terms, including any depreciations not yet realized in the accounts?"

"Yes. Bottom line. What's the sum?"

Silk named a figure.

Lancer sat up straighter.

Silk said, "Naturally, there is significant interest in Miss White's hand."

"Who? A few old baronets taking a pop? I can't tell Lord Rochester to send for his mother's engagement ring if he's going to get beaten to the altar. We put in all sorts of approaches to a girl from New York last year, but her family closed with a brewer instead. Complete waste of time." He scratched his chin. "What's the girl *like*? Is she a decent shot? What of her stock? Fertile? Has she ever been to Cowes?"

Truthfully, he and Quinn had never been to the Isle of Wight for the racing; it had always felt too far above their usual station. Silk dodged the question, draining his glass. "She will be the jewel of the season."

"And your objective…"

"Is to keep you informed. In the spirit of neighborliness."

Mr. Lancer gave him a quizzical look. "*Are* we neighbors?"

"In the spirit of fraternity," Silk said quickly. He disliked this sort of horse-trading; he disliked it intensely. But Quinn had pushed him.

"Don't be squeamish," she'd told him. "You're not selling *me*, not really. You're selling *Miss White*."

"It's crass," Silk had replied. "It's grubby. And besides, it's a waste of time. We have our mark. It's the *Kendals* we're after. And they don't need to marry a rich heiress for money. They've *got* money."

"Exactly," Quinn said briskly. "Which is why we need to drum up some competition, to attract their interest. I want an auction for my hand. A big one. By the time the world sees me, I want every great family gasping for my attention."

"Gasping?"

"*Gasping*, Silk."

Silk knew in his heart that Quinn was right: her powers of

negotiation were ferocious. So he'd sent out his tendrils, sprinkled his gossip, and set up these luncheons. He was holding them on the first day of the game for a reason. Whip up the market too early, and they'd lose control of the story. Leave it too late, and they'd generate no interest at all. Precision, as always, was everything. Besides, this was a new card, freshly plucked from the bureau. Nobody at the Château had ever played "False Heiress" before.

Mr. Lancer picked at his bread roll, leaving crumbs all over the tablecloth. "I suppose," he said carefully, "Lord Rochester might be inclined to look over this young lady's paperwork."

"He had better do so swiftly," Silk said. "Her diary is unutterably full. She is being presented at court this afternoon."

Lancer's expression was supercilious. "If she's out for a title, she won't do much better than the Rochesters."

"Will she not?" Silk said mildly. "We'll see." He laid down his butter knife. "I'm taking best bets, Mr. Lancer. Do let me know if you're in."

———

After luncheon, Silk spent a long time scrubbing his hands. The Earl of Rochester was a joke. An impoverished nobleman with a crumbling estate. Still, the exchange had done the trick: Mr. Lancer had scuttled straight off to discuss the matter with his master. The other secretaries and lawyers Silk had met with would be doing exactly the same. By three o'clock, Quinn would have achieved her design. The news would be out across the capital: a great and mighty fortune was coming on to the market...

But these were just the preliminaries. Stoking the fire, making sure their ground was piping hot. The true gambit would come this afternoon—provided Quinn gained entry to Buckingham Palace in time.

If anyone could, she could.

Silk was good at his job. He knew the rules. He kept hens in the backyard, minded the books, consulted the Rulebook on points of order. He preserved the old customs: dusted the portraits of past queens, indexed their games.

But Quinn kept them both alive.

He knew the world was changing, the century coming to a close. He couldn't very well *not* know it: ironworks closing, steamer routes opening, strikes, the endless prescription of anodynes. It wearied him tremendously. Mr. Silk had grown up among the old trades—silk weaving and rag fairs—he didn't care about dynamos and small arms and electricity. He didn't care for change. This was his great strength. Doing things in the proper order, to assure the queen's success.

He owed everything to the Château. This place had given him refuge when nobody else would, when even sixpence for roast beef seemed like an eye-watering sum. He had been hired on decades before—as a boot boy, scrawny and watchful. The Château taught him to read, fed him, gave him manners. It gave his life shape, warmth, *routine*. He became a true and faithful servant to the house.

Regardless of the cost. Regardless of the little voice that told him: *you've given up your life, your whole life—to play second fiddle.*

Regardless, too, of their mounting debts, and the threats posed by their more recalcitrant neighbors. Silk did all he could to protect the household, to preserve the Château's neutrality during gang skirmishes. Theirs was not the only criminal empire in East London, not by any stretch of the imagination. Mr. Silk paid a regular levy to Mr. Murphy, down in Bow, for the privilege of playing on turf the Murphy family otherwise controlled. But Silk was late on that payment; they'd received two reminders already.

The Murphys were not the sort to send a third.

Silk swept his concerns from his mind, dried his hands, buttoned his greatcoat. He felt a little woozy from the wine; he took a neat sip of tepid coffee. "Compliments to Mr. Russo," he said to the waiter, and then he beetled out into the city, ready for his next move.

4

Quinn

Quinn marched uphill to Piccadilly and boarded an omnibus heading toward Oxford Street. She sat on the top deck, ordering herself to enjoy the breeze. Fresh air would provide a stimulus. She needed to use her imagination now; she needed to hold her new character in her mind.

"Ticket, miss?" said the conductor.

"Portman Square," she replied, testing a new voice. Something clipped. Something that indicated wealth and refinement.

"Eh?"

"Portman *Square*," she repeated, clearing her throat. Evidently, she needed to warm up. The conductor punched her ticket and he leaned on the metal railing, studying the street below. There was an argument underway—someone had upturned a coster's barrow, sending his turnips rolling into the gutter. Quinn focused herself. Pretending to be a wealthy heiress wasn't difficult. *Maintaining* that fiction for more than fifteen minutes would be

very nearly impossible. Society would conduct the most ruthless due diligence on her. Parentage, reputation, moral rectitude,
medical antecedents, stock fertility, asset placement, stock and
bond certificates...

So Quinn needed a chaperone. An aide-de-camp who could
go places Mr. Silk couldn't. A person with an unimpeachable
reputation.

She had only one candidate in mind. A lady who was not
easy to pin down, not easy to persuade. Quinn had been leaving her visiting cards at her house for weeks, angling for an appointment, all in vain. Now time was running out. She needed
to settle this, at once.

Once this would have been straightforward enough to arrange.
At the start of Quinn's reign, the Château had a dozen people
living under its roof—old-fashioned dodgers, actresses selling
counterfeit maquillage, chiselers seeking funds for Spanish pris-
oners, girls trained in the Academy—sharing proceeds, running
jobs right across the capital. Quinn could have dolled any of them
up in long gloves and ostrich plumes and passed them off as a
decrepit countess or keen-eyed secretary. This was her prerogative. The Queen of Fives was supposed to have a whole band of
merry players at her disposal, to furnish her games, to feather her
nest—and inherit her crown, when she decided to set it aside.

But the old players had drifted away, one by one. Quinn accepted their reasons, though she cursed their disloyalty—and
her own failure to retain them. There was a time when Quinn
Le Blanc was famed for raising more capital in a single year than
any other swindler in Europe. Moreover, she spread the profits
around Spitalfields, earning loyalty as a beloved queen. It made
her heart thrum with satisfaction; it was the work that rooted
her to the city, gave her life meaning.

But the past two years had yielded poor returns: jobs kept stuttering, their marks getting scared off. Her debts rose; her influence waned. The Château's courtiers had started badgering her

for their dividends, pressing her endlessly to make changes to the way she ran the Château—to find new jobs, win bigger prizes, take risks outside the strict parameters of the Rulebook. Wasn't she going to consider steam power? Or phosphorescence? Or emotionometers? There was a man in Berlin using fluorescent prisms; couldn't she try some of that? Their pentagonal method was growing passé.

"Phosphorescence," Silk muttered. "Really."

"And you need a new steward," one of the old players had told Quinn, nodding toward Mr. Silk, bustling around the yard. "Someone with a bit of imagination."

This bewildered Quinn, although she was careful not to admit it. "Sign this," she said coldly, passing him his deed of confidentiality and dispensation. "And don't come back."

Quinn would never dismiss Silk. Could never dismiss him. He was as much a part of the Château as the Rulebook, as the bureau, as the games themselves. Still, she wondered whether he had everything in order.

"Do we need to take out a loan?" she'd asked him.

"Not in the least," he replied, poring over his ledgers. "We're simply fine, especially if it's just the two of us. No risk at all."

Quinn didn't call him a liar; she knew he believed his figures. But she knew they couldn't go on like this. She was twenty-six. She couldn't spend her whole life cutting costs, watching the walls closing in, seeing the light fizzling out of her life. She needed to place some bigger bets. It gnawed at her, night and day.

She touched the necklace at her throat, seeking the assurance it always offered. Her mother's initials were still monogrammed on the pendant: **L. Q. R.**

Lillian Quinn.

Quinn's mother—and one of the Château's best-loved queens.

Lillian had been twenty-seven when she died. Only one year older than Quinn was now. Her portrait stood on the staircase: a queen in pearlescent silks, sumptuous chocolate velvet trim and tassels. A young woman in the prime of her life, at the height of her reign—with a daughter barely two years old.

When she thought about her mother, Quinn felt as if her heart were tick-ticking ever faster—by the month, by the year...

It made her determined to win this game.

Her mind drifted, preoccupied, fizzing—and so she didn't notice the chap sitting three rows behind. She didn't see him slip a slender hand into his shiny blue silk waistcoat, checking the knife in his breast pocket; didn't realize she was being held under observation at all.

———◆———

Quinn got off the bus at Portman Square and went the rest of the way on foot, stopping outside a spindly coffee-colored house on Spanish Place. She steeled herself and rang the bell.

She heard movement on the other side of the door, sensed an eyeball watching her through the spyhole.

"Quinn Le Blanc for Mrs. Airlie," she called.

A shuffle of footsteps, as the person on the other side retreated into the house.

Quinn waited.

The sun was warm on her neck. The house stared down at her, flat-faced, anonymous—but she caught a tiny twitching of the blinds on the third floor. One of Mrs. Airlie's students had peeked out the window. This wasn't simply a private residence. It was the Academy.

The door opened. A housemaid stood there, wincing in the daylight. Her apron was a dazzling shade of white: handmade, exquisitely embroidered. Mrs. Airlie believed in taking care of the details.

"Come in, then," the maid said, unsmiling, and pulled open the door.

Quinn stepped inside.

The front hall was long and dim, the carpet as soft and dense as moss. Quinn could see her reflection in myriad oval mirrors as she unclasped her veil and lifted her hat. She removed her hatpins, letting her hair fall loose over her shoulders—her own dark waves, for she wasn't wearing a wig yet. Then she held up her arms while the maid swept her hands all over Quinn's blouse, armpits, waistline, down her thighs, nipping sharp fingers round the inside of her boots.

"I'm not carrying anything," said Quinn.

The maid rose, curtsied. "Mrs. Airlie says to come upstairs."

The drawing room was on the first floor. Here the light was golden, the furnishings swagged in yellow and green and brown velvet, the walls crammed with prints and miniatures. A lamp swung gently from the ceiling and beneath it, haloed, sat a woman—perhaps fifty, perhaps a little older—guarded by side tables and footstools and escritoires and armchairs. She was watching Quinn as she entered the room, counting every hair on Quinn's head, studying every muscle in Quinn's face.

"Le Blanc," the woman said with the faintest, most quizzical note of surprise.

"Mrs. Airlie," Quinn replied.

The drawing room door clicked shut.

Quinn could hear the tread of footsteps upstairs—Mrs. Airlie's girls returning to their desks and their studies. Unexpected visitors were an abnormal occurrence in the Academy. For this place kept the tightest of schedules. Routine was important. It was the stuff of life. Quinn had been taught that lesson herself: Mrs. Airlie had once been her own tutor.

"You've come seeking a favor," said Mrs. Airlie. It wasn't a question.

"You didn't return my cards," said Quinn lightly. "I thought I'd stop by in person."

Mrs. Airlie didn't smile. Her self-possession was absolute. She kept her neck collared, her hair artfully twisted and upholstered. Her skin glowed white under the light veil that came down to her chin; she almost certainly went in for the enameling of the face, and she was wrapped all over in muslin: hands concealed in fragile gloves. But it was still possible to see her eyes—large, dark, rounded.

"Tell me when you intend to leave," she said.

Not, *why are you here?* Not, *what do you want?* Long ago, Mrs. Airlie had taught Quinn a simple rule. Calculate the number of minutes you wish to remain in a room. Subdivide that number into thirds. At the end of the first third, you must create a surprise. At the second, a crisis. At the third, you must depart, leaving your hostess desperate for you to stay. It was the only way to manage a visit, to command a room. It was the method that Mrs. Airlie herself had developed as a young and wealthy bride—back when she moved in polite circles, before she disappeared from society and established the Academy.

Quinn considered it. "Twenty-four minutes," she said.

Mrs. Airlie raised a pristine eyebrow. "Eights," she said. "Ambitious. The girls upstairs are stuck on fives."

"So was I, for the longest time."

"You, my dear, are stuck forever." Mrs. Airlie reached for one of her side tables. Picked up a silver stopwatch. Jabbed the button with her veiled thumb. "Clock's ticking," she said, lips thinning beneath her veil.

———◆———

Mrs. Airlie was no longer a confidence woman, not exactly. She *had* been a player in the Château once, long ago. Rumor had it she'd even stood to be elected queen—she must have lost the vote. Later, she focused her energies on the London season, attaching herself to a certain Brigadier Cuthbert Airlie, inheriting his modest fortune when he died. But that life didn't agree with her: she'd unstitched herself from polite society before she even left mourning. She purchased a house for a whole new purpose.

"This is the nature of our world," she once told Quinn. "You can never leave it behind."

She didn't resume playing confidence tricks. She came up with a completely different enterprise: instructing the next generation in the arts of disguise. She bought the silent house on Spanish Place, selected her pupils with utmost care, trained them to run their own jobs in Paris, Monte Carlo, St. Petersburg. There were plenty of wealthy—and frankly rather criminal—families both in England and abroad who admired the Château from afar. They envied its profits, and happily paid for their own daughters to study at the Academy—in the hope that their girls might one day join the Château, or one of the other cunning firms popping up across the Continent. Silk had sent Quinn to the Academy when she turned eleven. She was one of Mrs. Airlie's most intelligent students, the most disciplined, the one everyone said was destined for greatness. She was Mrs. Airlie's best advertisement.

The Academy gave Quinn every advantage. Mrs. Airlie brought in professors—blindfolded, handcuffed—to instruct Quinn in rhetoric, oratory, the nature of the intellect. Beautifully schooled herself, Mrs. Airlie taught French, Italian, German, and Greek and farmed out Latin to one of her assistants. She raced Quinn through drawing, screen painting, embroidery—all those tedious accomplishments—and then drilled her in the true quadrivium: arithmetic, geometry, music, astronomy. For Mrs. Airlie's view was that a woman with a finely formed education could secure the confidence of anybody, anywhere, under any circumstance.

"You are a clever young person," Mrs. Airlie used to tell Quinn, "but a disagreeable student. You lack foresight. You operate *here*." She'd pressed her fingertips against the surface of Quinn's chest, above her heart. "Not *here*." She reached round and tucked a hard nail into the soft space at the base of Quinn's skull, making the girl wince. "*This* is where your finest machinery is located."

"I'm not a machine at all," Quinn had replied.

"More's the pity." Mrs. Airlie shook her head. "And modu-late your tone. If you had been raised by your own mother, you would have been taught manners. Rules."

Mrs. Airlie knew everything. And this impressed Quinn. She gave Mrs. Airlie her full attention. "Not too close, Le Blanc," Mrs. Airlie would say, when they took their brisk walks, arm in arm, around Manchester Square. Mrs. Airlie resisted affection. She possessed *heat*—you could see it in those black and rounded eyes—but it was contained, it was compartmentalized beneath the surface of her skin.

She never played mother. Nobody ever did. But she was a very effective sort of chaperone, indeed.

———◆———

Quinn explained the situation in simple terms to Mrs. Airlie, smoothing out the contours of the matter, including only the most essential details. She was targeting a gentleman of quality—and his family.

"I need someone to present me at the palace. So naturally I thought of you."

Mrs. Airlie's veil was clever. It made her look delicate and filmy when really her gaze was as sharp as the pointed end of a spear. "I see."

"Might you be amenable?"

"No," said Mrs. Airlie.

"Why not?"

"You are compromised."

"Compromised how?"

"The Château is in disarray."

Quinn glanced at the clock. "Says who?"

"*According* to who?" said Mrs. Airlie, drawing her fan from be-hind her cushion. She flicked open the metal catch at the base, revealing a blade beneath, and turned it toward Quinn's throat.

"Get this off me," she said, "and I'll know you're still worth my time."

A test. Tests had always been part of Mrs. Airlie's method. Quinn grimaced. "Aren't we past all that?"

The blade flashed. Mrs. Airlie sliced Quinn's collar: one careful bisection of starch and white cotton and navy bow tie.

"I'll have to bill you for that."

"Disarm me, Le Blanc."

"No. I came to initiate a collaboration, not a bloodbath."

Mrs. Airlie's face shimmered beneath the veil. "I do not care for collaboration."

"I thought you might appreciate it." Quinn paused. "I thought you might wish to salvage your reputation."

"My reputation?" The blade quivered at Quinn's throat.

"Yes. I hear *you're* in something of a bind, too."

Mrs. Airlie flinched.

It was true. Gossip had reached the Château by the usual channels, carried by Silk's scouts: one of Mrs. Airlie's students had been snared by the police. The girl had been taking her end-of-year examinations: a tidy little fraud on the manager of the Hotel Cecil. Obviously, a detail had been missed; the girl gave herself away; now she was in custody. Quinn didn't know how much it cost to maintain the Academy—a lot, she supposed, when you had to buy so many rare books and clever instruments and fine paintings. It wouldn't last long without student fees. And there wouldn't be any fees if the Academy was rumbled.

"Take the knife, please."

"No, Mrs. Airlie."

"Use your wits. I know you have them."

"No." Quinn was running out of patience. "And you forget yourself."

Mrs. Airlie blinked. "Forget myself?"

"Yes. Stand down."

"You're giving *me* orders?"

"We left the schoolroom eons ago. I've been in charge of the Château for eight years. You should have got down on your knees and kissed my hand the second I entered the room," Quinn said, "as well you know."

The room stilled.

"Hmm," Mrs. Airlie said, lowering the blade. "Nicely put, Le Blanc." She glanced at the clock. "Your timing is all off, though."

———◆———

Outside, leaning against a lamppost, a man in a blue silk waistcoat was studying Mrs. Airlie's house. The azure sheen sparkled in the sunlight; he buttoned his overcoat a little tighter.

He had watched Quinn Le Blanc go in. Now he would wait for her to come out. He did not mind waiting; he was the very living, breathing embodiment of forbearance.

Quinn. He repeated the name in his mind, testing it, weighing it.

She'd moved quickly, wending between crowds, leaping onto an omnibus. The man in the blue silk waistcoat was rarely puffed, and he wasn't puffed on this occasion, but Quinn Le Blanc left him very nearly out of breath, and this was worth noting.

Fast and dexterous, he wrote, noting observations in his tiny memorandum book. *Of moderate height. No distinguishing features.*

She did not seem particularly remarkable. It did not seem likely she could cause any great trouble. But she was edging into something that did not concern her. And this needed to be managed with care.

The man in the blue silk waistcoat checked his pocket watch. She was taking her time. He couldn't risk missing his next appointment. Clearly, Quinn Le Blanc was not a very fleet-footed sort of person. Not a very worthy queen.

The man in the blue silk waistcoat fingered the blade in his breast pocket. Then he turned and walked away.

5

The Duke

The Duke of Kendal spent his morning as he was so often obliged to do: meeting the family lawyers and his moneyman. The head footman set out the tea service in the library. It was not the grandest room in Kendal House, tucked as it was behind the ballroom, accessed by one of those windowless passages bisecting every floor, but it was one of the few rooms not filled with recessed arches and secret doors and hiding places. It was better suited to private conversation.

"I'll see them at eleven," the duke said. "Tell them to be punctual."

Tor and Lady Kendal would be safely ensconced in their own quarters at that hour—his sister in her sprawling suite on the third floor, back from her morning ride; his stepmother in her chambers at the back of the house. He'd once asked Lady Kendal if she wouldn't prefer to return to her former suite on the second floor, which she'd possessed when she first arrived as his father's new bride. "But I am not of your blood," she'd said gently. "The principal apartments belong to you now. Besides, I've grown accustomed to my own little hidey-hole. I'd be lost on your side of the house." Then she patted his hand. "Dear Max. It's kind of you to ask."

Before the meeting, he breakfasted in his own chamber, completed his correspondence, forced himself to read the newspapers cover to cover, and then took up his position in the library. He'd selected a sober neckerchief, scraped his hair flat to his scalp. He made his expression cold. The lawyers never came without pressing him to agree to something—a labyrinthine estate matter, the prosecution of a poacher, the sale of certain farms or leaseholds, requests for donations. It paid to greet them with a certain froideur, otherwise they would stay all morning.

They came in a pack, at five minutes to eleven: six of them clambering up the stairs, followed by one young laggard who tripped through the double doors, spilling papers. The duke sat at the far end of the room, legs crossed, preserving his distance.

"Good morning, gentlemen."

"Good *morning*, Your Grace." The eldest among them, a quite remarkably wizened fellow, crept forward.

The duke sipped his tea. "What do we have the pleasure of discussing today?"

"We are here, Your Grace, to discuss the matter of your marriage."

No wasting time, then. There was a click: the double doors opened, and a slim figure slipped in. Nattily dressed, waistcoat shining, cheeks pink from running up the stairs.

"Beg your pardon," he said. "Have we begun?"

The duke permitted himself a small smile. He had employed plenty of moneymen over the years, but Mr. Willoughby was by far his favorite—sharp-witted, good-humored, impish in his remarks.

"You, too, Willoughby? Anyone else? Send for Cook, if you like. You may as well all form a lobbying committee."

The elderly lawyer sniffed. "Lobbying, Your Grace? The matter of your succession should be uppermost in your mind. I hardly think we need to *lobby* you."

The duke said nothing. He wondered what these people saw when they looked at him. A man approaching thirty, in the prime of his life, master of all he surveyed? Or a moon-faced boy, ascending to the dukedom before he knew his own mind, requiring firm handling at every turn? He supposed the latter, and it made him grow weary. How long would it take to prove he could forge his own path?

The elderly lawyer must have seen something in his expression, for he attempted a smile. "Come, sir. Oblige me. I promised your father I would see this estate rightly handled. I only wish to make good my vow."

The duke gripped his teacup tighter. He said evenly, "Are the estates not being well handled?"

"They are. You have proven a most trustworthy custodian of it all."

"And are we not seeing excellent returns?" He turned his stare on Willoughby, who hesitated. "Well? Are we *not* in fine financial fettle?"

The lawyer waved this away. "Kendal credit is unimpeachable, nobody would dream of suggesting otherwise. So now you must do as your own father did, and look to the future."

The duke flinched, then tried to conceal it, reaching for a book. These walls were lined with thousands of volumes he would never read, would never have *time* to read. But, of course, that didn't matter. The library was tied to the estate. These books were supposed to be enjoyed by other future Kendals. No, that was not quite right, either: those future Kendals would preserve the books for *their* successors. On and on it would go, dukes begetting dukes—until the whole library turned to dust, until Kendal House stood on scorched ground in a crumbling city, guarded by ever-present lawyers. It made him feel more exhausted still.

"I'll think on it," the duke said, averting his gaze.

"No, sir, that won't do. The time is now. Another season is about to close. Even Lady Kendal has expressed her particular wish to see you married."

The duke was startled. "You've discussed it with my step-mother?"

"Of course, the Dowager Duchess has expressed a desire to see you safely settled, as part of her obligation to her late husband. But she is completely engaged with the prospect of your ball..."

"Lady Kendal has not mentioned a word about marriage to me."

"I daresay she considers it a personal matter, best left to Your Grace's trusted counselors."

"Perhaps she considers it a private matter, best left to me."

The lawyer raised a brow. "Regardless, sir, you really must make your intentions clear."

"Must?"

"Yes, you must." The lawyer softened his tone. "Your Grace's father was not minded to marry, either. Not at first. Do you know what persuaded him to wed your poor departed mother, in the end?"

"Your advice?" the duke said coldly.

"His *conscience*. Think of how many men you employ, Your Grace. Think of all your tenants. A man in your position must consider his obligations. To keep the peace, to care for his people. A firm line of succession will maintain your credit and put everybody's mind at rest. Your father would expect it of you."

"I have upheld *all* my obligations to my father's memory, and the Kendal name."

"Indeed you have, and you are a pillar in society, Your Grace. I cannot fault you for your immaculate conduct. But you know how people gossip."

"Gossip?" The duke felt himself growing hot. He looked at Willoughby. "What gossip?"

Willoughby shrugged. "The usuals, Your Grace. Debts and drinking and debauched behavior."

"*Just* rumors," the elderly lawyer interjected. "And most pernicious ones at that."

"People should mind their own affairs and leave me to manage mine."

"But will those people pay their rents, if they think the estate is going to crumble? Mr. Willoughby will back me on this point, I think."

Willoughby laughed shortly. "Don't look to me. His Grace knows my opinion."

The duke studied him. "Do I? Tell me."

"The estate is entailed. If you die without an heir, then these worthy lawyers will dig up some weak-chinned cousin to take your seat—provided he isn't carried off by financial ruin or typhus first. Your tenants will turn their loyalties to the next chap. The only people to suffer will be Lady Victoria—and your stepmother, I suppose, if the future duke chooses to quibble with her widow's portion."

The duke breathed, regulating his temper. "You are pushing this matter very hard."

Willoughby spread his hands. "We are men of business. A united family makes sound decisions and good investments. An unhappy one simply piles up debts."

The duke snorted. Kendals never had any reason to worry about debts. "Is that your scientific observation?"

"It is my personal experience, advising every family in Berkeley Square. You are the head of the Kendal family. Everything depends upon the woman you may take to be your bride."

The duke felt the blood pulsing at his temple. He spoke in the Lords when pressed to do so, presided over magistrate benches, attended meetings of the Privy Council, raised sums for his stepmother's good works, assumed the lord lieutenancy in Derbyshire when required. Of course, he had his sins and vices, the same as any other man. But he kept those in a box, out of sight and mind.

"Head of the family?" he snapped. "Don't let Lady Victoria hear you say that." Then he studied them more closely. "Have you spoken to my sister about all this?"

"Of course not," the elderly lawyer replied. "This is a private subject."

"Well," Willoughby said, clearing his throat. "I happen to have discussed it *very* briefly with Lady Victoria."

There was a moment of silence. The duke stared at him in astonishment. "Before me?"

Willoughby reddened, just a fraction. "An accident of timing. She had a few questions, nothing more."

"Questions?" The duke felt a prickle of unease. Surely, Tor could not support the lawyers in this? She'd always been vehemently against the idea of his marriage. "*Don't* throw me out," she'd begged him. "Whatever happens. *Don't* make me leave."

This was nine years ago, in the dining room at Kendal House, waiting for the carriage to take him to Westminster. He had been dolled up in his ermine robes, was staring bleakly at the cavernous sleeves dangling over his wrists. "Tor. What a thing to say."

She'd gripped his arm. "I'm your senior. If I'd been born male, you'd have to bow to me. But I wasn't, and you don't, and there's nothing I can do about it. But this is my *home*, Max. If you marry and have children, and throw me out, it will kill me. You understand?"

"Tor…"

"It will *kill* me, Max."

Tor was always ferocious. Everything was black-and-white, chalked in such brutal lines. She had been this way even when they were children. It was how they survived the nursery floor. You had to be alert, to know which of the servants were for you, which were against. So Max meant it when he pressed his hand to hers and said, "I will never make you leave. I daresay I'll never marry, come to that." He wanted to please her. Despite himself, despite his worst urges, he wanted to be good. He knew, even then, that there was a destructive force rising inside him. He had to do everything in his power to keep it contained.

"Is that a promise?"

He was not yet twenty-one, too young to make such a vow. But he'd said, "Yes, I promise."

Could Tor have changed her position so completely? He made his face blank, saying, "I see there have been some quite extraordinary maneuvers made around this topic. Tell me, how were you proposing to move it forward?"

The elderly lawyer's eyes lit up. "You should select a lady with great care. We recommend you make a survey of the field."

"You make it sound like horse-trading."

The lawyers laughed, not very pleasantly. "There is a Queen's Drawing Room this afternoon. The final debutante presentation before the season closes. I daresay your stepmother would be delighted to accompany you."

"Evidently." The duke felt as if he were being dipped into ice, turning slowly numb. "Very well. Send for the landau. Tell Lady Kendal to join me at the palace if she wishes."

———

The duke sent a note card to Tor before he left for the palace. He wrote and tore up several drafts. *We must speak... I wish to seek your counsel...*

His pen hovered over the paper, unable to form the right words. It had been too long since he and his sister had spoken frankly, openly to one another. He was forgetting how to do it.

This matter was best left in her hands. If Tor wished to raise it with him, she could do so. He wrote a stilted missive, dropped it on the silver tray in the front hall. *We wish you clement weather this afternoon.*

He met the dowager duchess at the top of the Mall. It was as if two foreign powers had met to sign an entente cordiale. Her carriage, a boxy dark-painted brougham, was stationed opposite the gates to Green Park. The duke's open-topped landau came in procession down Constitution Hill, preceded by six black destriers. Two police constables blew their whistles and held back the traffic. The brougham doors opened, and a tiny figure descended, crossed the road, climbed the silver-plated steps to the landau.

"Goodness," Lady Kendal said, arranging her skirts as she sat back in her seat. The footmen snapped the door shut; the suspension groaned as the landau turned. "You have a face like thunder!"

He gritted his teeth. "Have you had a pleasant morning?"

"Very pleasant, Max, thank you."

"Was it very busy?"

"A little busy, yes."

The duke knew his stepmother kept a brutal daily schedule, driving to inspect her improvement projects, visiting drains and sewers and schoolhouses, attended by an army of engineers and the directors of her many charities, all following her on bended knee in hopes of receiving her donations.

He said stiffly, "It's good of you to join me."

Lady Kendal opened her parasol. "You think I'd send you into the lion's den alone?"

She managed him perfectly, as she managed all things. She never pretended to be his mother. She preserved the necessary borders to their relationship, maintained her distance.

He and Tor had stared at her in wonder when she first arrived at Mount Kendal, this young bride with a heart-shaped face and tight dark curls. She looked like a grown-up doll: ruffled and layered, smooth as china. They couldn't comprehend why she had chosen to marry their father. "He has a nervous complaint," she told them. "You understand what that means?" They shook their heads, and she smiled at them, supremely confident, supremely calm. "It explains everything."

A nervous complaint. That made it sound like a weak thing, a pitiable thing—which is not at all what it was. His father's rage, his *resentment* of Max—for his wickedness, for the terrible thing he had done—permeated the air. Cold mist had hung permanently over Mount Kendal, seeping into the drapes, their clothes, their skin. Their father disappeared for months at a time. For a long while, the sound of his dogs—bloodhounds and mastiffs fighting in the yard—was the only sign they ever had that he was at home. He was now on the Continent, their new stepmother explained. Taking the waters. "Can you imagine? So dull for him. But a stroke of fortune for us. For now we can get to know each other much better."

She'd presented them with a gift, a dollhouse fronted with tiny red bricks, its rooms sumptuously decorated with miniature furnishings—lapis lazuli silks, delicate brocade. Tor crouched before it, pressed her palms to her knees, studying every compartment with a suspicious slant to her expression, as if she expected it to be filled with spies. Two small dolls had been placed in the miniature drawing room; she poked them gingerly.

Max's stomach was in knots. How to tell this smiling lady the truth, that *he* was the cause of his father's grief, his illness? Ten-year-old Tor explained it instead, in her usual straightforward terms.

"Mother died, having Max. It's not his fault. He wasn't to know. If he should say sorry to anyone, it's me. He's taken all my things." She crossed her arms, casting a wary glance at the dollhouse. "But I will protect him," she added severely. "He's my little brother. He has nobody else in the world but me."

She'd turned this ferocity on her new stepmother, too. "Papa has run quite mad because he misses Mama. Everybody says so. You have made a great mistake in marrying him."

Their stepmother's face had grown sorrowful. "I see you've

had to be terribly brave. But your father is a dear, good man, irrespective of his troubles." She folded her hands together. "I am
quite determined to make you all happy."

Tor had been unmoved. "You will dislike us and hate it here.
Everybody does."

Their stepmother had smiled sadly at them. "Dislike you? I
don't think that would be possible. And your poor papa loves you
dearly, too. Whatever anyone else may say about it."

Her gaze had flicked to the housemaids, hovering at the edge
of the nursery. Her voice grew hard. "I will permit no more un-
pleasant talk around these children."

She had always understood him, protected him. She knew
what to say, and what not to say, and how to say it—and he always experienced a sense of relief when she was near, certain
that she would take care of their affairs, pouring oil on troubled
waters, protecting them from charlatans and hangers-on and the
most odious of their neighbors.

Yet now, seated in the landau, opposite Buckingham Palace,
he perceived a hint of internal doubt. "I hear you're all for this
business," he said.

Lady Kendal adjusted her parasol. "Dear Max. I'm all for anything that brings you peace."

"Is marriage the only way to secure one's peace?"

"It secured mine," she said. "What a sorry life I should have
led, if not for your dear papa."

Papa.

Sometimes he could sense his father in the cracked leather of
these seats, behind the speckled mirrors. Jolting behind him, a
gaunt and silent ghost, judging his every move.

The duke exhaled. "Very well. Drive on."

6

Quinn

Quinn and Mrs. Airlie changed carriages incognito at Marble Arch to sign their contract—for Mrs. Airlie never undertook a commission without one, irrespective of her personal loyalties—and hired a brougham for the final approach to Buckingham Palace. Mrs. Airlie had transformed into a formidable shade of amethyst, fringed like a lamp. She made a tiny adjustment to her headdress: one sure, sharp move.

"I would like a drink."

Quinn raised an eyebrow, shifting her train. A fresh gown had been delivered by the seamstresses, who bicycled it furiously to Mrs. Airlie's house a little before two. Quinn fastened her buttons at top speed, thanking heaven for her own agility. "At this hour? Are you nervous?"

"Not in the least. I'm animated."

Mrs. Airlie didn't seem animated. She looked as bloodless as usual.

"Let's keep our heads on," Quinn said. She sped Mrs. Airlie through the details of her disguise: birth date, mother's name, father's name, nurse's habits, governess's predilections, pets, political persuasions, happy memories, bad ones, friends' names, the local priest—et cetera. "And we'll need to get your story straight," she added. "I propose you will play my maiden aunt."

"Absolutely not." Mrs. Airlie snapped her fan. "I will be your cousin, twice removed. Our mothers maintained a distant—a *very* distant—correspondence, but I have come to England out of a sense of Christian obligation, in aid of a very helpless woman, after an extremely long sojourn in…"

"Florence?"

"No, too obvious. I suspect I have been living in a very severe German principality. In absolute seclusion."

"Owing to your religious beliefs?"

"Owing to my extremely religious beliefs," Mrs. Airlie agreed, with warmth. "I am positively Lutheran."

"Your face: will anybody recognize it?"

Mrs. Airlie touched her chin, protected by her veil. "Oh, no," she said, well-satisfied.

"We should change your name."

"Unwise. We are engaging with the marriage market. We will both be scrutinized to within an inch of our lives. Best to keep everything close to the bone. What have *you* chosen?"

"Miss Quinta White."

"*Quinta?*"

"The fifth."

Mrs. Airlie sniffed. "Rather on the nose. But then, wealth breeds eccentricity. I follow your thinking. Now, tell me why you're obfuscating."

"Obfuscating?"

"We've discussed scripts and sobriquets and you've not said one word about the most critical question of all. Whom are we marking?"

The carriage bounced over loose cobblestones. Quinn replayed the moment, the night she and Mr. Silk had made their choice, and prayed she'd made the right decision.

———

It had been such a bad year: that was the first thing to know. They were struggling to find the right men to defraud—not least because the Château's Rulebook set such fierce conditions:

CLAUSE 1. *The manner and morality of a game cannot be in ANY WAY divided. A queen must be assured that her mark is of IMPROPER CHARACTER. And if she is at all doubtful on this point, she will stop all pursuit of his fortune at once, on pain of dismissal from the Château.*

"We haven't gone after any stockbrokers in a while," Quinn said to Mr. Silk, unpicking a blond wig from her head, wiping grease paint from her brow. She'd just returned from an extremely vigorous game of whist with a pair of magistrates in Marylebone—not a very satisfying evening. Now she and Mr. Silk were home at the Château, seated at the card table in the gaming room—shutters drawn, lamps dimmed.

"We've worked through all the noxious bankers we know," Silk replied, shoving his spectacles up his nose, peering at his ledger.

"Any government ministers?"

"We've exhausted our reserves there, too."

He closed his ledger with a thud. "Quinn, we have no fresh targets. No jobs afoot. No likely returns for another quarter. You shall have to learn to play biritch."

She gritted her teeth. The Château had thrived for a century; she wasn't going to let it collapse now.

"*Pax,*" she said lightly, extending her hand. "We'll find someone. We live in London. It's simply crawling with sinners."

She noticed a pamphlet on the table, carrying a very noisy headline. "What's this?"

"Another brochure," Silk said wearily. "Good Samaritans, come to rescue the East End from degradation."

Quinn flipped it over. It was a handbill, presumably shoved under the front door, shouting: *Who will bring Virtue to this Dominion of Vice?* Beneath the headline was a garish illustration of their own street, inhabited by demons and drunks and women showing off their ankles.

"Not a very flattering likeness of us."

"Nor a very friendly one."

"We should throw eggs the next time they come." Quinn couldn't abide these church ladies and missionaries, blocking the road with their broughams and landaus, scattering pamphlets outside the slaughterhouse.

"I fear that would simply spur them on. They're raising funds to build a new tenement on our end of the street."

"Impossible. We hold the lease."

"Unspent leases can be bought. Forcibly or otherwise." Silk was drumming his fingers. "Where would we go if they succeeded?"

Quinn studied the handbill. *Printed on behalf of the Committee for the Amelioration of Poor Housing.* She raised an inquiring eyebrow. "Who are they?"

"A philanthropic enterprise, I daresay. The usual frights."

"Let's see." Quinn ran her fingernail down the list of committee members on the reverse page. The names were impressive: Grosvenors, Beauforts, Churchills, Gascoyne-Cecils. *Chairwoman: Her Grace the Dowager Duchess of Kendal.*

"Kendal," she said thoughtfully, testing the name against her memory. "Pass me the peerage."

"Why?"

"Because I like to know who's meddling with our neighborhood." She flipped through the heavy crimson-bound volume.

"Guilford, Halifax, Harewood, Kimberley..." She turned back a page. "Ah. Kendal."

"Quinn..."

She scanned the entry.

KENDAL, Maximilian, *5th Duke in the second creation: b. Aug 4th, 1868; s. 1883; ed. at Christ Church Coll., Oxf (B.A. 1888). Residence—Mount Kendal, Derbyshire; Kendal House, Berkeley Square; Kendal Lodge, Loch Lomond; Kendal Park, Isle of Wight, &c. &c...*

She glanced up. "Plenty of property. Rather rude of them to bother with ours."

"Don't even think about it, Quinn. They're old money. Utterly unassailable."

Quinn knew he was correct. New money was malleable. Liquid. Easily syphoned. But old money, aristocratic money, was intractable—locked up in bogs and marshes and crags. It never indulged in speculation.

"But we've no fresh targets," she said. "No bankers to hoodwink. No adulterous cutlery makers."

"Quinn..."

"No underhand brewers, no shamefaced solicitors. It doesn't feel as *easy* as it did before, Silk. We might need to aim a little higher."

"Not *that* high."

"Whyever not?"

"We work with merchant bankers—not marquesses. We know our limits."

"Limits," Quinn said, "are made for people who lack imagination."

"No," Silk said. "They're made for people who need to pay the butcher."

Quinn held the handbill to her chest. "I'm not marking the

Kendals—*yet*. They might not meet the Rulebook's conditions. But I propose we inspect them a little more closely."

The light quivered, blooming in the lamp glass.

Silk said gravely, "This is not our usual habit."

Quinn screwed up the handbill, tossed it toward him. "Our usual habits," she said, "are going to be the death of us." She made her gaze firm. "Make some inquiries, Silk."

———

Silk did as he was told. He returned with a thick leatherbound pack of papers, which he slammed on the table with a thump.

"I have an informant in the Kendal household, who has furnished me with a good deal of paperwork. And I recommend that we do *not* proceed."

Quinn felt a quickening of hope. Silk never recommended they should proceed. His natural caution precluded it.

"Splendid," she said.

"Don't get excited."

"Do I look excited?"

"You look desperate, frankly." Silk unpicked the knot, unraveled the string, cast it aside. "Here. Photographs, to start you off."

He handed her a linotype with his own neat annotation—*Kendal party, en famille*—cut from a newspaper or a magazine. Quinn held it up to the lamplight. Three people seated on a vine-wreathed terrace.

"Stepmother, son, daughter," said Silk, pointing to them one by one. "The Dowager Duchess of Kendal, the present Duke of Kendal, and his sister, Lady Victoria Kendal."

"The duchess chairs the Committee for the Amelioration of Poor Housing?"

"She does."

The Dowager Duchess of Kendal was attired in a pale-patterned dress, gently pleated, arms hanging languorously at her sides. Silk had not been able to determine the date of her birth, but Quinn guessed her to be somewhere near five and forty: a handsome woman, whose hair remained dark and finely curled. She had turned her chin in such a way as to make her whole body appear soft, unthreatening, avoiding the camera—a rather clever maneuver, Quinn thought. She sat on her son's right.

In the far left position, the most inferior spot of all, sat the daughter. Lady Victoria. Her curls were wilder, more unruly, springing out in all directions. She had an angular face, a long neck. Her mouth was open, as if she had been distracted by something off camera. She looked to be in her mid-thirties.

"Rather a queer-looking woman. And this...?"

Between the stepmother and the daughter sat the duke.

"Maximilian Kendal," Silk said with a nod.

Quinn peered closer. "He cuts an—interesting figure."

Interesting was the word for it. Pale-haired, pale-faced, muscled: vast shoulders, thighs that might have splintered the chair. The picture had blurred his eyes, giving him a blank marbled appearance. There was a lantern-jawed strength to his face, but it seemed almost too much; he was too hard-hewn, too much like granite. He appeared to be a shade younger than his sister.

Quinn traced them with her fingernail. "Not a very cheerful-looking party."

"Nor a terribly accessible one. They're surrounded by lawyers and servants and hangers-on. They have a reputation for shunning society, for never entertaining. There may, however, be an opportunity to infiltrate their circle."

"Yes?"

"The duke will shortly celebrate his thirtieth birthday. His stepmother is arranging a ball. I understand the neighbors are in a state of high anticipation about it. They have not seen inside Kendal House for years." Silk tapped the folder. "On which point, here is everything I can glean about their portfolio. It is quite enormous, impossible to itemize. They're an ancient family, so you can assume all the ugly stuff: enclosure, razing villages, absorbing territory through capture, lots of boiling oil and executed peasants, et cetera."

"And now they're planning to raze *us* to the ground."

"In the spirit of urban improvement, yes. It's quite the fashion in the duchess's circle."

"Tell me about their property."

"How long have you got? A ducal seat in Derbyshire—Mount Kendal. A large freehold in Berkeley Square—Kendal House. A hunting lodge in the Highlands, a retreat on the Isle of Wight, a perfectly terrific set of coal mines, countless investments in overseas trading companies, and an enormous quantity of farms, docklands, and so forth. It would take months to scour it all."

Quinn wasn't concerned by that. Even Mrs. Airlie admired her excellent head for figures. "What's your general assessment?"

Silk closed the folder. "My informant in the household assures me that they're terribly, terribly rich."

"Clearly. Then why not proceed?"

"I have doubts."

"About?"

"Our capabilities." Silk regarded the Rulebook in its usual position in the bureau. "To target a principal peer of the realm… It may be beyond us."

"We need a rich quarry. Urgently. Without a fresh win, I hardly see how we'll survive another Christmas." Quinn examined the photograph again. "There must be a way into the Kendals' family circle. They'll have their secrets—and their sins. We simply need to locate them."

Silk pulled his leatherbound folder to his chest. "Very well. I'll see what I can winkle out about them." He got to his feet. "Leave it to me."

———◆———

Now, as the carriage sped toward the palace, Mrs. Airlie frowned. "Kendal?" she repeated. "Not *the* Kendals?"

Quinn folded her hands. "*The* Kendals, yes."

"But they're far too rich. *Abominably* rich. They'll be completely protected; there would be no way in. We all know their reputation: they shun society, never hold dinners; they live in a ghastly house in Grosvenor Square..."

"Berkeley Square."

"I stand corrected." Mrs. Airlie unfastened her fan. "I used to see poor Daphne Kendal going to church. Absolutely ravenous-looking. Pale as a ghost."

"She died."

"*Did* she? How unimaginative. At least she produced an heir."

"Two children," Quinn said. "Maximilian and Victoria."

"Yes, it's coming back now. Old Lord Kendal seemed like a terrific bore to me. And a very shabby widower. I do think that's a very perverse trait, don't you? To be rich as Croesus and still wear patches on your sleeves."

"He suffered the loss of his first wife very badly, by all accounts."

Mrs. Airlie scratched her chin. "But he remarried, did he not? A rather impressive young woman. Was she French? Perhaps it was her name...something foreign. It's so long ago."

"Marie Kendal. The Dowager Duchess."

"Of course! And then he died. What was it? Gout? Dropsy?"

"Consumption."

"And the present Duke must be—what? Twenty-five, twenty-six?"

"Twenty-nine. Very nearly thirty."

"I daresay he's packed his stepmother off to a nunnery."

"No," Quinn said thoughtfully. "She's still at Kendal House. So is his sister. They are about to throw a splendid ball to celebrate his birthday."

"All three of them? Still residing together, after all this time? How peculiar! I didn't know *that*. Well, there you have it: they're an utterly closed book, no peepholes at all."

"Not *very* closed. We have it on good authority that they'll be at the Queen's Drawing Room this afternoon."

"Whose authority?"

"Mr. Silk has spoken to his informant inside Kendal House."

Mrs. Airlie adjusted her pearls. "You're aiming terribly high, Le Blanc. The Kendals are the very top rank of society. If you misfire…"

Quinn smoothed her hair. Her forehead was warm, her muscles tingling with anticipation. Buckingham Palace loomed before them, hazy in the afternoon light: wide-slung, sprawling, the color of damp sand.

"I shan't misfire."

The carriage joined the queue lumbering into the smoke-stained quadrangle, and a footman unlatched their door.

"Mind your feathers," murmured Mrs. Airlie. "You can sell those if this all goes terribly wrong. Are you ready?"

Quinn considered the question. *Was* she ready? Provided the archdeacon had pulled the necessary strings, she'd be able to get through the palace doors. But could she pass muster with the crowd upstairs? Could she catch the Kendals' attention in the way she had planned?

"Of course," she replied.

7

The Man in the Blue Silk Waistcoat

The man in the blue silk waistcoat left the corner of Spanish Place, where he'd been spying on Mrs. Airlie's academy, and headed south. He walked briskly down to Duke Street, and thence to Balderton Street, and then to the Old Sarum Buildings—a new-made block of flats, chiefly occupied by artisans and mechanics and laborers, where he retained a room at a most economical rate: two shillings per week, locked in for ten years. His tenancy had been personally approved by the curate of St. George's Church and the board of trustees. It was a fine thing, in his opinion, to have his own little foothold in the heart of Mayfair.

Nobody observed him going in. He unlocked the door to his small flat, feeling the chill rising from the linoleum. There wasn't much time to waste.

He unbuttoned his overcoat, then his waistcoat, and then he opened the closet. Question: Could a man in a blue silk waistcoat be a man in a blue silk waistcoat if he had no waistcoat? It was remarkable, really, how easily one could accumulate skins. How swiftly they could be removed.

In the closet was a new gown. It had been ordered from Paris, made to regulation length with a regulation veil, everything wrapped as tightly as possible to eliminate the chance of creasing. It was an expensive fabric, pearl-colored, decked in velvet trim. And once the man in the blue silk waistcoat had unraveled himself from his former clothes, he was gone; he had never really existed at all. She stepped into her dress: she became the woman in the cream silk gown.

In her satchel was her wig, nicely fringed. She contorted herself into the dress, grimacing—it was not always easy to dress oneself without assistance. She squeezed the buttons through the eyeholes. Success! The gown adhered itself neatly to her skin.

On went the veil, pinned to the wig. Out flapped her train. She checked the time again. Her carriage would be arriving in three minutes, on the corner of North Audley Street and Providence Court. Providence, she thought wryly, was not something she cared for. She trusted in herself, and only herself.

She left, locking the door, concealing the key.

———

The forecourt loomed around Quinn, white awnings overhead, broughams and landaus crunching in across the gravel, lurching to a halt underneath a splendid but grimy-looking portico. The footman closed the carriage door with a sharp click.

"Card, ma'am," he muttered, passing her two admittance cards in his white-gloved hand. It would seem the archdeacon had obliged them. Quinn breathed a sigh of relief, giving one of the cards surreptitiously to Mrs. Airlie.

"Compliments to the Lord Chamberlain," she murmured in reply.

The footman gave her a knowing look. "Compliments to Mr. Silk," he replied.

Good: their friends and spies were in position. Mr. Silk had given her the description of his other informants; she recognized one of them lurking in the forecourt, studiously avoiding her gaze, his jacket blinking in the sunshine. This meant everything was in place.

"Not a very cheerful building," she remarked to Mrs. Airlie, casting a brief glance over her shoulder. Buckingham Palace seemed to be both very grand and very gloomy, a lot of heavy columns and carved pediments and prim blinds over the windows.

"You are the Queen of Fives, not a day-tripper," Mrs. Airlie said with some severity. "Come along."

They passed up the broad steps into a dim square hall, scented with camphor and chrysanthemums, a hundred ghosts coasting slowly up the stairs with their bouquets in hand. Quinn halted, clenching her own bulbous hydrangeas in a gloved fist.

"Shall we?"

Mrs. Airlie opened her fan. Like Quinn, she had removed her face veil, and attached regulation-length muslin to the back of her hair instead. She looked every inch the decorous chaperone.

"I'm going to enjoy this."

They glided upstairs.

The picture gallery was on the first floor. It hummed with desultory conversation, and the air was a little rank—the scent of champagne and sweat. Families eyed one another. This must have been the thousandth presentation of the season; the footmen were drooping as they held out silver platters of champagne. Mrs. Airlie swiped one.

"At least they provide the chaperones with refreshment. It takes some effort, bringing meat to market, you know."

A crowd of young men hovered nearby, rubbing their weak-looking chins.

"Market?" Quinn said. It felt more like the slaughterhouse. "This place is wretched."

Mrs. Airlie compressed her lips. "This, my dear," she said grimly, "is the summit of the earth."

The debutantes had been gathered in a sort of pen at the top of the gallery, clustered on low couches and ottomans.

"In you go," whispered Mrs. Airlie, shoving Quinn into the group. Instantly, there was a shift in the atmosphere, eyes turning. "Hold your nerve. You're a new face. They'll be watching you."

Around twelve young women were staring at Quinn. The youngest looked to be about seventeen. The eldest were still several years younger than Quinn herself. Mr. Silk had proposed they should be equivocal about the age of Miss Quinta White. Twenty-six might seem too outrageously decrepit.

"Good afternoon," she said with gravity.

"Sit down, if you like," said a girl close at hand. She was lounging on the ottoman, medieval in white satin. "We can shove along." She touched Quinn's bouquet. "Hydrangeas? Goodness, you're brave. My mother would have a fit."

There was a shimmer of agreement along the button-leather length of the couch. Quinn felt Mrs. Airlie stiffen.

"Hydrangeas stand for boasting, don't they?" the girl explained. "Hubristic flowers, Mother calls them. Better chuck them, if you can."

Quinn cursed inwardly. "Have we any others?" she murmured to Mrs. Airlie.

Mrs. Airlie tutted, trained her eye on the nearest girl. "Young woman, give me your bouquet. Yes, I'm taking the lily of the valley—don't fuss. String, please." Mrs. Airlie plucked the hydrangeas from Quinn's hands, unraveling, reordering. "Not terribly tidy." Mrs. Airlie kicked the loose stems under the couch and gave the room an implacable smile. "But we march on." Then she said, a little louder, "This is my dear cousin, Miss Quinta White."

Quinn watched the women registering her name, parsing it for meaning. Would they recognize it? Silk had been sprinkling intelligence among his spies and informants, planting seeds about the deliciously wealthy "Miss White" for weeks, to stimulate demand before he opened an auction for her hand. His labors had borne fruit.

"You're the girl we've been hearing about," said one, slapping her hands against her knees. "The Angel of the East, the girl simply dripping in gold. Our land agent can speak of nothing else. Mother is longing to get her teeth into you."

"Goodness," Quinn said evenly. "How kind."

One woman turned, voice sharp. "I say, look over there. Whatever are *they* doing out?"

Quinn felt a shiver of anticipation. Mrs. Airlie nudged her with her fan, whispering, "To your left, nine o'clock."

Quinn controlled her expression, taking care to conceal any undue interest, and spied two people entering the picture gallery, framed by the gilded architraves, causing the crowd to part for them. A very tall man, broad-shouldered, white tie glowing. And a delicate woman, perhaps fifteen years older, hand resting gracefully on his arm. They paused on the threshold, frozen as a tintype photograph.

It was the Duke of Kendal and his stepmother.

"Doesn't he look splendid in blue?" murmured one of the debutantes. "And *she* looks perfect, just like a doll."

"Just like a ghoul, more like. I heard she never goes outside."

"What nonsense! Mother goes poor-visiting with Lady Kendal all the time."

"He looks decidedly cross."

"Decidedly rich, you mean. Did you know his sister hung the Caravaggios in the stables?"

"How do *you* know? They've not held a dinner all season. Do you know, Papa's moneyman says the duke's a dreadful libertine."

"How splendid! Mama always said I'd be seduced by a rake."

Quinn could sense similar conversations circulating around the picture gallery. The men were gazing at the duke, puffing their chests; everybody was assessing Lady Kendal, pronouncing her ruffled gown and enormous diamonds to be decidedly charming.

Quinn fixed him with her stare. The duke shifted and looked straight past her.

The impact of him was startling. His photograph had shown he was a tall man. But in person he towered over the crowd, an Augustus or a Marcus Aurelius in white marble. It was the heft of his jaw and the close-cropped white-blond of his hair; it was the vast spread of his shoulders and the armored folds of his morning suit. He was not exactly handsome—there was something too colorless about him, and he made no effort to commence conversation with the crowd gawping at him. She had imagined him to be like other rakes: dandyish and louche, prowling around the debutantes. But clearly his mode of seduction was to give off an air of absolute standoffishness. His stepmother, in contrast, cut a tranquil figure in a cloud of ivory taffeta, and smiled serenely around the room.

A bell began ringing in the distance.

"Come, Quinta," said Mrs. Airlie. "To the ballroom."

The crowd surged and the Kendals disappeared from view. Quinn found herself crushed on both sides, swept with the tide into the palace ballroom. Figures stood on a raised dais, glittering in silver and blue. Royalty—surrounded by guards. Quinn's heart sped up, but she remained calm. She was a queen herself, after all.

Let this work, she prayed.

"Miss Quinta White, accompanied by MRS. AIRLIE," boomed a sonorous voice, and suddenly Mrs. Airlie was leading Quinn out into the full glare of the room, dust motes spinning in the air. She could feel herself being examined from all angles. A military man struck the floor vigorously with his white staff. Quinn sucked in a breath and faced the royal family.

The Princess of Wales was standing in for the queen today. There was something interesting about seeing a princess in the flesh. She acquired real dimensions, elevated on the dais: shortish arms, smooth skin, the same coiled hair you saw in photographs. She wore a low bodice spangled with ivory miniatures and ribbons and metal wheels and pearl drops. Her throat was encased in muslin and she was jeweled from clavicle to chin. Some of her diamonds were so big they looked to Quinn like boiled sweets—or teeth: ridged and dented, as if spliced straight from the rock. Her mouth drooped a little at the edges; it gave her a winsome appearance. She winced, putting a hand to her hip, as if she ached from standing up all morning.

"Go," whispered Mrs. Airlie.

Swiftly, train whispering, Quinn strode to the dais. She held her bouquet in both hands and curtseyed. Down—a pause—then up, supple as an engine rod. The princess stared into the middle distance, and flexed her fingers. "Peculiar name," she said. And it was over.

"The Honorable Sonia Hillyard, accompanied by MRS. HILL-YARD," boomed the sonorous voice again, and Quinn felt Mrs. Airlie dragging her offstage.

"Good," she muttered. "Very good."

Quinn felt a sense of anticlimax. "That's it?"

"That's more than enough for now. This way..."

Mrs. Airlie hooked her arm with Quinn's, leading them both to a position on the left-hand side of the dais. There was a nervous heartbeat in the air, fans pulsing. Quinn could smell sweat and violets and musk. She was now standing very near to the duke and Lady Kendal. They remained alone, talking to nobody, positioned at the front of the crowd.

Mrs. Airlie whispered in her ear, "Take a step leftward. There. Has he noticed you?"

"Not in the least."

It wasn't enough to stride into Buckingham Palace and flutter her fan. Quinn needed to command the room, make an entrance, make herself seen...

She rolled the dice in her mind. All she needed was a little luck...

Then the double doors banged open.

8

Quinn

A young woman charged across the parquet, advancing at speed. A debutante, in fact, dressed in white, veil streaming out behind her. She was reaching for something inside her bouquet. She drew it out, raised it aloft...

"A gun!" Mrs. Airlie exclaimed. "That girl is carrying a gun!"

It was like watching a zoetrope: flash–flash–flash. The young woman held her arm up, pistol out. Her attention was hard and focused. She was no longer facing the royal dais.

She had turned directly toward Quinn.

"Repent!" she cried.

Then she fired her pistol into the air.

It sounded like a thundercrack; it tore the room in two. The crowd froze, then gasped, shrinking back. Quinn felt fear slicing through the air and watched as people ducked for cover. Screams went up in all directions.

Quinn's mind slowed, snagging on every detail. A round-handled pistol with a high and flaxen catch. A lovely fleur-de-lis engraved around the cartridge. Expensive metalwork, finely crafted. French—almost certainly. Very difficult to trace.

A long black eye—depthless, dangerous...and a chamber filled with blanks.

Only Quinn and Mr. Silk knew exactly how this would go. They'd planned it together—poring over schematics, blueprints, floor plans. There were more bribes in circulation in this building than she had ever made before; she was simply praying she wouldn't have to cash them in at once. Quinn's eye landed fleetingly on the nearest footman, positioned at the double doors. His expression was stony—until he winked.

Her gaze shifted to the dais. The military man, bedecked in medals and bearing his white staff, touched his gargantuan mustache. A nearly imperceptible signal: *Ready?*

She gave a tiny nod, a signal of her own: *yes.*

This woman wasn't a debutante. She was Quinn's own age, or a little older. Her name was Maud Dunuvar, cellarwoman to a pub in Bethnal Green; provided very good wines to Quinn's table. She was also bullheaded and athletic and her undercroft made for an excellent hideout. "All right, I'll do it," she'd said, two weeks before, when Quinn offered the commission. "Because you're asking. But don't get me arrested."

Now she stood facing Quinn, pistol first, glint in her eye.

Quinn had orchestrated this with some care in her mind. She broke free of the crowd, hitching her train. Maud swung her pistol wide, per prior agreement—in the direction of the duke and Lady Kendal. The crowd shrieked again. The duke moved fast, stepping in front of his stepmother, protecting her. Sure-footed and graceful, Quinn strode toward Maud and kicked the cellarwoman straight in the shins. Maud let out a startled *oof* of pain, stumbling backward, dropping her pistol to the floor. It skidded across the parquet. Quinn bent, swept it into her hands, and rose smoothly to her feet.

"Detain this woman," she ordered. "At once!"

A soldier burst from the dais, followed by others ranged around the room—and then it seemed as if a crowd was running on to the field at a rugger match.

"I surrender!" Maud shouted in alarm, as they closed in. "I very much surrender!" Voices were raised in panic all around the room.

"Another agitator?"

"Here, in the palace…"

"Too dreadful…"

The chap in military medals shoved the teeming crowd aside, plucking the pistol from Quinn's hands. He was another patron of Mr. Dunuvar's pub, done up in stolen medals, bearing false credentials.

"Call for the police. We'll take this miscreant into custody." He kept a very tight grip on Maud Dunuvar. And then, loud enough for the crowd to hear, he addressed Quinn: "You are a young woman of remarkable courage."

The royal family were being ushered hastily from the dais. On her right hand, Quinn saw the duke bend down to speak into his stepmother's ear. She held his arm firmly—chin up, calm.

"I'm quite well, Max dear, thank you…" Then she extended a small hand in Quinn's direction. In a clearer voice, she said, "*This* young woman appears to have saved us all."

"Imaginary Assassin" was just a little flourish to start the game, but it always worked very nicely. The Queen of Fives was obliged to set clear terms of engagement, after all—to demonstrate her strength and attract the attention of her mark, all in the spirit of fair play. Quinn felt a hum of satisfaction as the Duke of Kendal turned toward her.

"We are indebted to you," he said. His voice was stiff, his expression stiffer. Quinn waited, but he said nothing more.

She always managed this moment with care. The first meeting with the quarry was of vital importance. A lesser player might have spoiled it, grinning and blushing, losing her nerve, breaking cover. Quinn's job, therefore, was to be ice-smooth, giving nothing away.

"Not at all, Your Grace," she replied, neither too demure nor too self-assured. "Anyone would have done the same."

"Not quite anyone," Lady Kendal said, peeping around her stepson's shoulder. Her tone was gentle now, but her mouth formed a sharp line. "You seem to be the heroine of the hour, Miss..." She hesitated, trying to recall it, a frown forming on her brow.

"White," said Mrs. Airlie swiftly. "My *dearest* cousin, Quinta White."

Quinn stole a hasty glance in the duke's direction. He was staring at her, as unreadable in person as he was in sepia.

Say something, she urged him silently. *Give me something to work with.*

Silk had made their usual inquiries into the duke's character, but the details were contradictory. His Grace seemed to be punctilious in his habits, going to the Lords every week, accompanying his stepmother to church on Sundays, eating plain foods, maintaining an excellent physiological condition. But the Kendal carriage had been spotted outside the least salubrious supper clubs in Soho—with huge dinner bills left unpaid, plates smashed against the walls, illegal baccarat games played for dreadfully high stakes—and Silk's informants spoke of several mistresses, reporting payments in the accounts to music hall singers, jewelers, flower sellers, certain ladies residing on Hill Street, Portland Place, South Audley Street...

Quinn had skewered plenty of people in her career, unscrewing their minds, refastening them with glee. Her early reign had been filled with those victories. But now, as Quinn examined the duke in person—taking in his pale blond hair, his starched expression—she found him more difficult than usual to read. *Was* he a veritable Casanova? Or insufferably haughty? Or simply reserved? She noticed that his hands, like hers, were encased in white gloves. He clasped them firmly behind his back.

"Miss White," he said, nodding briefly in response to Mrs. Airlie's introduction. "We are glad to know you."

Not a very lascivious opening. But some gentlemen held their cards close to their chests. Quinn said gravely, "You are kind to say so. Although I fear I've made rather a spectacle of myself."

His eyebrow lifted, just a fraction. "You think so?"

"I kicked her *very* hard."

The duke's mouth moved—whether in amusement or surprise, she could not tell. "The ends justify the means, perhaps."

"Indeed, they do," said Mrs. Airlie swiftly, fluttering her fan with some vigor. "Although I can assure you, my charming cousin is known for her modesty, her many accomplishments, her moderation…"

The duke's expression flattened. "I see."

Quinn opened her mouth to say more, but Lady Kendal touched her stepson's sleeve. "Dear Max," she murmured. "I fear we'll be consumed by the crowd…"

She had a point: people were already surging toward the stairs, causing a huge blockage at the doors. "Come, Quinta," Mrs. Airlie said briskly, linking herself to Quinn's arm. "Let us seek refuge, too." The pressure in her fingertips was clear: *Don't push too hard.*

Quinn sighed. "Good day, Your Grace," she said to the duke, all decorum. And to Lady Kendal, more seriously: "Your Grace."

Lady Kendal's gaze flicked away, as if already turning her mind to fresh matters. The duke dipped his chin, a near-imperceptible bow, saying nothing. Still, as Quinn departed, she could feel him watching her back, as if he were tracking her passage all the way across the ballroom.

———

The woman in the cream silk gown had a good eye for carpet, and a still better one for wallpaper, and so she was always very disappointed by the furnishings in Buckingham Palace. The carpet was thin and garish, the walls were glazed with a wipe-down syrupy sort of varnish, and the pictures—well, they were shockingly dull, an endless parade of Hanoverians. Most of the state apartments were filled with packing crates and dust sheets.

It had taken some effort to get here today—more cajoling and screw-tightening than she usually applied. Still, it was necessary to be here, to make sure matters were moving in the right direction.

She stayed close to the debutantes, watching Quinn Le Blanc. There was a stench of deception on the air; the palace was crawling with turncoats and spies. But the woman in the cream silk gown sliced through that rich and self-satisfied crowd without causing any commotion, making genial and forgettable conversation with anyone who happened to speak to her. She was very good at uttering banalities. She wasn't a show-off.

Unlike some people.

The girl's performance was ridiculous. A running leap across the parquet, knocking some trussed-up barwoman to the ground, swiping her firearms? What was the reason for it? The woman in the cream silk gown observed the hubbub from the crowd, finding herself jostled and jolted in all directions.

But, she had to admit, if Le Blanc's object was to garner attention and signal her strength of character—and clearly this was an Imaginary Assassin Opening, crudely done but efficient all the same—then the trick worked. Within minutes, all conversation was centered on the bewitching and courageous Miss White. It was infuriating.

The woman in the cream silk gown fought her way across the ballroom floor, dodging the constabulary—no doubt paid off—and the military attaché—suspiciously solicitous of Le Blanc and her chaperone—and the female agitator—pinned to the ground, clearly waiting for safe passage from the palace. She could hear the crowd babbling as she passed.

"Such elegance, such a fine carriage…"

"With such nice manners, too…"

"…for a girl raised in Cheapside…"

People were so endlessly predictable. And the girl had played them rather well. The woman in the cream silk gown felt a flare of envy.

In her reticule she was carrying a miniature self-portrait, concealed from view. It had a small inscription, carved in dusty letters: the Queen of Fives. She held it in her mind as she examined Quinn Le Blanc from the other side of the room. The girl would need to pay, and so would the Château.

"Marked," she said, under her breath.

Day Two
The Intrusion

1

Quinn

The boys planted the morning papers on the pavement at the corner of Bruton Street and New Bond Street, snapping the string with penknives. The stacks carried a warm wet-print smell. There was a juggler setting up shop on the other side of the road, putting his cap out for pennies. He began launching his skittles high, breathlessly high, into the air. The skittles flew up, up, and down, winking in the sunlight. The newspaper boys were so entranced they kept giving out the wrong change. Quinn searched her palm for the missing ha'penny as she flipped to the society pages.

This was the Wednesday edition, carrying that popular column, *Opera Glasses*—penned by H. Mellings, published on syndication. This week's sketch was the usual lovely rot: a piece titled "Virtue Unassailed," about the young woman who'd saved the royal family from an assassin's bullet.

I must conclude, wrote H. Mellings, *that true cultivation is not, after all, a product of education or breeding or even—forgive*

this truth!—blood, *but instead something utterly singular swelling
from a source more precious altogether: the soul.*

For when the world perceived Miss White—*in possession of
faery grace, of grave-eyed dignity, of boundless courage*—*take a
sure-footed step toward an agitator's bullet, well, the world could
not help but feel a stirring of the heart and all the senses, and cry
out, "Yes! There are still angels living in this city!"*

Quinn felt a glow of satisfaction. This was delicious stuff—just
as thrilling as the racing fixtures.

She found Mrs. Airlie in the gilt-and-cream morning room,
dividing a crumpet into infinitesimal pieces. The clock was chiming seven: Mrs. Airlie always insisted on an early breakfast.

"Success, Mrs. Airlie," Quinn said, brandishing the newspaper.
"The sketch writers can't get enough of us."

"Good notices?"

"Gushing."

"Bravo, Le Blanc."

Quinn had rolled the dice and approached her quarry. Now
she would need to make her second move, and advance across the
board. The Rulebook was clear: on the second day, she needed
to gather more information—and allies. A wise queen never
launched a direct attack against her mark without thoroughly
peeling back his layers, searching for intelligence to strengthen
her hand. Quinn always disliked the delay; it made her nose itch.
But the game could not be played too quickly. Nor too slowly—
few deceptions could withstand public scrutiny for more than
five days. Besides, the Rulebook put it bluntly: *the corruption of
a queen's character, engendered by willfully protracted falsehood, is No
Laughing Matter.*

"So," Quinn said. "Let us mount the Intrusion."

Mrs. Airlie nodded. "I concur."

"Have we had word from Silk this morning?" Quinn helped
herself to breakfast, the sideboard groaning with kedgeree and

grilled bloaters and egg fritters and crevettes *à la diable*. She could
feel Mrs. Airlie's students watching her greedily through the double doors of the connecting parlor: they'd risen early to catch a
glimpse of the Queen of Fives out of disguise. Quinn trusted
they wouldn't be too disheartened. Her hair was tumbling in
unruly waves, hastily brushed, and she was wearing her faithful old Norfolk jacket, its sleeves permitting far more movement
than "Miss White's" close-nipped gowns.

"He sent an express. Lord Rochester's agent requested a second meeting. Are you *really* playing the marriage card, Quinn?"

Quinn seated herself opposite Mrs. Airlie, grabbing a gold-
plated fork. "I really am."

"You have the stomach for it?"

"I will if I have a good breakfast." Quinn raised her knife.
"Besides, 'False Heiress' is quite clear. We *must* have a wedding."

"Very well. How will you manage the Intrusion?"

"I could do with your advice."

"Regarding?"

"On *whom* to intrude." Quinn took a bite of her breakfast.
"Oh, Mrs. Airlie—codfish pie! Heavenly."

"You haven't decided already?"

"I'm of two minds. Every instinct tells me to befriend the
stepmother. She accompanied the duke to Buckingham Palace;
evidently they have a good accord."

"How would you win her confidence?"

"Silk reports that she has a mania for poor-visiting. Perhaps I
could make a donation to one of her charitable causes."

"Could you afford to do so?"

"I could pretend to do so."

"Not very Christian of you." Mrs. Airlie nibbled her crumpet.

"Then again, I might be wasting my time. The Kendals are
an *old* family: to them, blood is everything. A stepmother is always just a hanger-on."

"So you wish to target the sister."

"Possibly. I suspect she has more weak spots; she must be in a very precarious position. A woman of advanced age, well on the road to spinsterhood, with a great deal to lose if she falls out of her brother's favor..."

"Advanced age?" Mrs. Airlie sniffed. "Good heavens, she's only thirty-five."

"Moreover, Victoria Kendal will understand her brother's nature better than anyone. Rather a useful person to have on side." Quinn fished out the tintype photograph of the Kendal family. She pressed a finger to Tor Kendal, studying her riotous curls. "But I'm undecided. I need to take a closer look at them both."

"So? How shall you proceed?"

Quinn studied the game in her mind. "Let me play as a pawn." She pointed her fork at the ceiling. "Tell me, Mrs. Airlie. Do you have any very old frocks upstairs I might borrow?"

———

Some queens assigned the Intrusion to other members of their household. But Quinn trusted her own powers of observation over anyone else's, even Mr. Silk's. The Rulebook put great weight on the importance of the Intrusion.

CLAUSE 2. The mark is an organism like any other, as fine and complicated as an orchid. It requires careful dissection to trace its vessels and chambers, to enter its splendid nectaries... To trap her quarry, a queen must know every inch of her vivarium; she must neglect no corner...

Quinn felt no scruples about poking about in the Kendals' business. They'd do worse to her neighborhood, given half a chance. She had memorized everything Silk had unearthed on the family—she prided herself on reading her papers at breakneck speed—but now she needed to pry Kendal House open, and look for ways to earn their trust.

So Quinn arrived at Berkeley Square just before eight o'clock, dressed as a flower seller—wearing a stained apron, and a skirt so hideous it might have been dragged out of a drain, with several layers of padding underneath. Her face was half concealed by a very disagreeable-looking shawl, and she'd changed into a worn-out pair of suede gloves. Her baskets were filled with delphiniums—rather wilted, but still a roaring shade of pink.

"Flowers?" she said to a tradesman in the mews lane.

"Try inside," he answered, thumbing in the direction of the gates. Laborers were passing in and out with ladders and packing crates. This counted as a fair invitation. Quinn made herself appear dim-witted, bobbing cheerfully and passing through the gate. Instantly, she felt it, the wriggle in her gut. Her game was alive.

The stable yard was surrounded by high brick walls. A stable block stood to the rear, whitewashed and brilliant. There was a stumpy clock tower and a chapel; a secondary wall concealed the privies, and there was a small porch leading to what Quinn guessed was the servants' hall. Exactly what she was after.

A handful of male servants were clustered in the doorway, wearing dark aprons and pale yellow liveries.

"Flowers for the lady of the house?" Quinn called, wagging her delphiniums.

"Clear off," said one of the footmen, flicking his cigarette butt on the gravel.

Quinn craned her neck upward, studying the dingy coal-stained backside of the house. The windows were strung with net curtains and striped awnings, stirring gently in the breeze. But there was no other movement. No life, no heart, at all. A glass-house stood on the southeastern side, its copper girders turning a stately shade of green. Quinn slipped behind the privy wall, tested the sash windows, and discovered one that was unlocked. Perfect. She nudged it open, swinging herself over the sill.

She found herself in a cool, dim pantry. The air had a whiff of vinegar, or boiled sherry—something coming from the kitchens. Quinn heard a burst of ragged laughter, a door banging, footsteps hurrying down a distant passage.

Then stillness.

She set down her delphinium basket and unpeeled her shawl. Underneath her filthy skirts she wore a dark twill dress, borrowed from Mrs. Airlie's own maid. From a pocket stitched into her petticoat, she tugged a second apron—starched and sparkling— and tied it neatly around her waist. She shoved a linen cap on the crown of her head, kicked off her clumpy boots, and put on a pair of plain black shoes pulled from her basket.

Thus, she became a perfect housemaid.

A pawn, ready to slice across the chessboard.

The front hall was dark, shuttered, the windows heavily draped. The ceilings seemed strangely low, as if the floors above were about to capsize; it gave the house a tilted, off-kilter feel. There was a sideboard bearing a white napkin, a long-handled spoon, and a tiny glass of red wine. Medicinal, perhaps?

She heard the distant *thwack* of a tablecloth being shaken out, the dull clank of breakfast things lifted from a trolley, and shrank into the dark recess beneath the stairwell. The staircase loomed above her, its crenellated galleries draped with banners, the walls hung with tapestries embroidered with swans and women wreathed in nettles, all with red-beaded eyes and frightfully distended necks.

She arrowed silently up the stairs, moving as quickly as possible, her tread absorbed by the thick red carpet. The light on the first floor was oddly refracted, twisting downward through a glass dome at the very top of the house. To the left she spotted a picture gallery, the walls congested with family portraits: a multitude of Kendals, done in chalks and oils, wearing powdered wigs and red coats. To her right stood a huge pair of sliding doors, leading to the ballroom. Beyond, she perceived a pair of double doors, facing the front: the drawing room, without a doubt.

Lowering her cap, she tapped on the door. Hearing no response, she nudged it open.

Light came crashing through the tall sash windows. The chairs were thorny, silver-painted; the chandelier was gigantic overhead. The walls were molded with plaster figurines, a host of whipped-up peaks and vines rushing from the floor. Not a very cozy room. Apparently, this was not a family who cared to gather around the fire.

She made again for the stairs. The bedroom floors might be more useful; they would reveal more intimate secrets. The second floor had a danker smell, tea leaves and potpourri and sugar water. She paused, wondering which way to turn.

A door on the other side of the landing opened. A housemaid, clearly doing her rounds. She looked gaunt, and even from a distance Quinn could see her painfully red hands. Quinn whipped behind a cabinet, nailing her spine to the wall, heart thudding in her ears.

She heard a door sliding open. When she peeped out from her hiding place, the girl had vanished.

Quinn couldn't afford to be spotted by one of the housemaids at close quarters; they'd detect a stranger in their midst immediately. Rapidly, she unbuttoned her dress and shrugged it from her shoulders, revealing a dark coat and trousers. She shoved the dress, cap and apron behind the cabinet, unpinned her mousy wig to reveal a flaxen, boyish crop beneath—and darted across the landing, edging open a pair of sliding doors.

She was in a large bedroom suite, three bays across, with a huge bed bearing a white satin canopy. Clearly, this was the principal suite, belonging to the duke—blanched and cold, glossy white floorboards, azure blinds. A floorboard creaked in an adjoining room on her left-hand side. The same maid, folding sheets. Quinn ducked into a third antechamber on her right.

The maid's voice called, "Who's that?"

"Just fetching a letter for His Grace," Quinn replied, voice deep, hiding behind the connecting door. "Won't be a sec."

A pause.

"Well, be quick about it," the maid called back. "I need to lock up."

Footsteps, a rustle of cotton and linen, and then the click of a distant door.

Quinn let out her breath.

Later, when things were well and truly underway, Quinn told herself: *you should have stopped when you saw the dollhouse.*

She'd guessed she was in a dressing room, but this chamber had no windows; it was more like a room within a room, with black lacquered walls and no furniture, save for a single circular table—polished oak, rubbed and glossy. And on it, yawning open: a model house.

It had several floors, a mansard roof, and sculpted pediments, almost a mirror of Kendal House. All the rooms were furnished with sumptuous, tiny things: miniature beds and chairs, walls painted in duck egg blues with ochre trim. In the heart of the house stood a central compartment with black walls, and in here sat three small dolls. Knitted figures made from yellow yarn, with wonky legs and arms. Black mismatched stitches where their eyes should have been.

Did they belong to the duke? Presumably, although she could not imagine what sort of gentleman kept a dollhouse in his private quarters.

Quinn felt the urge to rifle through his closets and drawers to search for more intelligence—but she feared the maid returning. She closed the door and left the suite as quickly as she could.

There was movement on the landing: more housemaids filing down the stairs. Once the coast was clear, Quinn crossed swiftly to the back of the house. Here the walls were mounted with hunting paraphernalia—truncheons and axes and brass horns and hideous pieces of taxidermy. One carried a small label: *The Duke of Kendal, 1866.* The old Lord Kendal, deceased father of the present duke. This was a family that enjoyed stalking, shooting, killing. It made her nostrils flare, as if sensing a spark of opposition from the house.

An interesting detail, perhaps. But she needed more.

Where was Victoria Kendal's suite? Beyond was a parlor, and then a bedroom, whose windows had been thrown open. A shadow moved, and Quinn flinched, looking for a place to hide.

There was none to be found.

Framed by weak light, back to the doorway, stood a woman. Quinn could scuttle away now. But instead she crept forward, heart ticking.

Not Victoria Kendal. This woman was at least ten years older than that, and curiously dressed, in a rough-laced tunic and silk trousers—and barefoot, legs planted wide apart. She held a contraption formed of two wooden handles and an elastic band, and she was stretching it back and forth, over and over. Scattered on the carpet were all manner of wooden rods and iron balls.

This was the stepmother: the Dowager Duchess of Kendal.

Yet, she appeared nothing like the gently ruffled lady Quinn had met on her stepson's arm at Buckingham Palace. Here, in her own house, she seemed lean and wolfish, muscles flexing in her forearms.

The duchess paused, elastic straining. "Thomas?" she called, setting down her contraption.

"Beg pardon, Your Grace," Quinn called back. "Just taking some post for Lady Victoria."

The duchess began to turn, a distant silhouette, drapes twisting restlessly in the breeze. Quinn swung on her heel, marching to the stairs before Lady Kendal caught a glimpse of her face.

She exhaled only when she reached the third floor.

This, surely, was where Victoria Kendal's suite was situated. Quinn's instincts flared again: someone powerful resided up here. The landing was lavishly appointed, the doors surmounted by gilded architraves, topped with splendid wings and pediments. Lady Victoria obviously did *not* have modest habits. She enjoyed her wealth; she'd licked the walls with gold.

So, Victoria Kendal prized fine things. This could be Quinn's way in.

She tried the door handle, very gently.

Locked.

Quinn took a step backward, frustrated. The walls on the landing were hung with horse brasses and modern paintings— mostly nudes, done on huge oil canvasses—electrifyingly ugly. A wooden frame, rather like a school prize board, had been engraved with gilt letters reading **CARRIAGE RACES**, with initials marked up in columns underneath: **M. K. D.—*First Place*... *V. K.—First Place*...** It meant nothing to Quinn. She tried to imagine the bedroom within: an enormous bed with a meaty tester and thick-swagged curtains.

Locked doors always sparked her curiosity.

She knocked very softly. But there was no reply.

She couldn't waste time: the game was ticking on. She sliced her way up to the fourth floor, which contained dimly lit guest suites; then the fifth floor, with the servants' quarters. At the top of the house, she spied a final dusty staircase, presumably leading to the attics. She stood on a square landing with shelves carrying water pails and decayed-looking brushes. Here was another locked door.

Quinn pressed her ear to the keyhole, heard the faint whistle of the breeze. Empty, she presumed—or full of old rubbish. Far less compelling than the live flesh downstairs.

"Here! Who's up there?"

She nearly jumped out of her skin. Quinn swiped some dust

from the banister, rubbed it on her cheeks, grabbed one of the brushes.

"I'm the sweep," she called, peeping down the stairs. "The chimney sweep."

A young footman was peering up the stairs, his pale liveries glinting in the shadows. "You need to go the other way." He jerked his thumb leftward. "Her ladyship won't like you poking around up here."

Which ladyship? Quinn wondered. But the footman frowned before she could ask. "That flue's not going to sweep itself, you know. Clear off!"

———◆———

Quinn made it back to the ground floor without impediment, taking the servants' staircase. She popped out on the second floor to reclaim her housemaid's disguise from behind the cabinet, then burrowed down to the basement. Scooping up her filthy apron, she clambered out the pantry window, refastening it as she crossed the stable yard, broke into a run when she reached Berkeley Square. She didn't stop until she reached Piccadilly, dodging a group of workmen who were taking up a portion of the road with a small steam engine.

Her mind was working, sifting information. The duke's bed-chamber: bleached and silent. The dollhouse and its knitted poppets. Lady Kendal, stretching her elastic rods, muscles tensing. All very odd. But Quinn could handle oddness. It was the golden door on the third floor that intrigued her most. Why did Lady Victoria keep her bedroom door locked? What was she hiding?

This question decided the matter. Victoria Kendal would be the target of the Intrusion. And the horse brasses on the wall provided Quinn with a clue about just how to approach her...

2

Tor

It took Lady Kendal a whole day to respond to Tor's request for an appointment. Tor heard nothing from Max, receiving only a cold card, wishing her a pleasant afternoon. In the old days he'd sent her letters, pages long, full of the horrors of school—beastly masters, mountains of prep—and the thrills of the rugger pitch. She'd sent her own extensive compositions by direct return, detailing news from the stud farm, peculiar weather formations, tenants who had died. Now it appeared they had nothing to say to one another at all. Had he met a suitable young lady at the palace? Tor was utterly in the dark. She was brooding on it as she returned from her morning ride, a little after nine o'clock, when the footman waylaid her on the staircase.

"Her Grace says she is terribly sorry for her tardy reply, but invites you to take tea with her now, if it pleases your ladyship."

Terribly sorry? Tor felt a flicker of anger. She unbuttoned her stiff-boned jacket, loosening her curls from their netting. Her top hat glistened in the looking glass reflection. "Tell her I accept."

It would be too bullish to simply go downstairs and give the reply herself. "It's always nice to allow someone a little breathing room," her stepmother taught her, when Tor was much younger. "It allows them time to make their excuses."

Tor had accepted this grudgingly. Some people needed time to concoct lies and stories to withstand the perils of dealing with one another. But it would be better if everybody said exactly what they meant, all the time, without compunction. She said as much to Lady Kendal.

"But this is not the world we live in," her stepmother had replied. She was rearranging the gladioli in the front hall, adjusting the position of each stem. Her tone was gentle, but her movements were not: she kept shredding the leaves. Tor found it unsettling. "Sometimes we are obliged to shift along with other people."

"I don't wish to shift along with anyone. Why should I?"

Her stepmother had sighed. "Why, indeed?" she said. But she'd taken the hint. The children of the neighboring houses were no longer invited for tea. All talk of Tor going away to school— a discussion that had swung into alarming view in the months before Papa died—came to a halt. Lady Kendal had granted Tor her heart's desire: the freedom to stay home, for as long as she wished, unimpeded by strangers.

Now, by engineering Max's marriage, she was snatching it away again.

Tor locked the doors to her suite and went downstairs. Lady Kendal's apartments were on the second floor, situated at the back of the house. Papa's stalking prizes had been stuffed and framed in glass, displayed on the landing: a stag's head, two shocked deer, a multitude of pheasants. They were decades old, and rather hideously done, but Lady Kendal refused to have them taken down, even after she'd remodeled the second floor. "They remind me of how splendid your father must have been in his prime. A fine hunter." Love was evidently a strange and mysterious business, Tor decided, if such ghastly trophies could carry sentimental value—but she'd sensed not to press her stepmother on the point.

A secretary emerged to greet Tor as she approached. "Lady Victoria, good morning! Her Grace will see you immediately."

Tor crossed the threshold.

Lady Kendal's personal drawing room was a hive of activity. Housemaids counted and tied sacks of silver paper for Great Ormond Street Hospital. Two footmen were crouched by the crackling fire, stacking tins of chocolate intended for one of Lady Kendal's favored regiments, the 19th Hussars. They stared dully at Tor as she passed. The dowager duchess still commanded the absolute loyalty of the male servants. Tor sometimes thought that the butler would gladly take down one of Papa's rifles and shoot her in the head, if Lady Kendal told him to do it. But this, she reminded herself, was a good example of irrational thinking, something she intended to avoid today.

The secretary pushed open the door to the inner boudoir, clearing his throat. "Your Grace? The Lady Victoria."

The room was draped in pale silks, cluttered with bric-a-brac—fresh magazines, novels, playing cards, envelopes for sending messages, a pair of rather menacing Dutch dolls in stiff blue skirts. It was like entering an oyster, Tor thought. Gleaming, pinkish, containing a single pearl. Lady Kendal sat on a low stool, skirts decorously spread, sewing fabric squares into a blanket. Around her, in far less comfortable positions, were the other housemaids, hunched and squinting, threading needles.

"Darling Tor!" Her stepmother smiled up at her. "How nice."

When the new duchess first came to Mount Kendal, Tor thought she was the most beautiful woman she'd ever seen. Her hair was raven black and beautifully curled. She smelled like a meadow, or a fruit basket. She'd pressed her palm over Tor's knuckles, transmitting warmth into Tor's bones. She did it now, reaching for Tor—and handing her a needle as she did so.

"Will you help us? I'm terribly afraid we won't finish these blankets in time."

Tor felt a quiver of recognition: the old reassurance that came from her stepmother's touch. She steeled herself against it. Today, she needed to be firm; she needed to protect her own interests, not Lady Kendal's feelings. She lowered herself to the ottoman, trying to be graceful. At close quarters, her stepmother always made her feel hulking and angular.

"I'm here to ask you for a favor."

"Yes?"

"Please—don't keep going out for calls with Max."

Lady Kendal tilted her head. "What sort of calls?"

"Mr. Willoughby told me why you both went to the palace. To search for a bride."

"Good heavens. The moneyman told you that?" Lady Kendal began stitching one fabric square to the next. "I wouldn't give him much credence, Tor."

"So it isn't true?"

Lady Kendal held up a silk jerkin, beautifully done in periwinkle and teal. "Aren't we doing *splendidly*? Don't you adore these little jackets?"

It was impossible to get underneath her surface. Tor dug her needle into her seat cushion. "Max doesn't wish to marry."

"Does he not?"

"I'm as sure about it as I can be about anything."

"Well then," said her stepmother seriously. "I believe you."

"Then please, don't take him looking for a wife. It's an odious thing to do and it sets false expectations in everybody."

One of the maids let out a sharp cry: she'd pricked herself on her sewing needle. Lady Kendal's face shuttered.

"Don't bleed on it. Go and wash your hands." The maid dropped the blanket, binding her finger with her apron. Lady Kendal's expression softened again as she addressed Tor. "Where is this all coming from, Victoria?"

"I told you."

"Have you spoken to your brother about all this?"

Tor shook her head. "Certainly not. He knows my opinion."

"Darling Tor, if Max chooses to marry—and it *is* his decision to make—it would safeguard this estate in perpetuity. Surely, that's not such a very bad thing?" Lady Kendal smiled. "Besides, you might make a match of your own."

"No, thank you."

"I know a good many gentlemen who would be honored to take your hand. Irrespective of your age."

"I know a good many gentlemen I'd like to see lined up in the yard and shot." Tor threw aside her ragged sewing. "Lady Kendal..."

"Mama, please."

Tor took a shuddery breath. "Mama, I wish you'd drop this matter. If Max marries, both of us will be obliged to leave Kendal House."

Lady Kendal threaded her needle. "Really, Victoria. What a silly thing to say."

"Silly? Not in the least. Quite truthful."

"Your poor father would hate to hear you speak like this."

"Would he? I don't recall any of his sisters lurking about Kendal House after *he* was married."

"Tor," Lady Kendal said. "I think you're worrying *quite* needlessly."

Tor knew their stepmother was benign. She had never made a move that was not to her stepchildren's advantage. She'd ensured they'd received a first-rate education, tended their father with absolute devotion during his last illness, gave exquisite care to the estate during Max's minority, and stepped aside graciously when he turned twenty-one. She was the very opposite of a wicked stepmother. And *yet*—Tor could not escape the feeling that somewhere, somehow, things were going wrong.

"Mama," she said helplessly. "I wish you would see—" She broke off. It was impossible to make herself understood.

"I think," Lady Kendal said, setting down her sewing, "that we've had enough disagreeable conversation for one morning, haven't we?" She reached for Tor, giving off the same old scent—lavender and heliotrope and phlox and cornflowers. She dug her small fingers into the soft parts of Tor's wrist. "*Haven't* we, Victoria?"

3

The Duke

The duke woke late, and ordered a cold bath in compensation. He breakfasted in his own rooms, ignoring the morning papers. His mind felt jagged. Clearly, he was on the brink of a dark mood.

To shake it, he ventured down to the glasshouse to work. Botanical science was only a hobby, but something about the practice soothed him. Really, botanists were quite perverse people, he thought, always peering at the sexual organs of unsuspecting flowers. But Papa had built the glasshouse at Kendal House for his mother, and she had imported such a wide variety of tropical plants that the duke felt obliged to catalogue them and give them proper care. She wasn't here to enjoy them, after all.

Apparently, the servants had guessed he might come downstairs, for he discovered his writing desk had been set up underneath the arboretum with a pot of tea and a bottle of fresh ink. But there was no opportunity to settle down to work, for an amused voice called out from the side of the room:

"Don't these steam pipes annoy Your Grace? So much hissing and puffing. I don't know how you can concentrate."

It was Willoughby, pushing through the mist and ferns like a panther emerging from the undergrowth. He was wearing a cobalt jacket, so bright it made the duke blink. Of course, Willoughby was prowling here, uninvited. He was irrepressible.

They shook hands very civilly.

"Have you breakfasted?" Willoughby asked.

"Yes."

"What a splendid teapot they've brought out for you. I've never seen anything like it. It's quite gargantuan." Willoughby seated himself opposite the duke, peering at the codices and reference books. "I don't know how you have the patience, truthfully. Such a lot of fiddly little words." Then he glanced up, said with greater care, "You seem rather out of sorts."

"Are you surprised? I didn't enjoy that little performance yesterday morning, Willoughby. It's bad enough to have the lawyers pushing me. I didn't expect you to be singing in the choir."

Willoughby sipped his tea. "Look here, it's a damnably tricky situation. You *must* marry, for all the reasons the old crows have been squawking on about for months. But you could take things in hand, you know. Make your own choice in the matter, select a lady of good breeding and fortune. I imagine it's awfully tedious for you, being managed by everybody else."

"*Can* you imagine it? Is anyone pressing *you* to secure the future of the Kendal estate? The last time I checked, you seemed to be a confirmed bachelor."

Willoughby pursed his lips in amusement. "I have a few years on you, Your Grace. I know what it is to be disappointed."

The pipes sighed, releasing more vapor.

"If it were only a matter of self-sacrifice," the duke said shortly, "I wouldn't put up a fight. But this has gone too far. It's running away from me."

"Good. You need to be rushed. There are all sorts of loathsome characters out there who *want* you to delay choosing a bride. The longer you wait, the more frauds they can rustle up to tempt you. Believe me. I know how these people operate."

"Do you? Have you been cavorting with charlatans yourself?"

Willoughby's eyebrows flew up. He cracked his knuckles. "Naturally! I sell information about you and your family from dawn till dusk. I could line up half a dozen confidence women to marry you this week, if I cared to."

"Don't joke, please."

"Then don't avoid the point. You went to the palace yesterday, yes? Rather a startling afternoon."

"You were there?"

"Of course! Lurking, in my usual dissolute fashion, so forgive me for not paying my respects. I do have other clients to spy on, you know. The Countess of Clare has two daughters just out in society. So does Mrs. Hillyard. Did you meet them? The Hillyards have less to offer in the bloodline department, but Sonia Hillyard is a splendidly savage little creature. I daresay she'd push your career magnificently."

"My career? I thought I was forbidden from having one of those."

"Why don't you take the Clare girls for tea? Court them a little."

The duke grabbed the teapot, filled his cup. "What is your intent here, Willoughby?"

"Truthfully?"

"Of course."

Willoughby flicked one of the nearby ferns with a neatly clipped forefinger. "To broker a quite extraordinary alliance for you at the absolute top end of society. To bring two great houses into one. To annex an earldom or a marquessate and absorb it into the Kendal estate. And thus to manage the largest portfolio in London."

"Isn't the Kendal estate sufficiently grand for you?"

"Nothing is ever sufficient for me," Willoughby said slyly, nudging the duke's foot as he uncrossed his knee. "I am unrelentingly desirous for marvelous things."

This was the thing about Mr. Willoughby: he was always diabolically frank. It was like being acquainted with a clear membrane; you could look right through him.

The duke said, not permitting himself to smile, "So your motives are, as always, purely mercenary."

"Well, yes. I have very plutocratic tendencies. I can't help myself."

"If it's a healthy portfolio you're after, why not chase that woman who caused a ruckus at the palace?"

"What, the assassin?"

"No, the one who stopped her bullet."

Willoughby cracked his knuckles again. "Who, the girl from Aldgate? No, thank you. Leave her to the Chathams or the Rochesters. They've got bills to pay and castles to rebuild. You don't need to marry a banker's daughter." He paused. "Besides, I know a little of her reputation. I wouldn't trust her as far as I could throw her."

"I heard she *had* no reputation. That she was entirely and spotlessly blank."

"Surely, you haven't been making inquiries?"

For a moment, the duke was tempted to provoke him. But there was no use being untruthful.

"No," he replied flatly. "But perhaps I should. If I need someone to push my *career*, a lady with mercantile antecedents could be rather helpful."

"Your Grace, this is not a laughing matter. You need to take action, now. Your stepmother tells the lawyers that she worries about your nerves—*not* a very happy narrative, for anyone who remembers your dear papa."

The duke flushed. "She ought not to worry."

"I quite agree, particularly as the entire household is devoted to the duchess, and inclined to do exactly as she tells them."

He felt a muscle leap in his jaw. "Perhaps they ought to remember their devotion to me. Or the title, at any rate."

"Perhaps you might give them a reason to do so. A wedding is always a happy affair for a ducal household. It brings everyone together splendidly."

"Willoughby..."

"Oh, I know what's holding you back. Your sister freely admits that she compelled you *not* to marry for wholly selfish reasons— namely the preservation of her income and her security at the expense of your future happiness."

"Tor said that?"

"Well, I put two and two together. Your sister's manipulations are not very cleverly disguised, I'm afraid."

The duke exhaled. "There are no manipulations when it comes to Tor. My sister may be brash, but she is not deliberately guileful."

"Perhaps not, but others are. This is the sort of slippery nonsense I'm employed to deflect for you. Yet, you obstruct my efforts at every turn. If you were a dog, you'd be put out of your misery—but you're not, you're a duke. And nobody dares to shake you, in case you snap."

"You forget yourself."

"Do I?"

"Yes. You're here at my pleasure."

"At *your* pleasure? I could give up your case this afternoon."

"My case? I'm not your patient."

"Then take your cure, sir. And listen to my counsel."

"Counsel? I don't need any more counsel. It's—" the duke felt his anger rising "—*friendship* I need. And if you won't provide that, then straightforward loyalty. Are we united or not, Willoughby?"

Willoughby's face darkened. "You're turning the screws on me."

"Yes. Now you know how it feels."

They stared at each other for a long moment. Then Willoughby clicked his tongue in irritation. "Yes, damn it, we *are* united. Someone has to look out for you." He let out a breath. "Very well, I submit. Put off the Clares and the Hillyards if they don't interest you. Go and visit the famous Miss White in whatever drain she resides in, if she's caught your eye. Better still, invite her to tea. We can put down some dust sheets. But you should know that your lawyers *and* your stepmother would advise a more elevated match."

The duke said coldly, "Tell me. Why *do* you think I'm avoiding marriage? To be petulant? To disoblige the world?"

"No," Willoughby replied, voice softening. "Your Grace is a gentleman of principle." He paused. "I suspect you feel your attentions are promised—elsewhere. Am I correct?"

The duke glanced toward the doors, checking the servants were not hovering in the background. He did not meet Willoughby's eye.

"Perhaps."

"Marriage need not interfere with a gentleman's private pleasures."

"I refuse to make a marriage vow," the duke said in a low voice, "that I cannot possibly keep."

"Good gracious! Gentlemen in your position always take a lover outside wedlock. I daresay your own father…"

"I am not my father." The duke could feel the heat in his cheeks. "Nor am I like other gentlemen."

Willoughby sighed. "No, you are not. But if you wish to honor Lord Kendal's memory *and* satisfy your nearest relations, *and* your dependents, *and* your neighbors—then you must set aside your principles. You *must* proceed, and marry. It is expected." He met the duke's stare. "I say this in the spirit of absolute unity with you."

"Well," the duke said, voice hollow. "I can't ask for any more than that. Send for them all, if you like. The Clares, the Hill-yards, Miss White. Bring them to tea, or to dinner, or the opera—who cares? Do it tonight. I daresay we can thrash out a settlement between us." He drained his cup of tea, masking a growing sense of unease. "Best to stride out across hot coals."

"There you are: fighting spirit. Shall we be friends again?"

"Clear off, Willoughby," the duke replied, returning to his books.

4

The Man in the Blue Silk Waistcoat

The man in the blue silk waistcoat scrunched himself into a barber's chair in a shop on Fournier Street. It was upholstered in red leather, cracked and lovely, warmed by the seat of its last occupant. His nostrils were filled with the sharp combination of Bristowe's soap and Makassar oil. A stove was pumping heat in the corner of the shop, despite the summer heat, and two old boys were sitting chatting in straight-backed chairs, perspiration running down their necks.

There was a flash of a metal razor blade. The man in the blue silk waistcoat glanced up to the mirror.

"Just a trim, sir?" asked the barber with a little frown.

"Just a trim."

He'd changed skins several times already this morning, taking a snaking route eastward to avoid observation—skipping to Aldwych, then Bridewell, then the Cheshire Cheese, then High Holborn. He was dancing the line of the old Fleet River, dodging omnibuses and goods vehicles and phaetons, peeling his layers as he went. He knew all the tricks: where to position his buttons, how to stack one garment on another. He kept an old collection of farthingale pins and *verdugados* for the trickier costumes. He didn't need a machine to make his clothes.

Now he watched the barber adjusting the scissors, studying his neckline with a little frown. *Go on*, thought the man in the blue silk waistcoat. *Say it's a wig. I dare you.* The pins were quite obvious, if you knew where to look, nestled beneath his silvery curls.

The barber pressed his lips together, spun his scissors on his thumb, and made the tiniest snip. "Nice weather we're having. You off on your holidays?"

The mirror was damp around the edges, flushed with condensation. "A man who takes a holiday is a man without purpose," said the man in the blue silk waistcoat. "Work is its own reward."

"I'm off down to Margate with the missus." The barber gingerly snipped another curl. "Just visiting, then, are you?"

"Correct."

"Got friends in the neighborhood? Family?"

"Are you a detective?"

"Detective? Ha."

"Are we in church? Are you taking my confession?"

The barber's expression stiffened, and the old boys fell silent. "Just making conversation."

"Let me ask *you* some questions, then." The man in the blue silk waistcoat waved away the scissors, getting to the purpose of his visit. "Does your tenancy cover the rooms upstairs?"

The barber hesitated. "Who's asking?"

"I can see there's a door to the rear of your shop." The man in the blue silk waistcoat extended a finger from beneath the protective cloak tied neatly around his neck. "I presume you have the key?"

The barber took a step back. "Look here. What is this? You've come in here for a haircut when you're not even—"

The man in the blue silk waistcoat knew how to be dexterous when required. He rose from the chair, hearing the squeak of the leather, and drew a blade from his jerkin.

"I would like the key to the back door," he said. "At your earliest convenience."

"Now, now. Don't be hasty."

"I won't," said the man in the blue silk waistcoat. "But I wish you would be."

The barber turned and scrabbled for the key. It was hanging on a brass hook right beside the mirror. The man in the blue silk waistcoat placed a five-pound banknote on the top of the big silver cash register. The edges fluttered in the warm air pumping from the stove.

The barber's mouth was agape. "You're joking."

"For your absolute discretion," the man in the blue silk waistcoat replied. "One more thing. I need the services of a young woman. Could you recommend one?"

The barber took another step back, face wrinkling in distaste. He didn't touch the banknote. "You can keep your money."

"Good heavens, it's nothing sordid. I need someone to take a message. Or rather to sit on it, until it's collected." The man in the blue silk waistcoat raised an eyebrow. "No? Very well. I'll ask around." He unlocked the back door, smelled the sharp tang of carbolic, felt a cool breeze trickling down the passage beyond. "*Do* enjoy your holiday," he added, closing the door behind him.

5

Quinn

"I need a horse," Quinn said to Mr. Silk. "And quickly. By three o'clock at the latest."

They'd met by appointment in the churchyard of St. James Garlickhythe. It was a little after twelve, and the sun was struggling into the midday sky. "A *horse?*" Silk repeated. He was sweating, running late. "How am I supposed to manage that? I've just come all the way from Stepney, calling in your debts."

They were aiming for an old stone-walled mansion just south of Cannon Street, designed to serve as Miss White's false address. The Château had reserved rights of occupation over this property for years. It once belonged to a loan shark deeply enthralled to the first Madame Le Blanc. It stood on a hilly patch of ground, connected to the churchyard by a narrow path, and from the gates Quinn could glimpse the smoky passage of the Thames, cargo boats chugging slowly both east and west. The rest of the street was inhabited by cloak-makers and fur traders, working in cavernous warehouses with their blinds and shutters drawn.

"I need props, not payments." Quinn kicked open the gate from the churchyard, making it clang behind her. "And I need a horse. A really very good one."

"But whatever for?" Silk wiped his brow with a handkerchief. "Oh, hang it. Here's the old skeleton, come to pay his respects."

A scrawny man of quite remarkable antiquity was creeping down the winding path, walking stick clacking against the nearest gravestones.

"Your Majesty," he said, clutching his walking stick, sinking into a bow. He stayed there, shoulders hunched. "I am your man of life and limb."

"Trusted friend, we greet you well." Quinn extended a gloved hand, permitted the old fellow to put his cracked lips to her fingers and then back away. To Silk, she added, "I need to give Lady Victoria a gift, to gain her trust. And she's horse mad."

They moved inside. The house clearly hadn't been done up in more than a century: the walls were a faded earthy shade of green, and the air smelled of mold. Silk wrinkled his nose. "I'll light some fires. We can burn some flower jars."

"Or the drapes. But, Silk, listen. I want to show Lady Victoria that I've got a pony. A really splendid one. One to impress her, earn her friendship *and* her admiration."

"A *pony?*"

"What else? I need her to vouch for me with the duke, assuage any concerns in the family about my low birth. The only way to do it is to convince her that we are like-minded, that we share the same refinements. Which means you need to pay a call on old Mr. Murphy about getting us a horse."

Silk raised his hands in the air. "Absolutely *not*, Quinn."

"Whyever not? The Goodwood Races are coming up, which means Murphy's gang will be running approximately three thousand rackets. He'll have more horses than he knows what to do with."

Silk shook his head. "We can't approach Mr. Murphy. He's a villain."

"But why shouldn't he help us? We pay our levy to him every year, don't we?"

He blinked, as if avoiding the question. "We never play on Mr. Murphy's turf. I advise another course of action."

"For heaven's sake, I'm not asking you to fix any bets. I just want you to go to Murphy's people and ask them to loan us a really *splendid* horse." Quinn took a breath. "And I need it this afternoon."

"Quinn..."

"Do you want me to go myself?"

Once they'd scored their winnings, she'd take Silk down to Monte Carlo. She'd book them into the best hotels and order peach Melba and ice cream for breakfast. She'd let him sleep in all day if he wished to. But at this moment, they were working, and the clock was ticking, and she demanded results.

Silk's fingers fluttered over his appointment book, cogs turning even as he flipped through the options in his head. "Very well. Let me see what I can do. Three o'clock, you say?"

"On Rotten Row. I'm depending on you."

Silk planted his bowler hat on his head. "Go to the church and see if they've got any incense to spare. This house needs a complete airing."

———

How Mr. Silk managed it, Quinn didn't know, but at quarter to three she spied him fussing his way around Hyde Park Corner, leading a gigantic dun-colored stallion down from a horse box at the foot of Rotten Row.

"He's a *beauty*," Quinn exclaimed.

"I fear he's quite wild," Silk replied as the horse stamped its hooves furiously, kicking up sand. "And he's a racer."

Quinn adjusted her top hat to examine him. She'd made a fast change at Mrs. Airlie's house, buckling herself into a riding habit richly made in lincoln green, braced in a stiff doublet and leather gloves that went right up to her elbows. She whisked her riding crop, making Silk flinch.

"What is he?"

A face peeped out from behind the horse's right flank. One of Murphy's boys, ruddy-cheeked and self-assured. "He's a Kochlaini, ma'am. Very expensive."

"How expensive?"

Silk waved this away. "If you *ask* about the insurance, then you *know* about the insurance, and I'd really rather keep certain facts inadmissible. He nearly destroyed the horse box, you know. We got him here just in the nick of—"

"He's perfect, Silk," Quinn said, squeezing his arm. "Well done." And then, to the Murphy boy, "Please send my compliments to Mr. Murphy."

"Returned, ma'am." The boy winked at her. "Mr. Silk promised us a very nice commission on your final receipts."

Quinn wondered how much. "Of course. We are pleased to share our largesse with Mr. Murphy. But not a word of this to anyone else, all right?"

"Likewise, ma'am. And I'll need this big chap back in his stables before midnight."

"You'll have him home by teatime." Quinn gathered her armored skirts. "Now, both of you, follow me."

———

Rotten Row ran end to end across Hyde Park, vast and sunbaked. Quinn stationed herself in the patch of ground between the carriage drive and the riding track. The sky was beginning to lose its bright blue confidence, but the heat was still rising. She could feel sweat prickling around her stiff white collar.

"Here, ma'am?" Murphy's boy was hauling the colossal race-horse into position.

Heavy broughams and open landaus and nifty little gigs were driving behind them, slowing to observe the huge stallion standing beside the lady dressed in green.

"Yes, here, behind the railings."

"You're sure she'll come?" Silk said.

"An afternoon ride, one hour before tea." Quinn nodded, checking her pocket watch, calculating how quickly she wished to be away, subdividing minutes in her head. "That's what the groom said."

"You're sure he didn't just take the cash and run?"

Quinn had crept back to Kendal House to bribe one of the lads working in Lady Victoria's stables. "No, but I'll string him from the rafters if he did."

"*Easy*, soldier," said Murphy's boy, placing a firm hand on the stallion's forelock. "He's a beast, ain't he?"

"Look sharp," Quinn said, raising her crop. "Here she comes."

And sure enough, wending her way around slow-moving broughams, cantering hard from the carriage drive into the track came Lady Victoria Kendal.

"Stand back," Quinn murmured. "Show off the horse…"

"She's not stopping," Silk said.

He was right. Lady Victoria came pounding right past them—riding sidesaddle, shoulders hunched, her own black top hat tilted hard over her brow. The hooves of her ladyship's gray mare threw dust and muck high into the air, almost spattering their faces.

A second later, she was gone, charging off into the distance. Quinn felt her stomach clench in disappointment.

"All done?" said Murphy's boy cheerfully. "Can I go?"

———

Both Quinn and Silk were in a bad humor by the time they'd returned to the horse box waiting at Hyde Park Corner.

"You should have listened to your instincts and aimed at the stepmother," Silk said.

Quinn cursed him inwardly. "I'll find another way to attract her attention."

"How, pray? Shall we bring a whole racecourse to Berkeley Square?"

"Hush. I'm thinking." She turned the plan over in her mind. But her thoughts were interrupted by the sound of thunderous hooves bearing down behind them.

The stallion reared again. Quinn turned fast, shielding her eyes from the gray glare. A figure on horseback, as tightly buckled up in navy as Quinn was in green, slowed on the approach. Curls sprang out from beneath the severe dent of her hat.

"Where," she called imperiously, pointing to the racehorse, "did you find *him*?"

———

Victoria Kendal was impressive. She dismounted from her mare smoothly, boots landing with a thud on the sandy earth beneath.

She moved with force, aiming straight for the stallion. It was clear she was in her mid-thirties. She had all the taut-cheeked, Cavalier-blooded, curly-haired confidence you'd expect of a woman who'd been brought up in one of the grandest houses on Berkeley Square. But it was clear, too, the sort of older woman she would become. Hard and upright and deft in her movements.

Silk removed his hat. The huge horse shied away.

"That *is* a Kochlaini," she said. "I thought as much." Her voice was clear, strong. Her fierce gaze swept Quinn up and down. "Surely, he doesn't belong to you?"

Quinn said, affecting nonchalance, "In a manner of speaking." She felt a burst of triumph. She'd done it: she'd snagged Lady Victoria's attention.

"But that's impossible. I tried to get a Kochlaini myself last year and the authorities in Cairo stopped me at every turn." Victoria turned to Murphy's boy. "Are you the groom?"

He seemed a little awed. "I'm nobody, mum."

Silk bowed, head shining in the sunlight. "Madam, good afternoon to you. I wonder if I may present Miss Quinta Whi—"

"But it's too extraordinary. He's a Kochlaini," Lady Victoria repeated. "Absolutely he is. Their trade is very nearly forbidden. He's *illegal*."

Murphy's man reddened. "Now look here. I didn't come all the way out here to be—"

"What's your price?" Tor said. "Money is no object."

Quinn could feel the minutes in her head ticking a little faster.

Her plan had been to flaunt her imaginary wealth by parading a lovely racehorse around Hyde Park. It would catch the attention of Lady Victoria Kendal, famed horsewoman, and Quinn would give her a very pretty gift: the chance to ride this lovely pony around Rotten Row any day her ladyship liked. Her ladyship's interest would be duly piqued, and Quinn would have made a new friend.

She hadn't expected Lady Victoria to simply buy the horse.

"He's not for sale," Silk said swiftly.

"Do you own him?"

Quinn hesitated a second longer than she should have. "I—"

Victoria fixed her stare on the groom. "Open an auction," she said. "You have two bidders."

Murphy's man looked helplessly at Quinn. She swallowed. Very well: if Lady Victoria enjoyed a fight, she could have one. Quinn knew exactly how to play this.

"Five hundred pounds," she said boldly. She had no idea what a racehorse would cost, but it felt like an extraordinary sum for anything on four legs.

"Ten thousand pounds," Victoria Kendal said, unruffled.

Murphy's man let his mouth fall open.

In that moment, Quinn understood. Lady Victoria Kendal was a different sort of human to anyone Quinn had marked before. Her honorifics had been monogrammed on her underclothes; she'd been taught to ride and hunt and shoot the way other children were taught to tie their shoelaces. She was made of blue blood, formed of stone and iron ore. She wasn't just rich, she was unbridled, unrestrained.

"Twelve thousand pounds," Quinn said coolly. She was counting minutes in her head, subdividing them into thirds, per Mrs. Airlie's training—and she wanted to be away as quickly as possible.

Silk blanched. "Quinn...*ta*."

"Fifteen," replied Victoria, lifting her chin.

"Seventeen thousand." That would surprise her, a nice little turn.

"Twenty thousand pounds."

"Twenty thousand *guineas*."

Murphy's man licked his lips in anticipation. The racehorse reared. *Fight me*, Quinn said inwardly. *Go on, take me down.*

She saw the flecks of blood in Victoria Kendal's eyes, and knew there was no possibility that this woman would permit her to outbid. They could lift twenty thousand from her in a heartbeat, in a single afternoon—and no doubt earn her confidence. People like Lady Victoria loved to win, regardless of the price: Quinn was simply giving her the opportunity. She flicked a glance to Silk. *Back me.*

His hands jerked, understanding her game. He imposed the crisis.

"Splendid, Miss White. You'll look quite marvelous on this fellow."

Victoria Kendal's nostrils flared. "Twenty-five thousand guineas."

Quinn smiled. Time to depart. "Matched. But we'll make it thirty, for the stud fees."

Lady Victoria laughed fiercely. "Don't you understand his value? He's a *Kochlaini*. Young man, I'll give you—"

Then her voice changed, becoming grim. "Oh."

Quinn felt a snag of alarm.

Lady Victoria *tsked* in impatience. Extended a gloved hand toward the stallion's head. "Too petite in the jaw. I should have noticed. And the ears—not quite as pricked as I had thought." She sighed, nodded to Murphy's man. "Correction: he's not a Kochlaini. He's a Varna." She turned, reaching for her own silver mare, striding away. Said over her shoulder to Quinn, "You can have him, Miss White."

A crisis—but not of her own making. Quinn could feel her heart pounding in her rib cage.

"You offered on him," Murphy's man said. "Fair and square. I can't tell Mr. Murphy otherwise."

"There's no contract," Quinn said. "Nothing in writing." She let out a fierce exhalation. "Besides, you *know* what I was doing. I was luring her in, leading her on."

"P'raps she played you."

"Nonsense. And I'm not paying a penny. You can take this bloody horse *home*. Now."

"I'll take him to the stables," the man said, "seeing as Mr. Silk can't handle him for love nor money." Silk was struggling with the reins, trying desperately to stop the stallion from bolting. "But I can't tell a lie. When Mr. Murphy asks me what happened, I'm telling him straight: you offered thirty thousand without batting an eyelid. And you know his terms: three days to pay up."

Quinn could feel a white heat at the edges of her vision. Thirty thousand guineas. It would take her years to drum up that kind of capital, even in a *good* market.

"I was acting, for God's sake," she said, voice low. "You know I was acting."

"*I* don't know anything," Murphy's man said. He fiddled with a brassy-looking ring on his left forefinger, eager to be off. "I'm nobody."

———

They stood together under the bandstand. Silk looked stricken. "Murphy will kill us if we default."

"He won't *kill* us."

"But, Quinn, we're behind on our levy."

She stared at him, aghast. He had never obfuscated before. "*Silk...*"

"I didn't wish to alarm you. But our debts are...rising."

Quinn raised a hand. "Don't tell me another word. We have no room for fears. No *time* for them." She shut her eyes. "We'll score our winnings. And then we'll repay Mr. Murphy whatever we owe."

"Quinn..."

"We *will*. We have no other choice."

Silk shook his head. "That blasted horse..."

"Don't speak ill of the horse." Quinn tried to laugh—a shaky sound. "He's part of the family now." She reached for him. "Come. We need to win this game. And fast."

6

Tor

Tor's mood on the return journey was unsettled. She was not a superstitious person, but the sight of that lady in green, lurking by the side of Rotten Row like a highwaywoman, had irked her. She'd felt, coming down the western approach, a powerful sense of being watched—not in the usual awestruck way of crowds, but rather through a microscope, as if being willed to stumble and fall. It had made Tor grip her reins tighter, hunch into her saddle, keep her gaze on the track.

Then, as she galloped into West Carriage Drive, she thought: that was a very fine horse. Graciously built. But it was being badly handled, rearing and scuffing in anger. *Can I leave it?* she'd asked herself. No, she decided, she couldn't. She reined in her own mare and turned back.

At first, it intrigued her, to realize that this woman was the same person the diary columns had been raving about: Miss White. And when she thought the horse was a *Kochlaini*, she felt her heart skip with pleasure. Thank heavens she had such an exceptional eye for horse breeds. Mr. Willoughby would give her a lecture if she'd spent so far above the market rate for a Varna.

This thought focused her. Alighting from her horse, striding into the house, she scratched a message on a note card: *Meet me in the smoking parlor. V. K.*

"Give this to Mr. Willoughby," she told the nearest footman, handing him her gloves. "And send up some coffee."

—◆—

The smoking parlor had been a seventeenth birthday present from Lady Kendal, remodeled during Max's minority. The walls were a profusion of giltwork, the seats stuffed with satin cushions in various shades of ruby and claret. "Smoking is not the *nicest* habit, Tor," her stepmother had told her mildly. "But if you must do it, you'd better enjoy your surroundings."

Tor had not been permitted to dine downstairs as a child. In those days, Papa threw huge dinners both in London and at Mount Kendal, packing the house with ministers and clerics and the more illustrious among his acquaintance. Tor used to hover on the staircase, listening to the ominous rumble of male conversation issuing from the floors below. They continued after Mama died, until Papa grew ill, and his moods became unpredictable. Then the dinners ceased. When Lady Kendal assumed the care of the estate, Tor had feared they would start up again.

"But, darling Tor," her stepmother said. "You expressly asked me not to invite strangers into the house."

Tor had felt a queer ripple down her spine. This was quite true. Yet, it was still a strange thing to find her wishes being obeyed, being listened to.

"Shouldn't you like to keep some company?" she asked doubtfully.

"Company?" Lady Kendal said, dark curls shining in the firelight, as the footmen cleared their glasses. "No. You are quite the nicest company for me."

Max was upstairs, presumably asleep. Lady Kendal began laying cards on the table, lights dancing in the deep-polished oak. She had been teaching Tor how to play a very ladylike game of hearts. "So you'll be able to go out in society, as and when you wish," she explained.

Tor studied her cards. "I'm glad you came to us," she said, voice small. "Awfully glad."

Her stepmother's eyes grew watery. She'd often cried, in those early years after Papa died. "Darling Tor" was all she would say. In Tor's memory, she had been impossibly beautiful, draped in half mourning, ageless and wise. Really, she must have been only twenty-seven or twenty-eight, her whole life yawning open before her. They finished their game and Lady Kendal escorted Tor down the long mirrored passage to bed. Her diamonds were winking dully as she nudged open the bright varnished door at the end of the hall.

"I have a gift for you," she said. And then, almost bashfully, "Happy birthday."

Tor had been unable to reply. Lady Kendal was the first person to give her birthday gifts since Mama died—brooches and lockets, small furnishings for the dollhouse. But this was something quite different. Tor stared at the gilded pillars and smooth mosaic and polished glass in this remodeled room and said, "You can't mean it."

"Why, Tor?"

"It's too much. I don't..."

Deserve it. The words weighed on Tor's tongue. The world considered her a spare part, an ancillary device—and this knowledge had wound itself into her skull, taken root there. But this gift proved what she knew to be true: that she *belonged* here, that this house was her *home.*

Lady Kendal presented her with a key. "Sometimes, Tor," she said, "it's nice to have a little room of your own."

She had earned Tor's absolute loyalty, and her trust, for life.

———◆———

The clocks were striking half past four in the smoking parlor. Willoughby was waiting for her in the passage, expression cross. Tor got the hint: he was annoyed she'd summoned him in such a peremptory fashion.

"Have I pulled you from an important matter?" she asked, throwing open the doors, admitting him to her lair. She was genuinely curious about what could occupy Mr. Willoughby all day long. Did he reside in a counting house? Did he employ clerks to itemize his banknotes? Did he dream of stocks and bonds and the mysterious nature of markets?

"Oh, no," he said, smoothing his face over, studying her cushions with intent. "Not at all."

"Did you see His Grace today?"

"I did."

So, Max *was* plotting. Designing marriage portions and land transfers and dowries. No wonder Willoughby was such a frequent visitor.

"You should know that I've spoken to Lady Kendal about the matter of Max's marriage."

Willoughby's eyes widened, just a fraction. "Oh?"

"I couldn't talk her out of it, much as I tried. So, I would like to understand my own position." Tor seated herself, reaching for the coffeepot, elbowing satin cushions aside. "I want to see Papa's papers. His financial provisions. All the settlements he made for me in the event of Max's marriage."

Willoughby perched on the edge of the couch, maintaining his distance. "I'm not an executor of Lord Kendal's will. You should apply to your brother to discuss that." Then his gaze narrowed. "Might I ask, why *haven't* you applied to His Grace?"

Tor felt her cheeks growing warmer. "Why should I *apply* to the duke for his permission? I would like to know what my father left me in ready funds. And stock. And property. Don't I have the right to that knowledge? *You're* the moneyman. If you can't tell me, then what is the purpose of keeping you?"

Willoughby looked sincerely puzzled. "But surely you know all those details already?" he said.

Tor breathed, mastering herself. "If I knew, I wouldn't be asking."

"Your ladyship's household expenses are covered by income held in trust."

"A trust? For me?"

"Indeed."

"I know nothing about it." Tor paused. "How might I access the fund?"

"It is governed by a trustee."

"You?"

"Good heavens, certainly not." Willoughby hesitated again. "I can speak to the family lawyers, if your ladyship wishes, to see if they are willing to release the name."

"What right does anyone have to keep these details secret from me? Tell me at once who governs the trust."

There was a brief silence. Willoughby chewed his lip. "Very well. But perhaps you might do something to oblige me in return."

"A bargain?" Tor stiffened. "I think not."

"Your brother is attending the opera this evening with several ladies. Might I seek your agreement to not disrupt those proceedings?"

"Max is courting *already*?"

"The season is almost over, Lady Victoria. There is really no reason to delay."

"Tell me who."

"The Countess of Clare's daughters. Miss Sonia Hillyard. And the young lady they've been going on about in *Opera Glasses*. Quinta White."

"Her? She's a very unsettling sort of person. I almost bought her horse."

Willoughby seemed startled. "Her horse?"

"Yes, just now. She seemed like a perfect charlatan to me. You should investigate her. I'd like to see if she has any credibility at all."

"In what regard?"

"Horse breeding," Tor said, surprised by the sharpness of his tone. "Clearly, she has no head for it. I wouldn't want her harming any stock." She leaned forward, reining the conversation back to the track. "Give me the trustee's name, Willoughby."

His discomfiture was written all over his face. "Your ladyship should consider…"

"The *name*, Willoughby."

He flexed his hands, as if giving up. "Lady Kendal."

Tor jolted. "My stepmother?"

Willoughby's ironic smile had faded. "I confess myself startled by this, Lady Victoria. Has Her Grace never mentioned the topic before?"

Lady Kendal had been appointed to govern Tor's personal fund? But if her stepmother knew how much money Tor possessed, if she knew the provisions available in the event of Max's marriage, why had she never mentioned them? Tor felt her gut clench.

"She has not." Then, taking a breath, she added: "Where will I find the terms of the settlement?"

"All of Lord Kendal's papers are held in the family vault."

"Are there any copies?"

He hesitated again.

"*Are* there, Willoughby?"

He sighed. "Yes. Several copies."

"Here? In Kendal House?"

He flushed slightly. "In my own personal files. For easy consultation, you understand."

Tor stood, drawing herself to her fullest height. "Bring them to me."

7

Quinn

Mrs. Airlie was waiting on the stairs when they returned to Spanish Place.

"Extremely significant developments," she exclaimed, brandishing a small card.

Quinn and Silk squeezed past the gimlet-eyed maid, putting up their hands to be patted down for weaponry, and Quinn removed her top hat. The collar of her riding habit was chafing her skin; her mind was still chewing on her failure to win over Lady Victoria in the park.

"Bad ones?"

"Good ones. Excellent ones!" Mrs. Airlie came down the stairs, extending the card. "The Duke of Kendal has invited Miss Quinta White to the opera."

Quinn took it. "You're not serious?"

"Quite serious. It came barely half an hour ago, directly from the duke's household."

Silk frowned. "Not Mr. Willoughby?"

Quinn glanced at him. "Your favorite informant?"

"Yes, the duke's moneyman. But he said nothing of this invitation to me. He ought to have given us fair warning, as a friend of the Château."

Quinn recalled spotting smooth-faced Mr. Willoughby at the palace. He had been lingering in the forecourt. She supposed Silk had instructed him to avoid direct discussion with the queen, unless she addressed him first.

"Well, let us forgive him," said Mrs. Airlie. "This invitation is a very helpful development."

Quinn studied the card with curiosity. It was more austere than she might have expected: a gray crest, mounted lions, a bloodred *K* with sober curlicues.

> *His Grace the Duke of Kendal*
> *requests the pleasure of the company of*
> **MISS QUINTA WHITE and CHAPERONE**
> *to a performance of The Marriage of Figaro*
> *in the company of a SELECT PARTY.*

"Very irregular," Silk said. "Willoughby has been instructed to give no indication of favor or friendliness toward you. We cannot have our connection exposed." He sniffed. "And the man is in no position to defy me. All sorts of rumors about his business habits circulate in the athenaeum. I have kept the worst of his secrets under very careful protection."

"I daresay this fellow has nothing to do with it," said Mrs. Airlie. "We made a very pretty spectacle of Le Blanc at the palace and she caught the duke's eye."

Quinn frowned. "I sensed no special attraction."

"Then this is moving too quickly," said Silk. "Today is the Intrusion. Our focus is the flank attack on a near relation, not a direct assault against the quarry."

Mrs. Airlie studied Quinn. "But has the Intrusion been successful? Have you secured the trust of Victoria Kendal?"

"No," Quinn replied.

"Or her stepmother?"

"No."

"Then you absolutely cannot decline," said Mrs. Airlie. "Besides, I've already accepted on your behalf. The gentleman wanted a response by immediate return."

Silk looked unsettled. "Perhaps the invitation comes from the duke in name only. It might have been sent by his stepmother, to round out a private party. She met you only very briefly at the palace. Perhaps she wishes to inspect you more thoroughly for herself."

"Perhaps," Quinn said, uneasy, too. Her preference was to slice her targets into pieces one by one, in perfect and inviolable order. Yet, this felt suspiciously like she was being pulled in a different direction, not of her own volition. "But she is not named on the card."

"It is immaterial," said Mrs. Airlie, checking her pocket watch. "You need to get dressed."

———

It was evening by the time they reached Covent Garden, taking another hired brougham that bounced and squeaked them all the way down Drury Lane. The sky was turning amber-gray, the air damp and clingy. As Quinn descended from the carriage, the opera house glowed before her, a mountain of steel and crystal and glass. Mrs. Airlie was close behind, sidestepping the flower girls and hansom cabs. Together, they joined the crowd as it passed up under the giant portico.

"Got everything?" Mrs. Airlie murmured.

Quinn had changed into a pair of fine gray gloves, sprinkled with steel studs. She ran her hands over the folds of her rented opera cloak, which contained a hundred useful things: notes, eyeglasses, playing cards, a pair of dice, a bashed tin of throat lozenges, a topographic map of London, and a few half crowns for tipping if the circumstance required. You could never tell what an invitation to a "select party" might entail.

"Yes," she said, feeling her confidence returning. The crowd thickened around her, a silky fog of velvet and bergamot and wine, and she felt her pulse thumping. "Which way?"

"Balcony." Mrs. Airlie raised her fan, directing them to the stairs.

Strangers turned toward them as they crossed the lobby. A shiny-faced man exclaimed, "Miss White! The heroine of the hour!" There was a smattering of applause.

"So shocking," Mrs. Airlie exclaimed. "My nerves have been shattered. But Quinta is dauntless, absolutely *dauntless*."

Quinn's opera cloak was ruffled all the way up to the chin, a brilliant shade of emerald green. Her wig had been teased and curled so that it bobbed precariously, miraculously high on her head. She was lacquered and varnished and she smelled of Parisian scent. *Confidence*, she reminded herself, was the most beautiful word in the world.

"How charming," said one woman dryly over her shoulder, as Quinn and Mrs. Airlie charged past. "Even the arrivistes can enjoy *Figaro*."

"Don't listen to the snobs," Mrs. Airlie whispered, looping her arm through Quinn's. "They're fearfully jealous of your cape."

Quinn glanced down at her silver opera gloves. "Did we overdo things?"

"For Covent Garden? Certainly not. You need to skewer the duke's attention."

But here was the tricky thing about not pulling off the Intrusion; Quinn didn't quite know whether she was aiming to attract or antagonize or attack the Duke of Kendal. The pathway to gaining his trust was not yet clear. She would have to improvise.

The crowd thinned out as they swept up to the grand tier. "Are those our footmen?" she murmured to Mrs. Airlie, nodding toward the waiters standing guard at the end of the passage.

Mrs. Airlie snapped her fan at them. "Look sharp, boys," she whispered. "What intelligence?"

One of the waiters tugged at his ill-fitting collar. "He's got a bloody nice supper in there. Will you save us some, Mrs. Airlie?"

"Don't be gluttonous," their mistress replied. "And open the door."

It was a terrific squeeze inside the box. Glazed walls, puffy chairs, crusty damask curtains open to the auditorium. Eight people. Two wiry-looking older gentlemen with near-identical mustaches. Three young women in a riot of fish scales and silver lamé and jet. One of them seemed familiar: a debutante from the palace—Sonia Hillyard. She placed her chin on her hand and gave Quinn a hard stare, taking in her cloak. A waiter—who gave Mrs. Airlie a wink—was setting out the supper things, and a final gentleman, wearing thick-framed spectacles and an aquamarine neckerchief, was already tucking into the very desperate-looking salmon on the sideboard.

And there, seated on a low chair at the front of the box, was the Duke of Kendal. He turned, as if sensing her entry to the box.

"Good evening," he said.

There was a dryness to his voice, Quinn realized, as if he was not used to speaking very often. Nobody else from the Kendal family was present. Just a couple of pinched-looking papas and young women Quinn supposed to be their daughters. *What's this, then?* she asked herself. *An evening of lordly matchmaking?*

The duke's expression was perfectly blank, giving away nothing.

"Good evening," she replied, matching his gravity.

He rose, paying courtesy to her chaperone. "Mrs. Airlie, I think?"

Mrs. Airlie extended a gloved hand. "Your Grace. So nice of you to invite us." She addressed the rest of the company. "Gentlemen."

They all bowed. The gentleman with the aquamarine neckerchief swallowed his food, peering at Quinn.

"Do sit," the duke said curtly, and returned to his own chair.

His back was extremely broad; his jacket fitted snugly to his shoulder blades. Quinn was not a fool: some women would swoon at this. She was not entirely immune to it herself. *What's in your head?* she wondered. *What can I work with?* She glanced around swiftly for an object, lighting upon a slender cabinet pressed up against the wall. Locked behind the glass was a gilded arrow, fastened to a hunting bow with the figure of a Greek god wrought in metal.

"Do you shoot, Your Grace?" she asked civilly, indicating it.

He raised an eyebrow. "Not with that." Then he said, a little weariness in his tone, "Yes, I shoot."

"And do you enjoy it?"

"Hunting?"

"Yes."

He seemed to debate this in his mind. "No."

Mrs. Airlie was shepherding the others toward the sideboard, locking them into separate conversations. Only Sonia Hillyard held back, eyeing Quinn from across the box. Quinn could hear the sound of the orchestra tuning up, the rising buzz of conversation. "Rather unusual."

"What is?"

"I thought all gentlemen were trained to hunt."

He flexed his fingers, as if surprised by her straightforward tone. Then said flatly, "You think being trained in something equals the enjoyment of it, Miss White?"

Quinn considered this. It was a frank question; she could give a frank answer. "I think it creates the habit. Habits, once formed, feel necessary. Necessity contains desire; completion brings reward." She retreated from the edge of the balcony, turning to face the duke. "Don't you find?"

"It sounds like you train dogs, not men."

She shrugged. "I train myself, that's all."

"Do you hunt?"

"I have seldom had the opportunity."

He gave her a long steady look. "You can find some good meets not far from town. I'll have my man pass on some names."

"Thank you, Your Grace," Quinn said. "You're too kind."

Mrs. Airlie was snapping her fingers for the waiter to pour everybody some wine. The duke glanced briefly over his shoulder, and lowered his voice a fraction. "You are fortunate to have a good friend to escort you around town."

"Yes, Mrs. Airlie is a dear relation."

"You don't find it tedious, being subjected to her constant companionship?"

It was Quinn's turn to raise a brow. "I am a very congenial sort of person," she said. "I don't care to be alone."

"Then we are unalike." His tone grew curt again.

"Yet, you must be surrounded by people," she said, examining him. "All the time."

"Here again we have a different way of looking at things. You suppose constant companionship breeds the love of it. I find the reverse to be true."

Quinn remembered the big sash windows in his bedchamber, the ones facing straight onto Berkeley Square. What would it be like to be watched and waited on, if you didn't care for scrutiny?

"Perhaps you need to find a disguise."

"Why do you think I came to see *Figaro*?" His mouth showed the glimmer of a smile. It vanished as quickly as it appeared. "Perhaps it will provide some inspiration."

Quinn could see faces gazing up at them from the seats below. People adored inspecting the grandees in the boxes. "I fear one is always gawped at, no matter one's disguise."

"Then stay at home," he said evenly. "If you don't care for it. I would."

"Would you?" Quinn kept her tone light.

"Yes. In fact, I do."

"No, you said it yourself: you ride to hounds. And I saw you at the Queen's Drawing Room yesterday."

"And I you. Congratulations on your brave performance."

"Thank you."

"I hear they let the woman go. Some confusion with the constabulary."

"How shocking. I hope they apprehend her soon."

He was silent for a moment. Then he said, more heavily, "Indeed."

And nothing more. Quinn decided she would need to unpeel him a little. "So tell me, Your Grace. How would you spend your time, if the choice was yours?"

He touched his lower lip with his thumb. "A rather bold question."

"Is it? I thought it a rather tame one. What's the answer?"

"What's yours?"

She laughed briefly, despite herself. "I would not change a thing about my existence."

"Now you are being untruthful."

"Perhaps," she said more seriously. "But I prefer to keep my counsel."

Something shifted in his face, and she felt a little wriggle of pleasure. She had done it: she'd planted a hook in his mind.

"I wish you would tell me," he said slowly. "As I mentioned, I am always seeking inspiration."

"Likewise," she said. "You can tell me when you're ready."

He wasn't used to being rebuffed. He smiled again briefly, as the lights began to dim. "Do you enjoy opera, Miss White?" he said.

Quinn folded her gloved hands. "It's very nice," she said. "Lucky you, to come here all the time."

She heard a footstep behind her: the gentleman with the thick-framed spectacles and the blue neckerchief.

"The *famous* Miss White," he began, oozing toward the plush velvet seat next to the duke. "Your reputation precedes you!"

Quinn opened her mouth to reply, but the duke was faster. "I think the performance is beginning, sir," he said, placing his hand over the vacant chair, indicating Quinn might take it. "And this space is reserved."

8

Mr. Silk

Silk pushed his spectacles high onto his nose, peering down at his appointment book. The light in the gaming room was weak, coming from an oil lamp that had seen better days. The air felt claggy, and he thought he could hear the scurrying of a mouse beneath the floorboards. With Quinn away, the Château felt far too big. But the queen was working on the other side of town, guarded by Mrs. Airlie, and he had taken the opportunity to complete this task at home, where he wouldn't be disturbed. The resolution of the game depended on its successful execution.

The card table was scattered with glass vials, brass measuring cups, and small jars filled with powders and colored chalks. Silk inspected each one, checking their contents, ticking off items in his book. These powders were harmless on their own. In combination, they could be very dangerous, indeed. Fortunately, Silk had an eye for precise details.

The evening had a febrile ready-to-jump feeling about it.

Worry needled his chest. This was the unfortunate nature of this work. One spent the greatest part of the year worrying about the imperfections in the latest scheme, twisting one's mind over the particulars. Of course, there would be a release, a breathing-out, on the fifth day of the Kendal game. But, before long, the next one would inevitably begin, and his brain would start chewing over fresh tricks and puzzles. Such was the nature of applying oneself to one's vocation, he reminded himself solemnly.

He went up to the roof to smoke one of his cigars. If Quinn were here, he would not have indulged the habit; this was a time for making necessary economies. He felt a wriggle of guilt as he took the cigar from its bashed and dented tin, lit it, chewed it, brought it up the winding, creaking stairs to his lookout spot on the roof. He adjusted his rotten little chair, the one leaned up against the chimney stack, and settled down to study the twilit sky.

It was then that he saw it. A light in a window. In the house backing onto the Château.

Mr. Silk discerned a prickling of cold sweat all along his arms and inside seams as he stared, disbelieving, at the House Opposite.

From the front, it was just a barber's shop with a cheerful sign hanging above the window. But from the back it was something else altogether. Silk knew, from studying the Château's bowdlerized deeds, that the upstairs rooms had been purchased by the Château. It was their hiding place, their priest hole, in case the constabulary ever stormed in. The Château's kitchen yard connected to the thin tapered garden of the House Opposite. Of course, nobody ever *lived* there.

Yet, tonight the shutters were standing open. And there was a light burning in one of the upstairs rooms.

Mr. Silk's whole body grew cold.

It'd been years and years since the promise had been made, but he retained the details, just as he remembered the clauses and stipulations in the contracts he'd designed. If someone placed a light in the upstairs window...

You'll know I've returned. You'll know it's my time.

Silk reminded himself that he was a pragmatic person. There could be a simple explanation for this. Somebody might have broken into the House Opposite—a squatter or a burglar. He didn't wish to get caught up in anything nasty, but he stumped downstairs all the same, crossed the yard, unlocked the back gate—and slipped into the garden opposite.

It was a strange thing, entering new territory. Although he could see the familiar landmarks of Spitalfields—the church spire, the backs of other houses—the angles were suddenly different, the darkness thicker. This garden had grown wild, in the way city gardens always did, which was to say the grass and thorns and rose briars and weeds had become so knotted as to be nearly impassable, and Silk had to use his stout walking cane to thrash himself a makeshift path. All the while, the light flickered in the window, high above the garden.

There was a small paved area at the top of the garden, and a privy building with a broken window. The back door was locked. Silk prayed the bolts would stick, denying him entry—for then he could say to himself, *Well, nothing doing, I can't get in,* and he could run away.

But the bolt didn't stick. The door opened smoothly, without resistance, as if the lock had been recently oiled.

He shivered as he stepped inside.

The air carried the chill you always sensed in unoccupied houses, dank and almost floral, with a top note of gas. Silk headed down the passage and climbed the stairs. Somewhere, on the other side of the wall, was the hairdressing shop. But the barber wasn't supposed to unlock the back door. He'd probably forgotten he even held the key. He probably never gave any consideration to what lay beyond his rented rooms. There were innumerable tenants in these old silk weaver's houses; plenty of people minding their own business, paying their rents to a shadowy landlord they never knew, never saw, like everyone else in London.

Silk went up to the fourth floor, to a tiny landing, and found himself standing outside a single room with a light coming through the crack in the door.

Silk wondered: Why now? Why *tonight*? There was no special significance to this date. He had thought—really thought—this moment might never come. That this person would never return. For a great deal depended on her absence. Peace and prosperity had come to the Château when she departed.

Silk felt a sudden stab of anger. It was so like her to have wrong-footed him, to have lulled him into a sense of false security. It was her great distinguishing characteristic, that she could trick one so completely.

He opened the door.

The room was small, square: a box room. The boards were stained the same dull rose pink as the shutters on the Château. If it had once been a bedroom, then it contained a bed no longer. It was illuminated by a single candle. The big shutters were flecked with black mold. There was mold on the window frame, too, and on the walls, and the air was cold and chalky. *Spores*, thought Mr. Silk grimly, wishing he'd brought his handkerchief with him.

There was a wooden chair in the center of the room.

Seated on it, hands folded, kicking her heels against the floor, was a young woman. She couldn't have been much more than twenty. She wore a canary-colored dress and her hair was dark and glossy and nicely pinned. Her eyes were fixed on Silk even as he entered the room.

"*You* took your time," she said tartly.

Silk didn't recognize her. He stared, uncertain of what to say. And then, when she tipped her head, puzzled, waiting for him to speak, he asked the only question he could.

"Who sent you?"

The young woman fished in her bodice, pulled out a rolled-up piece of paper. "Don't know *who* sent me," she said. "I was given half a crown to come sit up here and wait for someone. You, I s'pose. I had to buy a candle. Are you going to pay me back for that?"

I'll put a light in the window. You'll know I've returned.

Silk took the piece of paper, unfolded it. His hands were trembling.

Berkeley Square, Midnight, 4th August.

"That's all?" he said, half to himself.

"No," the young woman said, reaching around, picking something up off the floor. "This, too. Queer thing."

Silk's heart clenched. She was holding a wooden object in her hand. Long-handled. Plum-colored, varnished, ribboned with a strip of gold. She shook it and he heard that sound, that old familiar sound, a *hush-shushing* in his ears. Rice, beads, sand.

The rattle. Quinn's rattle, the one they gave her when she was very small. *Shake the rattle*, Quinn's mother used to say, when they were working, when Quinn cried. *Distract her.*

The young woman shook it again, chuckling. "Ain't it odd?"

She stood to leave, setting the rattle on her seat. She'd completed her job and would head back into the ordinary world, using whatever spare key she'd been given. She'd leave the House Opposite freely—as if it were not a secret hiding place, a memory box, a clause and stipulation, a place where time had fallen still. The light burned on in the window, the flame leaping.

As she disappeared through the door, Silk felt dazed, just like a child himself. He took the rattle, shook it gently, heard the rice *hush-shushing* in the ball, and he understood what it meant. He'd been given an instruction.

Distract Lillian's child.

9

Tor

The first message had come up on a silver platter around quarter past six: Lady Kendal would be dining alone, in her own quarters, and sent her warmest wishes to her stepdaughter for a restful evening.

The second message came up ten minutes later, on a copper plate: the Duke of Kendal would take supper at the opera house, and sent his best regards to the Lady Victoria, in the hopes that she had enjoyed a pleasant afternoon.

They were avoiding her, Tor decided. Basking in their own visions for the future. Well, she refused to be abandoned. She could dine out, too, if she wished.

In normal circumstances, visiting cards and party invitations and request letters were thrown straight into the wastepaper basket. But some evenings she felt an urge to escape, to stretch her own mind, and taste a little of the society she otherwise preferred to keep at bay. She marched across her boudoir and upended her trash bin, picking through the cards scattered on the floor. She plucked one at random. It was printed on immensely thick paper, with a very fulsome scroll: Mr. and Mrs. Charles Arnault, South Audley Street.

It was an invitation to dinner. Tor did not know the name—she guessed Mr. Arnault was another of those fearfully wealthy tradesmen building colossal houses all over Mayfair. Clearly, they held no mutual acquaintance. It was bold of them to seek her attention at all. The date Mrs. Arnault proposed was several days hence, on the eve of the Glorious Twelfth. Well, if they wanted her, they could have her. But it would have to be tonight.

Tor chose her own attire for the evening, modifying her riding habit, affixing a large whalebone-enforced hood to her shoulders. It gave her the appearance of having huge and ragged wings. She wore Papa's ruby ring, the one she'd inherited when he died. It represented the worst times, in childhood, when life was unrelentingly cold. A useful reminder, she decided, of the truth: that there was great danger in this world, that people could be very deceitful, but she alone would survive.

"Shall we send a boy on a bicycle to South Audley Street, my lady?" asked the head footman. "Just to warn them that you're coming?"

"No need," Tor replied. "If they don't want me, then they can tell me to my face."

Her stepmother would have been appalled. This was the very opposite of the advice to give strangers a little breathing room. But why should everybody else get all the oxygen? Tor's lungs were desperate for air.

"Send for the brougham," she said, dousing herself in Eau de Quinine.

"I believe it's being cleaned, Lady Victoria. Her Grace took it out yesterday afternoon. It's terribly dusty."

"The brougham," Tor repeated. "At once."

The brougham was indeed caked with mud and dust; evidently,

Buckingham Palace was no cleaner than a pigsty. It was a swift journey: the coachman pulled up the carriage at a large sandstone house on South Audley Street. One of the footmen leaped off the back plate, scurrying up to the front door. There was an intolerable delay while her footman tried to explain the situation to the Arnault footman. Then another one while the footman went inside—presumably to sound the alarm. Tor rolled her eyes heavenward. She was simply coming for dinner. Per their request!

A face appeared at the carriage window. "My lady? Mrs. Arnault asks if you'd like to come inside."

"At last," Tor exclaimed. She gripped the footman's hand and jumped to the pavement. Half a second later, she was inside. The lights jerked and fizzed as she crossed the threshold, and she squinted upward, spying movement at the top of the stairs. A crowd had gathered on the first-floor landing, gripping the balustrade, gawking at her. All conversation guttered, dying; an awed hush fell as Tor threw back her enormous hood.

A slender bright-eyed woman with a fulsome loaf of hair came hurrying down the stairs. "Lady Victoria? But this is too marvelous!"

She fairly tripped on the bottom step, reaching for Tor's palm, shaking hands ferociously. "Charles! Look at this! Aren't we honored?"

A whiskered gentleman, seemingly her husband, was racing after her. He wagged his pipe in the air, murmuring deferential greetings.

"*Do* come upstairs," said Mrs. Arnault with relish. "Have a sherry. Meet everybody."

———

It seemed the Arnaults enjoyed glittering dinner parties almost every night. In the drawing room, there was a terrific crush of very handsome-looking people—Americans and cutlery manufacturers and people who made their fortunes from brewing beer. She fell into combative discourse with a beady-eyed gentleman in a canary yellow neckerchief who told her he was a diamond millionaire.

"I expect I'm a millionaire, too," Tor told him sharply. "After a fashion. Don't be vainglorious."

He eyed her quizzically. "Who let you out of the house?"

"Don't listen to him," Mrs. Arnault told her. "I think you're marvelous. You say exactly what you think. So clever. More sherry?"

A servant banged the dinner gong with much more gusto than was ever permitted at Kendal House, and they all trooped downstairs to eat. Someone had hurriedly made a place for Tor at the top of the table; she easily outranked everybody in the room. She was seated beside a richly bearded solicitor who lectured her on the case of Mr. Wilde, freshly released from prison, apparently hiding on the Riviera.

"Clever fellow," he remarked. "Hope they don't catch him."

Tor stared back at him, fascinated. "So you approve of delinquents?" She'd sailed through the fish course at furious speed, Papa's ruby glittering on her right hand.

"Are we not all delinquents, madam, in our own way?"

"I suppose so," Tor said, sawing into her roasted grouse. "Now, tell me about your wickedest clients."

The solicitor began to recount the large number of scandals he'd personally managed, involving grand larceny and illegal baccarat games and never-ending probate cases, which he outlined in such minute detail that Tor was compelled to ask more and more questions. At length, she noticed the main courses were finished, and even the ices and candied fruits had been cleared, and the ladies were hovering around the table, waiting for the signal to retire. Of course, they were unable to do so until she rose from the table.

"Sit," she told Mrs. Arnault genially. "We're enjoying such a good conversation." Then she turned to the solicitor. "Tell me again about that dreadful old countess you mentioned."

"The countess wasn't dreadful, but her last will and testament—that was diabolical. We had to break the estate in order to fulfil it. Utterly break it, you know."

"Tell me quickly," Tor said, digging her cheese knife into the table. "How did you manage that?"

———

After the other guests departed, and Mrs. Arnault had shaken her hand very vigorously, the solicitor offered to escort her home. Tor knew pretty well what that meant. She took him in her own landau to his house, a narrow building north of Blackfriars, in a street as thin as a needle. It was dark as they crossed, arm in arm, Tor's hood creaking as she unfastened her cloak. The oil lamps cast a delightfully woozy glow against the walls. When he brought his lips to hers, she marveled at the density of his beard. Was it very lovely or very horrible? Hard to say. *A beard like a spinney*, she thought, enjoying herself. *A beard like a forest.* She slipped from her cloak and allowed her huge cracked wings to fall to the floor.

Afterward, they finished more wine, and he began lecturing her again, but she interrupted him.

"I have a decision to make," she said. "You are presumably a man of some perspicacity. You can help me."

The Kendal lawyers served the estate, not Tor. She wished to seek her own counsel.

He folded himself into a wingback armchair by the fire, sipping from a brandy glass. "Certainly."

"But you can't say a word."

"Very well."

Tor paced around his bedchamber, consumed by one of his brocade dressing gowns, and explained her situation. "As I see it, I have several options. First: do nothing. Wait for my brother to make a marriage, and be dismissed from the house."

"Surrender?"

"Yes."

"What is your second option?"

"If my brother marries, I might befriend the lady in question, and negotiate a settled position."

"Sisterly companionship," said the solicitor, nodding. "A harmonious outcome."

"I disagree entirely," Tor said, skewering him with her gaze. "What if I despise her? I cannot dissemble."

"What if you were to marry?"

"Why should I?"

The solicitor studied her. "What protections do you have?"

She hesitated. An agreement with Max, never written down, never signed—one she verbally coerced from him. A fund held in trust, governed by her stepmother, one she'd never concerned herself with until today.

The lawyer tilted his head, waiting for her answer. "No use mounting a battle if you don't have a gun carriage, madam. I suggest you marshal your defenses."

———◆———

By the time she left, the light was coming up, gray and accusatory.

"All right, my lady?" the coachman asked, leaping down from his seat to pull open the door. He'd waited for her all night, stationed on the north side of London Bridge—not for the first time.

"Never better," she muttered, climbing into the mud-spattered brougham, exhausted. Back at Kendal House, she went straight to bed, giving orders not to be disturbed, locking her door. A single resolve was turning in her mind as her head hit the pillow.

If Max did marry, if he did install a new duchess in Kendal House, then Tor would need to build new protective walls, a fresh existence, a life of her own making.

She needed to get hold of her money.

10

The Man in the Blue Silk Waistcoat

The hansom cab had drawn up on Bulstrode Street after dark. The man in the blue silk waistcoat unbuttoned his breast pocket, selected the proper change, and paid the driver. Then he strode down the road toward the Coach Maker's Arms. The cab driver, if he were ever questioned, would say that the man in the blue silk waistcoat had ducked into the pub. A neat alibi.

But then the man in the blue silk waistcoat turned rightward, into Hinde Street. Here he was again, he thought wearily, traipsing around the duller side of Fitzrovia. Not a very stimulating way to spend an evening. But this was his one opportunity to do a little digging, while the girl and her associates were otherwise engaged at the opera house.

Just as the clocks struck the hour, he entered Spanish Place, went up to Mrs. Airlie's house, opened the iron gate leading to the servants' entrance and descended the stone steps to the area. He rapped on the door.

There was movement behind the blinds, and he could see the low burn of a lamp. A voice, sharp, female, said, "No deliveries."

"Message for Mrs. Airlie," replied the man in the blue silk waistcoat in a carefully judged accent. Neither too grand nor too common nor too regional.

There was a shuffling on the other side of the door. Somebody was considering this, working out what to do with it.

"We're not expecting any messages."

The man in the blue silk waistcoat spoke the code words. "Flower delivery for the lady of the household."

It was past nightfall. Nobody was making any flower deliveries at this hour. Certainly not men wearing dark jackets and starched neckerchiefs and azure jerkins. Still, he heard the scrape of the bolt. A face peered out: Mrs. Airlie's housemaid, in a neat cap and dark dress.

"I'll still have to search you," she said sourly, recognizing him. "Rules are rules."

"No," said the man in the blue silk waistcoat, sliding inside. "They're not."

It was an ordinary kitchen. Dimly lit, red-tiled, with a big dresser and a long wooden table in the middle of the room. There was a rocking chair by the fireplace, and a mantelpiece swagged in cheery yellow velvet, and a passage leading to pantries and sculleries beyond. It was not a laboratory, nor a library, nor a treasure house. It was simply and entirely and *only* a kitchen. This depressed the man in the blue silk waistcoat. He'd expected more of Mrs. Airlie. The Academy had such a fierce reputation.

"I need to search around upstairs," he told the maid.

"Dressed like that?" she replied.

He cocked a brow. "What else," he said, "should I be wearing?"

The maid tutted. No doubt she saw plenty of queer comings and goings in her position, guarding the front door to the Academy.

"You've got ten minutes," she said curtly.

Her tone annoyed the man in the blue silk waistcoat. He wished he were *not* annoyed. He knew sensitivity of any kind was a very loathsome quality in a gentleman. But he couldn't help himself. He had his dignity or he had nothing at all.

"You've been late sending your reports, you know," he told the maid.

"I send 'em when I send 'em. It's not like there's much to report. Just a lot of silly schoolgirls playing dress-up."

"I like to know exactly who's being targeted. Exactly what jobs are afoot. And I was caught out by this one. Which I *don't* care for."

The maid's gaze flickered, a little sign of discomfiture. "Miss Le Blanc isn't a student here. She only turned up yesterday. Naturally, I was going to tell you."

"Naturally," said the man in the blue silk waistcoat pleasantly, fingering his revolver. Then he went upstairs.

———

He changed clothes in Mrs. Airlie's own dressing room. There was something satisfying about this. In this business, one was like a palimpsest, superimposing one's finest brushstrokes on the crude drafts one's predecessors left behind. He rifled through Mrs. Airlie's wardrobe and dug out a very plain cream silk gown. He hitched up his trousers, kicked off his black polished boots and removed his dark cotton jacket and blue silk waistcoat. He pulled the wig from his pocket and placed everything else in the back of the closet.

Then she buttoned herself into Mrs. Airlie's dress.

This gown was rather creased, but even great artists had to make do with second-rate garments every now and then. Unlike Quinn Le Blanc, the woman in the cream silk gown wasn't primped and pampered; she hadn't needed to go to Mrs. Airlie's *school* to learn her lessons.

The house was quiet, which meant the students were safely ensconced in the dormitories. So the woman opened the door, gliding down the passage to inspect Mrs. Airlie's study. She knew what she was looking for: paperwork, anything that would reveal the nature of the game, or intelligence the Château had unearthed on the Kendal family. She needed to guess Le Blanc's next move. So: What notes had she made? What ideas might she have given to Mrs. Airlie for safekeeping? If she could, the woman in the cream silk gown would have broken into the Château and searched it from top to toe. But she'd wasted enough time just trying to gain entry to the House Opposite—not to mention recruiting a girl, lighting a candle, waiting for Silk to raise his asinine head to spot it. But the woman in the cream silk gown was nothing if not patient. Besides, she knew how they played their five-fingered games—and how to unfurl her own dark reflections, one step at a time...

The study walls were lined with bookcases. The table was bare, and the desk drawers seemed to be filled with laundry bills and old receipts, nothing of any use at all. The drawing room contained a locked cabinet and a Davenport desk, but a swift search of the drawers revealed no key. She rippled away downstairs, frustrated, empty-handed.

"Done?" the maid said, as the woman in the cream silk gown entered the kitchen. The maid's expression narrowed when she observed the intruder's shift in disguise. "Don't tell me you're wearing Mrs. Airlie's things. That's a low blow."

The woman in the cream silk gown smoothed her rumpled skirts, adjusted her wig. The light in the kitchen was low and buttery; the windows were shuttered. It really was very warm and cozy down here. Such thick walls, such heavy doors. The girls in the dormitory wouldn't hear anything from the basement floor. Or if they did, they'd imagine it to be a fox, running through the back streets in the dark.

"You should learn to hold your tongue," she said.

There was a knock at the kitchen door, the one facing the street. The maid's eyes flashed toward it, alarmed. "Did you..."

The door clicked open. "Take her," said the woman in the cream silk gown, snapping her fingers.

The maid stumbled to her feet, toppling her chair, opening her mouth to let out a shriek of fear. One of the men clapped his hand over her mouth. The woman in the cream silk gown smiled. It was nice to execute the Intrusion properly. She would take a token—this girl, the one with the insolent tongue—right out of Mrs. Airlie's house.

"Quietly, please," she warned her servants, as they bundled the girl up the steps and into a waiting cab. The streetlamps were burning on the pavement. Anyone could have seen her coming, anyone could have seen her going—but she was not afraid. Everything would unfold as it must.

◆

Afterward, she went home. It had been several days since she had entered her workroom. She'd been allowing herself to fall into very sloppy habits. She lit one of the oil lamps, put on her finger warmers and settled down at her desk. It was encrusted with candle wax and awash with papers, notebooks, enameled cigarette boxes, dirty teacups, snuff bottles, bootlaces, gobstoppers, handkerchiefs, cigars, vials of cologne, powder, rouge, her mannequins—*too much*, she thought wearily. She needed to clear everything out.

Her workroom was at its strangest at night, the floorboards all purple and shimmery, catching strangely tilted shafts of light through high porthole windows. The moon was creeping around the house—but soon it would disappear, and even the clouds would be subsumed, for there was a fog coming. It would come in as fast and thick as factory smoke; she'd seen it happen a thousand times before.

There were dozens of faces watching her from the beams and rafters. All her little creatures, primped and polished, held in captivity—just the way she liked them. "It's not nice to stare," she told them, her pen scratching against the paper. "Not nice in the *least*."

She worked steadily, keeping up with her correspondence, settling bills, writing down reminders, sketching new designs. She didn't craft games for money. She made them because she needed to. Because she had dark humming tops spinning in her mind, and because she was *hungry*—to settle an old score, close off an old debt, win an old crown.

Day Three
The Ballyhoo

1

Quinn

Quinn woke with a headache, or something closely approximating it: a fogginess around the brow, a tension in the jaw. *Am I ill?* she asked herself, snapping awake. *I can't be ill.*

No, she decided, pinching her cheeks and studying her reflection in the glass, she'd simply drunk a little too much wine. The waiter at the opera house had been very liberal in his pouring of the claret, and Mrs. Airlie had been egging him on, keeping the duke's guests nicely intoxicated. The duke himself had sipped steadily from his own glass, earning some color in his cheeks. But when they rose, at the end of the final round of applause, he was steady on his feet. He towered over her. "Good evening, Miss White," he'd said with gravity—and they shook hands.

Now she washed, dressed, and descended to the morning room. Another day, another breakfast—but today the sideboard was empty.

"The maid has upped and left," Mrs. Airlie said, coming

through the double doors with a plate of burned-looking toast.
"You'll have to fetch your own eggs from the kitchen."

Quinn threw herself into the armchair next to the fire. "All I
need is coffee. Do we have the newspapers yet?"

Mrs. Airlie laid the plate of toast on the dining table with a
bang. "On the sideboard."

Quinn reached for the *Morning Post*, flipping to the society
pages.

"Another victory?"

"Read for yourself."

Quinn scanned the columns, looking for *Opera Glasses*. Mr.
Mellings had composed his usual daily sketch—an essay entitled
"Virtue Adulterated," a dense account of the performance of *Fi-
garo* at Covent Garden. Quinn skimmed it.

"Dreary costumes, bad lighting, yes, yes..." She frowned.
"Wait a moment."

"Indeed," muttered Mrs. Airlie.

> *I fear*, wrote H. Mellings, *that Mr. Pope may have put it best
> when he remarked, "Blessed is he who expects nothing, for he shall
> never be disappointed."*
>
> *What hopes we had for the grave-eyed female who lately caught
> our eye at Buckingham Palace! Imagine, then, the dismay felt by
> those who last night trained their OPERA GLASSES on the box
> situated on the west flank of the Grand Tier.*
>
> *They wished to spy a pale lily—immaculate, ungilded—but
> alas, they observed only a jade-colored virago, and her rouged
> companion, DRINKING beyond the boundaries of all decency,
> LAUGHING during the most pathetic love passages of the opera,
> demonstrating such tradeswomanly turpitude as to deter any man
> from trusting the female sex!*

"Dear me," said Quinn. "Were we introduced?"

"He was in the box," Mrs. Airlie groaned. "That awful little
fellow with the blue cravat. It was Mr. Mellings."

"You didn't recognize him?"

"Of course *not*! I was training all my energies on obstructing the Hillyard girl. She had a very determined aura."

"Did you get her people *very* inebriated?"

"Yes! Most assiduously. But now I rather fear I overdid it. We stand no chance of securing an offer of marriage from anybody if you're considered a liability."

Quinn ran her fingernail down the crease of the newspaper. "I *think* we've piqued the duke's interest."

"Are you sure? *Figaro* drags on so dreadfully."

Quinn nodded. "Call it intuition."

"Was it a very vigorous flirtation?"

"No," Quinn said slowly. "I don't think so. He doesn't make flirtation easy. He's too wooden."

"Other ladies say differently."

"We've yet to meet any of the duke's scorned lovers." Quinn mused over this. "Perhaps His Grace blossoms in the dark."

"I'm unclear, Le Blanc. Was last night a success or not?"

When Quinn had shaken hands with the duke, she'd noticed the warmth of his palms through her gloves. It was almost as if he were not made of cold marble, after all. And Quinn could always sense when someone was hiding their secrets; she was adept at doing so herself. Their conversation had been smooth, well oiled, a neat sort of sparring. But not lecherous. This had been a relief and a puzzle in equal measure. It appeared this job would need to be a seduction of the mind—not the heart, *not* the loins. And if the duke was guarding any deeper mysteries, she would need to find them.

"Will you be attending the Summer Exhibition tomorrow, Your Grace?" she'd asked him in an offhand tone as she looped the velvet threads of her opera cloak, getting ready to leave. "Mrs. Airlie and I will be there." Rather a blunt gambit, but Quinn liked to set her own invitations.

The duke said shortly, "Perhaps." Then added: "It would be pleasant to continue our conversation."

Pleasant? An anemic sort of word; it didn't give many clues. "Very pleasant," Quinn agreed. "Until tomorrow, then."

"Well?" Mrs. Airlie said now in the morning room, turning her bloodshot gaze on Quinn. "*Was* it a success or not?"

"I drank a little of his very expensive wine," Quinn said, checking the silver watch fastened to her bodice. "But not his very expensive blood. So we have more to do."

Mrs. Airlie sighed. "And further impediments to overcome."

"What impediments?"

"Didn't you finish reading *Opera Glasses*?"

Quinn reached for the newspaper and frowned again.

> At least some care is being taken to preserve the integrity of England's oldest estates. Word reaches us that the Duke of Kendal will very shortly marry a lady of patrician rather than mercantile extraction—a blessing, indeed, to all.

She glanced up. "Surely no other engagement has been formed?"

"Why did you think the Hillyards were there? Or the Clares? Clearly, the Kendals are lining up a nice blue-blooded alliance with a girl of good breeding *and* good fortune." Mrs. Airlie drummed her fingers. "My intelligence tells me that the Hillyards are close friends of Lady Kendal. Evidently, she's directing her stepson toward marrying a family she trusts, of good credit and fashion. We should have approached her much sooner."

Quinn suppressed any concerns, raising a hand. "No changing horses midstream."

"But…"

"You're quite right, I distracted myself fruitlessly by chasing after Victoria Kendal. But it's too late to start working on the stepmother. I need to focus on killing the stag."

"Rather a bloodthirsty expression."

"Rather a bloodthirsty business." Quinn chucked the newspaper aside. "I need to take more decisive action. The game demands a marriage proposal before midnight." She straightened in her chair, took a bitter sip of black coffee. The Ballyhoo was at the heart of the game. It was the moment when one parceled up a nice, shiny proposition for one's mark. Really, this was no different from securing any other sort of investment. The duke simply needed to make a pledge, agree to the terms of his engagement, ensure his financial commitments were properly underwritten.

And then they could proceed to the wedding.

"Le Blanc, are you certain, *quite* certain, that you'll be able to extract yourself from the altar?"

Quinn was startled. "Of course."

"Really?"

"I'd be rather doomed if I didn't."

"But if you gave me just a *hint* of how you're planning to get out of it..."

"You know the rules. The final twist will be mine alone."

Mrs. Airlie gave her a wary look. "That's what I'm worried about."

"We have no time for worries."

Quinn said it briskly, closing the matter. But her mind began turning over fresh concerns. Running the Ballyhoo and snaring a nobleman was all very well when one had pages of evidence detailing his stinking and undiluted corruption. But something about the duke's manner last night had given her pause. Quinn was no fool: she'd marked plenty of gentlemen who maintained one face in public and another in private. Yet, something nagged at her, the sense that she was missing some key piece of information. The Rulebook nudged her conscience. If the duke was not of improper character, then she was obliged to call off the game.

"Where have you put Silk's papers, Mrs. Airlie?"

"In my black cabinet. The key is in the davenport desk. Don't get ink over everything." Mrs. Airlie returned to her toast.

Quinn went up to the drawing room, rifled through Mrs. Airlie's walnut writing desk. *Don't get ink over everything.* Quinn smiled, fishing out a silver ink blotter. She shook it, then tested the handle. It had been screwed on with cunning. She unwound it, jiggling a slender key from the hollow space within, which fitted the lock of a japanned cabinet beside the window. Mr. Silk's dossier had been placed on the lowest shelf: sheaves of papers folded into a red morocco leather document box.

Quinn scattered everything on top of the velvet-swagged piano and began reading. At first, nothing surprised her: these were the same papers she and Silk had studied already. Relentless hiking of rates... Bullying letters sent to sick tenants... Schemes to displace people living in Spitalfields and Seven Dials... Sundry payments made to the private asylum at Swarkestone, to commit those persons of loose morals lately dismissed from our household at Mount Kendal... A whole catalogue of hateful papers, representing all the ways in which the Kendal family had caused misery and harm. Countless financial records—bills of sale, loans, repayments, credit memoranda; the Kendals seemed to owe as much as they spent. Old wealth moved in such a complicated fashion—but at least they had Mr. Willoughby's assistance to decipher it.

She dug deeper. One cache of letters, not yet disturbed, dated as far back as the 1870s. The hand was the same as all the rest—a stiff copperplate that belonged to the family's principal lawyer, discussing some murky business between a groundskeeper's daughter and the prior Lord Kendal, the details fastidiously blurred. It was the kind of letter that made Quinn's skin tingle with distaste. But there was an interesting postscript.

The duchess, it read, is minded to settle in this matter, subject to assurances that the parties will revoke their former threats against

His Grace, and provided that the magistrate will give orders for the young lady in question to be discharged from the county with every expediency.

Quinn did the sums in her mind. According to the date—1873—"the duchess" referred to the second Lady Kendal. Surely, it was an unorthodox thing for a young bride to be hushing up scandals, making financial settlements on behalf of her errant husband?

Quinn reached for her photograph of the Kendal family. Her finger hovered over the dowager duchess. Ruffled, curled, doll-like, and delicate. Her smile was so gentle. But Quinn remembered the figure she'd spied on the second floor of Kendal House: a woman surrounded by wooden rods and iron balls, her body whittled, ready for battle.

Quinn felt a quiver of apprehension. Here again, it seemed she had misjudged the family's character. And Mrs. Airlie was quite right: she'd paid entirely too little attention to Lady Kendal.

She folded up the papers and locked them away in Mrs. Airlie's cabinet. Then she went upstairs to her bedroom and began pinning her hair. One floor above, she could hear the students chanting through their Latin declensions, voices floating down through the ceiling.

What would my mother have done?

She rarely permitted herself the opportunity of asking this question. It was fruitless: there were so few remnants of Lillian's reign. Quinn had gone mudlarking through the Château many times, dredging up secrets from the cellars. She'd unearthed a document box, leatherbound, filled with note cards—the kind she recognized—marked Shopkeeper, Painter, Nun, in a fast but elegant hand. The box was a remarkably jaunty shade of red; it had a satin lining and myriad internal drawers. It seemed to tremble with playful, hidden intelligence. Inside, in the central compartment, lay the necklace: a small cheap thing—a silver chain with a small round pendant bearing the initials *L. Q. R.* Since then, Quinn wore it underneath her collar, where it couldn't be seen.

She touched it now, the metal cold against her skin. *Let the Rulebook be your guide,* she reminded herself. The Château did not permit a game to be rewritten, not once it had commenced. And to fold now would be a grave error. The Duke of Kendal was head of his family, accountable for its sins. He bore the Kendal title, he was an accessory to its crimes. If the dowager duchess had her hand in any of the family's darkest business, then she was culpable, too. Indeed, if she was negotiating an aristocratic marriage for her stepson, furthering his authority, cementing his bloodline, then she was obstructing Quinn's own design. She would need to be held to account.

Quinn had been civil; she had been smooth. Now, to advance, she would need to become serrated.

People so often misunderstood the Ballyhoo. They perceived only the dazzle, the glitter, the joy of presenting the proposition to one's mark. But truthfully it was a more delicate move than that.

CLAUSE 3. *The light and darkness of a game must be held in perfect equilibrium. For as the Queen of Fives turns her mind, she turns a coin: she carries both the head and tail. When she gives a gift, she takes a forfeit. For every kindness, a cruelty must be performed. For every truth, a lie...*

2

Tor

Nobody would have expected Lady Victoria Kendal to be familiar with Chelsea. Mayfair, yes. The northern side of Oxford Street, on occasion. Belgrave Square and its environs, without a doubt. But the redbrick, double-fronted environs of Tite Street? Not at all. Tor knew the sort of people who lived here: artists, playwrights, gentlemen of deliciously scandalous predilections. These things did not disgust her. If anything, she felt a lifting of her spirits. For she'd woken with an ashen mouth and a pounding headache—but a sense of clarity. Today, she would take charge of things. If anybody spotted Tor being driven toward the Thames, they would assume she was going poor-visiting in Lambeth. But they would be wrong—for the Kendal carriage turned, wending westward, eventually coming to a lurching halt on the Chelsea Embankment. Tor opened the door.

"Wait for me at the bridge," she called up to the coachman.

"You don't want me to follow you, my lady?"

Tor slipped out, squinting in the sunlight. She was outside the gates to the Chelsea Hospital, lawns stretching far into the distance, sun-yellowed and hazed in the heat.

"No," she replied. "Absolutely not." She wished to act alone; she wanted to move at pace.

The coachman clicked at the horses and the brougham creaked away toward the embankment—and Tor went hunting.

Willoughby's house was a new-built villa, made of dark red brick, with colored glass in the fan light. Tor tugged on the bell with gusto. A general maid opened the door, gawped at her card, and curtsied all the way down to the ground. Then she said, alarmed, "But the master's not ready to receive visitors."

Tor fixed the maid with a stony gaze. "Take me to him."

The maid bit her lip, then shoved Tor's visiting card into her apron. "This way, mum."

The hall was pristine, smelling of new paint. The maid opened a door at the end of the passage and led Tor into a square garden surrounded by high brick walls. Tor had to shield her face from the glare. She perceived white canvas, heard the clink of ice. Spied tables and deck chairs, big parasols tilted to the sky.

The maid hurried ahead, calling a low warning. There was the creak of a deck chair, a figure peeping out at her from the shade of the parasol. Willoughby didn't look much like a money-man today. He was wearing a quilted dressing gown, cornflower blue, and held a snuff bottle made of powdered glass, which he tucked hastily into his jacket.

"Lady Victoria? Good gracious, I fear you find me *en déshabillé*. I wasn't expecting callers at such an early hour."

Tor peered under the parasol. "I told you I wished to see those papers."

Irritation crossed his face. "And your ladyship should know that I fully intended to deliver them to you—today. At Kendal House. Where we customarily conduct our business."

"But I have no time to waste," Tor said. "Have you got them or not?"

Willoughby sighed, passing her a crystal jug. "Have some lemonade. I'll fetch the box."

Tor waited in the garden, under the watchful gaze of Willoughby's maid. Flies buzzed around the small square of lawn. She caught the hectic wingbeat of a tiny bird on the air, following its flight—and saw a movement in one of the upstairs windows, the briefest glimpse of a face. A servant? Or companion? A hand closed the curtain.

The garden door clicked open, and Willoughby sauntered back down the path, offering a document box.

"Here."

Tor swiped the leather case from him. The pages were all handwritten, in a faded and regular copperplate. "Tell me what these are."

"Lord Kendal's will, made in holograph. Then the particulars relating to your ladyship's settlement." He glanced back to the house. "I should take a moment to put on some proper attire. Will you excuse me?"

"Certainly not. Stay just where you are. I may have more questions." Tor turned her back on him, chest tingling. She placed the box on the garden table and began to read, taking care to make sure none of the pages would fly away on the breeze. The will was long and tedious and riddled with clauses relating to her father's possessions; she scanned it and then set it aside. The next paper, marked Composition of the Settlement for the Lady Victoria, was denser still.

"Explain it," she ordered.

He folded his hands. "It itemizes the five sources of income for your settlement. Inheritance from your maternal grandfather's estates. Inheritance from your maternal great-grandmother's estates. A stipend connected to the estate rents in Derbyshire. An annuity from investments. And—". here he paused "—private assets not connected to the formal estate."

"Private assets?" Tor said, flicking through the pages.

"Jewels, paintings, property held in the sea-bathing mansion, property held in the Scotland lodge, your horses…"

Tor looked up, heart skipping. "But this is a *great deal* of money."

Willoughby pressed his lips together. "Read on."

There was another paper lodged at the bottom of the box, written in the same slanting hand as all the rest. Notes in Advance of an Explanatory Memorandum. Beneath was a single paragraph, reading: *Question: what defects exist in the measures regarding settled estates, in respect of the disposal of a lady's property?*

Tor held it up. "What does this page mean?"

Willoughby hesitated. "That is a delicate matter."

"Tell me."

"You understand the Kendal estate is subject to an entail? It can be neither broken up nor sold save for an intervention by Parliament."

"Of course."

"This paper asks whether *your* settlement is held under the same protections. Whether your ladyship's property could be accessed—or disposed of—by another party."

"*Disposed* of?"

Willoughby said flatly, "The question is whether the Kendal family could break the protections around your settlement and spend the money against your wishes."

Tor felt her heart begin to tick faster. "Who asked the question?"

"Lady Victoria, you are placing me in a difficult situation. I serve at His Grace's pleasure. I am necessarily obliged to…"

"*Who asked the question?*"

He snapped back at her, "It's signed, is it not? Your ladyship can see for herself."

She glanced down. Felt a jolt. Willoughby was right: three letters had been inscribed neatly at the foot of the page.

M. K. D.

Tor felt the ground swaying beneath her. *Maximilian Kendal, Duke.* "Max."

"Lady Victoria. It seems to me this matter could be resolved if you were to apply to His Grace, *discuss* this matter as two siblings should. His affection for you is not to be doubted…"

"Discuss it? It seems to me that my affairs *have* been discussed, by everybody other than me." Tor's voice was hoarse. She shoved the papers back in the box, snapped the lid. "I'll deal with this myself."

3

Mr. Silk

Mr. Silk beetled down Brick Lane, starting every time a cart rolled across his path, every time someone shouted to a friend across the road. If someone were watching him, tracking him, plotting against him, then there were innumerable ways he could go...

Someone had breached the peace, sent a clear warning shot across the bows. He knew exactly what this person was capable of, how much they despised the Château. He could hardly believe they were still alive, still working; he wondered what disguise they could have possibly adopted. This person was as skilled in the arts of subterfuge as any player in the Château. They could have been interfering in their business for weeks, months, years, and he wouldn't have realized. Was this why the Château had experienced such a run of bad luck? So many marks getting frightened off, so many jobs falling to pieces...

He needed to gather some intelligence. And he couldn't

breathe a word of this to Quinn until he did. The depths to this, the complexities—she'd never understand.

Distract Lillian's child.

He knew what that meant. There was another game afoot, somewhere—and Quinn might be standing directly in its path.

Silk headed to Bethnal Green, to Mr. Dunuvar's pub. He seated himself at a corner table, his back to the wall. A boy was cleaning the counter with a rag. Silk's usual informants ambled in at the customary hour, just as he had expected. They were swaddled in their usual greatcoats and scarves despite the August heat, sweating profusely. Silk managed the usual civilities. The tankards came out on silver platters: a creamy round of stout, an order of bread and cheese.

"Please pass my respects to your mothers."

They bowed. Silk got down to business. "Gentlemen. Have you heard anything odd? Picked up any strange signals?"

Nope, they said, one and all, faces blank. *Not a peep.*

Mr. Silk frowned. "And...may I ask—has anyone caught a glimpse of our old..." he searched for the word "...trouble-maker?"

There was a ripple of unease around the table.

"Why d'you ask?" asked one of the men, adjusting the carnation in his buttonhole.

"No reason," Silk said swiftly. "Simply making sure." He wound his fingers tight.

"Long time since anyone worried about that person."

"Yes," Mr. Silk agreed.

"Long time since anyone *discussed 'em.*"

"Indeed. And how about that little place on Roman Road..." Silk cleared his throat. "The haberdasher's shop. No trouble there?"

The men reached for their tankards, drained them, one and all. Silence.

The boy was still rubbing down the counter, polishing it hard.

He was red in the face. Burning with concentration. Listening, Mr. Silk realized.

"Young man," he said slowly. "Have *you* seen anything amiss?"

The boy dropped the rag. "No, sir."

The other gentlemen didn't blink.

Didn't move, either.

Silk noticed where they were sitting. On his left hand, right hand—and blocking his pathway to the door.

"No?"

"No, sir. Like these men said. Not a dickey bird."

Silk felt something prickling all the way down his spine. "I see."

"We're all loyal to you, Mr. Silk," said the boy, still furiously polishing the counter. "Mr. Dunuvar sends his compliments, same as always. We none of us wants to see you getting into trouble."

Silk breathed. "Trouble? What sort of trouble?"

The boy glanced up, then—a long implacable stare. "Nothing, Mr. Silk. Nothing at all."

There was a great commotion, then: chairs scraping, tankards jolting, everybody rising to their feet. *Best be getting on, then, Mr. Silk,* they said, smiles fixed. *Good day to you...*

They ushered him to the door. There was a fierce jangle of the bell overhead as he was bundled courteously into the street. The door banged shut, and he heard the scrape of the bolt in the lock. He could see them on the other side of the frosted glass—conferring.

Someone had spooked them.

Which meant that his old friend was well and truly back in the neighborhood.

This was very bad news, indeed.

———◆———

The correct course of action would have been to tell Quinn all about it.

Our troublemaker.

It was a whimsical sort of name, one that belied this person's true nature. They'd been good at disguises from the start, able to play a chimney sweep or a flower girl or a prince or a pirate, whatever you asked for. The first time Silk met him he was a sullen-looking boot boy sitting hunched opposite the Château, in a torn and dirty waistcoat. It was made of silk, kingfisher blue. The toes of his shoes were splitting open, the heels worn down to stubs. Lillian Quinn had come to Mr. Silk and said, "There's a ragged sort of kid on the front step, wanting dinner. Can I bring him in?"

Mr. Silk sent the cook out to inspect the child for lice.

"Clean as a whistle," she reported. "Ever such nice manners."

"All right," Silk said. "Invite him in."

It was a noisy evening in the Château: all the players were gathered in the kitchen, feasting, drinking, trading insults. In those days the windows were flushed with condensation, the chimneys belched with smoke; you heard footsteps running up and down the stairs from dawn till dusk. The women with their ringlets done up in papers, smoking hard, boots drying on the hearth. Two hollow-cheeked chaps, spectacles clouded, buried in engineering manuals. The maid stacking pennies in teetering piles. The boy in the tatty blue waistcoat sat beside Lillian, tall for his age and very thin—watching everything, eating nothing.

"Aren't you hungry?" Mr. Silk asked him.

The boy had fixed him with a dark stare. "Are you going to strangle me?" he asked, gripping his fork hard.

Everybody laughed, except for Mr. Silk.

"No," he replied seriously. "You are quite safe here."

He understood the boy's fear. He'd been in the same position, once. Lingering outside the Château, kicking loose cobblestones with broken-toed shoes. Later, Silk realized how cunning the Devil could be. The child had *known* Mr. Silk's history. Had intuited it, or discovered it, had fashioned the perfect disguise.

They placed him in the kitchen, same as all the new starters.

The boy was a hard worker. He could be found at the cook's right hand, boiling fish bones and hammering slabs of meat, even negotiating in the market.

"You trust him not to steal the change?" Silk asked.

"Trust him?" the cook said. The air had been salty and steamy, stock boiling on the range. Cook moved like a prizefighter when she was making dinner, whacking the mutton with her rolling pin. "Not as far as I can throw him. But he gets the best prices of any of us."

The boy nodded gravely, flicking a dark curl from his eye, accepting this as his due. "I do, Mr. Silk."

Silk wagged a finger at him. "Pride comes before a fall," he said. "Don't you forget."

The boy had given him a look Silk never forgot: black and depthless, utterly uncomprehending. A look that said, *I'm the best, and I know it, and I won't be told otherwise.* It didn't chill Mr. Silk, not then. It impressed him.

It impressed Lillian, too. "How old do you think he is?" she asked Mr. Silk one day.

Silk hadn't given it much thought. "Eleven, perhaps? Twelve?"

Lillian shook her head. "Older than that, I'd say." Then she laughed. "He's not at all what we think he is. He's much cleverer than we realized."

Silk had never told Lillian's daughter about any of this. And there was no need to worry her now.

———◆———

Silk returned to the house in St. James Garlickhythe, the one belonging to "Miss White." It was still in a state of chaos, the arrangements not completed, every room covered in sawdust. The sound of banging and hammering came from every floor. Silk had arranged for Lord Rochester to come for a private dinner—to help drum up some competition for the Duke of Kendal—and he had brought in his usual hired hands to help with the set dressing. But they were falling behind schedule: missing tools, late deliveries, men crying off sick.

Sabotage?

He scrambled atop a stool, trying to help them take down the musty drapes to put up fresh scarlet hangings. They'd fitted gilded mold coverings to the dados and picture-rails, hammered emerald-green silks to the walls, laid an immensely thick carpet down to hide the pockmarked floorboards and placed candelabras and oil lamps and lanterns on every surface. The lights cast a brilliant glow against the walls—and distracted the eye from the very dubious-looking smoke stains on the ceiling.

"We need to bypass the shabbiest rooms," Silk told the ancient steward, stool wobbling dangerously. "Take Lord Rochester straight upstairs to the parlor for supper and cards—and wine. Plenty of wine."

The steward smiled, showing his gums. "Parlor ceiling's fallen in."

Silk blanched. "You're not serious."

But it was true: the upstairs parlor was a pile of dust and plaster and rotting wood, chewed by termites or vermin. The other rooms were in even worse repair and the smell of drains seemed to be rising by the hour.

"Fine. Enough. Send an express to Lord Rochester's house," he instructed the steward. "Tell them we'll be dining at a restaurant instead."

"No need," the steward replied, blinking his heavy-lidded eyes. "His lordship isn't coming." He held up a slip of paper.

Silk snatched it, scanned it furiously. *Sincerest apologies…his lordship unavoidably detained on business…* He glanced up, astonished. "He's sending regrets? On what possible grounds?"

The steward shook his head. "Her Majesty's performance at the opera, I daresay. Very scandalous. Not right for a lady. Perhaps his lordship wants to marry elsewhere."

The hammering overhead grew even more relentless.

"Silence!" Silk roared.

His heart was beating fast. This *was* a test; he could feel it. Worse still, it felt strangely, awfully, *familiar.* Things had been going wrong for months. The cogs in their games kept jamming, crunching, not turning as they used to. They hadn't grown slack in their methods. These preparations had been made with the usual care. His appointment book was as well thumbed as ever.

Which meant they were being subjected to deliberate sabotage. Someone was pulling the rug out from underneath them, right at the heart of this job.

Our troublemaker.

I will fix this, Silk told himself. I will put this right.

It had been his mistake to invite trouble into the Château, after all. Therefore, it was his price to pay.

4

Quinn

Quinn and Mrs. Airlie were determined to keep their planned appointment at the Summer Exhibition, since the duke would be there. But if Quinn was going to secure his confidence, and a proposal of marriage, she would need an immaculate reputation. *Opera Glasses* had cast aspersions against Miss Quinta White, an action that could not go unpunished. So, Quinn and Mrs. Airlie took a cab to the top of the Strand to put the matter straight.

Fleet Street was busy, churning like a river, secretarial workers and office boys dashing in both directions. Quinn had to jump to dodge an omnibus as she and Mrs. Airlie crossed the road, its destination painted in chunky, spiraling letters: **WHITECHAPEL**. It was trundling east, bound to its schedule; it could not be deviated. Quinn summoned the same sense of purpose, adjusting her bowler hat, shoving her newspaper under her armpit. She was here to curse the offices of the *Morning Post*.

"Spotted him yet?" said Mrs. Airlie, who was wearing a veil

of such implacable density she had to clutch Quinn's arm to prevent herself from tripping over.

"Yes! By the hatter's. Lurking."

"I can't see a thing."

"Hold on tight. I'm going to grab him."

Mr. Mellings had left the offices of the *Morning Post* and was turning into Shoe Lane—little realizing that he was being stalked. But he sensed Quinn coming a second before she caught him, spinning on his heel, spectacles flashing in fear.

"No, no, *no!*"

Quinn looped her arm through his and pinned him against the wall. He strained furiously, trying to bolt.

"Now, now," she said, keeping a good grip on him. "No need to be alarmed."

"Police! Help!"

Quinn pressed a gloved finger to Mr. Mellings's lips. "Shh."

"I've no money on me. Not a penny. Let me *go.*"

"We don't want your money," said Mrs. Airlie, voice muffled behind her thick veil. "We've got money."

"What we *want,*" Quinn said, "is your talent. Your art. Your *opera glasses.* There's such a lovely story you should be telling the world."

"What—story?" gasped Mr. Mellings.

"A *love* story. Between a gentleman of great and lordly bearing, and a young woman of fresh and—" Quinn paused "—*saintly* character."

Mellings groaned. "You beasts. Have you been sent by that awful girl from Cheapside? The one setting her cap at Lord Kendal? Well, you can clear off. I don't write columns to order. I'm not a *publicity machine.*"

"Yes," Quinn said. "You are." She twisted his arm, put her lips close to his ear. "We'll send you some notes."

Her eye fell to his tiepin, a handsome flash of gold.

"I wonder," she said, digging her finger into his chest, "whether I might borrow this?"

It gave her some satisfaction to terrify her enemies. As they re-treated down Fleet Street, Quinn could feel this mood thicken-ing. To be the Queen of Fives required a certain darkness, after all. To deploy all sides of oneself, in the service of one's ambi-tion. No queen could reign without some force. She pictured the Kendals driving down Fournier Street accompanied by their charitable committees and demolition men, set on capturing the Château, carriage wheels spattering filthy mud in all directions. It stirred her blood and focused her mind.

"Quinn?" Mrs. Airlie was still clutching her elbow. "Where next?"

"Lunch," she replied briskly, and took them to a chophouse less than ten minutes away, near St. Paul's—one of the few that admitted ladies. They entered by the side door, and were seated in the secondary dining room, curtains pulled tightly around their booth.

"What will you have?" said the waiter, poking his head through the drapes.

"Pie," said Quinn.

"Wine?"

"Yes."

The waiter disappeared. Quinn leaned back. Her seat was upholstered in cracked and sagging leather, dark green, padded with horsehair. The air smelled of ale and carbolic—homely and familiar. She breathed it in.

"You're nervous," said Mrs. Airlie.

"Naturally."

"And you're drinking liquor, really? We'll need to meet His Grace at the Summer Exhibition by two. *And* you need to change."

Quinn ran her fingernails through the grooves in the table. "It's not working."

"What isn't?"

"*Quinta White*. The way we're playing her. I misjudged the 'False Heiress' card." She grimaced at the memory of her description in the newspaper. *A jade-colored virago*. Mr. Mellings was insufferable, and so were his readers. "These fools don't want a girl who looks rich. They want a girl who *is* rich. But acts with modesty and decorum, never says boo to a goose. Someone pale and interesting. Jane Seymour in white muslin. You know the type."

Mrs. Airlie sighed. "I fear you may be right."

"Pie," announced the waiter, shoving two large plates through the curtains.

Quinn reached for her fork. Gravy oozed across her dish, piping hot. "But I won't play it that way. I refuse to be a complete blank."

"Couldn't you try?"

"No." She took a bite of meat. "Let us think. Today is the duke's birthday. The Kendals' moneyman, Mr. Willoughby, gave us good warning that they would be holding a ball for him tonight—planned by Lady Kendal. I had expected to secure an invitation by now, but..." She chewed, pondering. "It's clear I will have to take more direct action."

"How?"

"I will give the duke a birthday gift at the Summer Exhibition."

Mrs. Airlie's nose wrinkled. "Rather forward."

"Rather necessary. I need to claw his heart open a little. He must have invited me to the opera for a reason, but his manner still suggests he's holding me at arm's length."

"So...?"

"A thoughtful gift often wins great trust." She mused over it. "And perhaps I could make a calculated mistake, make him think that he's got the measure of me, encourage him to expose his desires in return."

"As usual, you are complicating matters. *Simplify* the game, Le Blanc. Set aside the marriage plot. It's far too ambitious, and it's riddled with risks. Revert to your usual design: present the duke with a nice, tidy investment and then run away."

"It's too late for that. Besides, the 'False Heiress' card insists upon a wedding."

"Then scratch it out, for heaven's sake. Write a new card!"

"I can't. I won't. The game has begun."

"You can adjust the game."

"No. We closed the bets."

"Closed the...? Oh, for heaven's sake."

"*Rien ne va plus.* We can't take it back now."

"You're being superstitious."

"Perhaps." Quinn didn't go to church; she could barely remember her catechism. But she'd pledged herself to Lady Luck, the first night she took the crown. Went to the back parlor of the Château, locked the door, pulled Madame Le Blanc's wooden dice from the bureau. They were over a hundred years old, carved in dark oak, their dots terribly faded. When Quinn held them in her hand, she could feel their warmth, their promise, the fire of queenship.

She'd rolled a pair of ones: the eyes of the serpent.

Temptation.

She knew what she needed to do: succumb to the game's embrace, not try to control it. Be a snake. Shed a layer of skin. Then pounce.

"Quinn," said Mrs. Airlie. "You have a very venomous look in your eye. If you do anything—*anything*—to risk my security, I shall have to withdraw my services. Regardless of my affection for you."

Quinn placed her elbows on the table. "I don't need your affection. I know exactly where your heart resides. I can see it through your skin. I could take a steak knife and get right to it. I'd eat it, right here at the table, with a bit of gravy, and a little salt, and perhaps some parsnips, too."

Mrs. Airlie thinned her lips. "Did I teach you to make such pugnacious speeches?"

"Yes, you did." Quinn straightened her back. "And you need to finish your lunch."

———◆———

They changed into afternoon dress on Spanish Place. Mrs. Airlie buried her hair underneath a sober but very expensive-looking hat. Quinn wore a jacket and skirt of pale malachite green with fierce, slender epaulettes, adding several drops of Crown Violette behind her ears—and attaching Mr. Mellings's tiepin to her buttonhole.

"Very smart," Mrs. Airlie said.

Quinn flicked her epaulettes. "Not too deadly?"

Mrs. Airlie raised a brow. "Would you change if I told you to?"

Quinn shook her head with a smile. "No."

They took the hired brougham to the Summer Exhibition. The skies were gray, but it was sweltering inside the carriage, and the forecourt of the Royal Academy was full to overflowing with a well-heeled crowd; Quinn could feel faces swiveling toward her as she and Mrs. Airlie marched toward the big doors and entrance hall. She was braced for sneers and laughter to accompany her progress, but she was faced with something more damning still: turned backs and cold stares.

"They're cutting me," she muttered to Mrs. Airlie.

"Don't lose your nerve," Mrs. Airlie replied as they passed through the main doors. "The winds will change the second Mellings starts to write more favorable notices."

"Let us hope so." Quinn surveyed the throng gathered in the hall. She spotted the Duke of Kendal immediately, standing tall at the top of the stairs, eyes on the crowd. *Give me your trust*, she thought. *Let me into your world…*

Mrs. Airlie's advice was still lurking in the back of her mind, to set aside the marriage plot. But she ignored it. Long odds and high stakes and great risks made for a magnificent reign. The kind her predecessors would be proud of. Conviction was everything.

The game coiled itself around her throat; she could hear the faint rattle of it in her lungs. Her mother's necklace felt like ice against her skin.

"Come," she said to Mrs. Airlie. She couldn't talk to the duke alone, not in public. They ascended the stairs, writhing through the crowd, lorgnettes glinting at them as they passed.

The duke turned, as if sensing her approach. He was dressed in another dark jacket, his collar perfectly starched. But as Quinn drew closer, she saw a tiny spot of color forming in his cheeks as he gathered himself. He unfolded his enormous arms. His voice, when he spoke, was as grave as usual.

"Miss White. Mrs. Airlie. Good afternoon."

What did he smell of? Quinn wondered. Cologne, she supposed. Something singular—like the flowers one found in a hothouse, faintly honeyed. Perhaps it was a warning. Dangerous organisms often produced a sweet nectar, the better to lure in their prey. She fanned herself lightly, stirring her own scent of violets. She smiled, feeling the tension in her jaw.

"Your Grace. Am I to wish you a happy birthday?"

She saw the flicker in his eyes.

"Yes," he said slowly. "It's kind of you to remember."

"Thirty. A whole new decade to enjoy!"

He smiled, his expression as taut as hers. "Indeed."

She took a half step closer to him, catching his scent again, feeling her own nostrils flare. She adjusted her voice down a notch.

"I have a gift for you," she said—her smile unmoving, her heart pounding in her chest.

5

The Duke

The duke had arrived at the exhibition with a feeling of anticipation, curious to see Miss White again. The entrance hall was
packed with people, far too stuffy, even though the glass doors
had been thrown open to admit a breeze. He climbed the stairs
so that he could find a spot from which to survey the pictures
without being required to enter any conversation. It was there, his
hand resting on the cold marble of the banister, that he glimpsed
her: Miss White, advancing across the hall.

She was dressed more simply today, in a costume that was either sea green or pale blue—it was made of satin and seemed to
shift in the light as if unwilling to make up its mind. She wore a
small neat hat and blisteringly white gloves. The duke felt something stir in him, a peculiar sense of relief. He'd feared she might
not come—he had seen the scornful notices in *Opera Glasses*, and
he knew she was being pursued by other suitors. Willoughby had
told him that the Rochesters were circling around Miss White,

presumably trying to put him off. But the duke was slowly recognizing a golden opportunity, and he was not willing to let it go.

"Miss White," he said to her in greeting.

The veiled, gimlet-eyed chaperone maintained a decorous distance, studying her program. Burlington House soared over them, the hum of the crowd echoing up the stairs. But here, nestled between the pillars, they were almost in private.

Miss White said, "I have a gift for you."

Plenty of men would have found her damnably attractive. There was a subtle curl to her mouth, a natural flush to her lips; there was both strength and delicacy in her throat. She placed a finger to her ear when she spoke, then touched the back of her hair—as if feeling for some missing ornament, some loose pin. He noticed this. He noticed all these things, these small gestures. They seemed to him to be like the movements of a clockwork mechanism, silver cogs whirring perfectly.

"A gift?" he asked.

Miss White lifted her white-gloved hands, her expression tranquil. She unfastened a small gold tiepin attached to her buttonhole.

"In honor of our very charming discussion last night."

He smiled. It was a hunting bow with a little quiverful of arrows. Rather cheaply made, but amusing all the same.

"Too kind of you," he said. "I'm only sorry I have nothing to offer in return."

Her eyes flashed. "Perhaps I might offer some inspiration."

"Certainly."

"I think you know that I was raised a little east of Berkeley Square. In great comfort, of course, and with every advantage." She paused. "But there has always been a good deal of wretchedness on my doorstep. There is a school in Spitalfields I have adopted, which is in desperate need of philanthropy. I rather thought you might like to assist them."

The duke felt a stab of disappointment. It was bad enough to have Willoughby pressing him constantly to give his signature to Lady Kendal's charitable payments. Rigidly, he said, "My stepmother is chiefly responsible for our philanthropic affairs. If she is occupied, I'll refer it to our moneyman."

She gave him a tiny smile, a glimmer of superiority. "It's a shame not to take charge of one's own pocketbook."

"I disagree," he said. "It provides one with a sense of freedom."

"Abandoning one's responsibilities is not the same as freedom."

She took a step toward him, just an inch. He could smell her: something hard and soapy and tinged with violets, as if she had scrubbed herself from top to toe before climbing into her sea green satin dress. Her eyes were crinkled.

"To give is better than to receive, Your Grace. Charitable donations provide an excellent balm for the soul. Consider me your conduit."

He laughed shortly. "Is that your birthday present? The preservation of my soul?"

"No, just the enhancement of it." She glanced toward her chaperone, checked that they were still alone. "Very well. I shall give you another gift. I shall make a donation to a cause of your choosing. Name it, and the price."

The duke raised a palm. "No need, Miss White."

"But I insist. You must have your schemes and projects. There must be a cause that pulls upon your heart. Well then, I shall adopt my own advice. I shall give to you without compunction, in any direction you ordain." She paused. "Think it over, if you wish. I could attend your ball, to hear your decision."

He was startled by the boldness of the suggestion, but he took care to give no indication of it. "Really, I have no cause in mind."

She smiled. "No cause? Or no heart?"

"Come," he said, proffering his arm. "We should examine the exhibition."

She didn't move. She gave him a level stare, one that seemed to pick right to the back of his head. Then she said, voice soft,

"I was not born with money. We have made a great show of dressing up my fortune to augment my coming-out, but if you go hunting through my papers, you'll find a great deal of dross. However, my offer is honestly and freely given. I will support you in any project you like."

Her chaperone was still standing several feet away, just out of earshot. But she stiffened, turning, as if catching the edge of this remark.

"Quinta, dear," she said, stepping closer. "Perhaps we should..."

"Dross?" the duke repeated.

"There, I have exposed myself! Your turn."

Was she teasing him? Lying? No, he thought: there was a bright candor in her eyes. It was the same light he'd observed the night before, seated beside her at the opera. Did she know *his* secrets? This made his breath quicken. For he had realized, late last night, how very badly he needed to unburden himself. How much he wished to be seen by someone, exposed to scrutiny. It frightened him, and because he was frightened, he hesitated.

"Your chaperone is waiting for you, Miss White," he said, folding his arms.

She furrowed her brow, as if disappointed. "Really?" The wrinkle vanished as instantly as it appeared. "Very well. Forgive me for any pert remarks. Good day."

She turned, beckoning her chaperone—and walked away.

———

What is happening to me? the duke asked himself, traversing the galleries. The paintings blurred before him, a thousand stormy seascapes, frenzied brushstrokes. Weedy gentlemen kept clapping him on the shoulder, their wives tapping him with their fans. "Your Grace, Your Grace..."

Leave me alone, he thought. *All of you...*

One of his headaches was coming on. Miss White must have stirred too strong a reaction within him. He had felt it gusting up inside, the desire to tell her the truth, to expose his greatest, deepest secret—just to see what she would say, what she would do, how fast she would run...

There was only one person he wished to speak to about this. In daylight hours, nobody would guess they were in love; they had taken such care to disguise it. Even when they were alone, things felt strangely repressed. They skirted it, avoiding it, as if it were not real. Sometimes he even wondered if he'd imagined them, those strange and moonlight nights. The duke craved his lover, hollow and hungry with desire. And yet, he'd learned to stifle it. To pack it down, deep in the earth, damaging the roots. This love could never flourish, never grow, and therein lay the longing, the desperation for it.

Everybody wanted him to marry. To bind himself in an illustrious alliance. To preserve the estate. To *honor his father*. It was making him sick. Every fiber in his skin revolted against it. He'd built himself to look nothing like his hollow, gaunt-cheeked father. He was training himself to be nothing like him, either.

Besides, he'd promised Tor he wouldn't marry.

It will kill *me, Max.* The idea of it, a stranger entering the house, displacing her—it had made her voice hoarse and ragged. He understood it, her fear. He felt it himself. It was the thing they shared, the two of them—the knowledge that they'd been forgotten, discarded, once before. That it could easily happen again.

Moreover, he'd felt something tremendous rising in him when she begged him not to marry. A huge and staggering relief. Here it was: the perfect excuse. He knew, even then, that he couldn't marry. That his desires were forbidden to him. So he made Tor a promise that seemed altruistic, that told her exactly what she wanted to hear, that seemed designed to protect *her* interests when really it was the most selfish act in the world. The most cowardly. A route to conceal his own desires with magic lanterns and double-sided mirrors.

But perhaps he had been fooling himself, thinking he could

go on like this forever. Perhaps it was time to give it up, bargain. He could go to Tor and seek forgiveness, make a settlement. He could take a bride. He *could* do it. He could remake himself, he could live completely in disguise—if it meant he could keep the person he needed most.

He touched the gold clasp resting in his palm, the hunting bow and quiverful of arrows. It glinted at him, taunting him. *What are you waiting for? It's your birthday, after all. Take your gift.*

6

Tor

Other people might have been willing to sit and wait for disaster to befall them, but not Tor. Her mind was whirring as the brougham dragged itself back to Mayfair. Her object was clear: to protect her fortune, keep her possessions, and live wherever she pleased. And as the carriage pulled into Berkeley Square—suspension ticking, heat rising, clouds gathering—the solution became clear, too.

Willoughby had helped her to understand the detail. Mount Kendal, up in the Peaks, was parceled up with the entail, tied to the male bloodline. She couldn't touch it. But the family's London possessions were not held under the same protections. Kendal House belonged to Max by dint of inheritance, but *legally* it could be carved up and sold off to anyone at all.

She descended from the brougham, slamming the door behind her. She passed the pointed railings, ducking into the porch. The dark hall beckoned, smelling of wine and wax. *Home*. The word thrummed in her blood.

"You have a visitor, my lady," said the footman, closing the heavy front door. "In the dining room."

"Good." She'd sent an express to Threadneedle Street, summoning the bearded solicitor. He was standing by the fireplace, fingers tucked in his buttonholes, peering at the portraits on the wall.

"Damned fine ponies, these," he said, turning. His beard seemed lustrous today, a wild and glinting thicket. It repulsed and thrilled her in equal measure. "Beauties."

"They're mine," Tor said, closing the dining room door. "All of them." The shutters were half drawn; the light was dim. "Now. I wish to instruct you to act on my behalf."

"In what matter?"

"War."

———◆———

The solicitor examined the papers, laying each one out on the dining table, perusing them with his hands folded behind his back. Tor watched him with mounting impatience.

"Well?"

"I recommend you seek a fresh financial settlement, Lady Victoria, disconnected from any prior provisions made by your father."

"Very well. I want this house and everything in it."

The solicitor raised an eyebrow. "I think the duke would need a peculiarly compelling motive to cede this property to you." He fingered his buttonhole. "That said, 'a man's gift maketh room for him.'" He pushed the box toward her across the table, leather hissing against polished oak. "Have you considered appealing to your brother's sense of charity toward you?"

"Charity? I have no interest in charity—neither his nor anyone else's. He's trying to break into my personal funds. It is an outrage."

"Then appeal to his fears. His character has been traduced in some of the better London clubs, you know." He winked at her,

saying gravely, "I have heard word of debauched dinners, of as-
signations after dark, of the Kendal carriage being spotted in the
more iniquitous corners of Chelsea…"

Tor reddened. Carefully, she said, "I don't know about that."

"Indeed, not. Now, who gave you these papers?"

"Our moneyman, Mr. Willoughby."

"Hm. I am acquainted with Willoughby. He is nothing if not
astute. If he's revealed your brother's designs against you, there
will be a reason for it—some way in which its disclosure aids his
own interests."

"He serves in our household. I compelled him to give me the
truth, that's all."

"And very few gentlemen could withstand your desires, I am
sure—but still it gives me pause. You're certain this attack on
your fortune *has* been precipitated by your brother? Not Willoughby himself?"

"Certainly not. Our moneymen do as they're told. They do
not act on their own instincts."

"But why should the duke require access to your ladyship's
funds? You're certain there's nothing off-kilter in his financial
affairs?"

"Of course not! Kendal credit is beyond reproach."

The solicitor put his hands behind his back. "Test that certainty. Inspect the duke's pocketbook. It is a mirror to a man's
character. And *if* you discover something amiss—any debts, any
defaults—you can use those against him."

———◆———

The library contained the various bureaus stuffed with family
papers—and, Tor suspected, all receipts related to the duke's financial affairs. She went swiftly upstairs—pausing at the junction to the ballroom and the picture gallery, listening for any
movement in Lady Kendal's quarters directly overhead. But all

was still. No doubt, her stepmother had retired to take her afternoon rest before dressing for Max's ball.

Quietly, Tor opened the double doors leading to the library, and slipped inside.

The room was filled with old books, collections passed down through the generations: faded flaxen spines in all shapes and sizes—folio, quarto, octavo, duodecimo. Her eyes swept over dictionaries and atlases, volumes on architecture, medicine, chess, poetry, history, canonical scriptures. The walls were lined with myriad cabinets, some hanging open, containing diagrams and prints and sketches purchased from Florence and Rome. On the far side of the room, placed under a porthole window, was a heavy desk made of polished walnut.

All of Max's papers were marked up and placed in envelopes: Political Correspondence... Estate Matters... Appointments and Diaries... Taxations and Duties... She rifled through checkbooks stamped with the Coutts crest, the stubs revealing mundane payments: doctors' fees, maintenance works on the chapel, repairs to the Lomond lodge...

As she flicked through these pages, she felt a sudden quiver of guilt. It could be no easy thing, managing an estate as large as this one. Opening each drawer, sifting the contents, her mind snagged on a memory: catching Max playing with her own private possessions on the nursery corridor at Mount Kendal. She had been eleven or twelve years old. "Put that down," she'd shouted, spotting him clutching one of her journals in his hand. "I'll box your ears!"

"Don't," he said, when she grabbed it from him. "I'll tell Papa."

Their father was dead. Did Max talk to Papa still in his prayers? Should she do the same? In the old days, when Tor heard footsteps above the nurseries, she imagined them to be her father's ghost. But today, she knew what they were: maids and footmen scuttling like mice between the walls.

She reached into one of the narrowest drawers, found a small

catch and spring. A compartment opened. In it, nestled in a lining
of red satin with black velvet piping, she found a packet of letters.

She pulled them out, unfolding the first one, feeling a tingle
of curiosity. The letterhead blazed up at her, KENDAL HOUSE,
in bloodred ink. The date, from a few weeks prior: July 9th. The
hand was muscular and hasty.

> *...my own darling, how dreadful it was to part this af-*
> *ternoon, when all I wished for was to be with you—*
> *just you, quite alone—away from everybody, and to*
> *tell you ALL the things I have been so desperately*
> *longing to say...*

Tor dropped the letter as if it had scalded her. She recognized
this hand: her brother's swift, slanting penmanship. Instantly, she
understood what it was: a love letter. But not sent, not delivered.

Or worse: returned to the sender, the message rejected.

Tor's fingers hovered over the packet. Page after page of black
ink, stamped with the Kendal crest, as if her brother had poured
his feelings onto paper—and then locked them away in a secret
compartment so they would never be confided.

Tor bundled the letters back into the compartment. The idea
that Max would realize they had been discovered, opened, *read*—
it made her nauseous.

He was in love with someone. Presently and currently and
absolutely *in love*—judging by the date. She closed the drawers,
affixed the clasps, breathed.

Was *this* ammunition? Could Tor use this in her favor?

No: it indicated one thing only. He had formed an attachment to a lady; he was seeking tenderness and intimacy—and
this frightened Tor; it showed her once again that she had misunderstood him. Max had grown so distant, so reserved—she
had started to forget he had a beating heart.

This distance had set in while he was still at school. He began
to transform his appearance, acquiring dumbbells and chest ex-

panders and spine directors. Tor had surveyed his strange new trunk and frame, wondering: *Why are you doing this to yourself?* He grew anemic; the family physician prescribed a glass of claret to be taken every afternoon. Max had flushed when Tor caught him sipping it. "You look at me as if I am a freak," he said, setting down the glass on the hall table. The napkin was stained, his lips dark.

She wondered *whom* he was doing it for. "You should not change yourself for anyone," she said.

Love, after all, was the most dangerous thing in their family. Papa was proof of that.

People imagined that Tor did not recall how her father adored her mother—but, of course, she did. The drawing room festooned with fresh roses; the birdhouse filled with turtledoves. There were no portraits of Daphne Kendal left now—the physicians had ordered them all to be destroyed when she died, for fear of inflaming the old duke's grief—but Tor had retained one miniature. It showed a fair-haired, doe-eyed lady, blurred by the softest oils, more cloud than a person.

Tor could still picture her father—as angular and pallid as she feared she might herself become—descending the stairs, trailed by his bloodhounds, howling for her mother. As if Mama was simply outside, standing on the byre road, waiting in the mist. Love and grief: these things were like cholera; they came and ravaged every corner of the household. If Max suffered the same fate, then he could not be trusted to make sound decisions.

Tor needed to tell someone about the letters. Surely, their stepmother of all people would understand the danger? Then again, perhaps not. She had met Papa at his very worst, and had loved and nursed him all the same.

Downstairs, in the depths of the house, a servant banged the gong. It was the dressing bell, Tor realized. Ordering the family to get ready for Max's birthday. The dull, ominous tolling reverberated upward through the house, through Tor's bones— a death knell.

7

Quinn

"You overstepped, Le Blanc."

Mrs. Airlie was in a dark mood as they rode home in the carriage. But Quinn's mind was distracted. She had thought she could read the duke—and yet now she was certain she was missing something; her gambits had not hit the mark. She'd disclosed a significant truth—that she was not born to wealth—to gain his confidence, but he showed no curiosity, no interest in her history. Instead, he closed up, screening himself behind a veil.

"Perhaps," she said to Mrs. Airlie. "But I wished to test him. Expose a little weakness in my armor. And seek an invitation to the ball."

"You must *tell* me if you intend to fly so close to the sun."

"Very well," Quinn said shortly. "I stand corrected." She had no patience for Mrs. Airlie's censure. "Not that it makes much difference. He didn't take the bait."

"You were being too subtle."

"Subtle?"

"Charitable gifts, birthday presents... I could hardly follow your tactics at all."

Quinn could feel her frustration rising. "It sometimes helps to find a gentleman's tender spots. His likes and wishes. The same sparring as before."

"You are an authority on these methods, clearly." Mrs. Airlie pulled the carriage blinds down. "But I will tell you this: the duke is *not* playing along."

———

Yet as evening approached, they heard a loud knock at the door on Spanish Place. A card was placed on the hall table.

"A boy bicycled it over from the city," said one of Mrs. Airlie's students.

"Whatever are you doing answering *the door?*" asked Mrs. Airlie, scandalized.

"We don't have a maid. Who else is s'posed to do it?"

Quinn flipped the card, felt her stomach jolt. "It's an invitation. Sent by express to the house at Cheapside."

Mrs. Airlie's gaze met hers. "To...?"

"His birthday."

"At Kendal House? Tonight?"

"Yes."

Quinn peered at the card, heart ticking. Dark ink, a fast and masculine hand.

The Duke of Kendal requests the company of Miss Quinta White and Mrs. Airlie to a BALL WITH SUPPER— response by return at your convenience, Yours &c...

There followed a postscript: *All candid remarks to be forgiven— nay, encouraged—this evening. M. K. D.*

"Quickly, child," Mrs. Airlie said to the student. "Run down

the street. Fetch an errand boy. We need to send our acceptance."
She turned to Quinn. "You hit your mark, after all."

Quinn could smell it: the scent of the game, sweet and rotten.
She didn't trust the duke, didn't trust this card. She needed to
find out exactly what he was concealing. The serpent was un-
coiling in her heart.

"Let's get ready," she said.

———————

Quinn hurried to the bedchamber allotted to her, took out her
gown to air, ate three pieces of buttered toast, had a hot bath,
swigged a half measure of cognac and sat down to pin, tease and
dress her wig. The light outside was turning amber, as if pre-
saging a storm.

"Mrs. Airlie?" she called. "Any word from Mr. Silk?"

Mrs. Airlie was in her own dressing room. "He sent an express. You didn't receive it? He's been keeping appointments in
Bethnal Green this afternoon."

Quinn sighed. It was typical of Silk that he would be fussing
over details on the other side of the city when she needed him.

"Leave a message for him, will you? Tell him to meet us in
Berkeley Square—midnight should do it. I want someone ready
with the carriage, in case we need to dash."

"What are you planning?"

"I told you," Quinn said, examining her gown. "To secure my
proposal." The seamstresses had outdone themselves: she looked
as lean as a dancer in a six-gored skirt of pale chiffon, the velvet
sash done in arsenic green. Fashionable—but sleek, not showy.
Nothing that could insult Mr. Mellings. The lacing went right
up to the skin; she needed Mrs. Airlie's students to tie her in. "I
am certain things will fall in our favor."

As night fell, the streetlamps came on. Mrs. Airlie had rented
a different brougham to take them to Berkeley Square: "We need
people to think you have a perfectly *terrific* fleet of carriages,"

she said. This one was bloodred, with that new-carriage smell of soap and lye, fresh from the harness room. Mrs. Airlie climbed in first, shimmering with rhinestones, her bodice embroidered with butterflies.

"Are we running late?" Quinn asked, following. She ran a swift finger over her neckline, grimacing as she found a pin over-looked by the dressmakers.

"Not in the least," said Mrs. Airlie. "Balls like *this* one will hardly begin until eleven o'clock."

The enormity of the night ahead presented itself in Quinn's mind. She had an invitation to the ball, certainly—but she was a long way off a proposal, particularly when women of more ex-alted birth were being thrown in the duke's direction. *He* might not be balking at her lowly origins, but others would be discour-aged by them, and would push him toward a different bride. She would need to face him, stare him down, skewer him into an offer of marriage—somehow. Without it, the whole scheme would collapse.

Trust the game, she reminded herself. *Trust* yourself. *You'll find a way.*

Queens did not accept impossibilities.

Berkeley Square was already crammed with carriages by the time they arrived at Kendal House a little before eleven. The front doors had been thrown open and the big electroliers were swaying, setting off brilliant light. The duke himself was stand-ing at the foot of the staircase, greeting the arrivals, encased in long trousers and white tails. Beside him stood Lady Victoria, wearing a decidedly peculiar costume: red satin, a great cloud of muslin thrown back over her shoulders, a velvet opera cloak streaming out across the floor.

"She looks like a very bad fairy," muttered Mrs. Airlie.

"I rather like it." There was a frisson of interest as Quinn crossed the hall; the crowd ogled her. "Well, at least they're not booing and hissing."

"Not yet." A receiving line had formed to shake hands with the Kendals. Mrs. Airlie frowned. "*Must* we wait?"

"Perhaps not. It's hardly moving." There was something raw about the atmosphere at the foot of the stairs: the duke and Lady Victoria were not facing one another. Between them, Quinn realized, was a smaller figure, almost invisible amid the crowd. Their stepmother. "Come. Let's dash upstairs."

They sliced directly toward the staircase. Quinn sensed the duke turning, spotting her. She raised her chin, shifting fractionally, just to catch his eye.

A woman's orange toque blocked the view.

"Mind your step," Quinn said to Mrs. Airlie. A fresh carpet had been laid on the staircase: a magnificent shade of scarlet, with brass grips sticking out at all angles. "It appears that our hosts want us to trip and break our necks."

Upstairs, the ballroom was filled with light and the smell of orchids, the pillars garlanded with white roses. It was colonnaded, mirrored, and presumably backed straight on to the stable yard. The windows were very high and very small and afforded absolutely no views at all.

"What odd proportions," said Mrs. Airlie. "One feels like the roof is about to fall in."

"Drinks?" said Quinn.

"Urgently."

They moved to the supper room, piled cold chicken onto their plates.

"The Kendals are plainly unafraid of gluttony," Mrs. Airlie said, surveying the sideboard with a shudder. Quinn agreed—there was a perfect feast here: a boar's head, game pie, fruited jellies and meringues, lobster salad, a towering charlotte russe. "But I just can't abide so much *tongue*. It makes one think of the nursery, and then one becomes terribly violent." Mrs. Airlie poked Quinn's arm. "Pass me those cherries."

"Do you recognize anybody here?"

"Some—although they have become dreadfully fossilized. I had better keep my veil on." Mrs. Airlie sucked in her breath, examining the crowd with a keen gaze. "Dull your eyes, Le Blanc. These are going to be some very tedious conversations." And she dragged them both into the fray.

Quinn worked the room with Mrs. Airlie, taking care to say nothing that could stir a single iota of controversy, allowing herself to be subjected to the same questions at least half a dozen times. Yes, she was entranced by hunting, shooting, fishing, riding, stalking, hymns, Cowes, dogs, lakes, children, her dear departed parents, embroidery, automobiles, and English beef. She smiled so prettily and incessantly her cheeks began to ache. It was clear the Kendals had summoned the absolute cream of society, and at first Quinn feared she would be exposed to the same froideur that had greeted her at the Summer Exhibition. But it quickly became evident that the company was far more engrossed with getting a good look at Kendal House for the first time in so many years.

"Aren't the tapestries frightful? All those ghastly swans, they make one feel quite nervous. I'd have thought Lady Kendal would have cleared them out."

"No, dear, she's put them in—and the banners on the stairwell. It didn't look nearly so medieval when Daphne Kendal was alive."

"Good heavens. She must have bankrupted the estate to pay for all this giltwork."

"Bankrupted? The *Kendals*? Impossible."

"What of the daughter? Isn't she absolutely superb?"

"If you enjoy diabolical fashions and a complete absence of reserve. His Grace was as haughty as usual. Huge as a mountain, pale as a ghost; it doesn't seem right at all, does it?"

After thirty minutes of circling the room, Quinn felt a hand pulling her aside.

"Will you dance?" Mrs. Airlie whispered.

"Are you asking?"

"No, but everybody else is clearly wondering."

Quinn glanced sideways. She could, indeed, see a few gentlemen creeping closer. "I thought they were running for the hills, owing to my rampant vulgarity."

"Well, yes, they are—but even snobs enjoy the polka."

Quinn could see Sonia Hillyard being steered around the opposite end of the ballroom by her redoubtable-looking mother.

"No. I'm going to get more chicken."

She turned and crossed the parquet, stationing herself beside a pillar, where she could keep a close eye on the crowd. There was no sign of her hosts. The most illustrious neighbors had been treated to a private dinner before the ball proper, following which the duke had by all accounts opened the quadrilles with one of the Countess of Clare's daughters. The Kendals had then vanished downstairs to greet their secondary guests, where they still remained. No wonder they disliked parties, Quinn thought. They had no opportunity to enjoy their own. Above her, situated in a gallery shaped rather like a conch shell, the orchestra was playing a brisk waltz.

"Dance?" said a tall fellow with drooping whiskers, extending a hand. His friends sniggered behind him.

"On no account," Quinn replied, peering over his shoulder. There were some stupendous-looking paintings in this room, and even better jewels on the women. Perhaps she could reformulate her business, switch to housebreaking, after all.

"Aha!" said a voice. "Look sharp. Here comes the infamous Lady Victoria!"

There was some commotion on the far side of the room; Quinn craned her neck to get a better view. Lady Victoria Kendal had arrived, charging across the parquet, her cloak rippling out behind her. There was something spectacular about her costume: a scarlet bodice decked in ropes of pearls, a gigantic cross of blazing rubies hanging from her neck. She halted in the middle of the room, surveying the crowd around her as if in some dismay—as if she had never seen so many people in her life before; as if she were as irked by them as they were fascinated by her.

Swallowing a final piece of cold chicken, passing her plate to the party of young men, Quinn strode into the crowd. It shifted for her. But halfway across the room, a shadow fell in front of her path; she caught a honeyed scent of cologne on the air, and a voice said:

"Miss White."

She turned.

Quinn was not a romantic. Nor a novel reader. She entertained no fantasies about catching eyes across a brilliantly lit ballroom. But even she, in that moment, was struck by the sudden appearance of the Duke of Kendal. He emerged from the crowd, blazing under the white-hot light of the electrolier, standing head and shoulders above everybody else in the room.

"Your Grace," she said.

A semicircle formed around them. In the distance, Quinn could see the whiskered figure of Lord Rochester, accompanied by his retainer, Mr. Lancer. A waltzing couple orbited her.

"I am glad you came," the duke said.

"I'm glad you asked," Quinn replied. "Many happy returns once again."

He tapped his lapel; she perceived a flash of gold. The tiepin. "Thank you." His eyes roved the room, alighting on his sister. Victoria Kendal was standing stock-still before a gigantic gilt-framed mirror, engaged in fierce conversation with various wide-eyed young gentlemen. "Will you dance?" the duke said, attention snapping back to her.

"Certainly," Quinn said. Dancing was useful. It provided proximity. Not for nothing had Quinn been schooled by Mrs. Airlie's own dance masters. "Now?"

"Now," the duke said, extending a hand. He, too, was wearing gloves: thick white cotton, stretched tight.

The music swayed, adjusting into the next waltz—and the crowd exchanged glances as Quinn permitted the duke to lead her on to the bright glare of the floor. She lifted a steady hand to his shoulder; he placed his own near her waist. They moved in tandem, in perfect symmetry.

Quinn's gaze was on the perimeter of the room, watching as Mrs. Airlie detached herself from her own conversation, keeping Quinn under her protective eye. Quinn blinked at her: *All's well.* Then she shifted her gaze back to the duke.

Dancing gave him something he had not possessed before: elegance. But his temples were dampened by a fine layer of perspiration. Touching the hard-hewn muscle in his arm, she was struck instantly by his temperature. She'd expected him to feel like marble—cold. But he was hot, sweating through the thick cotton of his jacket. It didn't show on his face, but his body betrayed him.

"Will you be engaged to Lord Rochester this week, Miss White?" he asked.

A blunt question. And a promising one. Surely, it signaled his interest? Quinn considered the answer. "Perhaps," she said. "I hardly know." *Lie.* She wondered if he could see through it or not. She decided to push back. "Are *you* intent on marriage, Your Grace?"

"I have been advised of the merits."

"But not persuaded?"

They turned with the music. "I am making up my mind. What is your position?"

"On marriage?"

"Yes."

"I do not plan to marry."

Truth.

"Whyever not?"

"Someone would have to ask. I would have to accept." She smiled. "These are mighty considerations."

"Perhaps you should do the asking."

"Carry the risk, you mean? Perhaps. I am someone who favors bold action."

"Regardless of expectations?"

"Whose expectations?"

"The world's. Society's."

"Oh," Quinn said, fingers hovering on his shoulder blade. "I don't mind those. My expectations of myself are high enough."

His lips were fuller, a shade darker, at this angle. "And have you met them?"

"My own expectations?"

"Yes."

"Of course."

Lie. A nerve leaped in her mouth as she spoke.

He spotted it, eyes narrowing just a fraction. "You have great self-assurance."

"It seems to me," Quinn said, "that one has little else in life."

The music swelled, and another line of dancers whirred into position, dark jackets and pale shoulders glinting in the mirrors all the way down the room. She'd lost sight of Mrs. Airlie; the crowd pressed in a little closer. The smell of the room—the orchids, the sweet edge to the duke's cologne, the fug of wine hanging over the vaulted ceiling—felt thick and rich and brimming with promise.

"You should ask," the duke said, brow furrowing.

"Ask what?"

"Ask someone to marry you."

His voice was restrained. But the heat was pulsing from him.

Quinn locked her gaze on his. "Should I?"

"Yes," he replied. "If you see the opportunity."

8

Mr. Silk

Mr. Silk was supposed to spend the afternoon recruiting men for Quinn's final flourish on her wedding day—a move they'd sketched between them the night before the game commenced. But when he'd descended from the omnibus at Bethnal Green, he hesitated, rubbed his earlobe—and deviated from the appointment book, heading east.

Their troublemaker could be anywhere. Lurking in Epping Forest, digging roads or railways, running casino tables in Monte Carlo. But Mr. Silk knew where to begin the search for a hostage. A small easy-to-miss sort of place.

A haberdasher's shop on Roman Road.

He slipped away from the main road, taking the alleyways and side streets. The sun had tilted downward, clouds thickening. Bethnal Green dissolved into Bow, the streets threading outward in long low-slung lines. The pavements were hoarded with black fencing, walls defaced with white chalk. Figures stood in doorways, watching him as he passed. Silk tipped his bowler hat down over his eyes. You never knew who was tracking you in this line of work.

The haberdasher's shop was at the eastern end of Roman Road. It had a small front window, strung with cheap shirts and blouses, and the front door was painted a grubby shade of plum. He took a sharp breath and pushed open the door.

A bell clanked overhead. Gloomy light, musty air. A face looked up from the workbench. A boy in his teens, tied into an apron so starched it crackled when he moved. A cash register loomed at the end of the workbench: nickel-plated, gray-glinting—American, probably. It was a reminder to anybody stopping by: this shop sold the most expensive, valuable product in the world.

Knowledge. Information. *Intelligence.*

Silk gave the boy a dead stare. "Open the back door."

The boy flicked a greasy lock of hair from his face. "Who's asking?"

"Back door."

The boy puffed his chest—but he fished a key from his apron, pushed open the door.

Silk entered. It could have been any back parlor in town. Pale printed wallpaper, kettle on the grate, mantelpiece fringed with velvet, a sturdy square table. Silk could guess the location of the kitchen and the privy outdoors. Two rooms upstairs, three rooms down. A small oblong yard and a thread-thin alley.

A young woman was sitting in an armchair by the fire.

Click.

The door closed.

The girl groaned. Her mouth was gagged, her arms and feet bound with rope. Silk recognized her at once.

"Good God," he exclaimed, and hurried across the room, untying the ropes around her wrists. "Does Mrs. Airlie know you're here?"

It was the housemaid from the Academy. She yanked out her gag, gasped, "They took me *hostage*, I've been tied up for..."

"Ah, good," said a clipped female voice from the other side of the room. "You have come to claim her, yes? Let us begin."

Silk swung around.

A woman was trimming the lamp. She was doing it with the fiercest possible concentration, adjusting the dial: he could hear the tiny *click-click-click* of the mechanism. She was in her forties, her face long and angular, her hair a shade of blond so pale it appeared almost white. She had an accent: Danish, perhaps. Very precise.

"Sit," she said, snapping her finger. She was wearing a smart afternoon dress, as if she planned to go shopping in town, as if she had all sorts of things to deal with besides Mr. Silk.

"What is the meaning of this?" Silk said, bristling. "This poor young lady—*who brought her here?*"

The woman shrugged. "You know what we do here. We sign for deliveries. We exchange them for payment. We don't discuss this."

"Deliveries?" said Mrs. Airlie's housemaid. "They took me clean out of the house, they *kidnapped* me..."

Silk frowned. "Has this woman been injured?"

"Grazing to the forearm, a little bruise upon the wrists, a scratch below the hairline," replied the woman. She pushed a piece of paper across the table. "I have itemized each abrasion." She smoothed her skirts. "Come. You want to take her home? Not a problem. My client has set the terms of bail." She pushed a second piece of paper across the table. "Here is the sum."

The woman reached for a cigarette, a box of matches, lit one. She wasn't a kidnapper. Nor a confidence woman. She was a bookkeeper. She could do this transaction with her eyes closed.

"Who is your client?" Silk asked.

"Who do you think?" she said, taking a drag, blowing out smoke.

Suddenly, Silk understood the fear of the men in Mr. Dunuvar's pub. He felt it himself.

"You know who *I* represent?" He lifted his chin. "The Queen of Fives."

The woman tapped her cigarette in her ashtray. "Well," she said. "Everybody seems to go by that name, these days."

———

Silk remembered what Lillian Quinn had said to him, years before, about the ragged boy they put to work in the kitchen. *He's not at all what we think he is. He's much cleverer than we realized.*

The boy had been reading the Rulebook, Lillian said, in secret—while the rest of the household was sleeping.

"But how did he get the key to the bureau?" Silk asked, shocked.

Lillian had smiled, patted him on the arm. "He must have pinched it off us. See? Very clever."

Silk had confronted the boy. "How old are you?" he asked.

"Thirteen."

"How old are you really?"

The boy stared at him, dark-eyed, smooth-faced, furious. *"Thirteen."*

"Mrs. Quinn tells me you've been deceiving us."

The boy gave him a baleful look—but his voice was small. "You wouldn't have let me stay," he said, "if you knew I was a *girl.*"

"How old are you?" Silk asked again, more gently. "Tell me the truth, please."

The girl sucked her teeth. *"Seventeen."*

They didn't realize the danger, not then, of letting her stay. Secretly, they were impressed by her subterfuge. "We can't very well turn her out for being a fraud, can we?" Lillian said. "It would be a bit rich, coming from *us*. Besides, she's tremendously good at cards."

"Is she?"

"Why do you think Cook agreed to keep her secret? She's got herself into terrible debt just playing rummy."

Silk had raised his finger to the girl. "I'll give you one chance," he said. "Spoil it and you'll go straight back to the kitchen."

But the girl didn't spoil it. She took elocution lessons, learned to waltz, began to wear wigs. Lillian shared her luxuriant wardrobe, dressing her in the same pearl-colored silks, in chocolate velvet trims. By the end of the year, the girl was running the best whist tables on Eaton Place, bringing home quite extraordinary returns.

"See?" Lillian said. "I'm training her in my own games next. She's devilishly good."

———◆———

Silk paid the ransom for Mrs. Airlie's maid. He presumed she was an innocent in all this; a token taken by the troublemaker, a way to signal she meant to play a dangerous game. He made out the bank order with a shaking hand, trying not to think about the risk of it defaulting.

"Pleasure doing business," said the bookkeeper briskly, passing him a receipt.

"Run home," Silk told the maid, giving her change for a cab. "*Home.* Not Mrs. Airlie's house."

She stared at him, eyes wide. "Are you in danger, Mr. Silk?"

"No," he said shortly. "Not in the least."

He knew what he would need to do now.

———◆———

Across town, the woman in the cream silk gown sniffed the breeze. It was fast approaching midnight in Berkeley Square. She could see the weather vanes shifting. She studied each residence one by one: thin, black-bricked townhouses on the southwestern side. Fawn-colored mansions to the east.

Right at the top, bloodred and watchful: Kendal House, blazing with the lights of the ball.

Softly, she opened the gate leading into the gardens in the middle of the square. Nobody heard her do it; the hinges were nicely oiled. She pressed into the thicket and vanished from view.

She'd sent a message to Mr. Silk. She'd snatched a token from Mrs. Airlie's house, to demonstrate the seriousness of her intent. And she knew Mr. Silk would take her seriously. She trusted the natural order of things, the sequencing, the five fingers of a confidence trick.

And she liked this part of the game. Liked it very much indeed.

———◆———

It took Mr. Silk some time to make it back to Mayfair. There was a pony and trap waiting outside the haberdasher's shop— unmanned, the horse simply tied to the lamppost. He'd stolen it, driven it westward, into the dusk and then the thicker darkness of night.

He stopped first at Spanish Place. Mrs. Airlie's house was quiet; the students were at their prayers—or casting spells. There was a message from Quinn: *Wait for us in Berkeley Square—at midnight. Q. R.*

He'd been given orders so many times by so many queens. Had received so many slips of paper, signed **Quinn Regina, Lillian Regina...** And the rest: ***V. R., A. R., T. R., E. R...***

But now he was following a different instruction.

There was no bedroom allotted to Silk in Mrs. Airlie's house, so he tidied himself in the drawing room, using the lamplight to study his appearance. He straightened his neckerchief, waxed his mustache, tried to smooth his bulky jacket. He fumbled with his buttons. Fear was making his fingers turn numb. He wasn't afraid of *her*, he was afraid of Quinn. Of what she would think when she found out what he had done...

He shook himself, put on his greatcoat, descended the stairs— and slunk into the night.

———————

Silk entered the Berkeley Square gardens through a narrow gate on the south side, peering into the gloom, looking for the troublemaker. He shivered, even though it was a mild night. The sky was thick with clouds—there was no sign of the moon.

A hand: gloved, waxy, calfskin, clapped itself against his mouth.

Behind him, a body nailed itself to his, pinning his arms and legs.

A voice, straightforward, familiar, right in his ear, said, "Hello, old friend."

Silk's instincts kicked in, fast. He staggered forward, trying to shake them off his back. He caught the dizzy, tender scent of flowers.

But the fist that met his skull wasn't tender: the impact blew his thoughts out like a dandelion stem.

The world went black.

———————

Behind Berkeley Square stood a row of small mews buildings, attached to the land owned by Kendal House. The woman in the cream silk gown ordered her men to bring in the prisoner: half helping, half dragging him across the cobblestones. She wore a heavy veil and a hooded cloak over her gown to conceal herself. There was a storehouse behind the stable block, smelling of old fruit and sawdust. In the distance, she could hear the noise of coachmen and drivers, drunken and raucous, waiting for their masters to leave the ball.

Mr. Silk was woozy, confused: it took him nearly a minute to come round. Perhaps she'd hit him a little harder than intended. She held up a candle and studied his face in the light. It was sad to see people growing older: to see their mouths droop and their necks sag. She smoothed her own jaw with her hand, satisfied with its tautness.

"All right," she said to the servants gathered at the door. "Leave us."

They backed out, shutting the door behind them. Silk groaned, eyes opening. He shrank back at the sight of her, cloaked and veiled.

"Now, now," she said brightly. "That's not at all how we pay our respects."

He didn't speak for a moment. That was something she had liked about Mr. Silk, back in the old days. He didn't try to impose his own opinions on her—unlike the other men in the Château. He took in her veiled face. She watched him piecing it together, the enormity of it, the *danger.*

He said shakily, "I never expected this."

"No?"

"Tell me your plan."

"You first," she said, crouching down beside him, resting her chin on her fist. "Didn't you get the rattle?"

"Of course I did," he said, his voice a croak. He looked terribly pale; there was a bruise forming by his temple. "A nice little threat."

She smiled at that, setting down the candle. The flame burned dangerously close to the sacking cloth piled by the wall.

"Not a threat," she said softly. "Just a reminder. That my time would come. Get Lillian's girl out of the way, Silk."

"But…"

"Do it." She leaned back on her heels, lifted her blade, and pressed it delicately to the softest part of his neck, directly under his chin. "Or I'll get *you* out of the way."

9

Quinn

Ask someone to marry you. That's what the duke said. The music stuttered, readying itself for the next dance—and in that moment the entire company seemed to turn in their direction, breaking into applause. They had been dancing beautifully, Quinn realized. She'd attracted grudging admiration from the whole room.

The duke gave her a small bow and then a steady look. He stepped back, as if waiting for her next move.

She was on her own. Lady Victoria had vanished. Mrs. Airlie, too, was lost in the crowd. Silk was presumably arriving in Berkeley Square, poised to negotiate her marriage settlement. Quinn could feel the clocks marking time, racing to midnight.

"May we talk?" she said. Her palms were sweating beneath her gloves.

"In private?"

"My chaperone seems to be otherwise engaged."

"Then let us search for her. If we choose to stop and take a little air along the way, then…"

She nodded, understanding. "So be it."

He offered his arm.

She took it.

They left the ballroom, the whole crowd parting to make way.

———

The hush enveloped Quinn and the duke as they passed into an unlit corridor running parallel with the ballroom.

"Out here," he said, dislodging her hand from his arm, opening a pair of French doors. "We can speak freely."

Cool air. Night sky. Quinn stepped out onto a little raised terrace perched above the outbuildings at the side elevation of the house. She could see the trees of Berkeley Square, hear the nighttime growl of the city beyond. They were forced into close proximity, penned in by a stone balustrade, sweet jasmine hanging overhead, plasterwork nymphs laughing on either side.

"What did you wish to say to me?" he said.

There was no hint of flirtation in his manner. It was just the two of them, and Quinn felt suddenly stripped back and exposed, snakeskin tumbling to the floor.

"I should be candid with you," she said slowly. "I came here tonight seeking a collaboration."

Truth.

"I will be candid with you in return." His voice was low. "I seek the same."

She held his gaze. "My object is to make a marriage."

And something changed. The duke's expression unraveled—and he said, the color rising in his cheeks, "That I cannot do."

The gloaming sky was thick with coal smoke. Quinn could hear the distant barking of a dog, offcuts of conversation floating up from the stable yard. Her heart accelerated.

"You...do *not* wish to marry?"

"I wish to marry, yes. And the alliance that would follow, with all the settlements required. But not a—not a full marriage."

Quinn said nothing. Her skin was prickling all over.

"Would you accept that?" His tone became more urgent. "I thought, from our very first conversation, that you—that you might be amenable to—" He broke off suddenly.

Strangeness, oddness, right up the spine. "An arrangement?"

"Surely, you're not seeking a love match, Miss White? You gave no sign of..." He pressed a finger to his temple. "You give the impression of..."

"What?"

"Of seeking a prize."

Quinn stiffened. "That is not the case at all."

Lie.

He stepped away from her. "I thought," he said, coloring, "that you had perceived an opportunity..."

The duke seemed to dissolve. It was a twisting of lights and colors and fabrics that Quinn recognized. She'd slipped out of her own skin too many times not to recognize when someone else was doing it, too.

An opportunity.

The shimmer to the ballroom. The dazzling glare of the electroliers. The thing she wanted being proffered on a gilded plate...

A perfect Ballyhoo. An intriguing proposition. Just not of her own creation.

"What do you mean," she said, "that we can marry, but have no marriage?"

He said nothing.

"Tell me," Quinn said, "or I shall go back inside."

Something crossed his face, a tiny flush. "A gentleman in my position is obliged to form an alliance. The appearance of marriage provides harmony to one's household. It provides an expectation of future issue."

Quinn recoiled, startled. "Issue?"

"Children. A line of succession." He paused. "Peace. Which is a hard-won thing, in any family."

"You want to have a *child*?" This was a good deal more than she had been expecting.

"No." He pressed his lips together. Then said briefly, "But one's obligations bear very heavily upon one."

There was a long silence. He lifted his hand to his cravat, adjusting it over and over.

Quinn said, studying him, trying to make sure she understood, "You wish to form a false alliance."

He said nothing. Then nodded—fast.

"You wish to do so because...?"

"I am attached to—another." His voice was hoarse. "I have pledged myself to someone else. But I cannot, I may not..."

Quinn reminded herself of the intelligence she had first received from Silk: that the duke was a charmer, a debaucher, a rake, and a flirt. Yet, this behavior did not seem to fit that description at all.

Doubtfully, she said, "You are...in love?"

He opened his mouth, then shut it again. "That is immaterial."

"Is it?"

"It should be."

"To whom? To me?" Her wariness was rising. "It seems rather a significant point, if you are seeking my hand."

"Why?" There was a spark of fire in his eye. "It seems this conversation has not been fruitful. I wish I had never raised the point at all."

Quinn paused. She decided to tread with care. "If you are in love with someone else, you ought to marry her."

The duke simply shook his head. "This person," he said, "is not available to me."

"So she is married already. You have been—engaged in adultery."

"No," he said, and it was his turn to look startled. "No, that's not it at all." He passed a hand across his face. "You should know," he added, "my liking of you is not wholly feigned."

"Your *liking* of me?"

"Yes. Our conversations. We have enjoyed most stimulating..."

She raised a palm to stop him. His capacity for concealment

alarmed her. "We've spoken three, four times at most. You do not know me at all, Your Grace."

Truth.

"Perhaps not, but…"

"This is an extraordinary proposition." Quinn felt heat rising in her cheeks. "And you have tricked me."

He started. "No."

"Yes. Absolutely *yes.*"

"Miss White…"

"Don't come any closer."

He extended a hand, then dropped it. "Madam," he said. "I unburdened myself in the spirit of candor. Because you seem to be the sort of person who prizes veracity."

Quinn felt her heart pounding. There it was again: the same sensation as when the duke invited her to the opera. The sense that she was being led down an unknown path. Dimly, through the frosted glass, she could see someone approaching, a figure creeping slowly toward the French doors. Mrs. Airlie, no doubt, ready to interrupt them, as planned.

"I do. And yet you are asking me to make false vows. It is— indecent."

The word made the duke flush more deeply. "If you wish to close this discussion, we shall. I ask simply that you exercise some discretion."

"I am not closing it. But we agreed to be candid with one another, did we not? So tell me. What do you want?"

"What do you mean?"

She very nearly laughed in astonishment. In the distance, she heard chimes—it was midnight. "By *marrying* me."

"Oh," the duke said—and his voice shifted again. It grew soft; it changed utterly. "That's simple. I should like to disappear."

Then he looked at her, his gaze straight and clear. "Miss White. Will you consider my proposal or not?"

Day Four
The Knot

1

Quinn

Life was a puzzle box. It was made up of innumerable little drawers—some locked, some not, with glinting clasps and metal teeth. Someone was playing a game with her. Quinn knew the signs.

There was a sharp tap at the door to the terrace. A female voice called softly, "Your Grace? Quinta?"

The duke's face immediately clouded over. "Anything you want—a contract, initiating payments in advance of dowry, you can have them. All I need is your hand. Do I have your agreement?"

Tap-tap-tap, more insistent this time. Quinn saw him turn toward it. He was reformulating his features, hardening over. It unsettled her. It made her realize what she looked like when *she* went into character.

"I—"

The door opened before she could reply.

"You're *here*." Mrs. Airlie was at the door, just as they had planned she would be if Quinn managed to secure a private meeting with the duke—ready to witness everything, close the deal, affirm her cousin's extraordinary virtues. Her eyes were bright and inquiring: *Done?*

"I have happy news," the duke said, before Quinn could speak—and he *was* the duke again: the words were drained of emotion. "The best."

Quinn felt her stomach lurch. There was a flare of victory across Mrs. Airlie's face. She shut her fan with a click. "But how *lovely*, Quinta, dear."

"I..."

A large crowd was spilling out of the ballroom. *It's in motion*, Quinn thought—*it's* all *in motion*. But her hands were not on the reins...

"I have not accepted," Quinn said.

Mrs. Airlie's chin snapped up. "You haven't?"

"No." Quinn blinked three times. *Some-thing-wrong.*

Not for nothing did Mrs. Airlie run the most formidable school in town. She turned, headmistress-like, to the duke.

"My cousin is overwhelmed with emotion. She requires a moment to recover her spirits."

The duke pressed his lips together, a tiny signal of frustration. But his voice was steady. "No matter," he said, pointing in the opposite direction. "I am sure my stepmother will put her mind at ease."

There were footsteps coming, a battalion bearing down upon them. It was Lady Kendal, accompanied by a retinue of footmen, her eyes glittering like her jeweled scarab.

———

They had planned the fourth move with such care. Quinn would secure a marriage proposal from the duke. His lawyers would meet with Miss White's faithful steward and family retainer, Mr.

Silk. These gentlemen would conduct the discussions around the bride's marriage settlements. Any questions on points of finance could be referred to that friendly moneyman, Mr. Willoughby. Any objections from the duke's nearest relations would be dealt with very smoothly by that charming chaperone, Mrs. Airlie. Quinn herself would glide through it all, on the arm of the duke.

Yet now, Quinn hesitated. The feeling of being shunted very neatly into position was absolutely foreign to her. It gave her pause.

The dowager duchess stood before them, eyes darting from her stepson to Mrs. Airlie, and back again.

"Max?" she said, her voice soft. "What is this?"

Lady Kendal was buttoned into an ivory-colored gown embroidered all over with locusts, a huge silver scarab clasped to her breast. The lamplight haloed her delicate heart-shaped face, making her dark curls shine.

The duke cleared his throat. "Miss White. You've met my dear stepmother." He paused. "Mama. I have—important news."

The duchess's expression shifted with the precision of a clockwork mechanism, landing on Quinn. Her gaze changed; it took on a dark and liquid quality. But she smiled. "Indeed?"

There was something impenetrable about Lady Kendal, something opaque, as if her roots had been dug deep, deep into the ground. She gave the outward impression of perfect, doll-like refinement—but there was absolute strength there.

"Your Grace," Quinn said, inclining her head.

The duchess moved closer. Her hair smelled of wood and oil. She wore no paint or powder. She was still youthful-looking, though her nose was faintly age-spotted.

"You," she murmured, showing little pearly teeth, "are the remarkable creature we saw at the palace."

Mrs. Airlie shifted. "My dear cousin Quinta was quite *astonishingly* brave…"

The duchess's smile was utterly cold. "Mr. Mellings reports

you were born in Cheapside. I hear your people made a perfect fortune. Yet, we've never seen you in our lives before."

Quinn glanced at Mrs. Airlie. "I've enjoyed an extremely quiet existence."

"But what is your motive, coming here?"

"My motive?"

"No woman goes wandering around Kendal House with my stepson late at night without intent. What is yours?"

The duke cleared his throat again. "Mama..."

Lady Kendal's eyes bored into Quinn. "I suspect you are seeking a husband."

The words hung like a dead weight in the air. The crowd was hovering at the end of the passage; the lamps buzzed overhead. A tense stillness descended over their circle.

"Perhaps, Your Grace," Quinn said.

"Perhaps?"

"I am considering the matter."

The duchess's eyes consumed her. "Good gracious, have you received so many offers you find yourself unable to choose between them?"

The duke flinched. "I am honored to have offered my hand to Miss White. And I am quite content to wait for her answer." He threw Quinn a look, as if seeking her approval.

Lady Kendal smiled. "Dear Max. Of course, you are." Her gaze switched back to Quinn, piercing. "Come, Miss White. Let us talk to one another. Alone."

———◆———

It was clear the duchess did not intend Quinn to be seen by any of her guests before this matter was resolved.

"In here," she said, arm linked to Quinn's. A door clicked open. "It is nice to be cozy sometimes."

It was a tiny room. Two lamps burned on a sideboard, casting a dull glow against silk-patterned walls. There was a delicate escritoire, bearing genteel clutter—an inkwell, several fat-handled pens, a stack of playing cards, notepaper emblazoned with the Kendal crest. This was a cabinet room, placed between two interior walls. The duchess squeezed her skirts around a small walnut table, brightly polished, pentagonal in shape.

"Sit," she said, indicating a tiny chair opposite. "Tell me your concerns."

The room was warm, heated by the gigantic chimney breasts rising through the central chambers of the house. The floor was thickly carpeted, and the walls were mirrored and gilded, creating the appearance of a dark jewel box. The duchess was repeated in the reflection a thousand times over, her silver scarab shimmering.

"Be absolutely frank."

Quinn sat down, sweat prickling her scalp. She examined Lady Kendal, wondering how to play her. She seemed too astute, her defenses too rigid, to be easily toyed with. More importantly, she might be aware of her stepson's affections for another person. She could even disclose the identity of that lady, if she was pressed with sufficient delicacy. Quinn did not wish to battle with an unknown rival.

"His Grace does not strike me as being ready to be married," she said, keeping her back straight, her chin raised. "Perhaps you can help me understand him better."

"Not ready?"

"I am not certain of...his affections."

"Has he asked you for your hand?"

"Yes."

"Then doubtless he is ready," she said, something caustic entering her tone. "Indeed, he is moving with greater alacrity than I could have ever anticipated. It is quite—" she paused "—disconcerting."

Quinn controlled her expression. "Is there any possibility he may be..." She was going to say *otherwise attached*, but she remembered the gravity in the duke's expression, the tone with which he'd asked for her discretion. *Don't press too hard, Le Blanc,* she warned herself. "He does not seem quite—happy."

Lady Kendal's brow furrowed. "You are young, Miss White," Lady Kendal said. "You are just beginning to learn the subtleties of life. Is the duke happy? No. I daresay he is *not* entirely happy. It wears upon him, this life, these obligations. He requires support. Marriage will provide that."

Quinn studied her. "His Grace said the same thing."

Lady Kendal smiled—the same cold line. "We are often of one mind, Max and I."

Quinn recalled the documents that Silk had gathered, the ones recounting the old duke's indiscretions, the steps Lady Kendal herself had taken to pay off his claimants. She remembered this woman was minded to tear down Quinn's own neighborhood. It seemed to Quinn that her most dangerous opponent was almost certainly facing her at this very moment.

"A marriage," she said, holding her nerve, "is typically accompanied by a financial settlement."

Lady Kendal smiled, unmoved. "A lady," she said softly, "does not generally talk about these matters."

Quinn knew she had to move with supreme delicacy. But she was determined not to leave this room without shoring up her position. "No," she replied, "but we are speaking frankly, are we not? Would His Grace be minded to make an initiating payment?"

Lady Kendal wound her fingers together. "An advance against your dowry?"

"Yes. A signal of his intent."

This was a crucial part of Quinn's plan. Any bride would be expected to bring her own fortune into a new marriage. But she wanted a little insurance, a first payment, just *in case* anything went awry.

"An advance against dowry is typically made when there is some expectation of the groom defaulting on a marriage settlement. Do you think us *likely* to default on any of our financial obligations?"

"My steward always counsels me to act with great care when it comes to signing contracts."

"Our name has been associated with honor and rectitude since time immemorial. Surely, that should give you confidence enough?"

Quinn spread her hands. "I hardly know. I am so ignorant of these matters."

Lady Kendal laughed shortly, an irritated sound. "Good gracious, how am I to set your mind at ease? Would you like to commission our moneyman to give you a close reading of the accounts?"

"Certainly, Lady Kendal, if you are offering it."

Her expression darkened. "I speak in jest, Miss White." She extended her hands across the lacquered, slippery surface of the table. "The world should have *no* concerns regarding the Kendal family's ability to meet a financial obligation." She hesitated, and then carefully pulled one of her rings from her finger. She held it up to the lamplight, a flash of amber. Slowly, she passed it to Quinn. "And neither should you," she added. "You may take this as a token of the household's intent." Her lips moved fast, as if correcting herself. "Of my intent."

Quinn didn't touch it. Lady Kendal's eyes were metallic: this was no token of friendship. Quinn knew people well enough to sense when they were trying to soften her up for the kill.

"I fear I am not quite the match you were hoping for, Your Grace."

"No," Lady Kendal said. "But I am bound to follow my stepson's wishes. His happiness is my only care."

Quinn studied the ring. "This is an extraordinary gift, Your Grace."

"Indeed, it is."

"Am I to take it that I have Your Grace's support?"

The chill in Lady Kendal's eyes had not lessened. But she said in a lower voice, "I was a stranger here myself once, Miss White. Kendal House is not always an easy place for a young woman to reside." She nodded in the direction of the ring. "Go on, take it. You can pawn it, if you really wish to."

Did Quinn trust her? Not in the least. Still, she picked up the ring. The gold had been warmed by Lady Kendal's hand; it glowed in her palm. Quinn knew jewels, but the ones she possessed were new-made, gaudy. This one was delicate and exquisitely crafted. It was an heirloom, old as the House of Kendal itself.

Hold your nerve, Quinn told herself. *Play on.* "Your Grace's generosity moves me very much," she said, folding the ring in her hand. She took a breath. "I am minded to accept the duke's suit."

The duchess's heart-shaped face was pale, focused. "Then surely," she said, "you should call me Mother?"

———

A great crowd had gathered outside the Duchess's cabinet room. The rumbling conversations died as the door opened. Lady Kendal smiled, ornaments tinkling softly, murmuring, "Goodness, what a lot of people."

The message could not have been clearer: a proposal of marriage had been made; it had been accepted. The duchess took Quinn's hand in her own and showed off the ring on Quinn's finger so that her guests and neighbors could see it. For a second, just a split second, Quinn wished it were all *true*. It was a very intoxicating thing, to soar above a flock of people as wealthy and exalted as these.

The duke emerged from the pack. His eyes met his stepmother's, and she offered him a microscopic nod: *resolved.* The relief on his face was clear. His eyes came to Quinn's. He bowed his head, a gesture of—what? Gratitude?

Mrs. Airlie hurried toward Quinn, arms outstretched, rhinestones glittering. "My dear child."

"*Now* you may say your congratulations, Mrs. Airlie," Quinn said, exhaling, touching Lady Kendal's ring. She decided to set any doubts very firmly aside. She would slice through the ocean like a liner, scattering tugboats, clearing impediments wherever they might arise. She faced the duke. "We have a wedding to prepare, Your Grace."

2

Tor

The heat and light coursing through the house repulsed Tor; the smell was revolting. Strangers everywhere, feasting on Kendal victuals.

She had spent the early hours of the evening in her private suite, dreading the night ahead. From the stable yard, she had heard clanking chains, trestle tables being winched into the ballroom, the creak of carts, the whinny of the horses. Part of her had felt a dangerous urge to seek out Max, confront him with his love letters. But she feared his dismay; that he would deny, deny, deny there was anything wrong. It was only ever Tor who spoke the truth. And this was always dangerous. She learned this as a child, tongue scrubbed with soap for speaking ugly words— while everyone claimed Papa was *not* sick, *not* cruel, that he was simply in mourning, not delirium.

So when she'd joined Max this evening to greet the arrivals— the first time in days they had crossed paths—she'd said nothing

at all. Their stepmother stood between them, smiling, already
locked in conversation with a wine-soaked archdeacon.

"Tor?" Max murmured. "Are you well?"

She nodded—fast, fierce. The company blurred, careening up
the stairs. Endless hands to shake; her skin crawled.

At last, she broke away from their party. "I need some punch."
She'd hitched her skirts and climbed the stairs, crossed the gallery
into the ballroom. "Yes, I will dance," she announced, advancing
on a gaggle of chinless young gentlemen lurking near the supper room. She pointed to the tallest among them; he gawped at
her as she approached. "You first." Papa's ring burned upon her
finger as he led her to the floor. While she danced, she observed
Max in conversation with Miss White, slipping off with her for
what appeared to be further private conversation. Tor felt a snag
of unease. First, the woman tried to sell them a horse; now, she
was nailed to Max's arm. Meanwhile, Lady Kendal was nowhere
to be seen, no doubt engaged in a thousand tedious conversations
in other corners of the house, in order to avoid any disagreeable
conversations with her stepdaughter.

I am completely alone here, Tor realized.

She selected another scared-looking gentleman to waltz with.
"And fetch me some wine," she said to a footman. She refused to
be a wallflower in her own home: if she had to suffer this ball,
she would do so with some vigor. The other guests were specu-
lating on the attraction between the duke and Miss White, but
she closed her ears to their gossip. She was still unsure what to do.

After several waltzes with a collection of thin-legged and un-
satisfying young men, she felt a flare of relief. Her bearded solicitor had entered the room and was standing by the fireplace.
She strode toward him, hand outstretched. He took it, sturdy
pressure against her fingers.

"Your ladyship appears to be enjoying herself."

"Not in the least. It is loathsome. I wish everybody would go
home."

He gave her a confidential smile. "Truthfully, I agree. I would far rather be sitting cozy by the fire. It would be even better if you were there with me."

"None of that, please," she told him. "You have a professional obligation toward me."

He sighed. "I do. And I'm a stickler for the formalities. Now, have you found your ammunition?"

She hesitated, wondering how to reply, but a voice spoke from behind her.

"My lady?" It was a footman, a blur of gray and yellow in his livery.

She turned. "Yes?"

"Lady Kendal would like to speak to you. With some urgency."

———

There was a crowd forming in the library passage, but they steered her in the other direction, to the blue room.

"Where is the duke?" she asked, glancing over her shoulder. "Where is Miss White?"

They didn't reply. "Her Grace says to wait here, if you please."

Tor felt a tingling of alarm. Had Max done it? Had he proposed marriage to a perfect stranger? She threw herself into an armchair, the ball booming through the walls, and watched the clock. Minutes passed. The suspense was gnawing at her: she jumped from her chair, determined to go and find Lady Kendal herself.

The door flew open; Lady Kendal swept in. "Tor, thank heavens."

"Mama? Whatever's happening?"

Her stepmother shut the door, took a breath. "Darling Tor. Abhorrent news. Max has just engaged himself to a perfectly dreadful woman. A fortune hunter."

Tor felt her chest tightening. "Miss White."

"Indeed—and I am most distressed."

She didn't seem distressed. If anything, she seemed angry,

rosebud lips pressed tight—and her voice carried a rigidity she never used with Tor.

Tor felt wrongfooted. "I thought you *wished* him to marry."

"To someone of suitable standing, yes. Not a spider who climbed out of a drain."

"Have you made an objection to Max?"

"Certainly not." Lady Kendal raised a hand, touched a smooth knot of her hair. "It is not my place to do so. I have shown the lady every courtesy, for now."

"For now?"

"Yes, Tor. But you must speak to him at once."

"Me?"

"Appeal to his reason. Tell him to remember what he owes his blood, his lineage, his ancestry. If your poor father were alive…" Her stepmother's voice shifted, modulating itself; her tone grew more sinuous. "A marriage to a lady of low birth, of poor standing, would leave an unutterable stain on the family." She straightened Tor's pearls. "On you, too, my darling Tor."

Tor could feel her body alerting her to something strange, something wrong. Her instincts told her that Lady Kendal was holding something back.

"You speak to him," Tor said with caution. "He listens to you most of all."

Lady Kendal shook her head, a tiny gesture of bafflement. "Whatever do you mean? You are his dear *sister*, Tor. His nearest blood relation. You must go to him *now*, before he ruins us all."

This room might have been made of china, it was so glazed and blue and cold to the touch. Lady Kendal never spoke with such force. Tor had always been dimly aware of the way her stepmother spoke to *other* people—in the household, or among her charities—with a certain reserve, even hauteur, befitting the Dowager Duchess of Kendal. But with her own stepchildren, she was always lenient, tender, soft. This change in manner unsettled Tor. She took a step backward, shaking her head.

"What if he is—in love?"

"In love? With a girl he's just met from—*Lord* knows where?"

"Perhaps."

Something moved in Lady Kendal's expression, something unreadable. "What makes you say that?"

Tor felt a trickle of sweat on her brow. "I found—several letters."

"To Max?"

"From Max. I didn't read them. Not all of them."

"To whom were they addressed?"

"I didn't look. They were—love letters." Silence, but for the crackling of the fire. "Perhaps they were intended for Miss White. I imagined they had been rejected, or else returned, but..."

"No." Lady Kendal raised a hand. "They were not sent to Miss White." Lady Kendal's clavicle was draped in gentle lace; her body was concealed behind soft taffeta. But her jaw was hard. "I know all about it."

Tor caught her breath.

"How *could* he have left us open to exposure like this?" Lady Kendal's face glowed in the light of the fire. "He has put me in an impossible situation."

Silence fell between them. Then Tor said, wariness still prickling all along her arms, "Exposure?"

"Your brother's heart will be his own undoing."

Tor exhaled. "Just like—Papa?"

Her stepmother's eyes darkened. "No. *Not* like your father at all." She came closer, reached for Tor's hand, pressed her fingers to Tor's wrist. Her grip was tight. "Victoria," she said. "You mustn't say a word to anyone about those letters." She squeezed Tor's arm. "Is that quite clear?"

Tor shook her off. "Whyever not?"

"For your own protection."

"Protection?" Tor almost laughed. "Protection?" Anger rose within her. "You offer me no protection at all."

Lady Kendal stiffened. "Whatever do you mean?"

"I know what you've been doing. You've withheld my trust from me. You've done nothing to safeguard my funds." Those initials were etched on her mind: *M. K. D.* She had presumed they referred to *Maximilian Kendal, Duke.* They could equally denote *Marie Kendal, Duchess.* Her cheeks grew hot. "Did you *know* that the household has been trying to break the protections around my inheritance?"

"Tor…"

"You make a very poor sort of governor if not. Papa left those funds behind for me. For *me.*"

She sounded like a child. She knew she did, and she loathed herself for it. But Lady Kendal didn't loosen her grip. She rubbed her thumb into the soft part of Tor's wrist, stroking it.

"Tor, darling…"

Tor shuddered. "Don't."

Lady Kendal retracted her hand. Suddenly, she looked smaller, wearier. "I've never taken sides between you children. I didn't when you were small. I have never done so since." Her expression changed again, looking pained. "On my honor, Tor, I have done nothing to betray your trust. Surely, you believe me?"

For years, they had lived together, dined together, slept under the same roof. Yet in that moment, Tor trusted only her own instincts, and they were needling her from top to toe. She was breathing more quickly.

"I hardly know what to believe."

Something firm passed across Lady Kendal's face. "I see. Well, I shall prove myself to you, once and for all." She pressed a finger to her neckline, nail snagging on the lace. "If you've discovered Max's letters, then others will do the same. I must take action." She turned on her heel.

"But who…"

Lady Kendal was heading for the door. "First, we need to put off this outrageous engagement to Miss White. We have no time for her, or her ghastly people. I've softened her up, in order not to antagonize your brother at such a sensitive moment. But we must dispose of her, as quietly and swiftly as possible. You'll help me."

"But…"

"Don't ask, Tor."

"*Who is it?* Who is Max's lover?"

"Tor…"

"*Tell* me."

Lady Kendal turned, eyes dark. "You truly wish to know?"

3

Mr. Silk

Silk staggered down the mews lane, back into Berkeley Square. A hansom came trotting around the bend in the road, and he hailed it in a croaking voice. It carried him east, back to the Château, against Quinn's instruction to wait for her outside Kendal House. She would be angry—but her feelings were no longer his greatest concern. He was serving different obligations now.

His skull felt as though it had been clamped in a vice; he was dazed and weakened by the blow to his head. When the cab reached Spitalfields, he stumbled out into the road, fishing for his key, trying and failing to connect it to the lock. The street was dark, figures moving in the brownish glow coming from the streetlamps at the end of the road.

He unlocked the door at last, slammed it behind him. The familiar scent of spirits and wax burned in his nostrils. His brain seemed to be stuttering.

His instructions were clear. To distract her, get her out of the way.

But Quinn was impossible to distract. She was dauntless, determined; she had always been so. Her face bloomed in his mind: watchful, laughing. He remembered the first time she ever tried on a wig. Curls, over-oiled, falling into her eyes. Her brow, furrowed, as she scratched her scalp furiously. *It makes me itch!*

He closed his heart to her. Lillian hadn't survived to raise her child. Silk had done his best to fill the void, to offer the sort of protection any child in the Château deserved. But his best efforts had their limits. He couldn't save her from this. Not if *he* wanted to survive.

Queens came and went. He didn't serve them. He served the Château.

For what was he without it? What was Silk without this house and its strictures, without the quiet, cunning rhythms of the Rulebook? Nothing but an empty vessel, a discarded old coat, worth nothing at all.

Certainty rose in him like bile, as he glimpsed the portraits of the prior queens lined up along the stairs. He knew what had to be done.

Silk entered the back parlor, feeling his way in the dark, unlocking the bureau with trembling hands. He withdrew the Rulebook, pressed it close to his chest. He didn't need to consult it. He knew exactly what it said.

CLAUSE 4. *The weaving of the Knot requires the ABSO-LUTE UNITY of the household—there can be only one hand upon the loom, one needle pulling thread. And if any CONTRARY FORCE should fray the silk, the household has full authority to halt the game, even deter the queen...*

Why do you do this? asked a voice in Silk's head. This work made him sick. It tarnished the soul. It was not a vocation. It was a disease.

But it was too late to change course now.

He locked the house, hailed a second cab, took the journey

westward to Spanish Place, trying not to doze, streetlamps blurring through the mist. Silk climbed out of the cab, muttering to
the driver to keep the change.

The road was silent, but there were threads of light visible
in Mrs. Airlie's house, behind her iron-barred shutters and her
weighted drapes. Something skittered across the pavement, a
mouse or a rat, as the hansom rolled off into the smoke-hazed
night. Otherwise everything was still.

He crossed the road and entered the Academy.

———————

It was half past four in the morning before he heard their voices
in the front hall. Silk stumped slowly across the drawing room,
trying not to stumble. There were still dots dancing in front of
his eyes. Distantly, he heard the doors opening, Mrs. Airlie's
voice exclaiming, "Victory! Well *done*, Le Blanc!" The lamplight swayed; the floor vibrated as they charged into the room.

"Good heavens—*Silk*! Where have you been?" A figure rustled
toward him, hands hovering at his temple. "You've been hurt!"

He tried to steady himself. "I had a fall, just a fall…"

Footsteps, faster than imagining; a whirlwind of silk. *Her* face,
blazing at him, all concern. "Silk?"

"Quinn…"

The drawing room collapsed upon itself; it folded in two—
and then it went black.

———————

He awoke on the floor, a fan flapping in his face, Mrs. Airlie's
voice in his ear, repeating his name, a buzzing sound… "Silk,
Silk, Silk…"

Struggling, he tried to sit up. Quinn swam into view, kneel-
ing beside him.

"You fainted. But you'll be quite all right." She turned, murmuring to someone. "Send for the physician. He must be examined."

"No, no, there's no need for that." A drink was pressed into his hand; Mrs. Airlie's fingers were digging into his back, helping him upright. His vision swirled again. "Good gracious," he said, feeling cold sweat all down his ribs, his thighs. "Good heavens, I'm so sorry…"

"You fell?" Quinn said, scrutinizing him. "Where?"

"In Berkeley Square, in the gardens, I…" He swallowed a sip of water, nauseous. "I tripped, clearly… Such an old fool…" He felt glad of his dizziness. This was the way to play it. Doddering old Silk, making half-witted errors…

"But you were on duty." Mrs. Airlie's voice cut across Quinn's. "You should have taken greater care."

Quinn glanced up. "Don't. No harm done." She patted Silk's shoulder. "We have made tremendous progress tonight, my friend."

His mouth was dry. "Ah," he said hastily, gulping his water, choking. "Tell me."

Quinn had removed her wig, and her real hair was falling untidily from where it had been pinned many hours before. Yet, her eyes were glittering; her face was glowing with resolve.

"No," Quinn said. "You need to rest. Mrs. Airlie and I will move matters forward." She rose. "Brandy, Mrs. Airlie?"

"Yes. A large measure, if you please."

A clink of crystalware; a gulp of liquor. The glass sparkled as Quinn handed it over; it made Silk wince.

"To the fourth move," Quinn said.

"To the Knot," Mrs. Airlie replied, sipping her brandy, grimacing as she did so. "And to thoroughly routing Lady Kendal."

"Well, that remains to be seen. She folded far too swiftly. I think we can safely assume she was dissembling, for the sake of smooth relations with her stepson. I would place bets on her making every effort to disrupt our game from here, to direct him to a bride of her choosing."

Silk's vision was blurring again. Dimly, he could see Quinn crossing the room, weaving around the sofas, light swaying.

Mrs. Airlie set down her glass. "I'm unsure. Lady Kendal will need to tread with great care, if she doesn't wish to sever friendly relations with His Grace. And she is known for her absolute allegiance to her stepchildren. I don't see how she could throw us off now."

"Nonsense, we know her type. A gorgon wearing kid gloves. She won't mount a direct attack—but she'll cause delays to the wedding; she'll obfuscate. I've no doubt she's holding out for a better match for the duke. Mark my words, there will be some impediment thrown our way by breakfast."

Silk nudged the leatherbound spine of the Rulebook with the heel of his boot. He had hidden it under Mrs. Airlie's couch.

"And what of your other love rivals?"

"Rival. Singular."

"He gave you *no* clue as to her identity?"

"None at all, other than to assure me she was not a married lady."

"Then she must be lowborn, or of very ill repute."

"Or an unseemly match. Like a widow."

Mrs. Airlie started. "You are not possibly suggesting…"

"I'm suggesting nothing. That is why *you* must search down all avenues. Meanwhile, I will think about how to separate the duke from his friends and relations, to tighten the Knot. Are we in agreement?"

Mrs. Airlie gulped her brandy. "Yes. But you need to rest, Le Blanc. We need our wits about us."

"I quite agree." Quinn aimed for the door. "Silk, get some sleep." In the next moment, she was gone.

The trembling in his hands grew worse; he struggled to lift his water glass to his lips. Hands helped him to his feet. It was Mrs. Airlie, lips close to his ear.

"For heaven's sake, Silk," she said, voice low. "What happened?"

He pressed a hand to his pounding head. "Your maid."

Mrs. Airlie's pulled back. "She resigned, she…"

Silk shook his head. "Abducted."

Mrs. Airlie sucked in her breath. "Is she…"

"Quite safe. Paid for."

"Paid…"

"She was taken to the haberdasher's shop on Roman Road." He leaned on the sofa, supporting himself. "There is an outside influence meddling in this job. Your maid was taken as a token of intent."

Mrs. Airlie's face became immobile. "I see."

"Mrs. Airlie…"

"My security has been breached."

"But the Academy is quite safe, I am certain there will be no further…" Silk allowed the words to trail off.

"Safe?" Two bright spots of color appeared in Mrs. Airlie's cheeks. "*Safe*, when my own maids are held to ransom?" She took a breath. "My loyalty is to the girls upstairs. My students. *Their* protection is of paramount importance. If your presence here has compromised their safety…"

Silk raised his hands. "Mrs. Airlie, please…"

"Go, Silk. At once. You *and* Le Blanc. I want you both out of the house."

"But Quinn…"

Silk watched with grim satisfaction as Mrs. Airlie's face hardened. "Tell the queen I have tendered my resignation."

———

He had to do it. The Rulebook demanded it: he needed to separate his quarry from her friends. Silk crept along the passage, knocked on Quinn's door.

"Who is it?"

"Me," said Silk. "I must speak with you."

"You *need* to go to bed—but come in."

He pushed open the door. A figure was changing behind the painted screen, hands waggling as clothes were slung across the room—petticoats, chemise, corset, velvet bows...

"Quinn," he said. "We must leave."

Her face appeared around the screen, shining with grease paint. The candle was bobbing under the eaves. "Leave?"

"Mrs. Airlie has—Mrs. Airlie has been taken ill."

Quinn emerged from behind the screen, frowning, adjusting her nightdress. "What d'you mean? I'll go to her."

Silk raised a palm. "She doesn't wish to see you."

Quinn looked bewildered. "Silk? What is this?"

He sealed his mind, made his face blank. "You need to pack your things. At once."

———

It was an odd thing, knowing someone. Knowing them so well, being able to predict their every move. Of course, Quinn obeyed him; she trusted him. It made his stomach writhe with guilt. But it had to be done.

They took their own phaeton, the one from the Château. Mrs. Airlie refused them use of the hired brougham.

"Silk," Quinn said. "Tell me what is going on."

"It's delicate." He clicked the horses off, praying his vision would hold. The moon completely shrouded from view by clouds. "The less you know, the better."

"The less I..." Quinn made an exasperated sound. "Don't *shelter* me, Silk."

He shook his head, biting his lip, turning them toward Oxford Street. They would head east, then dip toward the river, make for the house at St. James Garlickhythe.

"Silk! Answer me. I am the *Queen of Fives*."

She rarely used her title. There was no need to. The two

of them worked like cogs, teeth meeting, turning together as smoothly and regularly as any clockwork mechanism. Or so it used to be.

"Forgive me," he said. "I can say no more."

"My clothes, my things—they're all back at Mrs. Airlie's."

"She'll have them sent on."

"But I require Mrs. Airlie's assistance. You know how the fourth day must go. I'll need to separate the duke from his friends and relations. But I can't extract him by myself; I'll require a chaperone."

"Then we'll recalculate."

"How? We have two days left. Less than that—every minute counts." She twisted in her seat. "What were you *doing* in Bethnal Green?"

"Recruiting men. For the fifth move."

"But that should have been settled *days* ago."

Silk flicked the reins; the pony accelerated. "There's no need to concern yourself."

"*Concern* myself?" The sky loomed black and purple, empty of stars, thick with mist. The heat had dropped; there was a chill to the breeze.

"I am taking care of everything," Silk said, skull throbbing. "I always do. I always have."

———

Silk would never forget the election that had taken place at the Château twenty-five years before.

There had been two candidates.

Lillian Quinn—charming, clever, loved by all. She was nursing a daughter. The father had long vanished, as fathers in this city often did. The household had closed ranks around Lillian, protecting her fully.

And then there was the troublemaker. Stony-faced, ruthless, eternally unpopular. Yet, spectacularly talented.

She was the one who pushed for the vote.

"I want to be queen," she'd told Silk. "I'm running the best tables. Lillian doesn't even need to come with me when I'm in disguise. I'm twenty. I'm ready for it."

"I don't know," he said—as he said to all the queens-in-waiting. "We might need to wait a little while before advancing you."

She'd pressed him, goaded him, used every manipulation she could think of. She'd riled Cook, then every player in the Château; she'd worked them all into a frenzy so that finally Lillian came to him and said, "Good God, Silk. Call the election. The girl's right: she's running her own games, far better than the rest of us."

"Then we'll need someone to stand opposition."

"*I'll* put my hat in the ring, if that's what the Rulebook requires. But tell her it's just a point of procedure. She deserves the crown, Silk."

Elections.

They were sacred things.

He remembered the night as if it were yesterday. The players entering the back parlor. Silk's gloved hands hovering over the ballot box. Nibs scratching against paper, ink dripping on the stained floorboards. The fire, crackling in the grate. The smell of wax and resin, the note cards fluttering gently on the sideboard.

And afterward—in silence, but not alone, with Cook on hand to check the tally—he counted the votes.

"Lillian," he said to the assembled company, concealing the tremor, the surprise, in his voice. "*Lillian* for queen."

Quinn's mother paled. Her eyes went straight to their troublemaker, who was bunching her pearl-colored skirts in her fists.

"Me?" said Lillian. "Are you sure?"

She was right to be startled. Because their troublemaker was good. She was great. Not just at cards—at disguises, too. At modulating her voice, her face, her soul. Fast as the wind and made of snakeskin; she'd been trained by Lillian, but she was born to rule this place. Silk could sense a great queen in the making.

And he had voted for her.

But the rest had gone the other way. The troublemaker had started too many quarrels in the household to win the election.

Silk saw their troublemaker's eyes fix on the bureau, on the amulets and bits of string, on the fresh, clean note cards tucked into the drawer. She looked dazed.

"But I earned it," she said, voice cracking. "I'm—the best."

"Cook checked the votes," Silk said, uncertain. "Didn't you, Cook?"

"Fair's fair," said Cook. "Lillian won fair and square. Don't be sour about it."

"Come," Silk said swiftly to his troublemaker. "Come and talk."

He steered her from the room before she could say something she might regret. The others were already circling Lillian in the wavering candlelight, making obeisance, forming the sign of the crown on their heads as they bowed...

Silk and the girl went to the roof of the Château, where it was dark and cold. Christ Church steeple loomed over them, unreal in the mist.

"I'll have my revenge," the girl said.

Silk sighed. "Wait a little. Lillian won't want to reign forever. She has a child to think about."

"Did you vote for me?"

Silk pursed his lips. "Conclave is a confidential matter."

"Did you?"

He hesitated. "Yes."

"Liar."

He saw it then, the pain in her eyes. She wouldn't believe him. *Couldn't* believe him. Wouldn't permit herself to trust any living soul other than herself. He knew what she was feeling. He'd felt it himself before. He comprehended better than anyone what it felt like to be alone on the streets, alone in the world. To *long* for a place like the Château, a home.

"I…"

She didn't let him finish. She pointed to the House Opposite. "See that? It's dark. If you ever see a light, you'll know I've returned. You'll know it's my time."

Silk frowned, shaking his head. He underestimated her, he always did. "Look here, you mustn't leave now…"

She didn't jump. She didn't fly. But she ran away from him—lightly, rapidly—across the roof, with practiced steps, as if she'd rehearsed her escape, just in case she'd ever need it. As if she'd always imagined she'd be discarded in the end.

"Don't—" he began.

But she was gone.

The phaeton pulled up in front of the gates outside "Miss White's" residence at St. James Garlickhythe. Quinn jumped to the ground, not waiting for Silk to follow. He hauled himself from the driving seat, struggling with the reins.

"Silk," Quinn said, turning back to him. "This won't do."

"Good," he said as he picked his way across the cobblestones, fishing for his key. "That's good. It's all getting far too complicated. Let's simplify. Let's target those old shipping merchants again. We could even try…"

"No, Silk."

Her throat trembled.

But her voice was steady.

"Stand down," she said.

Hands shaking. Flesh leaping. *Go away, get out, don't come back…* Quinn hadn't used those words but that's what she meant when she made him return his keys.

What gave her the right? What gave any of them, any of these queens, the right to lord it over him? When all he did was serve their interests, protect them, keep everything tick-tick-ticking to *perfection*.

But then he reminded himself: this was how it had to go.

Sunrise was breaking overhead. Silk stood shivering on a muddy street corner at the junction between Poultry and Cornhill. He'd taken only one thing with him.

A man approached, per appointment. His scarf was pulled up over his nose, hiding his features. "Mr. Silk?"

Silk whirled around. "Here," he said, opening his greatcoat, extending the Rulebook with a shaking hand. "Take this to your mistress."

The man took it, frowning slightly, flipping it open. It made Silk's lungs burn, to see it treated with so little respect.

"Any message?"

Silk had a lump in his throat. "Tell her the Knot is underway. That I've distracted the child, separated her from her friends. She'll understand what I mean."

The game fizzed and crackled in his hands. He had never played it alone before.

4

Quinn

The news of the duke's engagement was carried in all the morning papers. *Opera Glasses* took a gushing tone, per Quinn's not-so-gentle encouragement. Mr. Mellings scolded the cruel gossips who suggested the marriage was being brokered for mercenary reasons, to unite two mighty fortunes in a single awe-inspiringly wealthy house. ***And it is our fervent hope the new Duchess of Kendal extends largesse to all those who count themselves among her greatest, truest friends.***

Quinn had woken with a start, rising abruptly from brief and ragged sleep. In the house at St. James Garlickhythe, gray light trickled through the cracks in the drapes, the distant sound of foghorns sounding far along the river. She crawled from her bed, mouth dry, head aching. The sash windows were smeared and dirty; they shuddered as she forced them open to let in a little breeze. The air smelled faintly sulfurous.

"Have we anything for breakfast?" she asked the ancient steward, as she came down the stairs in her dressing gown. "And have we heard from Mrs. Airlie?"

He averted his gaze from her state of en déshabillé, bowing low. "Porridge in the breakfast parlor, ma'am. And no message from Mrs. Airlie."

What on earth was the reason for her resignation? Quinn had banged on Mrs. Airlie's door before departing Spanish Place, to no avail.

"I've been taken ill," Mrs. Airlie had called back.

"So suddenly?" Quinn said, disbelieving. "Let me in."

"No. Please leave."

Clearly, she'd exchanged some angry words with Mr. Silk, no doubt over some point of order or protocol—but he'd refused to explain it. "She has every right to tender her resignation if she wishes" was all he'd said.

At first, Quinn had been exasperated, and then bewildered, and then she grew frightened. For Silk to obstruct her, to conceal information, was so out of character as to make her feel utterly wrongfooted. "Stand down," she told him—sure he would crumble.

Instead, he said, voice low, dangerous, "That is your prerogative, of course."

She took his keys to the Château, hands shaking, unable to believe it. Unable to *look* at him. "Just for now," she said.

"Of course. It is a point of order." He passed them to her, face cold. "I understand."

Then he turned and walked away.

No matter, she told herself now, heart hammering. She was sitting in the breakfast parlor, picking at her meager gruel, forcing herself to eat.

She would simply have to do this by herself.

Yet, to do it *alone*...

It wasn't pain she felt. It was something murkier, unhappier still—a sense of wrongness right in her gut. To lose *Silk*, of all people...

"Invitations and messages, ma'am," said the steward, placing a mountain of cards and letters on the table. She let out a shuddering breath and sliced open the first one. It bore the bloodred crest of Kendal House. The hand was strong and slanting, dashed out at speed:

I find myself obliged to attend a breakfast party offered in congratulations for my impending nuptials. If it would suit you to move our preparations forward with some expediency, will you suffer the tedium and join me? I understand the Archbishop is likely to attend, who of course will perform the service. Pray send me your favorable reply by return express and
Know me to be
Ever yours
Most sincerely,
Maximilian Kendal

A tiny card had been enclosed with the letter. Quinn made herself scan the particulars. *Cordially invited... Breakfast party at the house of Mr. and Mrs. Charles Hillyard... Bruton Street...* It seemed the Hillyards were determined to gloss over the fact that their own daughter had projected as a future Lady Kendal, and were determined to be the first to congratulate the duke on his happy news. Well, she decided, finding her resolve, they could congratulate his fiancée, too.

"Accepted," Quinn said, passing the card to the steward. She opened an envelope marked with the household banners of the Rochesters.

My dear Miss White,
It gives me great regret to tell you that urgent business

compels me to quit London for the remainder of the year,
leaving me ever very glad to be
Sincerely yours,
Hugh Rochester

"No reply," Quinn said to the steward, setting it aside. She summoned her strength, trying to cast aside her doubts. "Now, has our old friend the archdeacon arrived yet?"

The steward bowed even lower. "He's in the churchyard."

———◆———

Quinn dressed swiftly, buttoning herself into her most sensible dress—cabbage-colored serge, with very sober sleeves. She hastened down the winding path to the churchyard, pushing open the moldering door to the church.

"Archdeacon?" she called softly, boots echoing on the flagstones, eyes adjusting to the gloom.

The archdeacon was seated in one of the pews, clutching his walking stick. He turned, bench creaking, expression bristling with indignation. "It is *intolerable*, absolutely *intolerable*, that you should keep putting me in this position. What on earth am I to say if anyone asks me what I'm doing here?"

Quinn shut the heavy door, breathed in the musky smell of incense, and advanced on him. "You may tell them you've come to provide spiritual counsel to a bride on the day before her wedding."

"On the day before her wedding? Are you hiring a carriage to Gretna Green? You're only just engaged. Which, by the way, is the most loathsome piece of chicanery I have *ever...*"

"I need your assistance." Quinn slid into the pew, folding her gloved hands, making her expression pliant. "I need you to procure me a special license to be married. Immediately."

"No, no, *no.* This has to stop. You are imperiling every—"

"Archdeacon," Quinn said, raising her hand. "Time is not on my side. You know what needs to be done."

"You are a savage. You are utterly outrageous."

"Indeed, I am. Now, tell me. The Archbishop of Canterbury holds the authority to grant special marriage licenses, correct?"

"Yes, but…"

"He can override the usual procedures, the reading of the banns, the necessity to reside in a certain parish, and so on?"

"In *extraordinary* circumstances, and *only* to—"

"Peers and peeresses of the realm, yes, I'm quite aware. The Duke of Kendal meets that category."

"You would need a proctor to act on behalf of both parties, to present the case to His Grace. It would need to be a person of high standing within the church to…" The archdeacon flushed. "*No.* Absolutely not."

"Yes, Archdeacon. *You* must present our case to the archbishop."

"On what earthly grounds?"

"Christian duty, naturally. Our overwhelming desire to enter the holy state of matrimony."

"But it would take me weeks, months possibly, to secure an audience with His Grace."

"We are in luck. I am due to be seeing him for breakfast in—" Quinn checked her pocket watch "—ninety minutes." She glanced up, fixing the archdeacon with a gimlet stare. "I would hate to discuss your indiscretions with him."

The archdeacon's face clouded over. "I would like to discuss this matter with Mr. Silk."

Regret pricked at her. "Mr. Silk is not available."

"*Make* him available. Indentured servitude is one thing, but this is going too far. I insist on discussing fresh terms."

"You can discuss them with me. Although they seem quite clear."

"With you?" The archdeacon's voice echoed around the church. He lowered it, said through his teeth, "*You* are off your head."

Quinn folded her hands to keep herself still. "Archdeacon. We have done a great deal of business together. But you are not the only clergyman in the Church of England. I have eyes on priests and prelates in every diocese from here to the borders, and I *will* be married tomorrow, in one parish or another, come hell or high water, whatever *you* may say about it." She paused. "Are you refusing to oblige me? Once you renounce your oath of allegiance to the Château, there is no going back, you know."

The archdeacon regarded her with undiluted dislike. "You do realize that if you keep shooting your arrow so very high, you'll one day miss your mark?"

Quinn sighed. "I shoot my arrow where I must. Do I have your agreement, Archdeacon?"

He rose to his feet, wrinkling his nose. "Absolute chicanery."

Quinn returned to the house, thinking. This breakfast party was precisely the sort of thing she had been afraid of: that the duke's friends and relations would remain glued to his person. It focused her mind: she would need to extract him from their clutches, to avoid any risk of derailment.

She took a tepid bath, changed into a satin gown of emerald green, placed Lady Kendal's amber ring on one hand, and pinned her hair. She scrubbed any last remaining flecks of stain or powder or maquillage from her face, affixed a slender choker to her neck, and pulled on her French kid gloves. Her vision was fuzzy from lack of sleep, her headache was intensifying—but all doubts had to be set aside. Her eyes were now firmly set upon her prize.

"Carriage, please!" she called downstairs. "Quick as you can!"

It was a lonely drive to Mayfair; she drummed her fingers against the armrest, wondering whether Silk was awake. There was a mist hanging over Bruton Street as she descended from the phaeton, driven by a cab driver she'd bribed to play grooms-man. The Hillyards' breakfast party was being held in a flat-faced stone house on the right-hand side of the street, and the hall was already crowded with guests, and Mrs. Hillyard was positioned at the front door, clearly warned of her arrival. She was greeting Quinn with a steely smile, directing her straight toward the garden, when a voice said:

"Good morning, Miss White."

The duke was waiting for her in the hall. He smiled. "What a great pleasure."

Quinn's chest jolted. It startled her, the realization that she was *glad* to see him.

She kept her expression grave. "Your Grace."

He took her hand, offering a stiff but courteous bow under the cold eye of Mrs. Hillyard.

"Shall we go outside?" he said.

"By all means."

They were engaged, which meant they could walk together arm in arm without causing consternation. The party was being held in a dark square garden, and a long table had been placed on the terrace, laid with a blistering white tablecloth and surrounded by sun parasols. But there was no sun to speak of, only a dank breeze and a thunderous sky. The other guests looked as pinched and sleepless as Quinn, but there was a flurry of interest when she walked through the French doors.

"The principal matter we need to discuss," the duke said in an undertone, "is the date for the wedding. My people will speak to yours to settle it. To whom should they direct their inquiries?"

Straight to business, then. "They may apply directly to me. But I should tell you, I would not favor a long engagement."

"Nor I. A few weeks should be quite sufficient."

"Why wait so long?" Quinn glanced over her shoulder. "Tomorrow would suit as well as any other day, no?"

The duke's brow quivered, as if he was startled. Quinn raised her own in return. He pressed his lips together, as if making up his mind. "It would, indeed. And I have already given my household instructions to prepare a wedding."

"Excellent. Then let us expedite matters."

As if on cue, Quinn could see an eminent figure being escorted by Mrs. Hillyard on to the terrace, causing the general company to scramble to their feet. "Splendid," she said brightly. "The archbishop is here."

"With my stepmother," the duke said with a slight frown.

Quinn followed his line of vision. Sure enough, behind the archbishop was the Duchess of Kendal, in cobalt satin, ruffled with oyster-pink organza from chin to waist. Her hat was very small, topped with scarlet bows and blue feathers, perched at a quizzical angle. Quinn cursed her inwardly. She wished to speak to the archbishop herself.

Lady Kendal's eyes lit on Quinn and her stepson.

"Come," Quinn said, touching the duke's arm, indicating the table. "Let us feast."

———◆———

Some care had been taken with the seating arrangement, and Providence was shining on Quinn when she found herself seated directly next to the Archbishop of Canterbury himself.

"Your Grace," she said in greeting.

"Miss White," he replied. His long fair hair was combed neatly behind his ears; he had a calm, blue gaze. He was wearing a rather serious-looking morning suit, not his vestments and surplice— *Rather a disappointment*, Quinn thought. "I understand we have a mutual acquaintance."

"Oh?" Quinn said, with innocence.

"Archdeacon Green speaks very highly of you."

"The dear Archdeacon," Quinn said. "How nice of him."

"He sent me an express, advising that you young people wish to be married with some haste."

Quinn sliced her kippers. "He did advise it, yes."

"Is it your sincere wish to be married?"

Lying to the archdeacon was one thing, lying to the arch*bishop* was quite another.

"It is my sincere wish," Quinn said, "to act always in accordance with the dictates of my heart."

"Hmm," the archbishop said. And then, more carelessly, "You know there is the matter of a fee."

The duke was watching them from the opposite side of the table, frowning slightly, trying to follow the conversation.

"Is there?"

"Forty guineas. Dreadfully dull."

"Mm," Quinn said, swallowing her kippers. "Quite dreadful."

A footman approached. "Your Grace. Mrs. Hillyard asks if you will spare Miss White to come and sit with her and Lady Kendal."

The archbishop gave Quinn a level stare. "Your new mama awaits."

Quinn dabbed her mouth with her napkin. "She has been extraordinarily kind." She rose from her seat. "Good morning, Archbishop. We shall engage with you directly on the matter of the—fee."

Up the terrace Quinn went, passing sundry viscountesses and baronesses, sliding into the chair indicated to her. A small hand pressed itself to Quinn's glove.

"Miss White. My dear."

Quinn could have hardly been seated closer to Lady Kendal if she tried; she was practically perched on the duchess's lap.

"How nice it is," Quinn said, "to have breakfast al fresco."

"Isn't it?" the duchess said—smiling, looking perfectly well rested, but with an unmistakable tension in her jaw. Quinn felt her skin prickling, as if seated next to an electrical device. She lifted a butter knife, reached for some toast. The amber ring reflected the light.

"Lady Kendal," she said. "I wonder if we might use your family chapel for the wedding."

The duchess blinked, as if caught off guard. "A rather pert question."

"Forgive me," Quinn said smoothly. "I am a bundle of quite unimaginable nerves. I only ask because I originate, as I'm sure you know, from a very *different* sort of parish to yours. I could not sleep last night, thinking how dreadful it would be for the duke to be forced to marry in Cheapside."

The duchess slid the butter dish toward her. "I appreciate your scruples." She smiled again, showing all her pearly teeth. "The wedding chapel at Mount Kendal, in Derbyshire, is very fine. I was married there myself. It would make for a charming spring wedding."

Lady Kendal's strength was on display today: one could see the rigid lines of her arms, the tautness of her shoulders.

"I would *adore* that," said Quinn, slicing her toast. "Although I fear we cannot wait for spring."

She felt the duchess tense.

"No?"

"The archbishop told me all about the special license." Quinn nibbled delicately at her toast. "He seemed quite set upon the notion."

The duchess was silent for a moment, as if calculating. "A special license," she repeated. "I was not aware my stepson was minded to move at such extraordinary pace. It is very nearly— unseemly."

Quinn set down her butter knife, amber ring flashing. "I presume we still have your blessing?"

She saw a spasm of anger cross Lady Kendal's face. It was quickly masked.

"Of course, my dear," she said. "The Kendal family has never cared one jot about the gossip of strangers."

"Then perhaps we might consider the chapel at Kendal House, for the wedding?"

Lady Kendal chewed her own toast, then swallowed. "I am bound to your wishes, my dear Miss White."

"I am thinking to include orange blossom in the bouquet. Would Your Grace approve? For jewels, I have a few family pieces, but of course I know there is a certain tradition regarding the Kendal brides." Silk had shown her old pictures of the family tiara, which she guessed was now held in the bank vault at Coutts. It was formed of quite stunning diamonds, which could detach to form a rivière necklace.

"Yes," the duchess said stiffly. "I wore the Kendal tiara at my own wedding." She set down her own butter knife with a soft clang. "You have given this a good deal of consideration, Miss White."

"Oh, no, not at all. Everything is a perfect tumult in my head. I would much rather leave everything to you. But I would hate to impose *any* inconvenience upon you."

"Indeed. You struck me last night as a young woman who knows her own mind. And cuts her own path."

"In the matter of a wedding, one simply wishes to survive the day." Quinn sipped her coffee; it was bitter black. "But that is quite enough on the matter from me. I will refer further questions to the duke."

"Nonsense," said Lady Kendal. "I am completely at your service. You may direct any question you like to me."

There it was again: absolute power. Quinn smiled, matching it. "You are too generous." She caught a flash of movement in the corner. A guest, late for the breakfast, lingering at the top of the table. Hair slicked with wax, face shining and smooth, nattily attired in a bright cerulean jacket.

Willoughby.

Quinn felt a flash of surprise. Their informant—here? At the Hillyards' breakfast?

"Our moneyman, Mr. Willoughby," Lady Kendal said dryly,

following Quinn's line of sight. "I daresay he's here to grill you about your dowry."

Willoughby's eyes lit on Quinn's just for a moment. They both glanced away at once.

"How charming," Quinn said. "It will be a pleasure to know him."

Lady Kendal was watching her intently. "Indeed."

At the other end of the table, the duke rose to his feet. Then he crossed the terrace, shaking Willoughby's hand. Mr. Willoughby leaned in, murmured a brief word in the duke's ear. The duke listened, expression grave.

"More coffee?" said Lady Kendal, proffering a cup. The liquid was scalding hot.

By the time Quinn looked back across the terrace, both men had vanished inside the house.

———◆———

Fifteen minutes passed, but the duke did not reappear. Lady Kendal had turned her attention to the viscountess on her right hand, and Quinn found herself sucked into conversation with bright-eyed Sonia Hillyard—"Is it *very* smoggy in Cheapside? Can you even see out of your windows? Are you *really* richer than the Rockefellers?"—but her attention was distracted. She needed to keep the duke separated from his friends and relations, not ensconced with them.

"Excuse me," Quinn said, rising to her feet. "I must go and wash my hands."

The noise from the garden fell away as she entered the house. The front hall was dark, smelling of sugared fruit and beeswax. She heard the murmur of a male voice from the dining room: the duke. She held her breath, lingering by the door.

"I am set on this course," His Grace said.

Willoughby's voice was low. "And I congratulate you. But

speed is the enemy of prudence. You should wait a little before making any large transfers."

"No. Pay Miss White the sum she demands. I wish to move this matter forward."

Quinn's chest expanded in sheer relief.

"Very well. You can't blame me for sounding a note of caution. Somebody has to keep an eye out for your interests."

The duke's tone was warm. "You are *my* miser, and for that I blame you not at all."

Quinn peered through the crack in the door. The duke was seated in a chair, arm resting on the polished dining table, smiling. Mr. Willoughby faced him. In this weak light, Willoughby's age seemed to catch up with him. It made him seem more human, less brittle. His jacket was garish and foppish, his features pointed and impish—but there were lines and crinkles around his eyes, a slackness to the skin of his neck. There was something tender about the way he leaned down and placed a finger under the duke's chin, about the way he tilted it upward...

Quinn felt something tumble into place.

She turned and swept away.

5

The Duke

Willoughby kissed him. He smelled the same as always, of honeyed wax and his own skin. His mouth was the nicest thing about him. Soft, slightly swollen.

"Is that all?" the duke said, laughing, when Willoughby straightened up. "Be as parsimonious as you like with my money, but don't scrimp on the other things."

"Good heavens, we're in the Hillyards' dining room!" Willoughby returned the duke's smile. "Anyhow, many happy returns of the day for yesterday."

The duke flushed. Then he said calmly, "My birthday present will be seeing this business finally settled. We're nearly there, Willoughby."

Willoughby raised a brow. "And I really *can't* persuade you to slow down?"

"I see no reason for delay. Miss White is eager for a fast transaction."

"Apparently. But what does your stepmother think?"

The duke frowned. "I've made my choice. Lady Kendal knows my wishes."

Willoughby touched his chin. "I fear Lady Kendal may have hoped for a slightly more—elevated match for you."

The duke felt a flare of annoyance. "First, you pressed me to marry. Now, I've complied, you decry my choice. I have done exactly as Lady Kendal wished."

"And she has done the same for you."

"Indeed. We have an excellent accord."

"Then do not break it now."

The duke didn't care for the direction of this conversation. "She has raised no objection with me. Has she sent you to cast aspersions against my choice of bride?"

"Me? Certainly not."

"Then let us drop the matter. You can manage my pocket-book, but not my family relations."

Willoughby pressed his lips together. "Very well."

"I see I have offended you."

"Not in the least." Willoughby laughed shortly. "I am startled by your sudden alacrity in this matter. But your marriage is your concern, not mine."

"It's *our* concern, surely?" the duke said, tightness in his voice. "You have been all for it."

"For the sake of your estate, not for any reasons of—" Willoughby paused "—personal subterfuge."

"Subterfuge?" The duke's stomach clenched. "Is that what you call our—friendship?"

The real word was on the tip of the duke's tongue; he longed to say it.

Yet, he feared being rebuffed. Affecting coolness, he went on, "You fairly forced me into this position. You should be delighted that I've found a solution to please all parties. Who knew Miss White would be such a perfect candidate?"

"Nobody," said Willoughby grimly, touching the crystalware on the sideboard. "Certainly not me."

"What *is* your objection? Surely, it's not a question of rank. Miss White's low position in society is a decided advantage. No family, no questions to answer, no fear of annulment in the absence of a full marriage. Presumably, she wants this alliance quite as much as I do, for her own advancement. Do you think we'd have nearly as much room to maneuver with a girl born in Berkeley Square?"

Willoughby hesitated, adjusting his jacket. "You know so little about her."

"I hardly know Sonia Hillyard any better."

"But you've conducted no investigations into Miss White's background."

"The lawyers have been picking over her financial papers since last night. Although by all accounts, they're a load of nonsense."

Willoughby looked at him askance. "Whatever do you mean?"

"I hear there is a suggestion that her family history is a fiction, all concocted."

"Good gracious. According to whom?"

"Miss White herself."

A muscle moved in Willoughby's jaw. "You're not serious."

"She was completely candid with me. I presume she was born on the wrong side of the sheets, or some other murk. But what do we care? We're hardly in any position to judge her for presenting one face in public and another behind closed doors."

Willoughby kept his eye trained on the sideboard. "Your sister told me she thinks Miss White is a perfect charlatan. I'm astonished you don't have the same powers of perception."

"Oh, Tor thinks everybody is determined to destroy her."

"No," Willoughby said coldly. "Just you."

The duke felt a twist of guilt, right in the middle of his chest. Whatever he did, whatever action he took, matters always wound their way back to this. He was trapped, permanently, in the Kendal household, in all its tangles and briars.

"What did Tor say?"

"She summoned me two days ago, to demand sight of her inheritance. She turned up *at my house* yesterday to collect the papers in person, totally unannounced."

"Why shouldn't she have access to those papers?"

Willoughby flushed. "Max, I had a visitor. You understand? If she had realized—"

The duke could feel his heartbeat accelerating. "What *visitor*?"

Willoughby's smile faltered. "Max."

"Are you entertaining other gentlemen?"

Willoughby's eyes went straight to the door. "For heaven's sake. Lower your voice."

The duke rose to his feet. "Willoughby."

Willoughby's flush deepened. "I don't see how that is your affair." For a moment, he looked so uneasy, so awkward, as to appear almost like a stranger. His smooth, impish charm vanished. "For heaven's sake. This is very disagreeable."

And in that instant, everything became clear. This wasn't love—it was nothing *like* love. It was a physical transaction or—and here the duke's stomach turned again, realization plummeting like a stone—a business one.

"You have no affection for me," the duke said, voice hoarse.

"Dear Max, of *course* I do. Great affection. But not..." He smiled, hands twitching. "Dear fellow. I thought we were simply..."

The desire to grab Willoughby, to hold him, to root him to the spot and keep him, not permit anyone else to have him, was suddenly very great. It disturbed the duke, the force of the sensation. He pressed a hand to his face.

"I misunderstood you," he said. "Entirely."

Willoughby was not the first man he'd loved. Theirs had begun a few seasons before, the same way as all the others—

distantly, on account of rank. The first time they kissed, it was almost like an experiment, a pressing together of lips to assess the feeling, test the outcome. Certainly, they had been goading each other, egging it on, discussing every trivial matter under the sun rather than the central questions: *will we, shall we, dare we?*

Of course, they kept it perfectly and utterly secret. "Doesn't it frighten you?" Willoughby once asked, in the small hours of the morning. "Entertaining me in plain sight?"

They were in the duke's own rooms, half dressed, in their undershirts. But there was no risk of being caught; the housemaids only came to clean the grates at six.

"Not in the least. We're perfectly safe up here."

Willoughby was standing at the end of the bed, framed by the bedposts and the smooth muslins hanging from the sash windows. He had his arms crossed and gazed through the doorway into the antechamber next door. The little black lacquered room.

"You're sure?"

"Of course."

Willoughby wrinkled his nose. He tilted his head toward the antechamber. "It's awfully ghoulish, you know."

"What is?"

"*That.*"

The duke rose from the bed, letting his own sheets slip to the floor. He studied the dollhouse, positioned on the oak table, suffused in the half-light coming through the door.

"Oh," he said. "That's just one of Lady Kendal's gifts."

Willoughby said it unsettled him to see a grown man keeping a toy house in his bedroom. But the duke had laughed. "It belongs to Tor as much as me. It belongs to the estate, come to that." The dollhouse had simply been moved from Mount Kendal and placed in this suite years before, and so here it would remain.

The duke held out his hand. "Come back to bed."

A shadow of irritation had passed over Willoughby's face—as if he disliked being given orders. "Very well, *Your Grace*," he said in an arch tone. But then they'd both laughed, because really there was no difference in status between them, no difference in age, no difference in temperament. Not when they were together. On those long blissful nights, they were tangled up as one person, one entity—and the loneliness, the hunger, the emptiness of life in Kendal House was sated. At night, Max could be himself.

Not anymore, he realized now. Not with Willoughby, not ever again.

"I made a mistake," he said, vision blurring as he rose and turned toward the door. "Forgive me."

6

Tor

Tor did not think of herself as someone who was easily shocked. All things were shocking, when you put your mind to it, when you opened your eyes and looked properly at the world. Chewing slabs of meat, pouring intoxicating liquids down one's throat, covering one's body in dead skins, conducting thunderstorms to illuminate one's bedchamber, biting other people's flesh in search of satisfaction. London was sticky, built on clay; it was full of such vagaries.

She slept only a few hours. Max had departed for the Hillyards' breakfast in the landau. Lady Kendal followed shortly in the brougham.

"Saddle Patience for me," Tor ordered the head footman. "I have business of my own today."

She rode eastward, comforted by the rhythm of a steady canter, thinking over what her stepmother had revealed to her.

Her brother's absences, his silences, the impression he gave of having reduced his very essence—these things now made sense.

"You see, Tor?" Lady Kendal had said the night before, watching her intently. "It is really very bad."

"I should never have asked. You should never have told me."

"I did warn you."

"How can we—" Tor swallowed. "How can we protect him?"

"First, he must be managed. He *cannot* be permitted to marry Miss White. She won't understand Max's proclivities. She might even expose them. A woman of *our* station will be able to show more discretion. She will be able to make the necessary arrangements and preserve her own interests while fulfilling her duties as the chatelaine of Mount Kendal."

Tor rubbed her forehead. "Are you speaking from experience?"

Lady Kendal's eyes darkened. "Don't be disgusting."

Tor flinched.

Lady Kendal spotted it, gaze dimming. "Forgive me. You can see for yourself how this has strained my nerves. So: we need to sweep Miss White out of the way. I've arranged for Max to have breakfast at Mrs. Hillyard's tomorrow morning. Her daughter is eminently suitable—of suitable rank *and* fortune *and* temperament. I need to keep her in Max's sights."

"What if Max refuses to comply?"

"Then we must take stronger action to protect the estate."

Tor felt a prickling of doom. "What kind of action?"

"A depravity suit," Lady Kendal said calmly. "I have seen it done before. It could be done again."

There was a high whistling in Tor's ears. "You would...you would have Max *arrested*?"

Lady Kendal's face was expressionless. "Of course not. The suit would be made privately. Max would not even know who raised it. He would retire from public life, passing custodianship of the estate to a trusted party for his lifetime, and we would go on as normal."

"A trusted party? You?"

Lady Kendal said smoothly, "Or you, my darling Tor."

Tor froze. "Impossible."

"Quite possible. Extraordinary circumstances require extraordinary measures. I command the confidence of the family lawyers. They would arrange everything."

"Mama..."

"This is the emergency provision. I pray we will not need to exercise it." Lady Kendal tilted her head. "But if Max is exposed as a—" Lady Kendal closed her eyes. "I will not use the word. But *if* his sins were to be made public, and the police became involved, then the costs of the resulting legal actions, of battling the slanders that would undoubtedly follow—well, the damage would be enormous. Of course, I would support him. After your father died, I swore to myself that I would *always* do my best by the two of you. You in particular, unprotected as you are." Her voice shook a little. "And I am determined to ensure that *you* are safeguarded. Somebody must think of the women in this household."

Did Tor believe her? Did it even matter anymore?

"I don't know," she said slowly. "I'm not sure."

"Tor, darling, it seems to me that Miss White must know Max's secret already."

Tor flinched. "Whyever do you say that?"

"She could have discovered Max's predilections by stealth. She is clearly preying on him, hooking herself into his trust. How else did she manage to impress herself on him so swiftly? I daresay she gave him a false promise that she will not trouble him with the—*delicacies* of marriage."

Tor remembered the queer anxiety she'd felt, watching Miss White on Max's arm at the ball. "You think she is a charlatan?"

"Truthfully? I cannot tell. She may simply be a very bold young woman intent on securing a title and aristocratic progeny. Either way, Max is the victim." Lady Kendal sighed, held a palm to her forehead. "You see, Tor? All this has been weighing very heavily on my mind."

Tor took a breath. "Are you telling me, quite truthfully, that you have *not* been acting against me?"

"Tor." Lady Kendal pressed a hand to her heart. "Every action I have ever taken has been to your advantage."

"And you are certain, absolutely certain, that Max is compromised?"

"If I could wish this all away, I would. But yes, I am certain." She touched Tor very lightly on the arm. "Darling Tor. It grieves me to burden you with this."

Tor's senses were jangled; she could hardly decipher the truth of this matter. But she forced herself to come to a resolution.

"Very well. We are united. I'll get Miss White out of our way."

———

She rode all the way to Threadneedle Street, and then to the narrow road where her bearded solicitor resided. She leashed Patience to a lamppost and banged on the door. The maid pulled it open, staring at her in astonishment.

"The master's out," she said. "He's in chambers."

Tor handed her an envelope. "Take this for him. Tell him these are my instructions. He can reply at his leisure."

She had written her letter in a fast and vigorous hand.

My dear Sir,
I shall no longer be in need of your assistance in my affairs, and order you to destroy all record of our prior conversations. Given that your professional obligations toward me have now concluded, will you join me for the grouse shooting this month? I intend to quit London Thursday next for Lomond. Who knows when I will return?
With confident expectation of your acceptance,
Victoria KENDAL

Tor had underlined her surname several times, taking satisfaction in the sharp, vicious kicks of the *K*, the long sweep of the *L*.

"No need for a reply," she said. "He'll know where to find me."

Tor rode back to town. She had built a wall around Kendal House long ago, constructing it with painstaking care, brick by brick. She had believed it to be for her own protection. Yet, here was Miss White, cracking through, taking Max as if plucking a doll from the dollhouse. It angered her more than she could have possibly imagined.

There would need to be a retaliation.

The sky looked like it was sweating: it was getting darker, not lighter; perhaps there was a fog rolling in. As she reached Berkeley Square, people nodded to her, blinking, bowing. Look at them, she thought, these saggy-necked, empty-headed people. They took no care of their interests. They permitted themselves to be swept away on the tide. Not Tor. She dismounted Patience and handed the reins back to the groom.

"Bring out all the carriages," she said.

"All of them, my lady?"

"All of them. Every single one. Line them up in the yard."

The groom hesitated. "Why, ma'am?"

She smiled at Patience, stroked her forelock. "You'll see."

7

Quinn

Quinn sat at the breakfast table, waiting for the duke and Mr. Willoughby to return. Several minutes passed, and then several minutes more. Her heart was beating quickly.

Two facts had presented themselves to her with absolute clarity. First: the Duke of Kendal was in a dangerous, even vulnerable, position. Second: Mr. Willoughby was not the uncomplicated informant she had imagined him to be. He had disclosed no conflicts of interest, no personal attachments to the family. Yet, this was clearly an association of the most sensitive and delicate kind. *I have pledged myself to someone else*, the duke had told Quinn. *This person is not available to me.*

The duke had a right to his secrets, and so did Willoughby. But deception was *her* game—it irked her deeply in other people. Willoughby had furnished Silk with ledgers that revealed the duke settling payments to mysterious lovers. Had Willoughby discharged those payments himself? Had he falsified the accounts? If so, what else might he have misrepresented?

The French doors opened and the duke appeared on the terrace. His expression was identical to the one he wore the first time Quinn spied him, standing in the picture gallery at Buckingham Palace. Cold, blank, with the faintest sheen of sweat at the very top of his brow. He was working hard, powerfully hard, to conceal himself.

Quinn felt a flash of emotion. She knew what that was like. And she knew the damage it could cause.

"Ah." Lady Kendal's voice cut into her thoughts. "The duke is here. I fear we must depart. Sonia, darling—do go and say goodbye to Max. You know how he adores you."

Dimly, Quinn was aware of her companion at the breakfast table moving toward the duke, making laconic conversation with him, shaking hands. Quinn herself remained seated, thinking hard.

"Dear?" Lady Kendal called to the duke. "Shall we make our farewells?"

The duke crossed the terrace. There was something in the tautness of his huge shoulders that made Quinn feel a hollow sense of—recognition. *We're both liars*, she thought. *We're lying to the whole world. And yet, we dare not shed our skins, for fear we'll be destroyed.*

She rose to her feet as he approached the table. "Your Grace."

His eye avoided hers. "You wish to leave so soon?" he said stiffly to his stepmother.

Lady Kendal's laugh tinkled like a tiny handbell. "We have such a great deal to discuss." She lowered her voice, but Quinn could still hear. "Let us make our farewells to the archbishop."

The duke's fingers twitched, as if some mechanism in his brain had stalled.

"Max," Lady Kendal said more tightly. "Come along."

He looked up, as if startled by her insistence. Quinn perceived an opening, the first little fracture between Lady Kendal and her stepson. It provided the moment she had been waiting for, to separate them. She moved quickly, touching the duke's sleeve.

"Do you enjoy placing bets, Your Grace?"

"Bets?" he said. "What sort of bets?"

"I feel a strong desire to get out of town. There's still time to make it to Goodwood. Shall we?"

Lady Kendal's laugh was sharper this time. "Goodwood? Really, Miss White…"

Trust me, she telegraphed to the duke, keeping her face utterly calm.

He took a breath. "Yes," he replied. "Without question."

———

Not for nothing had Quinn always paid her seamstresses well above the average wage. There came a time, on every job, when one's wardrobe went completely out the window. And she realized, at breakfast, that it would be prudent to get the duke out of Lady Kendal's path altogether. She raced to St. James Garlickhythe, refusing the duke's offer to escort her home, and buttoned herself into a fresh silk blouse with the tightest possible reveres and a viciously narrow belt.

"I need theater," she said to the ancient steward, who stared, goggle-eyed, as she selected her coat. Silk would have been far better at this, she realized with a stab of guilt. "Parisian chic. An extremely high collar. Velour du Nord, with embroidery, and chiffon, and a boa. And an umbrella. And a carriage!" She changed into dyed yellow lace gloves and hurtled back to Victoria Station, ready to make the 12:20.

The weather was bad and there seemed no likelihood the skies were to become any clearer. But the mood in the station was festive and noisy, a blur of steam and engine smoke. A large and well-heeled crowd gathered on the platform, all in smart coats and jaunty capes.

Emerging from the steam was the duke. He had changed into a top hat and tails, same as every other gentleman present—but his waistcoat was an extraordinary iridescent green. Quinn experienced a brief feeling of triumph on seeing him: he was completely alone. She crossed the platform, feeling her neat-buttoned boots skidding on the wet ground underfoot. They stood in front of one another.

"I fear you have no chaperone," he said.

"Then let us take our seats," Quinn said as the guard blew his whistle. "Before society despairs of me forever."

Quinn led the way into a first-class carriage, praying nobody would recognize and spot them together. The duke seated himself opposite, placing his top hat on his lap. Silence fell between them. An entire train journey presented a conversational conundrum: how to fill the time? But the duke seemed withdrawn, his thoughts elsewhere. They sat together quietly, watching the skies darken outside. By the time they arrived at Chichester and attached themselves to the crowds heading for the racecourse, it had begun to rain in earnest. Still, Quinn congratulated herself on keeping him isolated from his stepmother.

"Luncheon?" said one of the stewards. "In the woods."

Through the trees, Quinn saw a large white tent, with tables set out for high tea. Distantly, she could hear flashbulbs popping, a bell ringing, and could see the gray-green shimmer of the racetrack, the white fences, and the hoardings. The rain was pattering steadily on the marquee roof.

"How will the horses run," she said, "if it's raining?"

He raised a brow. "I suppose they..." Then his features clouded. "Ah."

Someone was approaching, striding across the canvas flooring, shaking out her umbrella so that the droplets spattered Quinn in the face.

"Miss *White*," said a voice.

Quinn turned. Victoria Kendal was bearing down upon her—rigged as if for battle, in an extraordinarily blood-colored coat.

"I've caught you both," she said, teeth glinting. *"Good."*

———

Lady Victoria did not seem to be dressed for the races. Her costume had the dimensions of a tea gown, sack-backed and luridly patterned, with strange slits and cuts in the skirt that might have been made with a shearing knife. The pattern clashed violently with her hair; it blanched her skin. Quinn cursed her inwardly for following them. But there was still something magnificent about her; she held herself as if a steel rod had been sliced right down her spine.

"My stepmother told me you were here. She thought somebody ought to keep an eye on the formalities. Good thinking on her part. Where *is* your chaperone?"

Quinn held her nerve. "Mrs. Airlie has been taken ill. I fear she's had to confine herself at home."

"How ghastly," Victoria said before the duke could interject. "I hope it isn't catching." Waiters were circling the tent, proffering champagne on silver trays. A fashionable crowd was drifting into the tent, aiming for the tea table. Tor took a glass, then said bluntly, "Walk with me."

The duke's expression darkened. "Tor…"

"I just want to *talk* to her," Victoria said, head whipping round. "That's all." She caught Quinn's arm, linked it with her own. "There are things we should discuss."

"Of course," Quinn said, gripping Victoria's arm in return. "How lovely."

———

"I don't know *anything* about you," Victoria said, eyes fixed straight ahead. "But don't lie, don't make anything up."

The trees formed a canopy overhead, shielding them from the worst of the rain.

"Good gracious," Quinn said. "Nothing could be further from my mind."

Victoria's brow furrowed. "What do you want with us? Be truthful."

"Whatever do you mean?"

"You can't be in love with Max. Do you intend to harm him?"

Quinn pulled her arm away. "Lady Victoria..."

"*Not* a very good reply. Tell me."

"Tell me what you suspect me of."

"Fortune-hunting. Blackmail. *I* don't know. But I don't trust you. Not one iota. And I *will* protect my brother."

"Blackmail?"

"*Don't,*" Victoria said. "Don't trick me into saying it."

The duke had broken free of the crowd and was advancing toward them. Quinn felt a jolt of alarm: evidently, Victoria Kendal knew her brother's secret. But how could she possibly have guessed that *Quinn* knew? Clearly, the duke's relations had intimate knowledge of his affairs, whether he realized it or not.

"Lady Victoria," she said, gathering her breath. "Your brother has shown me nothing but courtesy. I have no intention of..."

"Liar."

"Lady Victoria..."

"Liar. I can smell it on you." Lady Victoria swung round. "Max!"

Quinn's chest was pounding. The duke was coming up the track. He called to his sister, his tone indicating a note of alarm. "Tor?"

Victoria turned back to her. Said, voice low, "Do you cut deals? Here's one. Don't give him away. Don't shame him. If you agree, I'll spare you."

"*Spare* me?"

"Max!" Victoria said again. "We're plotting against you."

He came to a stop, several feet away. "Miss White?" he said. "Are you well?"

"Yes." Quinn's breath was constricted. "Just—plotting."

"You'd do well to come back to the tent," the duke said slowly. "The rain—they're calling off the race."

Victoria was startled. "Before the afternoon has even begun?"

The sky was darkening by the second. "Yes. We'd best turn back to London." The duke studied Quinn. "I'm sorry to have dragged you all the way out here, Miss White."

"I fear I did the dragging," Quinn said, taking a step toward him. "Very well. Let us return directly." If Victoria was intent on protecting her brother from his potential bride, Quinn would need to stay close.

Victoria crossed her arms, an odd light in her eyes. "But we've had no sport!" She stepped into Quinn's path, blocking her from her brother. "I propose a carriage race. If I win, you pay nothing. If you win, I pay any sum you desire."

"Tor..."

"Come now, we need *some* entertainment today."

Quinn frowned. "A carriage race?"

The rain was coming down hard now. Victoria regarded Quinn with a pitiless look. "Haven't you studied our motto? *Our blood, our laws.* You want to join the Kendal family, you may as well learn our traditions."

———

They took the express train back to London, in a first-class coach cleared of all other passengers. As they approached the city, Quinn could see the sky changing: a pale haze turning dark. They alighted from the train, conducted by a line of porters to the Kendals' own enormous carriage. It groaned as it left the station, heading north to Mayfair.

"Tell her the rules," Victoria said to her brother.

Quinn felt the duke shift beside her. He seemed uneasy.

"Family tradition," he said. "A private one. Whenever we have something to celebrate, we hold a race." Then he glanced at his sister. "But the weather is very bad, Tor."

Victoria was holding on to the leather straps on the door handle. "You're not a coward, Miss White. You'll race me, won't you?"

Quinn remembered the boards affixed to the walls outside Lady Victoria's bedchamber: the ones with scores etched in gilt. If this was a test of her mettle, the only way to keep the duke under her thumb while he was in the Kendals' company, then Quinn could see no other route but to concur. Besides, her heart was still jolted by the venom in Victoria Kendal's voice when she'd said the word *liar*.

I need to prove myself, Quinn decided. *I need to match their power...*

By the time they reached Kendal House, it was late afternoon. Quinn could hear the noises from the stable yard: grooms shouting, the crunch of wheels on gravel. She rattled the carriage door handle, but it spun feebly on its axis. Evidently, there was some special mechanism required to unlock these doors.

The duke moved fast. He pressed a quiet-clicking button underneath the window. The door sprang open.

"Come," Victoria said. "Let's race."

8

Quinn

The air in the stable yard smelled strange; there was something caustic on the breeze. Quinn could taste it on the roof of her mouth, a little like blood.

"Choose your carriage," Victoria said.

The grooms hauled open the mews doors. Broughams, landaus, phaetons, an ancient barouche, even sedan chairs over a century old.

"That one," Quinn said, pointing at a light two-wheeled gig, painted a vivid shade of tangerine. It was too small to permit more than two passengers.

The duke raised a brow. "You're sure?" he said.

"It seems to be the only one to permit a private conversation." Quinn could feel a skittering sense of anxiety. To maintain the duke's confidence, she would need to keep hold of his trust. "And I would like to speak to you, alone."

"Unchaperoned?"

"We are engaged."

The grooms seemed excited; the news had traveled around the yard: *a race, a race!* Quinn chose her mare, her whip; she was handed gloves, a fur-trimmed cape. Victoria Kendal went inside to change and came out in a tight-buttoned scarlet riding habit.

"My sister is the best rider I know," the duke said. "You should bear the risks in mind."

Quinn watched Victoria climb into the driving seat of an enormous brougham, barely assisted by the grooms. The horses reared, restive. Quinn hauled herself into her own driving seat.

"I will." She slid across the plank. "Get in."

The gig quivered as the duke hauled himself aboard, thigh pressed to hers, the seat creaking beneath them.

"Go," he said, and Quinn clicked the gig forward. A cry went up; Victoria turned her own dark mares in the direction of the gates. They were off.

———

The gig moved so quickly it sent Quinn's heart into her mouth. She tightened her grip on the reins. The pony was sure-footed; it whipped them downhill, across Piccadilly, making for St. James's. Quinn heard the thunder of carriage wheels. Victoria Kendal's black brougham had given them a head start, but now it was bearing down the hill behind her.

"Where to?"

"Your choice," said the duke. "You're the quarry."

Quinn felt the breeze streaming through her hair. "You called it a race, not a hunt."

The gig hurtled over a loose cobblestone, jolting them violently.

"There's no difference, with Tor," said the duke.

Quinn steered them hard across the Mall, making for Whitehall and then the Thames, where the roads would be more open.

The duke swung his arm behind her, not for comfort, simply holding them in position.

"You said this marriage was an arrangement," Quinn said. "That it was an opportunity."

"Yes."

Quinn adjusted the reins. "You should know that I am privy to your secret."

He stiffened beside her. "I have no secrets."

So he told lies as smoothly as she did.

"I saw you with Mr. Willoughby in the Hillyards' dining room."

The gig leaped forward. The duke's knuckles turned white, clenching the rail.

Eventually, he said, "I see."

"I don't intend to harm you by circulating this intelligence."

The wind whipped past them. The duke said, "But you feel duped."

"No," Quinn said, catching her breath as the wheels rattled over a pothole. "I interrogated you last night before accepting your suit. I asked you to tell me the name of your lover. You told me it was immaterial. I accepted those terms."

The gas lamps were blurring the edges of the park.

"I will deny this story if you ever put it out into the world," the duke said.

"I told you, I have no intent of exposing you." Quinn forced the gig into a hard turn, lurching on to gravel, racing for the stone archway at the top of Horse Guards. "Whatever your sister may think."

He grabbed the side rail. "Tor... Tor knows nothing of this."

"She told me directly."

A second jolt, a fast exhalation from the duke. "Halt the carriage."

"Your Grace..."

"Halt it at once." His voice was thick.

Quinn maintained her grip on the reins. The gig sped onward.

"Your Grace. We are united. You have nothing to fear."

But she could feel something shifting, could see him glancing over his shoulder, looking for his sister.

"How could... When could Tor have..." The wind whistled in their ears.

Quinn had shocked him deeply. And in that moment, she realized she had misplayed him. He was scrabbling with the gig's side door, as if he meant to leap straight into the road, as if he intended to run back and face his sister. She needed to regain his trust—and quickly. Her mind rattled with the wheels of the carriage.

"I have secrets of my own, Your Grace," she said, keeping her eyes on the road. "Beyond those I've already shared. Just ask Mrs. Airlie."

He let out another breath, focusing himself. "Your...chaper-one?"

"My one-time chaperone. She has abandoned my cause. So has my steward. Or rather, I have temporarily suspended him from my employ. Imagine what Mr. Mellings would say if he heard I have no chaperones. But then, Mr. Mellings is under indentured servitude to my house."

"Indentured...?"

Quinn's heart was racing. The truth might be the only thing that would secure his commitment to her game.

She heard a whoop behind them. Victoria Kendal's brougham was chasing them, as if trying to gain ground, approaching the archway at a colossal pace.

"She can't make it," Quinn said. "It's too narrow."

"She can."

She did. Quinn saw a flash of scarlet: Victoria ducking, driving the brougham with terrific speed, gravel flying into the air.

"Coming for you!" she shouted, slamming the brougham into a hard turn. Quinn grabbed her reins and her own gig sped down

Whitehall, aiming for Westminster. The other grooms were in their own carts and phaetons, trailing behind.

"Whatever do you mean, indentured servitude?"

"I mean, I have Mr. Mellings under my thumb. Willoughby, too."

The duke's voice was constricted. *"Willoughby."*

"Believe me, he has not breathed a word about you. He allowed my associates to believe you are the greatest Casanova that Mayfair has ever seen. I suppose that story was a rather useful smokescreen for you both. Perhaps he has greater capacity for loyalty than I realized."

"Willoughby spoke to you about—*me?*"

"He is my informant. I am—a fortune hunter, a charlatan," Quinn said, taking a breath. She could feel the strange heat of him, the way it passed through her own skin. She wished to shift away from him and yet there was no room to do so. She continued to focus on the wide and empty road. "I am every dreadful thing you can imagine."

The duke's leg moved beside her. She glanced sideways, met his gaze for half a second. She could feel the bite of the reins, the bitter chill of the metal railing through her skirt.

"There," she said, heart faltering. "I have unburdened myself to gain your confidence. I have arranged your freedom if you wish it. We may be married in the morning. So tell me: Are we still in collaboration or not?"

"Miss White…"

Quinn pulled hard on the mare's reins, turning the gig. The wheels shrieked as she did so; the duke nearly fell out of his seat. The whole vehicle tilted wildly, rearing on to one wheel, and Quinn clenched her jaw, steering them toward Westminster Bridge. She saw Victoria Kendal's brougham slowing, as Quinn changed the direction of the chase.

"My name," she said, "is Quinn Le Blanc."

The wind was whistling in her ears, streaming through her

hair. Her pins were slipping, her curls disarranged. She knew she was playing a dangerous game, breaking every stricture of the Rulebook. But her instincts were singing to her: *Tell the truth.* It felt strange, unutterably strange, unutterably thrilling, to do so. She felt it, bolts of unfamiliar pleasure shooting through her chest.

The duke straightened himself, finding his balance. "I see."

He said it quietly, carefully, in the second before Victoria's brougham screeched up behind them, just as her face was looming out of the mist, just as she cried, "Caught you!" in triumph. He said it just as another small gig—painted a vicious shade of blue—came pelting toward them in the opposite direction. Quinn turned, startled.

"Whatever is *he...*"

The driver's face was obscured by a high scarf and a low cap pulled over his bald head; he was whipping his horse hard, paying no mind to the traffic, aiming straight for them. Quinn's own mare reared in alarm; her gig clambered onto the pavement as the wheels of Tor's brougham thundered up alongside her. Quinn's reins slackened; she felt the breath leaving her lungs.

"Yes, we are still in collaboration," the duke said, right before the smash.

9

Quinn

The impact nearly threw Quinn from the carriage. She heard the crunch of the wheels, felt her body slam into the metal bar on the driving seat. There was a strange suspended moment, the reins unraveling from her hands—and then the gig turned over.

Cries went up in all directions. The horse whinnied; the world tilted. *Help*, she mouthed—or perhaps she had no time to form the word. The pavement rushed toward her—and saved her, too. The curb balanced the gig as it toppled sideways. Quinn tumbled from her seat into the road; the duke fell directly after.

A voice called from the pavement: "Quickly, help her! Help the lady!"

Hands reached for her.

"I'm all right," she gasped. "I'm not hurt…" There was a sharp pain in her wrist. She lunged forward, grabbing the mare's reins before they became twisted around its neck. It reared, nearly wrenching Quinn's shoulder from its socket.

"Don't harm her." A forceful voice. Black gloves, cracking leather. Victoria Kendal—leaping from her own brougham, diving across the pavement, wrestling the mare's reins from Quinn's hand. "Don't touch her."

"Who hit us?" Quinn said. For she knew she had been hit: she turned and saw the blue body of a second phaeton, its wheels splintered, straddling the road.

"Him," said the duke, panting, pointing into the distance.

Get that man! was the general cry. For the phaeton driver, whoever he was, had leaped from his seat even as his bright blue carriage had smashed into Quinn's gig—and now he was running, limping, in the opposite direction, hurrying furiously toward Whitehall. He'd pulled off his cap, his bald head shining in the lamplight. Several others took chase.

Quinn kept her distance from Victoria Kendal. "You were trying to run me off the road," she said.

Victoria's eyes were bright and furious. "Just a little sport. That fellow ruined my fun."

The duke looked pale. He crouched next to Quinn. "Are you hurt?"

She shook her head. "Just my—wrist." She moved it gingerly, winced.

"You need to see a physician. At once."

He helped her to her feet.

"Are you injured?" she asked.

"Not in the least." His voice was steady.

The race was called off; there was no question about that. Victoria's attention was on her horses. Quinn and the duke climbed into the enormous Kendal carriage.

"Drive on," the duke called, rapping sharply on the roof. His attention was fixed on Quinn. "Let us speak. With absolute candor."

Quinn could see everything blazing in brutal detail. She counted the buttons in the seats, ran her fingernails along the hairline cracks in the morocco leather. Small mirrors had been fixed to the doors, encased with silver plating; she could see hundreds

of versions of herself shifting and turning in the light. The silver
had been polished and carried the faintest whiff of turpentine.

Everything she had ever done, everything she ever aimed for,
had depended on her disguises. In concealment, in the sheer
rippling delight of shifting skins. And yet she had known, back
there in the gig, wind streaming through her hair, that she could
claim a greater prize. To be herself, just herself, just for once. Just
to see what it was like.

Now she wondered, in the burn of the duke's expression,
whether she had played it correctly.

"Candor?" she said. "Certainly." Her mind was ticking fast. She
had given him her name, but she wasn't about to disclose her whole
history, not her whole scheme against him... She felt a fierce jolt
of pain in her wrist. The carriage swept down the road, clearing
traffic aside. A brougham this large, carrying the Kendal crest, carried all before it. *This is power*, Quinn thought. *This is wealth. This
is supremacy.* She tried to summon it into her own veins.

"I have told you the truth." She lifted her chin. "And now we
must decide what to do about it."

He laughed, a fast and brittle sound. "You read my mind."
Then he added: "It seems to me that both of us could still destroy the other. If we wished."

Quinn nodded slowly. "If we needed to. If we wished to. Do
we wish to?"

"I hardly know."

"Nor I." Quinn nursed her wrist.

They studied one another, saying nothing.

There was chaos in the stable yard. The grooms had taken their
own horses and gone ahead to warn the others: "There's been
a crash, the master's coming now..." Servants were streaming
down the stairs from the house, bringing towels and plasters and
bandages—as if they expected Quinn to be lifted limply from
the carriage, wounded and gray with shock. She threw open the
door with her good hand and stepped down onto the gravel—
back straight, gloves buttoned, collar up.

The duke followed, waving the servants away.

"We are quite all right," he said. "But send for Dr. Rowe." He put his hand on Quinn's upper arm—the lightest touch. "Come," he said. "Let's talk inside."

They marched across the gravel yard, servants' eyes on their backs. Kendal House loomed overhead, like a bruise against the sky. It was not at all like coming home.

Something uncoiled in Quinn's mind. Dusky pink shutters, a yellow door, the creak and groan of a winding stair. The scent of Mr. Silk's cigar smoke on the breeze...

The Château.

Home.

The idea of losing it, losing Silk, failing on a job—it always made her throat grow tight.

And yet—Silk had already gone. She could no longer trust that old sense of belonging.

I can only trust myself, she thought.

They went to the thorny, silvery drawing room. Quinn sat on one of the low couches; the duke sat directly opposite. The physician came and inspected her wrist, bending it, judging her grimaces.

"A sprain," he said. "Nothing more. I shall bandage it up."

"Need I delay the wedding?" she asked.

"Not if you can carry your bouquet in one hand," he said, fastening his Gladstone. He gave the duke a sharp nod. "Good day, Your Grace."

They were left alone, in that huge metallic room, silent but for the quiet ticking of the clocks. The light was draining away from the sky outside. Time, Quinn realized, was running out. She could feel it, the old pressure on the air, inside her heart.

A small pack of playing cards rested on the side table. Quinn reached for it.

"Come. Let's amuse ourselves." She shook the cards, set them on the table.

"But your hand..."

"I can play one-handed."

He seated himself close to her. She could see his heartbeat thumping in his neck. "Very well. You choose the game."

"Nothing complicated." She turned over the first card. "Snap."

His own hand came out fast to meet hers, his skin touching her glove. They began working methodically through the deck.

"Tell me," he said, and there was a strain in his voice, "the whole truth about Mr. Willoughby."

The question startled Quinn. "You wish to discuss him, above all else?"

"Yes." The duke's eyes were dark. "Do you—think me a fool?"

So it was love. Or had been. For the duke, at any rate.

"I hardly know you. And I barely know Willoughby at all."

The duke studied her with a fierce concentration, as if willing her to say more. "I take it Mrs. Airlie is not really your cousin?"

"Mrs. Airlie," Quinn said, pointing the sharp end of her card toward him, "is to be considered immune in this discussion."

"Are you in any position to decide who is or is not considered immune?"

"Yes, as are you. Who do you choose?"

He lifted a card. "Tor."

"Snap." Quinn swiped the cards. "Why?"

"Need I give a reason?"

"No. But I should like to know all the same."

"You first. Why have you protected Mrs. Airlie?"

"Because she is an old and loyal friend, as close to me as family."

"Did you really lose your parents?"

Quinn pressed her lips together. "No further questions. Your turn. Why Tor?"

"For precisely the same reason. She is my sister."

"But *why*?"

"Because she…" The duke's voice carried a certain strain to it, a shadow of doubt. "We were close as children. I owe her a good deal. And I feel a sense of—obligation."

"She appears to navigate the world rather well without your assistance."

"Incorrect. Tor has no freedoms. Her life is tied to Kendal House."

"Is it? Or has she chosen to make it so?"

He didn't answer this at first. "One's family can only be comprehended by oneself."

Quinn sighed. "I will grant you that. What of your stepmother?"

The duke's gaze narrowed. "She is beyond reproach. I do not think you could touch her even if you tried."

"Beyond reproach? My word."

"Snap." The duke's heavy palm hit the table; he collected his cards. "Here is another question. You tell me you are a fortune hunter. Once you have your fortune, what happens next?"

"What do you mean?"

"Tomorrow we will be married. You have the rest of your life ahead of you. What will you do?"

Quinn laid a card. "What will *you* do?"

His eyes rested on hers, as if he was considering this with care. "I am reformulating my intentions."

"Without Willoughby?"

Silence.

Quinn nudged him gently. "Lay your card."

He unpeeled it from the pack, turned it over.

"Hearts," she said with a short laugh. "And diamonds."

Love. Money.

And a pair of fives.

"Snap," he said in a low voice, eyes coming up slowly to meet hers.

She spread her hands. "Your win, Your Grace."

He took the pile.

Quinn could feel a choice sparking in her chest, one she hadn't previously considered. To execute her plan as it was originally designed: to lead the duke directly to the altar—and then bring about the final flourish, saving herself, leaving him to deal with the broken wreckage of her game. He would survive; his fortune and his title would assure all that. She would order roast beef and claret for dinner, reconcile with Mr. Silk. She would put herself up in a first-class hotel, send flowers to Mrs. Airlie's house, enjoy a week of fine sea bathing. She'd feel sun on her face, fling herself into icy waters, rejuvenate her soul. She'd return to the Château reinvigorated, replenished, ready for the next great chapter of her reign. The bureau would hum with promise; her portrait would glow next to her mother's on the staircase wall.

But then she would drag a chair to the table, pull out a large sheet of paper, lift her battered old pen from its vermilion case. Silk would list their debts still not settled, warn her they might never pay off their debts to Mr. Murphy, tell her that they needed to retrench unless she could write and win another game...

She'd clench her teeth and rack her brains to force the next card into reality. She'd pace the dressing room, trying on silks and furs and veils, and the sun would not touch her face, and her hands would be sweating inside her gloves, and she would carry on hiding, hiding, hiding all her life...

Or she could go through with marrying the duke.

"One final question," she said.

His eyes were on hers in an instant. "Yes?"

"If you give up on Willoughby, have you any need for our arrangement?"

He pressed his lips together. "Do you think I shall never find affection again?"

"I think that is up to you. What do you desire?"

"Desire?" His gaze darkened, growing wary. "You could not possibly imagine."

She began to reshuffle the cards.

"How would you like it," she said, "if we could both disappear?"

10

Mr. Silk

Mr. Silk had been told which door to open. He knocked softly, listened, heard nothing. Gently, he nudged it open.

A candle trembled against the far wall. He was standing in a pantry, the air smelling of sawdust and herbs, the shelves piled high with ordinary things. Bath bricks and bottles of ebonite and polishing paste. Packets of Hudson's Extract and sticky-looking bottles of brandy. Tinned meats and biscuits, various types of beef essence, candied peel, a tin of Assam Pekoe. So, he thought dully, this was where he would do it. Where he would put an end to things. In this dingy room in this dingy corner of the city.

He'd adhered himself to the wrong rules; he'd allowed himself to be cut open and used—and now he was too old to sew himself back up again. *I've wasted my life*, he realized, skull hammering. *I've wasted the whole thing.*

Mr. Silk adjusted his neckerchief. Then adjusted it again. He ran his hands down his jacket, taking comfort in the fit, in the bones.

It felt necessary to be dressed, *properly* dressed, for this discussion. Men judged other men on their clothes. Silk knew what to wear.

He'd lied to Quinn the night before, when he said he'd been recruiting men to support her fifth move. But now he would finish that task, although not in the way she had ordered. He entered the goods yard near Mr. Murphy's offices, on the side of Aldgate he generally avoided, doubts writhing in his gut. A dozen men stood watching him, smoking. The air was stale and blueish and designed to make him cough. He did cough, the second he entered; it made his eyes water.

"Mr. Silk," one of the men had said—short, amber-eyed, wearing a dark cap. He smelled powerfully of tar soap and peppermints. "What news?"

Silk rubbed his mouth with his fist, mastering his breath. "You know the Château is running a debt."

"Yes, Mr. Silk. A large one, getting larger."

"I am authorized to make a payment in kind."

The men exchanged glances again. "You've come all the way down here to tell us that?" Mr. Murphy took cash, and cash *only*.

Silk swallowed. "The payment is—the Queen of Fives."

When it was done, when they'd agreed how many men to spare, when they'd signed the papers, Silk journeyed back to the center of town. He slipped into the mews house behind Berkeley Square, down an alleyway, and then to this pantry on the ground floor of the big house.

He could smell brine and cooking sherry on the breeze—and something darker, too, something rolling in from the Thames, from the park. His vision was distorted; he thought he was going to be sick.

"Done?" said a voice.

The man in the blue silk waistcoat was sitting on the tiled floor, his knees tucked up under his chin. He looked pale, but it wasn't from fear; Silk could tell that much. It was queer excitement, coming off him in waves. The candlelight reflected in his inky eyes.

"Done," Silk replied. "Murphy's men will do what's required."

And then, stomach turning, he said, "Why do you bother to change your clothes? I—I *know* who you are."

The man said disdainfully, "I don't dress like this for you. I dress as my whims require." Then he scrambled to his feet. "Now go away. I'll tell you when she's been taken."

"Will you…" Silk couldn't form the questions out loud. He felt weak. *Traitor*, he told himself. *Weasel*. Always the lieutenant, always shifting his allegiance. First this queen, and then this one, and then this…

"What? Hurt her? Kill her? Worse still…tell her who betrayed her? Oh, yes, I'll certainly do that."

Silk's heart juddered.

There was no calculation. Just motion. He put his hand to his jacket.

The man frowned, wondering what Silk meant to do—because he didn't know Silk well enough; he knew several layers but not the ones at the very bottom, not the darkest, locked-up chambers. The ones schooled in running, hiding, fighting, killing…

Silk took a blade from the inner lining of his jacket. Fluid, fast: he came for the man in the blue silk waistcoat. He aimed the knife directly at the man's throat.

"Ah," said the man. His hand went up, a sharp and jerking defense, knocking the knife from Silk's hand.

And because Silk was still dizzy, still nauseous, he stumbled. His knife missed the gentleman's throat.

The man in the blue silk waistcoat had his own weapon. A pistol, cleverly made, not noisy. Silk didn't see the man lift it up. He was scrabbling, falling, holding his lovely waistcoat carefully in place. All he thought, in the split second before the gun went off, was: *Quinn*.

The pistol exploded—quietly, furiously, aimed straight at Silk's heart.

Something went out then, in that room; some curtain fell hard upon the stage. A worried old soul—honest, trying—vanished. Silk was rubbed out, his name and self unraveled; he became a thing that might never have existed at all.

11

The Duke

Max closed the door to the bedroom suite, shutting out the servants and the secretaries and the lawyers. He exhaled. His body was tense, all his muscles locked—and his mind was fizzing; he had barely slept since the ball. He needed time alone, before supper, to think.

Miss White—or Miss Le Blanc—intrigued him utterly. He could see it now: the falseness and the artifice in her costume, the clever pinning of her hair, the layers of fabric she wrapped around her wrists, her throat, to keep herself apart. It reminded him of the grim comfort he found in his own dark jackets, his starched and ironed collars.

And yet, she had seen through all that, after all.

His breath quickened in his throat. She was wrong and marvelous and dangerous in equal measure. And so was he.

He crossed the room, pulled down the blinds, lit the lamps. His mind circled around his options. *How would you like it,* she asked, *if we could both disappear?*

She wouldn't tell him her plan. She simply asked him for his trust. Coolly, brazenly, as though she were not a self-made liar.

He didn't know if he could give it.

"*Decide*, Max," he said to himself, voice low. His jaw was aching from clenching his teeth. It was always in him, this tension. He could never relax his guard, not even in this room. He had lied to his lovers, Willoughby included, when he said they were quite safe in this suite. Truthfully, he always lay awake beside them, staring up at the forked tongues and popping eyes carved into this monstrous bed—this bed that had once belonged to his father. How could he sleep, when his father's ghost was circling the room, his fingers trailing along the walls? He heard it, so many nights: the whispering shuffle of a specter's footsteps.

Only the dollhouse comforted him. He often pretended it meant nothing to him, that he only kept it out of courtesy to Lady Kendal. He laughed, going along with the family joke that Lady Kendal had presented her stepchildren with a toy mansion, only to remodel the real one in its redbrick image.

But this was the greatest gift: Lady Kendal had painted over his father's lines for him; she'd remade these rooms; she'd concealed the past with gloss and varnish and blazing plasterwork.

He went into the dark anteroom and studied the dollhouse, with its three small dolls inside—always there, always united...

Something had shifted at the Hillyards' breakfast. Startled anger flashed across his stepmother's face when he agreed to accompany Miss White to Goodwood. He understood why: she wanted a fine match for him, an illustrious wife. And he had never gone against her wishes before. In normal circumstances, they might not have spoken at all; they would have simply sent a nicely worded message by way of a note card. Miss White's arrival seemed to have disturbed all that.

Better to let her down this way, than for her to discover his other sins.

"My blood, my laws," he said to himself now, quitting the room, leaving the dollhouse in the dark.

12

Quinn

A late supper was served at nine o'clock. Word came down via a monogrammed note card that Lady Kendal was dining in her own room.

"She does not wish to join us?" said the duke.

"She begs leave to be excused, Your Grace," murmured the head footman.

A look of concern crossed his face. "Granted, naturally. And my sister?"

"Lady Victoria dined alone, Your Grace."

The duke exchanged a look with Quinn. "It seems we have been given license to spend our wedding eve by ourselves."

"Lucky us," Quinn replied.

Yes, he seemed troubled. To Quinn, the message was perfectly clear: their expedition to Goodwood had offended Lady Kendal deeply. Now there would be no grand dinner, no reception, no champagne, no congratulations made. The gloves were off:

the Dowager Duchess of Kendal would not assist in the wedding preparations. The Lady Victoria would rather see the bride driven off the road than eat a little supper with her. The duke rearranged his cutlery, lost in thought; he was clearly forming the same realization.

"I fear you are about to suffer through a rather sad and silent wedding," she told him gently. She was calculating how to get a message to her seamstresses in Spitalfields. She needed the dress, the one they'd designed with the greatest care, the one that had already incurred the greatest expense.

The duke looked up sharply. "You think I was standing idle last night? I've never given so many orders in my life. And now we've set the date—well, I daresay the household is reeling." He reached for his wineglass, threw back a swift gulp. "Thomas," he said, calling to one of the footmen standing guard at the double doors. "Let us show Miss White what the House of Kendal is capable of."

The doors slid back and the servants came in, bearing notes and lists and bolts of fabric.

"Confectionery," he said, clicking a finger for the pastry chef, who laid sketches of the cakes, sprigged with myrtle.

"And look here," he added, offering Quinn an arm, walking her across the hall, pointing up the first flight of stairs. The picture gallery and reception rooms were being draped in fresh silks and garlands of lilies. The ballroom—newly scrubbed and aired and waxed from the ball barely twenty-four hours before—was being fitted with a huge white carpet and what looked like a thousand pink roses. A canopy was being erected between the garden steps and the chapel, and footmen were issuing forth from the glasshouse, carrying palms and lilies to place in huge bowls throughout the drawing room and picture gallery.

"You have *not* stood idle," Quinn said, feeling her heartbeat accelerating. "All this, Your Grace? For two people?"

"Two people? Hardly. I daresay the whole world will descend

on Kendal House tomorrow morning." The duke flushed with something that resembled satisfaction as they returned to the dining room. "I have put the word out that the archbishop has granted us special license to be married on the morrow. Berkeley Square will be agog." He flexed his hands. "I am throwing the doors open at last."

Quinn adjusted her necklace. "So you are satisfied with our arrangement? You will proceed?"

He did not meet her eye. "You wanted a wedding. If you keep your bargain, I'll keep mine." Then he wrinkled his nose. "We should bolt the windows. There's a bad fog coming in. I can smell it."

Quinn watched him cross the dining room. He'd discarded his jacket, was dressed in his shirtsleeves and trousers. She could see the muscles moving in his back as he unbolted the shutters, drew them carefully over the big sash windows, affixed the drapes.

"Can I trust you?" he asked softly.

"Can I trust *you*?" she asked in return.

Neither replied.

Instinct was needling Quinn all over: she needed to be alone. Indeed, she desperately needed to *sleep*. She had caught sight of herself in the glass on the way through the picture gallery; she was running the risk of looking exhausted—not at all the appearance she wished to display.

"I would like to retire," she said. "Do you have a room for me?"

"Of course," he said. "We'll show you up."

"And I have a message to send to—my people."

He nodded. "You can entrust it to my man. He will see it safely delivered." His expression was inscrutable. "I trust his discretion."

Quinn supposed he was obliged to, if he'd been making appointments with Mr. Willoughby after nightfall. She scribbled a note to her seamstresses, folded the paper, stuffed it into an envelope. Her pen hovered over the envelope. Dared she write the address? Give herself away so fully?

"Here," she said, passing it to him. And then, feeling a sudden stiffness in her cheeks: "I thank you for it."

The duke and the head footman accompanied her all the way up to the third floor. The footmen came, too, and a pair of housemaids designated to her service for the night. The duke unlatched the double doors, pushed them gently open. The room was ready for her, fuzzed with lamplight, the bed piled with furs and pillows.

"I think," the duke said, "it is customary for us *not* to cast eyes on one another, before the ceremony." He stood aside, permitting her to enter. "Good night, Miss White."

Day Five

All In

1

Tor

Tor never entered her stepmother's rooms without making an appointment. She knew the proper procedure: to scratch a message to Lady Kendal's secretary, to await a reply, to agree to a time. But the evening had stretched on and on, and no reply was forthcoming. At last, when the house was quiet, and the clocks began striking midnight, she decided she could wait no longer.

She went downstairs without seeking permission.

Tor's mind had been fizzing and spitting on the ride back from the carriage race. The sky had grown dark, obscuring her view of the streets ahead. Her thoughts were darkening, too. Her intent had been to drive Miss White off the road, to demonstrate the strength of Kendal blood, to frighten her into submission or even call off the engagement. The woman smelled like a cheat and a liar and Tor had been certain she would crumble at the first sign of violence.

Yet, she'd driven faster and with more skill and accuracy than

Tor had expected. And then, just as Tor was gaining ground, a secondary driver had hurtled out of thin air, colliding with Miss White's gig, nearly crashing into Tor's brougham—and Tor had realized something was wrong. It was clear Miss White had her own nefarious connections. She'd swerved too neatly, too cleverly, to have been in any real danger. *Tor* was the one who had been at risk of harm: *her* brougham could have collided with the pavement and overturned—it would have been a very severe crash.

Which made one thing quite clear.

Miss White was dangerous.

Not dangerous in the way Tor had first supposed—as a person in possession of feminine wiles, weaseling herself into Max's confidence. Rather, by being a blunter force altogether, out to cause serious injury as well as exposing the Kendal family's secrets. Lady Kendal had underestimated her: she was more than a distraction; she was the enemy.

This realization had taken root in Tor's mind as she rode home. "Don't fret," she told Patience, who was huffing as they turned into the stable yard at Kendal House. "There's nothing to fear. I'm here."

The household was a hive of activity. There was movement everywhere: servants pushing crates, wheelbarrows, tea trolleys; footmen lifting boxes and trunks; tradesmen delivering baskets of flowers, foodstuffs, wine. It was as if the world had gone mad. She left Patience with the grooms and she strode into the house.

The servants were coming up and down the stairs, carrying linens, packing cases, hatboxes. There were so many of them they didn't move out of the way for Tor; she had to fairly fight her way through the crowd. She hastened up to the third floor, passing under the radiant architraves of her own doorway. Her skin was tingling. Was anyone in here? No, it was undisturbed.

For now.

Tor faced the truth. Preparations were clearly being made for

Max's wedding—without delay. And however high the walls, however thick the glass, however dense the drapes, Kendal House would be spoiled by strangers again. Imposters would scale the roof, dig through the cellars, scuttle up the drains.

She studied herself in the glass—pinched, worn, buckled into her armor. This *house*, her *home*—fighting for it—was sucking the life out of her.

She crossed the room, plunged her hands in the bowl of cold water on the washstand. Splashed her face, pressed her palms to her neck, trying to cool her skin. It reminded her of the earliest days at Mount Kendal, on the nursery corridor. Icy water in the bath, the chill tiles on the floor, condensation on the taps. Surrounded by servants who disliked them, enjoyed taunting them, *knew* they were weak because they'd been forgotten by Papa. Her only duty then had been to keep watch over Max.

Max.

She straightened, letting droplets of cold water fall to the marble washstand. A feeling of deep unease passed through her.

There was no way of getting Kendal House, keeping Kendal House, without harming Max. Without exposing him, or at least threatening him with exposure. What had her stepmother called it? *A depravity suit.*

Her brother was not depraved.

Her hands jerked; she stepped away from the washstand. Reached for a towel, rubbed her face roughly.

When did she stop speaking to her brother? When did they start sending stiff little messages on gilt-edged cards?

Who had caused them to become so divided?

Depravity suit.

The words were ugly, wrong. Should never have been spoken…

Tor could hear footsteps everywhere—overhead, underfoot, in the walls, in her skull. She and Max had been overrun, invaded, gently pried apart. She needed to nail things back together.

———

The clocks finished chiming midnight as Tor reached the second floor. The doors to Max's suite were thrown open, servants passing in and out without compunction, atmosphere prickling. But the rear of the house was quieter. It seemed to Tor that there was a crafty stillness to the air, that the scent of rose water was just a ruse, designed to cover a more dangerous smell underneath. Her nostrils flared.

She didn't knock.

Lady Kendal had not yet retired to bed. She was standing on the far side of the suite, framed by the architrave of her own double doors, which were a mirror image of the design upstairs. Her gown was unbuttoned at the back; she was pinning her hair into place, digging her fingers right into the scalp.

"Mama?" Tor called. "May I speak with you?"

Her stepmother was not alone.

It took half a second for Tor to realize. Then she heard the tread of a footstep on the left-hand side of the room. Her gaze swung sideways and she saw him—his blue jacket, pale face, expression as startled as Tor's own.

"Willoughby?" she said.

And in that moment, in the strange, hesitant way he looked straight to Tor's stepmother—as if seeking permission to speak, to move, to act, to explain—Tor understood.

These two were locked in some form of collaboration.

Tor closed the door behind her. "Lady Kendal?" she said, voice hard. "What is this?"

Her stepmother's hands fell away from her fringe. Her arms were bare, her skin taut in the lamplight.

"Tor," she said—and her voice was soft. She was obviously caught off guard: it showed in the way she compressed her lips. But she was going to conceal it. "How nice."

"What is he doing here?" Tor said, extending a finger in Willoughby's direction.

Lady Kendal's eyes were dark, unending pools. "Oh," she said. "Nothing to concern you, Tor, darling."

She moved, skirts rustling, her loose sleeves shifting as she came. Her hands were outstretched. Tor recoiled.

"Don't." She took a step back, closer to the door.

Lady Kendal had never given any indication of a private friendship with Mr. Willoughby. None at all. And suddenly, Tor was quite clear: her stepmother was not to be trusted. Danger ran all the way up her spine.

"Tor," Lady Kendal said. "Don't be alarmed."

Tor swallowed. "I'm not alarmed at all. In fact, it's as well you're both here. I'd like to settle a business matter."

The lamplight swayed. "Business?" said Lady Kendal.

"My trust. I want access to it, all of it. At once." She turned to Willoughby. "Lady Kendal will sign it over to me. You may fetch a pen and ink."

He opened his mouth. "Lady Victoria..."

Tor turned to her stepmother. "Mama, I insist."

"You insist?"

"Yes. If you please."

"I don't please."

Tor shivered. "Lady Kendal..."

"I don't please, Tor. I don't care for this at all. It's far too late. Go upstairs and rest, and we can speak at breakfast. I am occupied."

"Occupied?" Tor let out a harsh laugh. "Is he going to help you do up your buttons?"

Lady Kendal laughed in return. "Is that what you think this is?" She turned to Willoughby. "You see?" she said. "My stepdaughter's nerves are *quite* destroyed." Her expression contracted. "I think we will have to consult with Dr. Rowe. It must be a dreadful sort of complex. I would call it very nearly hysterical."

Tor felt her vision getting sharper and sharper until a pain started in her head. Kindness. Softness. Gifts. Lady Kendal had provided Tor with *everything*, every kind of security. Tor's anger billowed outward, like a boom swinging across the centerline.

"*You* are acting against me, aren't you? Not Max. *So give me my trust.*"

Her stepmother's rooms smelled of her: roses, ferns. And other things, things that Tor had not paid attention to before. Brandy, and boot polish, and resin, and musk.

"No, my darling." Lady Kendal said mildly. "You've had things your own way for too long."

Fear rose in Tor like a gale, but she didn't let it out. Lady Kendal was going to take her pictures, her jewels, her money, her *horses*, her *freedom*, her life…and Max.

"We are no longer on the same side," she said. "At all."

"No," Lady Kendal said, adjusting her sleeves, muscles flexing in her upper arm. "We are not. Willoughby?"

Willoughby hesitated, just for a moment. Then he took three fast steps toward Tor. He gripped her wrist and clapped a handkerchief over her mouth.

2

Quinn

Of course, Quinn didn't go to sleep. She longed to, but she needed to rehearse. She paced her boudoir barefoot, scrunching her toes into the thick pile of carpet. *Enter the chapel… Then time for the vows… Turn to the organ… Find the glass vials…* She timed it, counting seconds in her head.

As soon as she'd marked the House of Kendal, she'd planned this move. This was her way, the very heart of her method: to paint the final scene in vivid colors before she'd even sketched the rest. It was like peering through a telescope at a far-off shore: it gave the whole journey a sense of promise, the knowledge that despite all impediments, one would arrive at one's destination. This was the faith of a queen: that her mind possessed rare faculties, that the game clung to her skin like silk and whalebone, that she held perfect mastery over it all.

First, she and Silk had recruited the men. They were essential, the vital component. Half a dozen of Mr. Dunuvar's sturdiest, fastest, youngest associates, in brown jackets and peaked caps, bearing the queen's colors: lincoln green ribbons in their buttonholes. She had directed their steps like a dance master. They would come brandishing the weapons she'd paid for. They'd bare their teeth and raise their fists and the crowd would scream—and in the noise and the confusion, they would abduct Miss White from her very own wedding.

Just before she made her vows.

For even Quinn, cavalier as she was, would not commit herself in the eyes of God—or worse still, the law—to anyone. Not even for a confidence job like this one.

Then, once she was free and clear and on the road, a message would be sent galloping back to Kendal House: *Miss White will be freed in return for payment of the following ransom…*

There was never any doubt in Quinn's mind that the Kendals would pay a ransom for Miss White's freedom. Indeed, it was vital that they did. The "False Heiress" card proposed two payouts from the mark: an advance against dowry as an initiating payment, and a secondary settlement *to be paid in cash, not kind, on conclusion of the wedding.* A ransom was by far the neatest solution. Quinn was rather proud of herself for conjuring it up. For the Kendals would *have* to pay up. Their honor would depend on it. What sort of family would abandon a new bride, an orphaned one at that, and leave her to the cruel mercies of her kidnappers? Or worse still, risk her death? The ransom note would be very shocking, very alarming; Quinn would put her most violent penmanship into it.

The kidnappers would release her. But she, of course, would do what the queen always did on the fifth day: disappear.

"The principal risk, however," Silk had said, weeks earlier, "is that they shun society. They don't care about their neighbors' good opinion. They may *have* no honor." He chewed his pencil. "What if they simply don't pay?"

Quinn had waved this possibility away. "They will. They must. Let's name the sum."

She and Silk had agonized over this. He had pored over Willoughby's reports, calculating what the Kendals could afford to yield. The Rulebook was strict on this point.

CLAUSE 5. *Only an intemperate queen would impose arbitrary taxation upon her marks. A prudent queen will be satisfied that the rewards she seeks are sufficient to discharge her debts and augment her commonweal, but GREED is not the purpose of her reign.*

"Fair?" Quinn had said, penciling a sum, swiveling the paper for Silk's final agreement.

"Eminently," he had replied. "We would be safe again. Back on top."

She'd wanted nothing more. But now she was playing with an alternative ending. One that gave the duke *his* freedom, too. Of course, His Grace had no notion what she was planning—she had not run completely mad. He had pressed her—sotto voce, while the servants were parading the newly ordered linens—for the particulars, but she rebuffed him.

"How will you make us disappear?" he'd asked.

"You'll see," she replied. For here was the tweak, the adjustment—the one she'd need to mutter to Mr. Dunuvar's men, as soon as they grabbed her. *Take* him, *too.* "All I need is your agreement."

"To what?"

"To whatever may happen."

He'd frowned, unsure if she was jesting with him. "I think not."

She fixed him with her stare. "Agree. Else I can't go through with it."

Confidence tricks could be carried out for all sorts of reasons.

To raise necessary funds, recoup lost earnings, settle bad debts, acquire a very particular piece of knowledge, test the discretion of certain friends. They might be used in the reappropriation of property—but only in the most select circumstances; the Château was not in the habit of engaging in petty larceny. But abduction—this was a different matter altogether. She had not tried it before. She could take no risks.

"Very well," the duke had said, although he appeared unsettled. "I agree."

Quinn paced it out, step by step, squeezing her fists tight. Downstairs, she could sense the house writhing, humming; the preparations would go on long into the night. Overhead, she heard the whisper of footsteps, the distant banging of doors.

At last, she exhaled, threw herself onto the bed. She'd prepared all she could. What else could she do but sleep?

———

Dreams came and went, wickedly edged. There were figures moving in and out of her room, opening the doors, bringing trunks and luggage cases and hatboxes. She could not tell, drifting in and out of consciousness, whether they were real or not. At one point, she imagined there was a figure standing at the very end of her bed, framed by the bedposts. It shimmered, bluish in the moonlight.

"Silk?" she said, her tongue tasting like chalk.

It was too slim: a navy shadow. It melted away into the dark, and she fell back into sleep.

3

The Man in the Blue Silk Waistcoat

The man in the blue silk waistcoat always made firm decisions. This was a necessary condition of his existence. But it had startled him, on some dim and distant level, to see Mr. Silk fall to the ground. "Dead?" he'd said to himself, really wondering, holding the pistol in his hand. Silk looked so small, crumpled, like a wolf cub.

"Get one of those crates," he'd said to his men.

They hesitated.

"Now."

They obeyed, lifting Silk into one of the huge packing crates stacked in the corner of the pantry, and covering his stiff body in sacking. Silk would have hated being taken away like old rubbish. But he sealed his fate the moment he lifted his blade. Besides: Quinn Le Blanc was the mark. Her friends and associates had to be swept away.

"Gently," he said to the men as they hoisted the crate into the

air. "Take it up the back stairs. You won't attract much observation now." There were so many deliveries being made today,
after all.

They clenched their jaws, straining, shuffling from the room,
avoiding his gaze. They were disturbed by this, by all these developments. But he had no doubts about their loyalties. Those
had been cultivated with great care, like the orchids in the hothouse. And the man in the blue silk waistcoat could read people
perfectly. He had honed this skill from his earliest years, dis-
secting their quarrels and loving words alike. He could intuit
what people were thinking, what they needed; he could get it
for them.

The Château taught a person how to aim high, how to become a man in a blue silk waistcoat—or a woman in a cream
silk gown. It was like any other sort of acting; it was the greatest, grandest sort of *play*. He studied people's voices and gestures
and fears and desires. He paid equal courtesy to the weavers and
the shoe finishers and the rabbi and the scholars and the women
on the market stalls, and he improved his conversation and his
knowledge of the world.

Lord Kendal had been easy to understand, too.

A widower with a funny sort of constitution. Not a physical
affliction. More like very bad nerves. He had a young family—
two children, a boy and a girl, ensconced on his dreary estate in
the Peak District. He couldn't bear to see them; they reminded
him so dreadfully of his late wife. He was eaten up with grief;
he was consumed by anger and loss.

The man in the blue silk waistcoat didn't forget him. After
he left the Château—for it was his choice to leave; they didn't
throw him out, regardless of their election—he set his mark on
the House of Kendal.

The Rulebook said one had to conclude a job in five days.
But Lord Kendal's estate was enormous, his fortune vast. There

were hundreds of thousands of little drawers and hidey-holes. One could burrow into a place like this and never come out.

It was the most splendid game he ever played. It took extraordinary effort to disguise himself so magnificently, to gain the trust of the household, to give wise counsel. And to spend, spend, spend their money...

For a long time, he convinced himself that he had forgotten about the Château. That the memory of his departure no longer made his lungs burn. He was safe now, he was enriching himself, he was clambering to the top of society.

But then he heard that Lillian Quinn's daughter had been crowned the Queen of Fives.

It startled him, the way it stung—it was such an old wound, after all. It exposed an unwelcome truth: that he had not yet buried his old self in the ground. He still loathed Silk and the Château. He still yearned to deface the Rulebook, to set fire to the bureau, to smash the portraits on the stairs. It was a low-burning fire, unquenched; it required satisfaction.

He left Lillian's girl alone for a while. But then he couldn't resist meddling in her games, spooking her marks, sending anonymous letters warning them of her low reputation. He watched as her debts mounted, as her players departed, as Silk spun around and around, trying and failing to set things right. The man in the blue silk waistcoat encouraged the House of Kendal to spend liberally on its charitable projects, to start tearing down the East End, demolishing old silk-weaving mansions in Spitalfields...

And then he learned about Quinn Le Blanc's new game.

————◆————

At first, it seemed like a joke. As if it couldn't be real. The rumors were circulating around Berkeley Square: there was a fine young lady, unimaginably rich, residing in a lovely old mansion in St. James Garlickhythe. She was an orphan, born of merchant banking stock, quite delightful in her manners...

False Heiress.

He remembered the old card in the bureau. He hadn't seen it in years.

Was it a coincidence? It was too extraordinary that, after all this time, after all he'd done to disguise himself, the Château would have turned around and marked the Kendals. They were *his* mark. And if Le Blanc mounted an Intrusion, searched the house from top to toe, picked through the family's correspondence, its financial papers, its secret drawers...

Then they might expose him.

Lady Luck moved in such mysterious ways, imposed such strange tests on her players. Perhaps this was a gift, he told himself—a miracle in disguise. For the Château owed him a debt, not settled. He still deserved that crown—stolen from him in the vote, all those years before.

When he fired his pistol at Mr. Silk, he did it because the game demanded it. Quinn Le Blanc was the mark, the undeserving queen, and her court had to be dissolved.

"Get one of Murphy's men to chase down Lord Kendal's gig," instructed the man in the blue silk waistcoat. "Get Le Blanc off the road. Injured or worse—up to you."

He'd wondered whether Silk would obey the order. He could scarcely believe it when Silk did. *That loathsome little worm*, he thought. A filthy turncoat all along. He'd served his purpose; he was better off dead.

—◆—

Afterward, the man in the blue silk waistcoat went upstairs. The circularity of the route soothed him; he wound himself into the knot. He sped silently up the servants' staircase to the second floor. He crossed the landing, passing the truncheons and hunting axes and rifles, and opened the Duchess of Kendal's bedroom door.

The light was low and soothing: there was a fire burning in

the grate, even though it was such hot and sweaty weather. The drapes had been drawn over all the windows, which disoriented him. Sometimes, when you climbed into a new skin, it took a moment to climb out again.

Still, he pulled himself together, changed clothes, ready to get to business.

Then Victoria had arrived.

Her voice: so unbearable. So unmodulated. In the end, there was no helping her. She made a good many grand pronouncements, a good many threats; she stood there blazing in all her self-righteous glory—dressed as always like a fool. But when all was said and done, she had to be removed.

They took her upstairs by force, bundling her up the servants' staircase.

———◆———

The house was a wild, living thing at night. It had an underside, a second skin. You could move between the internal walls, the cabinet rooms; you could take the back stairs. There were footholds and iron ladders built into the chimneys, and double doors that led to the central compartment wedged between the second and third floor. At this point in his life, he didn't need a lantern to guide his way; he could navigate Kendal House by touch and memory alone.

He squeezed himself into the slender, pitch-black corridor on the second floor, the one adjoining the duke's suite. This passage wound its way around the anteroom that contained the dollhouse. He peered through a crack left between the paneling and the plasterwork.

Max.

He was standing in the half-light coming from the bedchamber beyond. He was still dressed, and he was staring at the dollhouse as if it would provide an answer to his questions.

The man tiptoed on, a whisper of blue silk brushing against

the plasterwork. If Max heard it, that susurration between the walls, he would think nothing of it. He had heard it a thousand times before.

———————

Morning. The man in the blue silk waistcoat changed, became the woman in the cream silk gown. First: the hum of voices on the third floor. Next: footsteps coming up and down the main stairs—housemaids, bringing the bride her morning tray, her flowers, her dress.

The woman in the cream silk gown hunched herself into the tiny airless passage circumventing the bride's boudoir. Through the walls, she heard a tap on Quinn Le Blanc's door. She sucked herself in, holding her breath, listening.

She could hear them dressing Quinn. Heard the snap and crunch of the corsetry, the sigh of the chiffon, the smooth rustle of the lace. She knew it was a very fine wedding gown. Violently embroidered, encrusted with pearls and beading, a riot of silver lamé. Plenty of cream silk, too—the kind fit for a queen.

It should have been me, she thought calmly. The title, the Château, the portrait at the foot of the stairs. Not Lillian's. Not Lillian's daughter.

The woman in the cream silk gown was the true, the rightful, the reigning Queen of Fives.

Quinn Le Blanc was just a pretender, same as her mother.

She pressed her eye to the peephole, the one set into the looking glass. She stared right at Quinn Le Blanc, watched the housemaids lacing Quinn into the dress. *Tighter*, she willed them, grinning to herself.

Distantly, in the upper reaches of the house, she heard a sound. A cry like the caw of a bird.

4

Quinn

At seven, the maids came with hot water. By eight, the boudoir was crammed with strangers. It was clear Quinn would not be permitted to get ready for the ceremony herself. The maids stripped her out of her nightdress, folded her into a furiously hot bath, toweled and perfumed her.

"There's a right crowd outside, ma'am," one of them said nervously.

"I'll have a look," Quinn said, making to open the drapes.

"No, ma'am," the maid replied swiftly, batting Quinn's hand away. "His Grace said we weren't to open the windows."

"Come along, then," Quinn said. "Bring me the dress."

It took hours to get ready, to be brushed and curled and laced and buckled, taking care not to hurt her wrist. The duke's message reached her seamstresses; they came with the dress just in time, not long before twelve. Her heartbeat accelerated when she saw herself in the looking glass. Miss White. Immaculate and dangerous.

The clocks chimed every hour, on the hour...ten, eleven, twelve...

At noon: the wedding breakfast. The dress constrained her; the skirt was heavy, weighted with beading on all sides, clinging to her knees. Quinn held her bouquet aloft, clenched in her fist, safe behind the gauzy screen of her veil. As she came down the stairs, she could sense the servants marching through the house. There were still chores to do, even on a wedding day. Changing the linen, transporting the butter kegs, brushing the duke's tweeds, blacking the grates. The lawyers closed ranks as she reached the first floor, hemming her in on both sides as they sailed past the ballroom. This she understood. There were papers to be signed.

"Is the duke in good spirits?" she asked.

The lawyers hesitated. The groom's temper was beyond their purview. "His Grace is in raptures."

She gave them a very gracious smile. "As am I."

Together, a phalanx of men around a single bride, they descended to the front hall.

It was nice to be veiled. Quinn's slippers met the parquet, gliding on beeswax. She could smell ferns, jasmine. The dining room loomed before her, double doors thrown back. Here came the heat from all those bodies: dark-suited men, plumed women, clerics in their vestments. A hush fell as Quinn crossed the threshold, the crowd sensing her arrival. She could feel the walls pressing in. Diamond chokers on leathery necks, wrinkled satin, the tang of kippers. The footmen were pouring champagne: she could hear the bubbles fizzing, popping, all the way down the room.

There was the duke: a formidable blur at the other end of the table, attired in midnight blue velvet, a sharp white collar, gold buttons. He was beautifully dressed, she thought: as smooth and elegant as she had ever seen him.

The company fell back, making way for her as she entered. The duke rose from his own seat in the middle of the table, and bowed.

"Miss White," he said.

"Your Grace," she replied.

Their voices were heavy in the hush.

He had outdone himself; there was an enormous crowd present. She recognized some of the ministers' faces from the sketch magazines and the newspapers. Some of the rigid women, too—and among the clerics she could see the bristling, indignant stare of the archdeacon from the other side of the table. The smog outside was obliterating the light and the servants were turning on the electroliers. It might have been evening, not morning.

"Your seat," the duke said, indicating a chair opposite his. And then, with a tiny intake of breath, "You look—" He paused, and his neighbors turned, expectant. "You look—beautiful."

The word sat awkwardly upon him; he flushed as he said it. But the crowd seemed enchanted. Was he playing them? Had he calculated exactly how to whip up the world's interest in his affairs? He had always seemed so repressed, restrained, as if he found public exposure supremely odious. But perhaps she had underestimated him. Perhaps he had a natural taste for these types of games, after all.

Quinn raised a brow. "You look quite splendid, too." She scanned the room. No sign of the duchess. No sign of Tor, either.

Quinn touched the thick white damask cloth. She inhaled the scent of pink roses, jasmine, ferns. The table gleamed like an altar, festooned with family plates: great metal dishes, silver falcons, a gold cup winking at her, studded with pearls. A serious show. The light swayed, milky, heavy. The servants sprang into action and began to bring in the food.

The conversation picked up again, a taut low hum. The electroliers flickered overhead.

"Where is your dear stepmother?" she asked the duke across the table. "And sister?"

His gaze was tense. "Lady Kendal has sent a message to say they are indisposed."

Quinn was surprised that Lady Kendal had not at least shown her face at breakfast. To signal her opposition to the match so openly, when yesterday at the Hillyards' she had taken care to show reluctant but necessary courtesy—this felt like an odd development. She could hear the other guests whispering, remarking on it. "Lady Kendal told me she was perfectly shocked... Absolutely browbeaten into it by her stepson..."

Around them, the footmen were placing mountains of food upon the table. Collared eels, roast fowl, slabs of tongue, joints of beef, biscuits, wafers, ices, cream, and water. The mayonnaise shuddered, glutinous and sick-making. Everything smelled tart, stewed, drenched in vinegar...

Quinn frowned. "They are—*both* indisposed?"

The duke nodded tightly. "But I must trust they will come downstairs presently."

The other guests were eavesdropping on this conversation greedily. Quinn understood their delight: this was the stuff the gossip columns were made for. A family of great antiquity and stupendous wealth, hidden from view for so many years, being cracked open by a banker's daughter... Quinn could see Mr. Mellings at the end of the table, watching her furiously, longing to rebuke her with his pen. They all looked dreadful, these gawping guests. Sunburned and wine-soaked, veins bursting, eyes bloodshot, skin worn, hair lank. Clearly, none of them had slept in weeks, lurching from dinner to dinner, ball to ball, as the season raced toward its close.

"We shall have to save Lady Kendal some kedgeree, Your Grace," Quinn said, and raised her champagne glass.

The duke's features remained taut. *Be calm*, Quinn told him in her mind. *Have faith.*

"Indeed we shall," he replied, and raised his glass in return.

5

Tor

Tor woke.

The light had changed, was changing. It was gray, then amber, spiraling down through a porthole window.

Her nostrils felt sticky, carrying the honeyed scent of lilies or orchids—and they burned.

She moved, legs tangled in her skirts. Her palms brushed against dusty bare boards.

She was lying on the floor, on her back.

Pressing a hand to her spinning head, gasping, she pushed herself upright and studied her surroundings.

The floorboards were scarred and scattered with dead leaves and wood shavings and chipped-off plasterwork. There was a fine coating of pale dust over everything, giving the room an eerie, moonlit appearance. Lamps had been set, church-like, in high brackets around the room. There was a spiral staircase in one corner, rising to a rickety sort of gallery, which ran around the perimeter of the room and gave Tor the unsteady feeling of being in a surgeon's theater.

She peered upward, heart hammering. In the roof itself, there was a small turret with a glass cupola, its windows open to the sky. It was morning; she could see the clouds scudding overhead.

I'm in the attic...

She'd never ventured up here before. It was a strange space, double height, with timber rafters rising high into the mansard roof. It was pentagonal in shape: she counted the walls slowly, one to five, each furnished differently: scarlet hangings, lacquered green paper, plain redbrick like a chimney breast, plasterwork, pale blue silks...

Tentatively, she clambered to her feet, extended a shaking hand toward the silks. And then—with a gentle sigh, as if released by a clockwork timer, she heard the rippling sound of fabric being freed from high-strung hooks. The blue silks fell smoothly to the floor.

Behind them, braced against red brickwork, were iron girders—rusted and peeling. Above those, braced to the wall, were huge plasterwork panels. Peering upward, Tor realized they had been fashioned to resemble the frontage of a large and stately house—pillars, pediments, high sash windows... She approached slowly, reaching up on her tiptoes, touched the nearest pillar. The whole display seemed to have been fixed to the wall merely for effect. It looked awfully like the frontage of the dollhouse in Max's room.

Letters had been daubed in white paint on the drainpipes: **L... A... L... N... I...** Tor squinted, trying to make them out. Her head ached, vision swaying.

They drugged me...

Tor tried everything to escape: banging on the door, climbing the spiral staircase and attempting to scale the walls to smash her way through the glass cupola, shouting and shouting—for help, for Max, for the police, for the servants, for anyone. Downstairs, she guessed that guests would be gathering for that abominable wedding breakfast. It seemed unbelievable that she could be trapped up here, above them.

"Help!"

Her voice grew ragged. Nobody came.

The light shifted, and something else caught her eye.

There was a small figure sitting in the wooden gallery overhead, watching her.

The hairs on the back of Tor's neck stood on end.

But in the next moment, she realized: no, this wasn't a person. It was a strange creature—a *doll*.

China palms up against the railing, poised and still, like a watchful child. She wore a bulky sort of skirt made of coarse striped material.

Tor took a step backward, away from it. The letters on the drainpipes shifted, swimming.

A... L... L... I... N...

The words came together with a clicking sound.

All in.

A real clicking sound. An actual *tick* in the air.

Gears: teeth meeting teeth.

Tor's mind grew cool and clear. Someone had placed a mechanism inside this room. She could feel it: the verve in the air, a ratchet and a twisted coil. Something was ticking slowly, steadily. Like clockwork, on a timer...

She peered up at the doll. It seemed unusually large, the size of a real child. Underneath its bulky skirts she could see something else: packets, wrapped with wire and string.

"Want to place any bets?"

Her heart leaped. She wasn't alone.

Her captor was watching her from the little gallery overhead—smiling.

"Why are you *doing* this?" Tor said, trying to keep her voice from shaking.

"Doing? I didn't want to do anything to *you*. But you got completely in my way."

Tick-tick-tick.

The sound drew Tor's attention back to that queer little mannequin, up on the gallery. "What *is* that?"

"What do you think it is?"

Tor had never seen anything like it before. She'd only heard of bombs in newspapers and novels. The doll had a bright varnished face, cherry-red lips stretched in a brutal grin.

She felt her vision swaying again.

In the gloom, hanging from the beams, stacked on high ledges, were countless other dolls—of shapes and sizes in all varieties, some monstrously large. They wore crooked wigs and rich fur stoles; they carried fans and lorgnettes. Some were Russian dolls, spilling out of each other, their eyes wide and sightless.

"What is this place?" Tor said, disbelieving.

"My workroom," her captor replied. "A place for playing games."

Tick-tick-tick.

Tor glanced up. There were beams running underneath the mansard roof. Where the beam met the wall, there was a door, suspended high above the floor, the sort you'd find in a stable loft. It was studded with thick black iron hinges and it was hanging open, revealing a room beyond. A ladder ran up to the door.

"Do you sleep up here?"

"No. But you will."

A black rope was connected to the doll, uncoiled and snaking along the gallery, slick and dark. Oiled, Tor realized. A flame would come licking up that line in a heartbeat, the second someone lit it...

"Please," Tor breathed, taking a step back. "Let me go..."

"But this is your house, Tor," said her captor, treading slowly down the stairs toward Tor. "Don't you want it? All for yourself?"

6

Quinn

Breakfast passed swiftly. At last, the servants lurched forward, shifting plates and spoons and cups and glasses with such speed and accuracy that it felt as if someone had whispered, *"Exeunt,"* and brought out a perfectly enormous broom to clear the stage. The guests dabbed their mouths and clambered to their feet, a great creaking of chairs and flashing of metal studs and diamonds.

Quinn felt the duke's hand on her arm. "It is time," he said.

His eyes met hers. No camaraderie. Just tension.

"Yes," Quinn said, chest humming. "It is."

Not for the wedding ceremony. Not yet. They had a business transaction to complete first.

The dining room doors opened. The guests crowded around her, a phalanx of women on every hand. Quinn could feel the sheer force of them: wire, whalebone, belts, buckles, chokers, every sort of reinforcement; skirts sprung and starched and hard-ruffled, pressing into hers. Hands, everywhere, guiding her forward: kid gloves, the sticky-stretchy sensation of leather on her forearm.

"Ladies," she said courteously, every inch the duchess-in-waiting. They stood aside.

The lawyers were in the library. Outside, overhead, Quinn heard a cry. The distant shriek of a bird, perhaps. Fog was creeping in and pressing itself against the library windows. Quinn and the duke walked quickly across the room, aiming for the escritoire and the pile of papers waiting for them. The eldest of the family lawyers bowed as she approached, an old lackey greeting his next duchess. Then he glanced up toward the door.

"Ah, Willoughby," he said. "You're just in time."

Quinn swung around. The duke did the same, face tightening. *Betrayed*, Quinn thought, studying him. But Willoughby strode toward them, expression untroubled, not meeting Quinn's eye.

"Forgive the delay. Carry on."

He was good. Unruffled and easy-mannered. It was not impossible to see the attraction the duke might have felt: there was something sportive, mischievous about Willoughby's manner, something neat and muscular about him. His face was so smooth and unlined, almost ageless.

We should have used him long ago, Quinn realized. He was a master of concealment.

The lawyers moved, blocking Willoughby from view. "Miss White, do sit down," said the eldest. She snapped her attention back to the desk, taking a gilded chair. A single piece of paper glided its way across the green leather inlay. "The marriage settlement. For your initial and autograph, ma'am."

Quinn didn't touch the pen. She tilted her head, peering around the lawyers, examining Willoughby. "Do you have the receipt?" she said. "Of the advance payment made to me?"

They had never spoken directly. All their transactions were managed through intermediaries, principally Mr. Silk. Willoughby was clearly startled to be addressed by her in this setting; she saw a tremor in his eyebrow.

The lawyers stood aside, glancing toward the moneyman. "Willoughby?"

Mr. Willoughby swallowed. "Certainly, Miss White."

"May I have it?"

Quinn did not trust Willoughby. Not because of his attachment to the duke; that was a private matter. But because he was clever—cleverer than he had let on. And she would not permit there to be any further surprises.

He gave her a smile. "I authorized the bank order myself, acting as proxy for His Grace. Copies of the paperwork will be sent by messenger to your house in the city this afternoon."

"No need to do that," Quinn said smoothly. "Just give it to me."

Willoughby laughed, a faintly brittle sound. "Good gracious, I should not wish to trouble a bride on her wedding day with *paperwork*."

"No trouble." Quinn pushed the pen aside. "It would seem rather irregular of me to proceed to the altar without being satisfied that the preliminaries had been settled to everybody's satisfaction." She smiled at the lawyers. "I do not believe you would think very highly of me, gentlemen."

The lawyers turned to Willoughby, their faces expectant.

He glanced swiftly toward the duke. "Your Grace. Perhaps I..."

The duke frowned, cutting him off. "Let us do exactly as Miss White wishes. Fetch the papers."

Willoughby flushed, just a fraction. "I am afraid there may be a delay."

"How much of a delay?"

Silence in the library.

"Willoughby?"

"Your Grace," Willoughby said, voice strained. "May I speak with you—alone?"

Quinn examined the duke. He seemed nonplussed. "Whatever is the matter, Willoughby?"

Willoughby kept his gaze fixed to the duke. "Your Grace..."

Quinn felt a tingle of alarm. She rose from her seat. "I am troubled by this."

The men stared at her, eyes widening. The duke moved fast, snapping his attention to the lawyers.

"All of you, wait outside. Willoughby, stay here. Miss White, let us interrogate this matter together."

The eldest lawyer cleared his throat. "Your Grace, you may wish to retain our counsel for..."

"Leave us," the duke said sharply. "At once."

The lawyers looked at one another, then the duke, then Willoughby. Then they scuttled out of the room. The door clicked shut behind them.

Willoughby smiled. It was a strange, glassy grin. He said, very softly, "The bank order has been given. But I cannot fully guarantee that it will be obeyed."

Quinn spoke before the duke could. "Why not?"

Willoughby faced the duke. "This is a *private* matter, sir."

"You can speak freely in front of Miss White," the duke said. "She has my absolute trust."

Quinn perceived trepidation in Willoughby's expression. Clearly, the duke could see it, too.

"What *is* this, Willoughby?" he said, more roughly.

"You should know," Willoughby replied, "that there have been some troubles regarding the estate."

◆

The Kendals were rich. They were utterly and absolutely *rich*. Everybody knew this. But what Willoughby told them was almost beyond comprehension.

"Debts?" said the duke, still frowning. "What debts?"

Willoughby had laughed—he really laughed, when he said it. "They were just the tiniest little things at first. I didn't even pay them much attention. The first sign of trouble was an outstanding bill I noticed last winter, which was owed to a milliner in Stockport."

"Stockport?"

"It's not far from Mount Kendal. One of the hat works produces caps for the maidservants. There was a bill owing to the factory for several years' worth of goods."

"But not a material sum?"

Willoughby drummed his fingers on his thigh. "Not in relation to the estate's overall worth. But it troubled me. Why should the household not have paid it? I could see no evidence of a dispute. She simply neglected to settle."

"Who?"

"Lady Kendal."

The duke took a breath.

Quinn said, "And did you discover other debts?"

Willoughby hesitated. Then said, "Yes. The factory in Stockport is not the estate's only creditor. I've found other charges outstanding in the accounts—not amortized, not properly listed. I see losses from the coal interests; I see defaulted rents; I see land sales commenced but not concluded. Large pledges made to Lady Kendal's charities, some paid, some deferred, many canceled..."

The duke seemed bewildered. "But nobody has mentioned these debts to me." His face darkened. "*You* certainly have not."

"I have, of course, been working rather assiduously to see what we could *do* about the matter. I would not bring you a conundrum I had not first tried to solve." His eyes flashed. "Whatever else you may think, I do take some care with Your Grace's affairs."

"Not enough," the duke said flatly, "if we cannot even sign a marriage settlement."

"But you're rich." Quinn turned to the duke, flinging her arm wide, indicating the whole extent of the house. "You're plainly rich."

"*One* member of the Kendal family is rich," said Willoughby in that same strange, tight voice. "I'll grant you that."

"Who?"

"Your sister."

"Tor's fortune is held in trust."

"Indeed."

"Is Tor aware of all this? Have you spoken to her already?" The duke looked up to the ceiling. "I should go to her."

"No," Willoughby said lightly, raising his palm. "I wouldn't do that." He exhaled. "If you really wish to settle an advance against dowry today, then it would be advisable for you to access Lady Victoria's funds."

"Spend *Tor's* money?"

"There are some legal impediments. But the *good* news—" and here Willoughby's smile became quite rigid "—is that Lady Kendal and I have been seeking advice on how best to overcome them."

Quinn felt alarmed. Here again was an alliance she had not been made aware of. "Have you been collaborating with the duchess, Willoughby?"

His reaction was immediate. "Collaborating? Whatever do you mean?"

Quinn's mind was ticking hard, trying to piece this together. "You discovered the estate had mounting debts. You chose not to bring the matter to His Grace. You went instead to Lady Kendal."

"I..."

"Why? For what possible reason? Did you mean to impose yourself upon the duchess? Machinate with her to unearth fresh income from the household?"

Willoughby stiffened. "Sir," he said, facing the duke. "This is outrageous."

"Answer her question, Willoughby," the duke replied, voice dangerous.

"Tell me," Quinn said. "Did you frighten the duchess into this collaboration?"

Willoughby's expression grew ugly. "*Frighten* Lady Kendal? I do not think that would be possible." He mastered himself. "Or necessary. The duchess shares my wish to see the House of Kendal's affairs safely settled."

"Through marriage," the duke said slowly. "To a lady of good standing—*and* great fortune." He put the heel of his palm to his forehead. "I see now why you have been pressing for my nuptials so assiduously."

"If you are not forcing Lady Kendal's hand," said Quinn to Willoughby, "then I presume she is forcing yours. What hold does she have over you? I will support you, if required. You are under obligation to me. It provides you with protections."

Willoughby's eyes flashed toward her, startled.

"Yes," she said. "The duke knows of our arrangement. And I am abreast of your private friendship with him."

"Our former friendship," the duke said, voice flat.

Something huge billowed in Willoughby's gaze—several calculations, running one after the other. But his voice, when he spoke, was terse. "Good gracious. I have no notion what you're talking about."

Then he turned to the duke, blocking Quinn. "Your Grace, your sister's fund will satisfy your creditors. Give me the authority to break the trust, and we shall have this matter settled before the banks close their doors."

"*Break* the trust?" the duke repeated. "You would have me destroy my sister's future?" He turned to stone. "Get out."

———

The door slammed. "I will not oblige him," the duke said to Quinn. "Don't ask me to do it."

She could hear the pain in his voice. "Lord Kendal…"

"He's gone quite far enough. I've been backed into a corner too many times. I won't make Tor suffer, too."

"That could not be further from my mind." Quinn straightened. "But I must ask you plainly, do you wish to proceed with our arrangement?"

He ran a hand through his hair, shutting his eyes. "This is not how I imagined things would go."

Quinn could feel the clocks ticking on every floor—they were due in the wedding chapel. She longed to cajole him, press the point, force him to fold, as she usually did. But a voice in her head warned her: *wait*.

"Yes, damn it," he said at last. He was hungry for his prize, the grail she'd offered him. "Yes, we will proceed."

She breathed. "Then I will be absolutely candid with you. I need to secure that payment—at once. You're not the only person in this town carrying a debt."

"Very well. I will guarantee your funds."

"How?" She pitied him, trusted him, but she was determined not to be duped. "If Willoughby is to be believed, you have no ready cash."

"Good heavens, I'll sell this damnable house if I have to."

"Very well." Quinn indicated the escritoire. "Write me a promissory note for the sum we agreed. Then we may proceed."

Trust the game, she reminded herself. *Conclude this business, secure the investment. Get it done, Quinn. Now, before it's too late…*

All in.

7

Quinn

There were servants everywhere: maids on the staircase, footmen lined up in the passage like a guard of honor. In the stable yard stood the grooms, grasping brooms and shovels. Peering at her, all of them. Fog shrouded the neighboring houses, bringing with it a strange hush, broken only by the popping of umbrellas in the crowd as Quinn emerged from the house.

A carpet had been laid out across the cobblestones, beneath the canopy, marking the way between the house and the chapel. It was damp underfoot; Quinn could feel water seeping through her soft-soled wedding shoes. Her veil clung to her face. The chapel looked small and squat from the outside, built in the same bloodred brick as the house. But as Quinn passed under the portico, it seemed to unfold itself, shuffling its aisles and pews and transepts into a spidery, pentagonal web. At the top of the nave, Quinn could see the organ, pipes rushing up to the roof, surrounded by black-oak lecterns. She spied the altar, a riot of gold leaf and terracotta and marble, decked in silver plate and candles. The paneling was so dark as to appear boot-blacked, everything smelled of varnish and resin, and the air had been pumped with incense.

She halted at the doors, abruptly queasy.

There was the archdeacon, standing in the nave, consulting with the family chaplain. There were the guests, cramming themselves into the fine-carved pews, kicking kneelers and prayer books aside. Here came the duke, marching across the foggy yard, his face shining, his pale blond hair plastered to his scalp. He swerved, avoiding her look, marching straight up to the nave. The organ gasped, stuttered, thumping out its first few notes.

Where were the Château's men, the ones Silk had been recruiting for her? Hiding behind the stable block, she guessed. Or crouching on the roof? She had not seen them—but then she never did, when she was planning a fast getaway. The grooms closed the chapel doors, hinges creaking, and the light fell away. Quinn tightened her grasp on her bouquet—favoring her good hand, feeling a throb of pain in her injured wrist. Suddenly, it seemed that the whole chapel was sucking on her; the old generals were adjusting their red coats, the viscountesses were fanning themselves furiously. Quinn dug her fingernails into the soft parts of her palm.

"My dear Miss White," said a voice in her ear.

She jumped. "Archdeacon?"

He was staring at her, furious-looking as always. "Are you ready?"

The organ music swelled.

"Yes," she said. "Quite ready."

The floor was pale sandstone, still rough, not age-worn at all. It clung to Quinn's slippers as she moved up the aisle. She moved quickly, calculating how few minutes she had left before her men arrived, subdividing it into thirds. The guests murmured in surprise at her pace; the family chaplain was left behind. *First surprise.*

Quinn glided up to the duke and the altar. The lectern loomed in the backdrop, surmounted by a great blood-colored eagle.

The duke towered above them all. He was silent, his face immobile. The archdeacon began working his way through the wedding service. The words carried no substance; they might have been hieroglyphics for all they meant to her. *Am I going to do it?* Quinn asked herself silently. *Are we going to manage it?*

She could feel him, the vibration of him. She could sense his heat, his absolute concentration.

"Do you, Quinta White, take this man to be your wedded..."

Now, Quinn thought. It had to happen *now*. A moment of crisis before her departure...

"...husband?"

Silence.

Complete silence, utter stillness.

A whole company of players, ranged out behind her, powdered and painted and pinned and beribboned. The guests. The servants. The archdeacon, eyes twitching, fingers trembling on his prayer book.

Waiting for her answer.

The duke raised his gloved hand, very slowly, and touched Quinn's.

Fabric, separating them. They were encased in layers of cotton. But for a second, she could feel an electric charge passing through his skin to hers.

"Miss White?" muttered the archdeacon. He repeated the words. "Do *you*, Quinta White, take this man to be..."

A ripple of interest crossed the chapel, as if the crowd had noted her hesitation, had begun to parse it for meaning. Quinn felt hotness rising up her neck, prickling her scalp. Where were the men paid by the Château? Where *were* they?

"...your husband?"

She studied the duke's glove. He hooked his finger to hers, steady, warm.

ALEX HAY

"I…"

Bang.

The chapel doors flew open. There was a gust of wind, the smell of sulfur; a cry went up at the bottom of the nave.

The duke dropped her hand.

As she heard the footsteps coming, the cries from the pews, Quinn breathed in, grabbing her skirts, taking one giant leap sideways. She knew exactly what she was aiming for: this was the moment she'd designed, after all. *Second surprise.*

"Good gracious," she exclaimed. "What is *happening?*"

The organ loomed over her, fat and splendid, tall as a house. She fell—deliberately—into the organist, who was knocked from his seat. Quinn kicked the organ pedals underneath his stool and prayed that Silk had managed it, that he'd had those little glass vials placed exactly where they'd arranged. *A little burst of color, at the all-in. A little fizz and noise, for the close…*

She stamped down hard on the pedal, felt the resistance underneath: yes, there it was. Glass, shattering. A little cache of exploding powder, gusting up into the pipes.

Crack.

She felt it. The vial breaking, gas releasing. She scrambled backward.

There was an enormous thundercrack. The archdeacon ducked, and the guests cried out, and the vibration in the air seemed to increase tenfold, and suddenly the organ let out a terrific roar, shuddering violently like an engine boiler, shrieking, whistling— and then, with another terrible crack, the top blew like a volcano, a massive uprush of steam and vapor and gas.

Quinn saw figures running toward her across the transept.

My men, she thought in triumph. Time for her departure.

It was a perfectly clear image: silhouettes charging toward the altar. Strangers in dark jackets and thick boots. A cry went up: *Get out, get out!*

But something was amiss.

Their buttonholes.

They weren't wearing her colors, not the ones she'd ordered. Not her lovely shade of lincoln green, in bright satin.

Blue silk, *blue* ribbons.

The organ belched and roared and poured out brightly colored steam and smoke and violent sparks, obscuring the duke from Quinn's view. The guests began to scream and run for the doors.

The men came for her side-on, like bulls, shoving her bodily to the ground. She smelled flowers; the chapel went dark.

———

She was on the ground. Dust, the feel of it on her fingertips. Pain—a dull ache, right across her forehead, behind her skull. "Where..."

Her tongue was too heavy, as if she'd been drugged.

She'd been played.

There was a moment, approaching the climax of a job, when you were always trapped. When it was just you and your quarry, facing each other down, the prize dancing in your eyes. But this felt different. She wasn't dangling stocks and bonds tonight. She was pinned to the flagstones.

The men from the chapel, the ones who'd knocked her to the ground—they'd vanished. A small group of servants surrounded her, housemaids in dark twill dresses, footmen in yellow-gray liveries.

Pawns, making their attack moves, slicing across the board...

She looked up. Beams, rafters, tiny porthole windows... She was still in Kendal House.

But up in the roof.

Quinn struggled to her feet, head spinning.

There was an oil lamp burning in the corner. Around it were several rich-looking mattresses, piled high with pillows and eiderdown, and the floorboards were scattered with goose down and feathers. The air smelled fruity and sour, and there were several indignities in the corner: pewter bowls, and basins, and rags and towels. Close at hand, two figures were seated on chairs and bound in ropes and gags.

The first was Lady Victoria—skin blanched, red curls springing out in all directions, bolt upright in her seat. The second was the duke—massive shoulders hunched, eyes trained on Quinn. He was straining furiously, trying to loosen his restraints.

"Miss White," said a voice. "What an unsatisfactory transaction this has turned out to be."

A figure moved into the lamplight.

Willoughby.

He took short jerking steps—expression rigid, fingers fluttering at his side.

And behind him, peeping over his shoulder, the person who had spoken. A small woman, half in shadow.

For a second, Quinn's legs grew weak. This woman was wearing a cream silk gown—an old-fashioned dinner dress, full in the back, puckered and ruffled along the hems. There were brown tassels on the sleeve, chocolate velvet ribbons at the throat. An echo sounded in her mind, a portrait from the Château...

Mother...?

The illusion dissolved. A heart-shaped face emerged from the gloom, framed by dark curls. Quinn heard the whisper of the gown as it swept against the dirty floorboards.

It was Lady Kendal.

8

The Duke

The duke watched his stepmother cross the room. It was as if he didn't recognize her, had never seen her before.

An unsatisfactory transaction.

The servants had stuffed a length of dirty cotton in his mouth. He could taste the fabric—sour. His wrists had been tied with rope—brutally so, digging into his skin, forming welts. They'd strapped him to the chair like a beast, lashing him around the waist.

Silenced.

Tor sat beside him. Tall, straight as a tree, unbending. He'd watched them tie rope around and around her waist, but the tighter they bound her, the more upright she became. Her hair was burning red-gold, her eyes were black. He began to fight, trying to shift his chair toward her, trying to do *something*.

Men wearing blue ribbons had pinned his arms, dragged him from the chapel to the attic, then pelted away. The servants were the ones who assumed his custody, and they'd laughed at him—two footmen, two housemaids, and a scullery maid. They were the ones who tightened the knots, tied the gags. The housemaid was the tallest of them all. Gaunt, with red knuckles—a combination of bruising and carbolic and the cheap tar soap they ordered for the servants' quarters. Now she stood guarding him. She had tough forearms, a spot on her forehead, dry skin around her nose.

I see you, he thought.

Willoughby was staring at the ceiling, saying nothing. He couldn't meet the duke's gaze.

Behind Willoughby stood the duke's stepmother.

"A transaction?" said Miss White—no, the duke remembered. Miss Le Blanc. "Is that what this is?"

Lady Kendal laughed. "What else?"

The duke watched Miss Le Blanc struggling to make sense of this.

"Who *are* you?"

"You know who I am," said Lady Kendal. "You should go down on bended knee." She did something curious then. She lifted her right hand, splayed her fingers.

Five.

Then curled them into a circle, thumb to forefinger. Raised her arm as if placing an invisible crown on her head.

Queen.

The gesture meant nothing to the duke. But it had a curious effect on Miss Le Blanc. Her mouth opened in disbelief. As if Lady Kendal's gesture symbolized something the duke did not, could not, understand.

His stepmother laughed softly. It was so familiar, so entirely her, that it made him shiver.

"This is an old game. Old, old, old. Much older than you. And who are you to ask *me* questions?"

The lamps buzzed.

"You're from the Château," said Miss Le Blanc.

Lady Kendal gave her a long steady look. "No, I'm not *from* the Château. I stopped in, just for a little while."

"You were never crowned. I've never seen your portrait."

"Crowned, queened." Lady Kendal made a noise of disdain. "Irrelevant. I was the best then. I'm the best now. That's enough."

Miss Le Blanc seemed to be piecing things together. "How long have you been here?"

"In this house?"

"In this *skin.*"

Lady Kendal's face glowed with triumph. "This is my silver anniversary."

"Twenty-five years?"

"Five times five, indeed. With many more to come."

"But you must know Mr. Silk…"

"Ha! Yes. I once knew Mr. Silk." There was something crafty in her expression. "But alas, no more."

"Did you—did you know my mother?"

Lady Kendal's lips tightened. "Oh—*yes*. Lillian." She smoothed her skirts. "Did I make you stare, wearing her old gown? Rather a cruel trick, I suppose. She shared all her gowns with me, taught me the queens' games."

"But I've never heard your name. I've never seen you before."

Lady Kendal moved. She grabbed Miss Le Blanc by the chin. "Never seen me? Of course you have. My fingerprints are all over your work."

Miss Le Blanc grimaced, pulled away. "All your good works, those pamphlets, those building projects. You've been trying to tear us down."

"And run you out of town. Spook your marks, spoil your jobs. Yes, why not? Silk could have made me queen, but he let the vote go the other way. *Your* mother took the crown. My crown. You deserved to be frightened." Lady Kendal shook her head. "What were you thinking, coming here? Marking this house? Interfering in *my* games? You're a fool."

"Your games? You never signed a card in the bureau."

"Never signed a card..." Lady Kendal made a scoffing sound. "Child, who do you think wrote the game you're playing now?" She spread her arms wide, as if beckoning something. "I *designed* False Heiress."

"You...wrote it?"

"Wrote it, played it, *am* playing it."

Miss Le Blanc paled. "Tell me."

"How I did it?"

"Yes."

Lady Kendal laughed, the same tinkling sound. "By playing whist, in the beginning. For very high stakes. Lots of little card parties. Lord Kendal enjoyed my tables."

Papa.

"You marked this family?"

Lady Kendal turned and faced the duke and Tor. "Look at them both," she said, to Miss Le Blanc. "They so desperately needed my help. I was glad to give it. Really, I was." Her expression changed. She looked, in that moment, like her old self. "Dear Max. Darling Tor." Then she glanced back at Miss Le Blanc. "Yes, I marked them. I'd do it all again. They'd be quite safe, if *you* hadn't spoiled things."

The duke could see Miss White's pulse throbbing in her neck. "What type of heiress did you play?"

"A girl of good gentry birth. Niece of a country squire with a few humble church connections. That was your first mistake, you know. Coming in like an electric wire, fizzing and biting— rich and *showy*. The card doesn't call for all that. Far better to play it cold. Play it clean."

"So you deceived Lord Kendal. What did you do to him?"

The duke felt his blood turn cold. Surely, she hadn't *deliberately* harmed their father...

"Nothing at all! He was sick when I met him. This family has been weak in the blood for centuries." Lady Kendal tilted her head toward the chairs. Something flickered in her eye, some sympathy, quickly flattened. "Tor remembers what it was like."

Again, the duke tried to turn around. He could just make out Tor's expression—hunted, ghastly.

Miss White's voice was hard. "But you marked him, hounded him, gained his trust. And smoothed over his indiscretions."

"You really have been through all the family papers! Yes, I took very good care of everything. I have been a quite magnificent mistress of this house. Look at my darling Tor. She was misunderstood by everybody before I came along." She pointed at the duke. "Look at *him*. Such a stunted little boy, born before his time. Milksop, the servants used to call him. Do you know, when I first went to Mount Kendal, they told me he had some impediment, some twist upon his tongue? But he *could* speak. I gave him every advantage, every kind of support, and *look at him*. He's blossomed, he's radiant."

But I'm not, thought the duke. The stronger he became, the more he'd dissolved inside. The more silent, the more useless, the more despised...

Their stepmother was a charlatan, had bankrupted the estate, fooled them all...

Grief, betrayal—they crashed through him like a wave.

He was not a monster, not a beast. He could not split his ropes or spit his gag from his mouth; he did not let out an almighty roar.

But he could stand.

He leaned forward onto the balls of his feet, the ropes burning his skin, bringing his chair with him. He rose, half squatting, straining all his muscles. Willoughby let out a warning sound.

His stepmother turned—and laughed.

The duke tried to break into a run; he aimed his chair, his weight, all the force in his body, at the door. He heard the lock groan. He pulled back, sucking in his breath, ignoring the pain shooting up his shoulder. He tried again, meeting the lock's resistance. He staggered, losing his balance.

The door did not give way at all.

9
Tor

Tick-tick-tick.

The doll grinned down at them, slick with grease. Tor's mind was filled with mumbling noises, her thoughts shifting like pigeons in the rafters. This conversation was pointless. Absolutely futile.

There was a rope slicked with oil, waiting to be lit...

"Max! Don't be foolish. For heaven's sake, Willoughby, bring him back..."

That was Lady Kendal. Dimly, Tor perceived Max trying to break down the door. *No use*, she told herself flatly. No use Willoughby chasing him, either. What good could it do?

Tick-tick-tick...

She'd always heard the footsteps in the attics. She knew there were people living in the walls. Ghosts. Or rather, a single phantom.

Papa.

For surely he was up here? Surely, surely, he couldn't have

simply *died*? With nothing settled, nothing forgiven? Nothing resolved between them, any of them?

If it were me, she thought, *I'd tell the whole world I was dead, and then I'd live in the attic. I wouldn't be mad, I'd be quite sane. Quite* safe. When she saw the doll, she'd imagined for a second that it was *him*. Shrunken with age, abominably withered, starved of sunlight.

But no, that was her imagination. He wasn't here. He'd forgotten about them again.

"Max..." she said.

They'd gagged her, so the word came out as a grunt.

No, Tor didn't want this place anymore. She *didn't* want to live up here in the attic. Tor needed to get out of London, and taste the bitter tang of moorland sky, and ride as far and hard as she could. Up, up, into the woods, along the track, up the misty byre road, back the way the strangers came...

In that moment, she could feel the whole house straining, filling her mind. She could sense the grooves in the oak paneling, the whorls in the plasterwork, the chill in the gold basins, the zigzagging threads in the brocade. The black railings smoldered in her mind. They were singing to her, a dangerous siren call.

Stay.

No, she told the house.

It didn't belong to her. Nor to Max. It was possessed by something older and emptier than either of them: their name. She and Max were simply stiff-faced dolls, dressed in ermine and coronets, stored here as their parents had been before them—and *their* parents, and *their* parents. Their blood, their laws, none of it meant anything.

I give you up, she told the house.

Something cracked open in her heart; some small and bitter thing was released.

Tick-tick-tick...

She sensed a movement overhead, a shadow in the rafters.

She looked up, vision blurring. Nobody else noticed; they were facing Max, who was being dragged back into the center of the room by the servants.

The dolls grinned from ear to ear; the mannequins hulked in the shadows. Nobody there.

Across the room, Miss White rounded on Lady Kendal. "Enough! Let us parley."

10

Quinn

Lady Kendal whirled around, skirts billowing. "Parley?" she repeated, staring at Quinn with derision. "With *you*?"

The servants were tightening the duke's ropes, forcing him
back into his chair. It made Quinn's flesh crawl, the sight of her
mark being gagged and bound. This was a wicked business, she
realized, mouth dry. Not a game at all.

Tick-tick-tick.

Dolls overhead, their sightless eyes drilling into her skull.

"What is that sound?" she asked, lifting a finger, following
the restless beat on the air.

"Time," said Lady Kendal, mouth stretching into a smile.
"Running out."

Quinn didn't understand. "For you, perhaps. You've outplayed
your hand."

"Outplayed it?" The smile vanished. "I think not. You're at
my mercy."

Quinn breathed, trying to make her voice steady. "You know this game. So you must have a proposition. What do you desire?"

Lady Kendal moved closer, her silks catching the light. It seemed suddenly obvious that her hair was a wig: Quinn could see how carefully she'd pinned it to the scalp. When you looked closely at a charlatan, you could see all the joins and edges.

"Abdicate your crown," she said.

Quinn held her ground. "And give it to you?"

"It is mine by rights."

"You really care? After all this time? When you have this house?"

The amber ring glowed upon Quinn's finger. It caught Lady Kendal's eye and she frowned, as if momentarily disconcerted. "Why should I be made to choose?" she said, voice shifting. "Why pick *this* life over *that* one? Why mayn't I have them all?"

The mannequins shimmered behind her. She raised her hands to her face, smoothing her temples. "First, I was the boy in the blue silk waistcoat. Then, the girl in the cream silk gown. But before that, I used to sit by the shore, kicking my heels on the tub boats, watching people coming down the gangplank from the steamer. Have you never done that? Watched a crowd from a distance, picked them off one by one? Asking yourself, shall I eat you? Or you? Or *you*?"

Yes, Quinn thought. She had. It made her chest burn, a dangerous sense of kinship. She repressed it. "You had such power here. Wasn't it enough?"

"Power? Yes, I suppose I do have that. Old blood, old land, old laws, utter deference. Yet, I appeared so *gentle*, so *lovely*, didn't I?" Her eyes swirled with darkness. "Nobody could turn me out of *this* house for being too hard, too clever."

"So you found the perfect hiding place. Not a soul knew you were here."

"Well, I disliked society. You've seen our neighbors and the way they pry. It's far better to cultivate acolytes and lackeys, peo-

ple who need your money. *You* know that better than anyone."
She cast a hand in the direction of Mr. Willoughby, who stared
back at her, white-faced and silent. "Don't pretend you don't
have your spies and servants, the same as I do."

Quinn felt stung. "At least I do some good with my winnings."

Lady Kendal flinched in return. "As do I! I am quite the finest philanthropist London has ever seen. Even the Rulebook
couldn't punish me for my largesse. I have reshaped the ground
under your feet."

"But you've run out of funds. You've worked through your
moneymen like seed cakes and sweetmeats." Mr. Willoughby
sucked in his cheeks, avoiding Quinn's gaze. "Furs, jewels, gowns,
dark wigs, remodeling this house—am I correct?"

Lady Kendal's voice tightened. "All that and more. I gave a
great many gifts to my stepchildren." She glanced at Lady Victoria. "Did I not?"

The duke and Victoria could say nothing.

"I don't doubt it," Quinn said with scorn. "We would do anything to please our marks, to earn their favor."

"They are not simply my marks." For the first time, Lady
Kendal's hauteur wavered. "They needed someone to be kind
to them."

Tick-tick-tick...

Quinn laughed aloud. "This is your notion of kindness?"

Lady Kendal flashed a look toward Willoughby. "*He* can vouch
for me. We considered three actions. First, arranging Max's marriage to a suitable bride, with a dowry large enough to clear the
estate's debts. Second, breaking into Tor's trust, to release the
funds it contains. Third, a contingency action, to seek an end to
the entail on Mount Kendal." She held Quinn's stare, unashamed.
"We agreed we would need to gather some testimony relating
to Max's...private pursuits. In order to mount a case for his re-
tirement from public life."

"You planted Willoughby in your stepson's path?" Quinn said, sickened. "How much did you agree to pay him?"

Quinn saw the duke watching Willoughby with revulsion. Willoughby swallowed, averted his gaze.

Lady Kendal said sharply, "What do you think? A very fair commission from the eventual receipts." She sighed. "Of course, things would have never gone that far. These steps were merely for insurance. Had things followed the path I designed, Max would have married a lady of my choosing, our debts would have been quietly cleared, Tor's trust would never have been broken, and peace would reign. Peace, my dears," she repeated, voice going up a notch, as she spread her arms. "Your happiness has been my only care."

She really believed it, Quinn realized. Lady Kendal had told herself fairy stories, she had crafted this fantasy right out of her head.

The Rulebook was correct: prolonged deception rotted the soul.

And there was no going back now. Lady Kendal's game had been exposed. The realization came to Quinn with perfect clarity: she would never free them now.

The duke and Victoria stared at their stepmother. They were alone now; they had nobody to protect them—and neither did Quinn.

She could feel her mother's pendant at her breastbone, the silver chain cold against her throat. Quinn had ordered herself to be strong, to work harder than anyone, to form her own protections—to revel in her disguises, to follow the Rulebook—even though time was running out, the Château was failing, she was nearly twenty-seven, who knew how long she had left...

Tick-tick-tick...

She couldn't fail herself now.

"Enough," Quinn said, voice shaking, screwing her hands into fists. "Let us end this."

"End it?" Lady Kendal said. "It has only just begun."

Lady Kendal turned, climbing the winding staircase, gliding her fingers along the railing. She crouched beside the large doll, cradled its head in her hands. Quinn could hear her fingering the packets rustling underneath the doll's skirts. A rope trailed from it, wet with oil.

In that moment, Quinn understood. "Stop!" she exclaimed. And then, nausea rising, realizing she had only one proposition left, she cried: "I will—I will abdicate the crown."

It was the greatest sacrifice she could make. The thing she had yearned for, worked for, existed for, all these years.

"It is already mine," Lady Kendal replied.

She drew out a matchbox.

11

Mr. Silk

The dolls stood in the gallery overlooking the attic floor. Among those, there was a movement.

A stealthy, clever, cunning little movement.

When the man in the blue silk waistcoat fired his pistol, Silk knew that he would fall. And when the bullet struck him, he knew he hadn't died. He always wore his plated, crusted jackets, lined with whalebone and strips of steel and little diamonds, wrapped a dozen times in cotton and satin—and silk, naturally. The bullet struck him in the chest and the impact knocked him backward to the ground—but his breastplate deflected the blow.

Extraordinary, he thought. Quinn always laughed at him for his padded jackets, believing him to be unreasonably anxious. And yet, here it was: proof positive. He was *right* to be afraid. As he fell, some old self dissolved; the old Silk melted away. He fell to the ground and took the deepest breath.

He knew that the man in the blue silk waistcoat was studying him, wondering if he were really dead. Silk could hear him breathing—in, out, a quickening of excitement. Silk had stared at the wall, fingers splayed, leg twisted, knowing the bullet was nestled nicely in his waistcoat. *Go away*, he thought desperately. *Go, go, go.*

But instead he was dragged into a packing crate; sacking was thrown over his body. It took every fiber of his being not to flinch, not to groan; his head was still pounding; he hardly dared to breathe. Eventually, he felt a whoosh of air, saw the floor swaying through the cracks in the crate, heard footsteps shuffling against the stone floors.

He had been carried all the way up to the attic. The men groaned, stopping at regular intervals. There seemed to be a good deal of noise and confusion in the house, other goods and parcels being lugged up and down the stairs in readiness for the wedding. Silk squeezed his lips together, making not a sound.

At last, they deposited him on the floor of the attic.

"Are we just going to leave him?"

"What d'you think?"

"Is he a goner?"

"If he isn't, he soon will be."

"Fine. You got the key?"

Boots echoed on the floorboards; a door creaked open, then slammed shut. Silk heard the rusty click of a key turning in the lock. The footsteps retreated—and he was left with nothing but silence.

Silk uncoiled himself, bursting out of the crate, taking a gasping breath as he threw off the sacking cloth.

Alive, he told himself, triumph coursing through his veins. *I'm alive.*

He was playing his own game at last.

Now all he had to do was wait.

Later, as night thickened, he heard footsteps coming up the distant stairs, and he had to scurry up to the gallery, concealing himself among those ghoulish mannequins. From this vantage point, he could see the door opening, a woman being dragged in, thrown unceremoniously to the ground. Quinn?

No, he realized, exhaling. Victoria Kendal.

He quelled the urge to go down and help her. He crouched in the shadows, watching in awed horror as Lady Kendal prowled her workroom, waiting for her stepdaughter to wake up. He pressed his fist to his mouth when Victoria hammered on the walls, screaming for help.

He needed to hold his nerve.

And when they dragged in Quinn—unconscious, followed by the duke—he nearly cried out in anguish. He bit his lip so hard he tasted blood. He listened, heart thumping, as Quinn faced down Lady Kendal, conducted herself with the sort of courage he longed to possess. It gave him a quiver of envy, and then guilt, for having allowed her to stray so far into danger.

He remained silent, hidden.

It was only when Silk saw Lady Kendal mounting the gallery, fumbling for her matches, that he realized his moment had arrived. He watched her from the gloom, her limbs supple and glowing in the stormy light. Her shadow loomed against the wall, wild and enormous, far bigger than her frame. It made him shiver.

The Queen of Fives.

The name was myth, it was legend, and yet in that moment, he wondered if it was something more than that. The shadow seemed to move of its own volition, spreading like a stain.

There was an echo in his mind, something calling him from boyhood. The old tallyho on the wind, the burning air...

He was eleven years old, lurking at the end of Fournier Street, trying to navigate an unfamiliar and threatening part of town...

A woman had crossed his path, heading east, her face concealed by a veil. A high-waisted gown, a dark pelisse, cropped hair and muscular arms...

Something peculiar about her, about the speed with which she glided through the fog...

Her shadow rippled, long and bony, against the low brick houses...

He'd followed her, curious, and spied an old mansion with dusky pink shutters, its front door opening and spilling candle-light onto the cobblestones—and the woman dissolved from view, as if she'd never been there at all.

A ghost, or Lady Luck herself, welcoming him to the Château. Indenturing him to servitude, for life.

The memory shimmered in his mind as Lady Kendal hoisted herself up on to a ledge, clutching her demonic china doll in one hand. Her cheeks were coal-stained, her gown mussed and torn.

"Martha!" he called, using her old name. "Stop!"

She turned, blanching at the sight of him. The match hovered in the air.

"*You,*" she said in disbelief.

Then her face changed; the old expression. Depthless, scornful, molten black. "You can't slow me down now."

Her disdain for him was absolute.

There was movement below, a voice saying in astonishment, "*Silk?*"

"Wait," he called to Lady Kendal as she lifted the match.

Not just for himself, not just for Quinn, but for *her,* too. Because Martha had been great, she had deserved so much more than they had ever given her.

She didn't need to destroy herself—not here, not now.

But Martha had never listened to him before, and she didn't listen to him now. She was an artist, a worker. Her eyes were on her own games, her own creations, and nothing else at all. She placed the doll on a ledge, coil trailing beneath its skirts.

And then she struck the match.

12

Quinn

"Quinn!"

It wasn't the duke's voice, it wasn't Tor's. It was a voice she knew as well as her own.

It came from every good memory, every triumph, every card game in the Château, every sip of victory claret, every dark day, every quarrel...

"Quinn, stand aside!" He was hastening down the stairs, windmilling toward her. "Get back!"

The relief, the unbridled guilt, the anger at herself, the love for him she felt; they all billowed in her. The scent of his cigars, his taste for horrible blancmange, his neat-pressed waistcoats, his stubby pencils. His *loyalty*...

"Silk..."

Above them, Lady Kendal was holding her match, tiny flame leaping. She hadn't touched the rope—not yet.

"Tell her," she called to Silk, pointing to Quinn. "Tell Lillian's girl what you did to *protect* her."

Silk whirled around. "Everything," he cried, voice hoarse. "Everything in my power!"

Quinn's heart leaped. But Lady Kendal began to laugh, bending, bringing her match flame dangerously close to the rope. The duke grunted, trying to rise to his feet again.

Willoughby darted forward, speaking for the first time. "Your ladyship..."

The servants shrank back. One of them shouted, "Don't let her light it..."

The rope was like a serpent, darkly oiled. Lady Kendal crouched, silks billowing, and grinned at them. "I told you. This is just the *beginning*. I can't have you all exposing me now."

And because she was distracted, she did not see a shadow cross the gallery. New faces appearing overhead, peering down at them through the porthole window in the roof. Quinn felt her throat tighten. Urgently, she said to Silk:

"Those men abducted me, they took me from the altar..."

Silk gripped her arm. "Murphy's men," he whispered.

"Murphy?"

"All in!" he cried, beckoning to them. *"All in!"*

Was it...a signal? One of the men spotted Silk, nodding sharply. He was bareheaded, scarf rippling around his neck, a smudge of color on his breast.

Green scarf.

Lincoln green.

They'd changed their colors...

"I hired them," Silk muttered, his face close to Quinn's. "To trick *her*. To kidnap you from the altar at her request. But I told them *not* to harm you. Just to—twist the game."

Quinn's gaze flew to Lady Kendal's servants, and she saw that they were lurching forward, staring up at the porthole window with the same astonishment. Lady Kendal peered upward, too, her face contracting in dismay. The match sputtered in her hand. Above her, one of Mr. Murphy's men lifted his boot in the air, brought it down on the porthole window.

The glass cracked right down the middle, and a second later he drew out a hammer, smashed the rest from the frame—and Lady Kendal cried out, raising her arms above her head, as the panes fell in jagged portions all around her, smashing into thousands of pieces on the floor below.

"Gentlemen!" Silk cried, pointing to Lady Kendal. "There!"

The Queen of Fives.

Not crowned, not truly—but when he'd realized the true identity of the woman in the cream silk gown, he'd known what to do. He would hire Murphy's men to abduct the greatest player of her generation, the troublemaker who never became queen, while she was disguised as the Dowager Duchess of Kendal, to earn a magnificent ransom…

"My God," Quinn breathed. "You double-crossed her."

"I played the final flourish," Silk said, releasing her arm. His cheeks were flushed, eyes bright. "I played the serpent, the traitor, a grand deception. As the game demands."

The men descended on their ropes, landing with a thud, flinging themselves toward Lady Kendal. Her servants cried out in fear; Willoughby's mouth was hanging open in wonder.

"Quickly!" Silk charged forward. "Untie these ropes!" He drew a knife from the lining of his jacket, sliced Victoria Kendal's restraints open.

Quinn launched herself toward the duke, tore the gag from his mouth.

"Behind you…" he gasped, as a shadow fell across them both.

Quinn spun on her heel. Willoughby was right behind her, spittle flying.

"Stop," he said, clawing at her. "You cannot…"

Quinn's fist met Willoughby's jaw with a sickening crack. He crumpled to the ground, shrinking from her.

"Foolish," she said to him in disdain, "playing one mistress against another."

Another voice, high, shaking, cried out: "Mama, *stop* all this madness!"

It was Tor Kendal, kicking aside her chair, gag falling from her mouth. But her stepmother was fighting, scratching, wrestling Murphy's men.

"Traitors!" Lady Kendal cried, tearing away from them, a shout of fury. "You are done! Finished!"

The duke called out to her: "Do *not*..."

His stepmother ran from Murphy's men, pulling a box from her sleeve. She tore out a fresh match, struck it in one fast deadly movement.

Quinn felt her heart freeze, heard the hiss and crackle of the flame as it sprang into life.

Saw the whir of silks as Lady Kendal lifted the match...

...and lit the rope.

13

The Man in the Blue Silk Waistcoat

The man in the blue silk waistcoat was Martha's oldest disguise. Her inner self, the deepest drawer in her mind. He was the one who wrote her games, collected the dolls, dressed the mannequins. His brain guided her hand; *he* brought the flaming match toward the rope.

She watched, fascinated, as the fire touched the knots and cords, so wet and dangerous. Blueish-reddish heat snaked its way up the coil, along the fuse, racing for the clockwork bomb. Her doll beamed down at her, its smile ferocious, beckoning disaster.

She rose to her feet, hearing cries across the room—but dimly, as if from a great distance. A strange emotion gusted through her heart. Not pain, or not exactly that. Just astonishment—that it could have happened again. That once again she was running away from home.

"What now, Marie?" she asked herself. But Lady Kendal's skin seemed slack; she no longer trusted its dimensions. She'd worn this disguise out; it would have to go.

Tick-tick-tick...

She could not look at the children. She heard their voices, pleading with her, and she felt her heart yearning back. But she had made a choice long ago: to protect her own self, first and foremost, at any cost. The dolls grinned down from the rafters. They were all her precious creatures, locked inside this house...

Hands grabbed Lady Kendal, pulling her away from the rope.

The man in the blue silk waistcoat simply smiled, safe in the small compartments of her mind. He waited for the dice to land.

All in.

14

Quinn

"Run!"

The others seemed frozen, staring at the rope, watching in horror as the flame licked upward, straight toward the doll. But Quinn moved, dragging the duke with her. "We need to *run*."

Tick-tick-tick...

Quinn's mind grew cold. She could guess how clockwork bombs were made. The mainspring would have been ratcheted up impossibly tight. But Lady Kendal had lit the fuse; it would override any delay. Gray smoke was already drifting down from the gallery. The servants were pelting across the floor, shouting to one another.

"Keys! Quick!"

They hauled the door open. Murphy's men dragged Lady Kendal down the stairs, her shoes slipping from her feet, her toes skimming the dusty boards.

BOOM.

An explosion rocked the air, resounding inside Quinn's skull, and a bright light broke overhead as the doll's china face shattered.

"Tor…" The duke broke away from Quinn, reaching for his sister. She cannonballed toward him, eyes blazing.

Silk fairly shoved her through the door. "Out, out, everybody *out*…"

But Quinn paused. The explosion had sounded loud, violent—but not devastating. White smoke filled the attic—but the roof was intact.

"The beams." It was the duke, his voice raised, pointing upward to the rafters. "She laid ropes along the beams…to give herself time…"

Quinn's mouth was dry. Another flame was licking along an oiled line…

A second flash of orange light, another pack of dynamite, another china face cracking open…

"The dolls," she said, backing through the door, pulling the duke with her. "She's set up *all* the dolls…"

They turned and ran through the open door, following the others, aiming for the stairs. Three terrific booms resounded overhead.

CRACK.

As they fled down to the servants' quarters, they heard it: timber and masonry collapsing overhead. The duke stumbled at the top of the principal staircase, grabbing the richly carved banister, sending a tremor through the stairs. "We'll never make it."

The house yawned open beneath them. It suddenly seemed endlessly deep; the stable yard felt like miles away. She could hear voices below her, figures spiraling downward through the floors—servants, Murphy's men, Silk, Tor…

CRACK.

"Courage," Quinn breathed. *"Run."*

They hurtled forward, skidding down the stairs, pelting for the third floor, then the second. There was a brutal explosion as the glass dome shattered overhead. Plasterwork, moldings, gilt architraves—they began plummeting down the stairwell, crashing down to the ballroom floor.

"Front door," the duke shouted.

"No, servants' stairs," Quinn cried, her train soaring as she raced down the final turn. "If your main apartments collapse…" The scent of orchids filled her nostrils, wedding blossom everywhere, linens blowing in the breeze coursing through the house. "We need to go deeper…across the stable yard…"

There was a terrible groaning, keening sound overhead, as if the upper half of the house had been fractured.

"If it falls…" Quinn thrust open the door leading to the servants' stairs, retracing the steps she'd taken only a few days before. "Then we'll be trapped. *Go.*"

They hurtled down the brown-papered, varnished passage, circumventing the servants' hall, aiming toward the reddish light of the world outside, staggering through the portico and into the yard. But they weren't safe yet. Quinn could hear noise, confusion: the Kendal grooms shouting orders to one another, the horses whinnying from the stable block. The fog was dense, curdling now; it took people and it swallowed them.

"Which way?" Quinn shouted. She could glimpse the pink-tinted outline of the chapel; she couldn't remember the way to the gate.

"Quinn!" Silk was beckoning for her from the murk. "Quickly!"

The house loomed behind them, its edges blurred by fog, dissolving into sky.

The duke's gloved hand met Quinn's. "I have you." He turned his face to the crowd: grooms, the remaining servants. "To the gates! All of you! Run!"

Quinn felt it, the coil tightening, right in her gut. Time, running out.

The roof blew apart, like the doors on Pandora's box, exploding upwards and outwards. Black soot and ash and a million upon a million tiny things; the most almighty cloud. The noise was colossal: bloodred bricks shattering on every floor, glass erupting in all directions.

Kendal House was torn wide-open.

15

Quinn

One week later

The ruins shimmered in the morning haze. Quinn stood on the
opposite side of Berkeley Square, listening to the sounds of Mayfair
waking up, watching a procession of bowler hats bobbing down
the pavement. She stood there patiently, just breathing, making
up her mind: go in or not?

"Now or never," she said to herself, under her breath, and
crossed the pavement.

The message had come on fine paper, thick cut, in an envelope addressed to her: *Q. Le Blanc*. Silk presented it to her, doubt in his eyes.

"Delivered by hand," he said.

"By whom?" Quinn asked.

They'd been sitting in the back parlor of the Château. Mrs.
Airlie, after some persuading, was out in her landau, paying calls
across the capital, mitigating the damage. The wedding of her
dear cousin had been despoiled by agitators; Quinta White had
retired immediately from society, she might even enter holy or-

ders; Mrs. Airlie was quite horrified by the hideous events on Berkeley Square...

The envelope had been sealed with old-fashioned red wax, stamped with a crest. A bird of prey, an eagle, its wings spread wide. Quinn glanced at Silk.

"Kendal," she said.

She had not seen the duke for a week, but she had followed his movements in the newspapers. They were full of him. A vicious assault had been mounted on the House of Kendal by a group of agitators at the duke's wedding. Not only had they attempted to seize His Grace and his bride, but they had scaled the roof— "Like demons!" Archdeacon Green declared, a breathless witness to the scandal—and had broken into the quarters of the dowager duchess, who had been delayed in her arrival at the chapel. They had abducted her from the house, setting a terrifying ransom for her safe recovery.

"Has she been safely delivered from harm?" Mr. Mellings had asked, deeply alarmed. "Is she quite well?" Quinn had come to visit him in his office at the *Morning Post*—fully veiled, immediately after the wedding.

"She has not returned," Quinn said gravely. "I fear the ransom is too high."

"Too high?" Mellings's pencil hovered in the air, his expression aghast. "You mean to say her captors are still—*at large?*"

"I regret to say they are."

The idea that Lady Kendal, patron of the arts, chairwoman of multitudinous committees, embodiment of grace, could have been so cruelly apprehended—it was too shocking. Yet, word was out: the ransom was unutterably high. Higher than the Kendal estate could presently afford.

The following day, Parliament moved to break the entail on the ancient estate of Mount Kendal.

"For my stepmother's sake," the Duke of Kendal said, voice clear, in his plea to the House. "For the sake of one's *family*, my lords—the most ancient and honorable estate of all."

Such legislation would dissolve the protections around the Kendal estate, permitting Kendal properties and possessions to be sold off for the first time in generations. Funds would be released to satisfy the estate's attackers. *The duke's sacrifice was the measure of a great man*, wrote Mr. Mellings, who published a gushing paean to familial devotion printed in a special elevenpence edition of *Opera Glasses*. *Praise be to His Grace's sister*, Mellings added, *the good Lady Victoria, her virtue unassailed, unmatched, by any woman in the kingdom.*

Bank loans were duly granted to the Duke of Kendal to pay for the recovery of his gracious stepmother. But was she well? the world asked, agog. When would she next be seen in society? The story had broken out beyond the *Morning Post*; it was carried in the *Times*, and in New York. Newspapermen took photographs of the ruins of Kendal House, interviewed the dumbfounded residents of Berkeley Square.

"My family desires nothing more than peace, my lords," the duke said in a second address to the House. "And *absolute* seclusion."

Where he was staying, Quinn did not know. Now she tore open the envelope. She unfolded the letter within. The handwriting was neat, steady: a clerk's hand.

Dear Miss Le Blanc,
It would be in your Personal Interest to attend a meeting with ONE WHO WOULD WISH TO MAINTAIN YOUR FAVOR—*at the address below, in Berkeley Square, at any hour you propose, by return of post.*
Yours &c.

"A meeting."

Silk frowned. "Is that wise? Can he truly be trusted? He knows so much…"

"We need *all* commitments secured, Silk. This is the final piece."

Quinn arranged the appointment, and at the allotted hour, she took a hansom westward. The last remnants of the fog were beginning to clear. She wore her piquet skirt and a sharp-cut blouse and her mousquetaire gloves, trying to steady the beating of her heart. There were children running down Piccadilly, whipping hoops along the pavement.

It was quiet on Berkeley Square. The London season had stuttered to a grinding halt; the big houses were already shuttered; the neighbors had fled for the country. Quinn approached Kendal House—or what remained of it—through the mews lane, where the breeze gusted around the stable yard and dry leaves came rolling in across the cobblestones.

She studied the large and broken building before her. The sky seemed huge, peering through the massive gaps in the roof, the walls. It was a big ancient London sky, of indeterminate color, like sacking or linen—as if the city had temporarily forgotten that it was in debt to the Gas Light and Coke Company, and would soon be filled again with another brown-orange haze.

"I fear I can't sell this place to anybody now," said a voice behind her.

Quinn whipped around.

The duke's collar was turned upward, his expression grave.

"Your Grace," she said, chest tightening. And then: "I fear you're right."

He grimaced a little—a look that could've signaled displeasure, or regret, or uncertainty; she couldn't tell. But he said only, "I have your payments here."

"Truly?" Quinn studied him. "But I defaulted on our agreement. I failed to fully execute your abduction. I didn't set you free."

"No," said the duke. "You did." There was something restless in his gaze. "May I ask, is my stepmother..."

"She is unharmed."

Silk had managed a flourish that even Quinn could not have

conjured up. On his instruction, Mr. Murphy's men had over-powered Lady Kendal's servants, abducted the duchess from the rear of the house in an armored brougham, and taken her to the hostage shop on Roman Road. The ransom note had been issued within the hour. The moment the bank loans were authorized, three days later, a payment of forty thousand guineas was made from Lord Kendal's office directly to Mr. Murphy. It cleared the Château's debts, with a very healthy surplus besides. Murphy's alliance with the Château would never be questioned again.

Lady Kendal's release was a condition of payment. Murphy's men told Quinn they'd unbolted the doors, bracing themselves, expecting her to hiss and curse and flee—but she marched out, head high, and simply dissolved into the tangle of streets beyond.

"Without a word?" Quinn had asked.

"Not a dickey bird," they'd replied in awe.

The duke appeared to chew on this intelligence. "Will she... return?" There was something complicated in his expression: hope and trepidation, intermingled. Max and Tor would be wrestling with the truth about their stepmother for a long while, Quinn realized. It made her flush with unease. She had never witnessed the scars left behind by a grand deception.

"Lady Kendal vanished the second Murphy's men released her. I do not think you or your sister will ever be seeing her again."

"Will you?"

"I surrendered my crown. I pray she will not seek further retribution.'

He turned to face his broken house and said, voice strained, "You know my suite is one of the few not totally damaged by the blasts? Tor's was destroyed, and so was Lady Kendal's. But *mine* lingers on, intact."

Quinn studied him. "And?"

"My stepmother's gifts remain."

"I'm not sure I understand."

His expression was not easy to read. "There were two new dolls placed in the dollhouse."

Quinn felt a chill pass through her. "From her?"

"Who else? Wrapped in ribbons, wearing very beautiful little jackets. I am sure she sewed them herself." He cleared his throat. "Completely covered in dust, of course. But one was carrying a little slip of paper in its hand…"

"What did it say?"

"A twist on the old family motto. *Your blood, your laws.*" He frowned. "I cannot make it out at all. I hardly know whether she loved us, or loved tricking us, all long."

"Perhaps it was both of those things, at different times." Quinn folded her hands behind her back. "It does strange things to a person, shifting skins."

"I permitted her to rule our household; I abdicated my own responsibilities to the estate, to my tenants…" He was still facing the ashen wreckage of the house. "I shall have to atone for that, somehow."

Silence. Then he said, "Extraordinary to think that we were so very nearly married, you and I."

"Hardly, Your Grace."

"Two words. That's all that separated us."

"What words?"

"*I do.*" His eyes flicked sideways. "It was on the tip of your tongue."

They were quiet for a moment. Then Quinn said, "Your sister…"

"She will be spending the rest of the year in Scotland. She has summoned her own companion to give her entertainment. A solicitor with rather incendiary politics." He sighed. "I still cannot make Tor out at all. But she is well."

"And rich?"

"Indeed. When the trustee of her personal fund was abducted, the governance of it dissolved. She has now gained rights over her own fortune. And we shall split the remaining spoils of the estate between us."

"And have you spoken to..."

Something complicated crossed the duke's face. "I do not think," he said carefully, "I can discuss Mr. Willoughby. But he has gone to ground."

"Good." She reached out, placed her hand on his arm. He did not flinch.

"You're wearing old gloves," he said.

She glanced down, surprised. "Am I?"

"Every time I met you, you were wearing fresh ones. I noticed. I thought it was rather interesting."

"I always do, when I'm on a job."

"So you are not on a job today?"

Quinn recalled the thrill she'd felt, nearly two weeks earlier, when this game commenced. And she remembered, too, the sickness in her gut when she abdicated her crown. And though Lady Kendal had rejected it, disdaining the sacrifice, Quinn had felt something shifting—as if Lady Luck had turned her cold and lovely face away from her, as if the dice were being thrown in a fresh direction...

"I'm not sure I will be on a job ever again," she said.

The breeze riffled the duke's pale hair. "Will you miss it?"

Quinn took a breath. "I am not sure," she said, "whether I am quite ready to discuss that."

"It is not so easy to give things up as one might think."

"Indeed. How goes your disappearance?"

"Well, I'm still here. So, perhaps not as smoothly as I would like."

"Why *are* you here?"

"I don't know," he said intently. "I rather wondered if you might help me work it out."

She sensed a skittering between her ribs. It was the same as she felt when she first became queen: the desire to leap, boundless and infinite, into silks and satins. To make oneself up, to pretend to be new.

To be safe, always—cloaked and veiled from the world.

But something had changed. She no longer trusted that old desire. She wanted to breathe without a serpent coiling around her throat. And surely, no amount of money earned, no quantity of good works performed, could be worth sacrificing her entire self. The thread tying her to the Château was fraying. It pained her; it was the only home she'd ever known. But underneath she felt something else, something unexpected: a sense of resolve. Her mother may have been a great queen, Silk may have been her oldest protector—but Quinn knew, with fear and certainty humming in her heart, that she needed to forge a fresh path.

"I am afraid," she said, "that I provide very untrustworthy advice."

Something crossed his face, faster than she could detect. He smiled—a little sadly—looking to the sky. "But I hope we may remain friends."

"This is my hope, too." She risked a smile. "And I am indebted to you. You could have summoned a police constable to detain me for being a charlatan."

Stiffly, he replied, "You might have done the same to me."

Quinn felt her smile falter. She said, voice low, "No, that I will never do."

They did not speak for a while. Then Quinn said, more brightly, "Now, Your Grace. You would not think me a very capable confidence woman if I did not badger you very vociferously for my remaining monies."

She still had her other debts, after all: to her seamstresses, Maud Dunuvar, to the archdeacon, and the rest. And Silk. More than anything, she needed to know that Silk would be all right, if she wasn't around to quarrel and jest and work with him every day.

The duke's lips twitched. "Quite right. Here." He reached into his breast pocket, pulled out a slim envelope. "Your advance against dowry."

The clock began chiming above the chapel. Quinn held the envelope. Delicately, she said, "The sum is…?"

The duke wrinkled his nose. "It would be a little vulgar to name it, surely?"

"I am a very vulgar creature." Quinn tapped the envelope against his arm.

"No, I shall let you peruse it at your leisure." The duke turned his attention to the sky. "But it would give me pleasure to know how you spend it."

"Your liberality knows no bounds," Quinn laughed as she pocketed the envelope. "But if you ever lose another fortune, you know what you need to do."

"What?"

She raised a brow. "Set a mark."

"I could not…" He shut his mouth, amusement playing on his lips.

They faced one another. He extended his hand. "Good day, Miss Le Blanc."

She unbuttoned her gloves, freeing her own. She gripped his palm, felt the heat there. "Until we meet again."

Then she turned and crossed the stable yard, passing through the iron gates into the square beyond. The duke's envelope was tucked safely inside her coat; her mother's pendant rested above her heart. For the first time in years, Quinn felt no clock ticking behind her ribs. It was a wide-open, dizzying sensation. She glanced down, studying her own hands, her own self—and smiled. Her life stretched out before her, thrumming with possibility, to be played any way she liked.

Here was how it began.

★ ★ ★ ★ ★

Author's Note

I have discovered there is a particular thrill in sending a second novel out into the world. They are tricky beasts—and so sharing this one fills me with glee and terror in equal measure. Huge and undiluted thanks to you for diving into Quinn's world with me, and here is a little more about how this story took shape...

My first book, *The Housekeepers*, was a heist novel—and, oh, how I reveled in the twists and turns of that plot structure. So, diving into this book, I was itching to conjure up yet another devious scheme—and I began to sketch a con featuring a gang of Victorian swindlers. I wanted to tell a story filled with diabolical deceptions—and to explore what it might feel like to live life in disguise.

But it fell apart. There was something cold about the cast, something turgid about the plot—it just wasn't coming to life. So I threw my plan out the window and re-sketched the scene.

Two houses emerged. First, the Château, shimmering at the edge of Spitalfields, run by a sharp-witted young mistress and her faithful steward. Then, across town, a splendid redbrick mansion looming on the north side of Berkeley Square—glittering with treasures and thrumming with secrets.

It was the first time I ever wrote a whole novel by instinct rather than a plan on a spreadsheet—following my protagonist as she stalked her prey, circling and circling to find the story within. It was gleeful and head-scratching in equal measure—a book that shifted skins nearly as often as its cast! Thankfully, I had the Rulebook to guide me: the five movements of a confidence scheme, as imagined by the first Queen of Fives, which gave the book its five-day structure. It was the Rulebook, too, that prompted more games within games, spinning new threads in my mind as I put fingers to keyboard. From the start, my mind was fizzing with ways to twist and play with some delicious nineteenth-century tropes: big attics, rich heiresses, grand weddings... And the 1890s felt like the perfect staging ground to devise a rackety con—for here was a world swept with high Victorian gloss, giving texture and drama to a game of high deception—populated by characters rushing toward the brand-new century with their own hopes and dreams and secrets.

Quinn is a fictional character with her own unique take on morality—but some of her methods do take inspiration from nefarious fraudsters operating in the nineteenth century. Cassie Chadwick, born in Ontario in the 1850s, was accused of countless confidence tricks, supposedly passing herself off as the illegitimate daughter and heiress to the millionaire Andrew Carnegie and forging promissory notes to secure stupendous bank loans. James Whitaker Wright, born in 1846, infamously associated with the "Wright Panic" on the London Exchange in 1900, was accused of promoting companies that frequently failed to return any decent profit to their shareholders—a method Quinn deploys to lift investments from her own corrupt gentlemen.

The Château exists only and entirely in my imagination, but it springs from a flight of fancy, pondering what might happen if a group of professional swindlers came together under the well-ordered protection of a single queen, sharing profits and plugging dividends into the community. The result, in this novel at least, is my play on an elective monarchy infused with the spirit of the gaming table, its economics nodding to the late Victorian cooperative movement.

I purposely blurred the Château's address for the sake of my story, but curious readers will find it in Spitalfields, shimmering somewhere between Princelet (formerly Princes, or Princesse) Street and Fournier Street. It would have likely been built in the early 1720s, granted to its first inhabitants on a ninety-nine-year lease, occupied by glovers or brewers or silk weavers—and its oak-paneled walls, narrow, creaking stairs, and plunging views of the Christ Church steeple could survive unchanged to this day. I am indebted to Volume XXVII of the *Survey of London*, edited by F. H. W. Sheppard and published for the London County Council in 1957, for detailing the construction and early ownership of the Wood-Michell estate in such detail. Volume XL provides further detail on the construction of properties in Mayfair, notably on the north side of Berkeley Square, which forms the rough location for my fictional Kendal House.

Lady Kendal's "good works" in Spitalfields take inspiration from philanthropic projects such as the Charlotte de Rothschild lodgings and building works carried out by the Four Per Cent Industrial Dwellings Co., where tenements were erected over so-called "rookeries" or "slum dwellings," ostensibly for the purpose of improving desperate living conditions, but often displacing existing residents along the way. It is a truism of London that its socioeconomic picture can change radically from one end of a street to another, and so I am indebted to the Charles Booth poverty map, which surveyed the western end of Princelet Street in 1898 and classified its residents as being "fairly comfortable [with] good ordinary earnings." In other words, Quinn would have been fortunate to enjoy warm fires and a good diet and the services of a general servant, even though she was raised cheek by jowl with desperate poverty. I must also express a debt to Hallie Rubenhold's *The Five*, which provides the most poignant and vital picture of the area as it would have been in Quinn's youth, when the Jack the Ripper killings cast a devastating blight over the neighborhood.

A few other historical notes: marriage brokering and inheritance battles form the spine of this plot, and the engagement of the American heiress Consuelo Vanderbilt to the Duke of Marlborough provided particular inspiration on the types of debts and financial constraints associated with estates protected by the terms of entail. Quinn accuses Mr. Silk of holding an irrational terror of agitators, but his fears were not entirely unfounded: clockwork-timed bombs, powered by dynamite, were deposited at railway stations and illustrious dwellings in the 1880s. Mrs. Airlie's habit of using veils and cosmetics to conceal her identity and appearance was also not unusual: the Princess of Wales (later Queen Alexandra) was reputed to go in for "face enameling"—the application of paint to produce a younger, smoother complexion. I have adjusted the dates of the Royal Academy's Summer Exhibition and the Goodwood Races to aid my plot.

This novel deliberately plays with some of the tropes of "sensation fiction" or fin de siècle literature, a genre that revels in duality and savagery and repressed desire, pressing on the anxieties associated with change and the dawning of the twentieth century. *The Strange Case of Dr. Jekyll and Mr. Hyde* is, of course, one of the most famous examples, and I am indebted to Robert Louis Stevenson for showing me the delights of playing with holographic wills, glass phials filled with dangerous liquids, and very dense fog. On which note, I am duty bound to note that I have brazenly adapted the meteorological conditions of August 1898 in the service of my story.

Writing Quinn's story and inhabiting her world has been such a joyous experience. Thank you so much for reading along with me—I'd be so delighted to hear what you think. Do contact me on X or Instagram (@AlexHayBooks) or email me at www.alexhaybooks.com. And one of these days, I must tell you one of the stories left untold from *The Queen of Fives*—those deadly students lurking in Mrs. Airlie's academy, those female impresarios getting ready to make their fortunes, and a new glittering century opening up just around the corner…

—*Alex Hay*, London, March 2024

me on X or Instagram (@AlexHayBooks) or email me at www. alexhaybooks.com. And one of these days, I must tell you one of the stories left untold from *The Queen of Fives*—those deadly students lurking in Mrs. Airlie's academy, those female impresarios getting ready to make their fortunes, and a new glittering century opening up just around the corner…

—*Alex Hay*, London, March 2024

Acknowledgments

Mammoth thanks to super-agent Alice Lutyens, who read the first chapter of this book hot off the keyboard and championed it from day one. Thank you as always for your counsel, care, and boundless thinking. Hugest thanks also to Olivia Bignold, Rakhi Kohli, and the whole magnificent team at Curtis Brown.

Heartfelt thanks must go to this book's remarkable editors, Frankie Edwards at Headline and Melanie Fried at Graydon House, aided by the epic Jessie Goetzinger-Hall at every turn. You have offered limitless wisdom and ingenuity and love to this story, from madcap first draft to final version—and there is nobody I'd rather devise a devious con with than you. Thanks to Sharona Selby and Dana Francoeur for such thoughtful and invaluable copyediting and to Samantha Stewart and Vicki So for proofreading this novel with such care.

At Hachette UK, I owe very special thanks to the wonderful Rebecca Folland, Grace McCrum, Sophie Jackson, and the phenomenal rights team, who have taken my work and sold it around the world with such ambition over the past two years. It's been one of the most extraordinarily special parts of the publication journey so far, and I am eternally grateful. At Headline, absolutely colossal thanks must be given to Caitlin Raynor, publicity director extraordinaire, who leaves no stone unturned and has done so much for this book and for me; Becky Bader and the brilliant sales team for reaching retailers and readers everywhere; Marta Juncosa and everyone in marketing for the most incredible support; Ellie Wheeldon for audio; Tina Paul for production. Thank you to the very wonderful Jen Doyle and to Mari Evans for your wholehearted support.

At Graydon House, I am indebted to the brilliant Leah Morse for publicity—you have unlocked countless opportunities and I am so grateful; to Pamela Osti for marketing, and to absolutely everyone in the sales, production, and subrights departments who have done so much to help *The Queen of Fives* fly. I'm also so grateful to Quinn Banting for designing our beautiful covers.

One of the greatest delights over the past year has been meeting so many magnificent book bloggers, reviewers, booksellers, wondrous librarians, and fellow writers who all invest such time and commitment to recommending and sharing books, enabling readers to discover and connect with authors. This is such a rich and special community—I'm so grateful to be part of it.

Thank you to dear friends and colleagues who provided love and support. Special thanks to my wonderful mother, Dale Hay, for encouragement and enthusiasm throughout the writing of this book.

Finally, and most importantly, thank you to Tom—my splendid husband and greatest support. You are the first person to hear about my ideas; your instincts are unfailingly right (even when I'm loathe to admit it)—and you let me bang on about Every Single Detail of the publishing journey with boundless love and enthusiasm. You are generous and unswerving in your support, in both happy times and hard times, and I am truly grateful. I love you.